PRAISE FOR MARIA V. SNYDER

"Shyla Sun-Kissed is back, and is just as bad-ass as ever in *The City of Zirdai.* Starting off where *The Eyes of Tamburah* finished, this sequel from Maria V. Snyder is not something to be missed! I had super high expectations for this sequel, given that I absolutely loved (and devoured, honestly) *Tamburah,* and I wasn't let down at all. Full of the action, magic, and Snyder's style I know and love, it firmly has a place in my 2021 favorites, for sure!" The Nerd Daily on *City of Zirdai*

"An enriching mix of fantasy, adventure, suspense with a touch of romance filled with witty dialogue that made it very easy for me to grasp the new world and terminology...The fast-paced plot made it almost impossible to put down." The Nerd Daily on *The Eyes of Tamburah*

"Oh. My. Stars! I just raced through Maria V. Snyder's *Navigating the Stars* and *Chasing the Shadows,* and I'm blown away! ...The plot is fantastic, the pacing spectacular, the intricacies, the snark, the banter...oh my! Go, go, go. You'll love this!" Amanda Bouchet, *USA Today* bestselling author on The Sentinels of the Galaxy series

"This is one of those rare books that will keep readers dreaming long after they've read it." Publishers Weekly, starred review on *Poison Study*

"Snyder deftly weaves information about glassblowing into her tale of magic and murder." Library Journal on *Storm Glass*

"Filled with Snyder's trademark sarcastic humor, fast-paced action, and creepy villainy, *Touch of Power* is a spellbinding fantasy adventure." *USA TODAY*

"A wonderful, thoughtful book full of vivid characters and a place—Inside—that is by turns alien, and breathtakingly familiar." Rachael Caine, *New York Times* bestselling author on *Inside Out*

ALSO BY MARIA V. SNYDER

Study Series
POISON STUDY
MAGIC STUDY
FIRE STUDY
SHADOW STUDY
NIGHT STUDY
DAWN STUDY

Glass Series
STORM GLASS
SEA GLASS
SPY GLASS

Inside Series
INSIDE OUT
OUTSIDE IN

Invisible Sword Series
THE EYES OF TAMBURAH
THE CITY OF ZIRDAI
THE KING OF KORAHA

Sentinels Series
NAVIGATING THE STARS
CHASING THE SHADOWS
DEFENDING THE GALAXY

Healer Series
TOUCH OF POWER
SCENT OF MAGIC
TASTE OF DARKNESS

Discover more titles at
MariaVSnyder.com

MARIA V. SNYDER

The King of Koraha / Maria V. Snyder—1st edition
Cover design and interior art by Joy Kenney

Published by Maria V. Snyder

Digital ISBN 9781946381118
Print ISBN 9781946381101

To those who started out as my readers, became my friends, and then transformed into a part of my family: Kathy, Nat, Jo, Reema, Renée, and the self-proclaimed Maria's Girls: June, Sarah, Sheree, and Tori. Mama Bear is honored that you're a part of her herd.

Ever since Shyla was six circuits old, she'd wanted to visit all the vast underground cities of Koraha. At that time, her world had been very limited. Raised in a monastery by the Monks of Parzival for eighteen circuits, she'd only ventured out to the nearby city of Zirdai on the rare occasion. Her desire to travel never dimmed as she researched the history of each city, their various famous and infamous inhabitants, and catalogued the underground wonders of Koraha. In her dreams, she'd plan her visits, listing the sights that shouldn't be missed.

It was a nice bit of dreaming that failed to factor in one crucial detail—visiting those cities required traveling over the hot sands of the desert for far too many sun jumps in a row.

Far, far too many.

Now, Shyla trudged up yet another sand dune, hot, sweaty, and tired of the unending vermillion sands that stretched out in all directions. They were endless, rippling out to the horizon and beyond. As Shyla followed a step behind Lota, she wondered, not for the first time, how in the seven hells the caravan owner knew where she was going.

According to Lota, there was a road underneath the layer of sand. And Shyla had to admit—grudgingly—her dillo leather boots didn't sink in quite so deep. A good thing, as walking would require more effort if she sank up to her calves with every step.

Shyla glanced back at Lota's caravan trailing behind them. It was considered an average size, with fifteen wagons filled with goods and one for Lota's family. Each wagon had its own driver and was pulled by two gamelus. Then there were eight extra people that Lota referred to as her "muscles." They performed various jobs like taking care of the gamelus during stops and unloading and loading merchandise. There were also eight guards, counting Shyla and Rendor. Actually, as a captain, Rendor should be counted as three at least.

Opposite her point guard position, he marched in the rear guard location, scanning the sands for potential threats, but he caught her gaze and smiled. The warmth inside her heated, and it had nothing to do with the sun jumping toward apex. She returned his smile, wishing for the millionth time they could have some privacy. But the travel shelters along the route only supplied protection from the killing heat and the freezing darkness, with nothing fancier than a communal scattering of cushions.

There were two ways a person could travel across the vast desert that blanketed Koraha. Either you hired a guide, who arranged everything and escorted you safely to your destination, or you signed up with one of the many caravans that crisscrossed the world. Hiring a guide cost an outrageous amount of osmiums so only the deep-level wealthy could afford it. The second option gave you two choices: you either accompanied the caravan as a passenger or you joined as a worker, the latter being the cheapest way to travel and the easiest way to blend in. Too bad it was almost impossible for Shyla and Rendor to travel incognito.

As a sun-kissed, she stood out. Her sun cloak's hood helped hide her blond hair and kept the harsh rays of the sun off her golden-brown skin. However, she'd decided before this trip that she'd no longer worry about what other people thought of her. She hoped the citizens of Qulsary, the capital of Koraha, no longer believed that sun-kisseds must be sacrificed to the Sun Goddess right after birth. The new Heliacal Priestess of Zirdai had already outlawed the abandonment of sun-kissed babies on the sands.

Thinking about the new priestess, Shyla grinned. Not only was the woman a sun-kissed, but she was Shyla's mother. A pulse of love swelled in her heart. After circuits of thinking she had been abandoned and rescued by the monks, Shyla now had a family. Which she'd promptly left behind in Zirdai. Not because of her desire to travel. No. Because the King of Koraha had ordered her to report to him in person.

The knot in her stomach tightened and her gaze returned to Rendor. He too failed to blend in. At one hundred and ninety centimeters tall, Rendor was broad shouldered and pure muscle. And he was all hers. His solid presence helped steady her nerves but couldn't banish her fears completely.

What if the King had her arrested as soon as she arrived? There was nothing Rendor could do in that situation. She and her Invisible Swords had overthrown Zirdai's Water Prince and Heliacal Priestess—two very corrupt and power-hunger people who deserved to be usurped. Unfortunately, two hundred and sixty-four people died during the defeat—many of them Shyla's good friends.

Was the King worried her organization would set their sights on him? As far as she knew, he wasn't a despot. He was over eighty circuits old and preferred to rule from a distance, keeping an eye on the cities through the monks. The King only interceded in a city's politics when their tax payments stopped. Then he would send his legendary soldiers to deal with the problem. Otherwise, he seemed inclined to leave the cities alone, which had been unfortunate for Zirdai when it desperately needed his help.

To keep from fretting, Shyla concentrated on the fact that the King's emissary had investigated the events leading to the change in leadership and had approved Jayden as the new Water Prince and Kaveri as the new Heliacal Priestess. Yet Shyla's thoughts kept circling back to why the King wanted to see her.

Perhaps she should be more concerned about the sun nearing the danger zone. They had usually found shelter by now. If they were caught on the surface between angles eighty and one hundred, they'd be cooked alive. A few of the drivers muttered unhappily as other members of the caravan exchanged worried glances.

Shyla scanned the pink sky, searching for flocks of velbloud.

The fuzzy white creatures rose into the air about twenty angles before apex to escape the killing heat, remaining attached to the sands by their long tethers. Tethers she'd used once in desperation to ascend with them. If it hadn't been for them and Zhek's healing goo, she would have died and joined the Sun Goddess.

"Beacon spotted," Yegor, Lota's husband, shouted. The tension dissipated as everyone relaxed.

"'Bout time, Yegor," one of the drivers called in a teasing tone. "Thought you'd gone sand blind."

"I wish," Yegor shot back. "Then I wouldn't have to see your ugly mug every sun jump." Laughter rippled through the caravan as Yegor urged his gamelu team to pick up the pace.

Yegor drove the first wagon, which contained his and Lota's two children. Actually, "contained" wasn't quite accurate as the little boy and girl rarely rode inside, preferring to either cling to the sides, lie on the roof, or ride one of the gamelus—which they had all named.

Shyla squinted through the brightness. Good thing they hadn't depended on her to find the tall obelisk that marked the entrance to a travel shelter. Even though they rose high above the dunes and had been built of black granite to contrast with the reddish-orange sands, they were still hard to find.

Lota led the caravan over to the beacon. As soon as they reached it, everyone burst into action. The gamelus were unhitched and brought over to the stone corral. They were given water and brought under the massive sun shade made from velbloud skin that the muscles erected. The gamelus were well equipped to handle the killing heat during the danger zone, however, due to the extra effort they expanded pulling the wagons, the shade allowed them to recover from their exertions faster.

Once the animals were settled, everyone climbed down the ladder into the shelter. Before joining them, Shyla scanned the horizon one more time, using the power of The Eyes to sense if there was anyone nearby. Not that she expected attackers to be hiding in the desert this close to the danger zone, but the shelter only had a single exit, and if it was blocked, they would be trapped. When Shyla had mentioned this to Lota and the other guards, they'd shrugged it off, unconcerned about the possibility. Only Rendor had understood the danger.

Satisfied they were alone, she descended into the cooler air. It was a straight shot down, ending in a long rectangular chamber about seventeen meters underground. By the time she reached the bottom, the temperature had dropped to twenty degrees Celsius. She waited at the base of the ladder for her eyes to adjust to the semi-darkness. The yellow glow from the druk lanterns hanging around the chamber were weak compared to the sunlight.

Once the black shapes inside the shelter solidified into the caravan members, Shyla nodded at Rendor, giving him the all-clear signal. He had waited nearby with his hand on his sword just in case. This habit of theirs amused the other guards, but they didn't know what magic could do. They had no idea that magic wielders could hide under the sands or disappear inside a dune.

The chamber was about five meters wide by fourteen meters long and identical to every other shelter they'd stopped in since Zirdai. Cushions for sleeping and sitting littered the floor. A few long low stone tables lined the walls.

Shyla and Rendor headed to an empty sleeping cushion, weaving through the small clumps of caravanners. Some were already sprawled on cushions, others shared meals and gossiped, while a few rolled dice in order to pass the forty angles until the surface cooled to a safer temperature. Unaware that Shyla and Rendor had been involved in the turmoil in Zirdai, they didn't pay them much attention. Only Lota and her husband knew the truth because Shyla had wanted to be honest with the owner.

Once they reached the cushion, Rendor stripped off his sun cloak. Underneath he wore a sleeveless tunic. The soaked fabric clung to his well-defined chest. She relished the view as he wiped the sweat off his face, watching his muscles flex. Before he could catch her ogling him, she removed her own cloak.

Shyla welcomed the cool air that caressed her overheated body, sighing with relief. Too bad the water in her water skin was beyond tepid. Any hotter and she'd use it to make tea. Rendor handed her a couple rolls of velbloud jerky.

Taking her blanket from her pack, she spread it over the stained and lumpy cushion before lying down. Rendor joined her. This was one of the few times they spent together in relative privacy—not that they could do anything other than talk quietly and sleep.

"I don't think I'll be able to take fifty more sun jumps of this," she said, snuggling close, breathing in Rendor's unique spicy scent.

"This?" He squeezed her tight for a moment.

"No. The endless sameness sun jump after sun jump for the last twenty jumps."

"Traveling the world not as glamorous as you'd hoped? Or is it the lack of rebellions to lead? I could ask if the others want to overthrow Lota and her husband to generate some excitement," he teased.

"All right, you made your point. I just..." She searched her emotions.

"You just want to be there."

"Yes! The wait is killing me. Why couldn't the King say why he wished to see me?"

"It could be standard procedure when there's a change in leadership. Maybe he wants to get the details from a reliable source. Or to thank you for your help."

"Or to arrest me for murder."

"Ah. Tell me again how many people *you* personally killed?"

None, and he knew it. "You know what I mean. They died because of *me*."

"No, they died *because* the Heliacal Priestess set off gas explosions."

"Because she wanted *me*."

"She wanted The Eyes of Tamburah. It didn't matter whose eye sockets they were in, she was going after them regardless. You have to stop blaming yourself."

Except if it hadn't been for Shyla, Ximen, Elek, and Lian wouldn't have been on level ninety-seven when part of it collapsed, killing them.

Rendor must have sensed the direction of her thoughts. "You're not going to be arrested."

"And if I am?"

"Then I'll rescue you."

She smiled at his confident tone. "What if I'm guarded by one of the King's elite squads?"

He huffed in derision. "I'll still rescue you. Just might take me a few more angles."

"Their fighting skills are legendary. They can't be beat."

"Everyone can be beat, sunbeam. And I would be *highly* motivated." His words hummed in the air like a promise.

No doubt the big brute would try. She gave Rendor a quick kiss. "Thanks."

His voice dropped to a husky whisper. "Thank me again when we're alone."

She nibbled on his ear before saying, "That'll be in fifty more sun jumps."

He groaned.

"Do you still think it's not that long?"

"Can't talk. I'm sleeping."

She'd punch him, but she'd end up just hurting her knuckles.

After the sun moved from the danger zone, the caravan continued its journey. Once again trudging through the sands, Shyla scanned the horizon. The routes between the cities of

Koraha were lined with shelters. However, with the constantly blowing sand, you'd never know they were well traveled. The only time the sand stopped moving was when the sun reached the apex of its jump. Most times a steady breeze blew the grains, but on rare occasions, they were blasted by a howling sandstorm.

When the sun hung low in the sky, Lota stopped them at another shelter. This time the wagons were parked in a circle to keep the gamelus inside. The sun shade was draped over all the wagons, creating a thin ceiling for the herd. It also blocked the wind and trapped the sun's heat emanating off the sands and off the animals. Enough warmth so the guard on duty didn't freeze.

Shyla admired the design as she circled the outside of the hut during the start of her twenty-five-angle shift to protect the wagons, checking that all was well. Then she turned her attention to the wider surroundings. The starlight from the Five Brothers constellation illuminated the sands just enough to spot the approach of any sand pirates without having to use a druk. But Shyla still used her power to seek the souls of any hidden attackers. Rendor and the others were just a shout away. He wouldn't admit it, but Shyla knew he remained awake when she was guarding the wagons.

Satisfied no threats lurked nearby, Shyla practiced manipulating the sand with her magic. Sand was a powerful weapon, and she still hadn't mastered moving large quantities of it. Starting with the easiest task, she focused on her footprints in the sand and used the magical command *return*. Her prints disappeared. Then she moved on to the more difficult task of hiding her body underneath the sands by creating a furrow she could lie in, before settling a layer of sand over herself so the ground appeared to be undisturbed.

So far, her attempts to walk through a dune had not been successful, but not for lack of trying. Shyla climbed to the top of the nearest dune. Using her magic, she removed the sand underneath her feet so she sank down into it. At least she no longer panicked when the sand closed above her head. In fact, she took a moment to savor the protection and warmth that built from her body heat. But when she focused on creating an exit in the side of the dune, the sand exploded from the hole instead of pouring gently out. The noise alone would alert anyone nearby that something strange was going on. Stealth was key for this maneuver. Frustrated, Shyla smoothed the gaping hole, returning the dune to its unblemished state. Jayden had done it with nary a ripple. Then again, Jayden also had eighteen circuits of practice. Except now his magic was gone.

As the new Water Prince, he couldn't have an unfair advantage over his citizens. Shyla didn't regret taking his magic from him. Her worries focused on how he would handle the job without his power. Mojag promised to keep an eye on him from a distance. The boy hadn't forgiven Jayden for betraying the Invisible Swords. And Aphra, Jayden's new archeologist, also said she'd watch him for signs of trouble. The citizens of Zirdai deserved a qualified, compassionate, and incorruptible leader.

When it grew too cold, she ducked inside the hut to warm up and check the gamelus. They had curled up together with their long legs and snouts tucked in tight, looking like an oversized yellow bush. A few gave her sleepy half-lidded looks.

Shyla wondered how anyone could tell them apart. But Faizah and Anwar knew them all by name. Come to think of it, so did Rendor.

Once warm, she returned to practicing with the sand until Rendor arrived to take his turn. Another reason she enjoyed guard duty was when he pulled her close and kissed her like he hadn't seen her in circuits. Heat immediately speared her and she deepened the kiss, wrapping her arms around him.

Rendor's sense of duty always kicked in and he broke off the kiss to scan the surrounding desert for trouble. She rested her head on his chest and just soaked him in, listening to the thrum of his heart.

"Go inside and get warmed up," Rendor said.

She reluctantly let go. If she pushed to remain with him, he'd insist she get some sleep. If she stayed despite his protests, he'd physically escort her to the shelter. She could use her magic to stop him, but she'd never do that to him. In fact, she'd promised not to use magic on him without his permission. Unless it was an emergency. As for the power of The Eyes, she didn't need to read his thoughts and emotions. Over the last two hundred and thirty-three sun jumps they'd been together, she'd learned to read his body language pretty well. Besides, she already knew his heart.

"Go," he ordered.

He wasn't in charge, but he could out-stubborn her. So she stole another kiss and went into the shelter.

The sun jumps blurred together, piling up. Shyla was both comforted by the routine and frustrated by it. Soon after they left the travel shelter at the start of their fifty-second sun jump of travel, Shyla sensed a strange thickness to the air. Beside her, Lota appeared unconcerned. Shyla glanced back at the other guards and caravan drivers, but no one acted anxious. The kids were having fun pretending to be racing the gamelus. Yet there was a hum of anticipation and excitement that danced on her skin.

It took her a couple of angles to spot the small shapes in the distance. Monks? Had they traveled close to another city? The monasteries were always built near a major city so the monks could spy on the people and report any problems to the King. They also wore special clothing that blended in with the color of the sand when they were out on patrol.

Rendor moved up from his position, joining her. "Do you see them?"

"Yes."

"I count ten," he said.

"I see a dozen."

"There's eighteen," Lota said.

"Are they monks?" Shyla asked her.

"Not out here."

"Sand pirates?" Rendor gripped the hilt of his sword.

"No. They don't strike in sunlight, and they wouldn't be lying half buried in the sand."

Shyla squinted. The woman had a keen eye. "The King's guards?"

Lota scoffed. "No. If the guards ever bothered to leave

Qulsary, they wouldn't hide." She paused. "We are near a major crossroads so there are travel shelters in each direction."

"Who are they?" Rendor asked.

"I've no idea, but they're lying in wait for us." She signaled the rest of the guards to get ready. "I hope you two are as good as you claim. This is going to get rough."

Lota yelled at her kids to get inside the wagon and stay there. Then she ordered her muscles to arm themselves. The caravan slowed but didn't stop. They were on a tight schedule and stopping could result in death.

Shyla considered their odds. They had eight trained fighters and eight without experience against eighteen unknown opponents. With her magic and Rendor's skills, she guessed that their caravan still had the advantage. She hoped. The thought of anything happening to Anwar and Faizah made her sick.

Without any discussion, Rendor took charge of the defenders. Lota's official "captain" creased his brow as if he'd like to protest, but Rendor's calm professionalism soon overrode his discontent.

"They're going to wait until the caravan is well inside their attack zone before they initiate hostilities," Rendor said. "This will allow them to surround us."

"If their goal is to steal from us, they'll be planning to take the wagons and leave us behind," Lota said.

"And if they have another goal in mind?" Uma asked. She drove the third wagon.

Lota glanced at where her children were hiding. "Then I've no idea what will happen."

Rendor straightened. "Whatever their objectives are, they will *not* be successful."

His words energized them. They stood taller and gave him their undivided attention as he positioned the sixteen of them in a ring around the caravan, alternating a skilled person with an inexperienced one. Shyla and Rendor took point with Lota.

When Rendor politely suggested she stay with her husband and children, Lota said, "It's *my* caravan."

Shyla scanned the desert with her magic as they neared the ambush, counting the bumps hidden in the sand. Lota was right: there were eighteen.

The temperature increased as the sun jumped toward apex. Shyla hoped the fight, if there was one, wouldn't delay them too much.

When they reached the first of the hidden figures, nothing happened, just like Rendor predicted. Since she was much closer to them, Shyla considered sending all the ambushers to sleep. Lota and the others would just believe that they weren't the target and happily continue on. Except there was nothing stopping them from following the caravan and trying again. Best to find out why they were here and what they wanted. And to then scare them away from planning a second attack.

They kept walking, pretending they didn't see the figures in the sand. Shyla noted their head scarves had been wrapped to cover everything except their eyes. It was a clever design. One she'd take a closer look at if she had time afterward.

"Get ready," Rendor said in a low voice.

Two angles later, a battle cry sounded and the figures jumped to their feet and rushed toward the caravan.

Shyla and the rest of the guards braced for an attack as the enemy surrounded them. Except the eighteen armed people stopped about three meters from the ring of guards. They each held a short sword with a slightly curved blade in one hand and a thin dagger in the other—a slashing weapon and a stabbing one. Unease swirled in her heart.

One figure stepped forward. His eyes were the color of honey. Shyla met the leader's gaze and read his immediate intentions. Not violence. At least not yet.

"Give us the sun-kissed and you can go," he said to Lota with the confidence that the caravan leader would readily agree.

Shyla suppressed a frustrated sigh. Why did they want her? Did they know who she was, what she could do, or did they hate sun-kisseds that much? She couldn't pick up anything more from the leader; he was too focused on completing his task and getting paid. He was a mercenary. That was unexpected. The King's soldiers had defeated all the mercenary troops in Koraha over two hundred circuits ago and they continued to ensure no new troops formed.

"And if I don't?" Lota asked.

He gestured to his people. "We'll take her by force. In that case, you'll risk injuring your workers and your children."

"Touch the children and die," Rendor growled at the leader.

"An interesting offer," Lota said in a calm voice. If she was upset by the threat to her kids, it didn't show. "Allow me to consult with my advisors." She turned to Rendor. "Captain, what do you think?"

It was a nice bit of intimidation, calling him Captain. Shyla approved.

"I think we should give them the opportunity to leave before we pound them back into the sand," Rendor said.

Then she asked Shyla, "What do you think?"

"I'll go with them to avoid bloodshed."

Rendor gave her a questioning look. She sensed his inquiry: *Can you handle all of them?*

She nodded.

Lota faced the leader. "Guess I'll be the tie-breaker. The answer is no. Shyla is under my protection."

The man sighed then stomped on the ground. Odd. His gang stomped as well, like they were all having a temper tantrum. Was that supposed to scare them?

Sand exploded into the air and a dozen more figures stood behind the ambushers. Shyla started at their sudden appearance. She hadn't sensed them. Did they have magic? She tried to catch one of their gazes without luck.

"What about now?" the leader asked.

Shyla picked up on his frustration, but he was determined. He'd been hired to do a job and he never failed.

"Captain?" Lota asked. This time a slight tremor shook her

voice.

"My answer remains the same."

"Shyla?"

Could she influence thirty people? Probably not. But she was curious about who had hired them and why, and that required her to spend more time with them. It appeared they wanted her alive. Plus she didn't want Lota's children or the caravanners to suffer. "I'll still go."

"No," Rendor said. "I won't let you."

Well then. Shyla concentrated on the sand under the ambushers' feet. Might as well even the odds.

"Don't be stupid, Lota," the leader said. "She's willing and you're wasting time." He gestured to the sun.

"You're right, we're wasting time. Captain, make it fast." Lota stepped back as Rendor surged forward, stabbing his sword toward the leader's neck. The man blocked and lunged at Rendor's stomach with his dagger.

Shyla wrenched the sand from underneath six attackers' feet. They sank into the ground up to their chests, crying out in surprise. The other ambushers charged toward them. Two of them reached her within the blink of an eye.

Stop, she commanded with her magic.

They froze in place. Next to her, Camlo, one of Lota's muscles, clutched a mallet to his chest, gaping at the fighting erupting all around. She tapped him on the shoulder, borrowed his weapon, and struck the frozen men on their temples. Hard. They crumpled to the ground.

She handed the mallet back to him. "Stay close to me."

He almost trod on her heels, but he caught on quick. Shyla froze attackers, and he knocked them unconscious. They sidestepped various skirmishes, ducking blows and dodging a few sword thrusts. The air filled with the hot metallic scent of blood and sweat. Grunts and curses peppered the air as weapons clanged. The caravan's guards knew how to fight with a sword, but they were loath to take a life. Shyla sank a few more ambushers.

Knocking everyone unconscious and leaving them to cook in the sun went against her oath to only kill in self-defense. Between her efforts and that of the other guards, half of their assailants were trapped in the sand and the other half would wake up with horrible headaches. Overall, the fight was over quickly. Only Rendor still fought with the leader.

He was holding his own and appeared to be enjoying the match. The man had some skills, but nothing compared to Rendor. As she watched, she figured out the real challenge that Rendor faced was fighting in a way that led the leader to believe he had a chance to win. Which was harder.

"Is the caravan secure?" Rendor asked. Even though sweat streaked his dark skin, he wasn't winded from his exertions.

"Yes. You can stop playing. I've questions for him," she said.

The man increased the pace of his attack. Rendor countered with ease. Then all Rendor's flourishes and fancy feints and blocks disappeared as he went on the offensive. Quick, efficient, and intense, Rendor unarmed the mercenary and knocked him down in three moves.

Staring at Rendor in astonishment, the leader raised his

hands as the point of Rendor's sword touched his neck. Shyla yanked off his head scarf. Tight ringlets of sweat-soaked brown hair clung to his scalp. He looked to be around twenty-five to thirty circuits old.

Rendor stepped back but kept the tip of his sword aimed at the man. "Get up," he ordered.

A kindness, since the sand was hot enough to burn skin even through clothing. The danger zone was quickly approaching. The leader moved gracefully as he stood.

When Lota joined them, Rendor asked, "Do you recognize him? He called you by name."

"No, but I'm well known throughout Koraha. Shyla, do you know him?"

"No. But you should get your caravan moving or you'll be cooked. We'll catch up and report in."

"Are you sure?" Then she noticed the state of the mercenaries. "Are you going to—"

"No. We're not."

Lota paused another moment, but then she ordered the wagons to go. "Don't take too long," she said to them.

The drivers and muscles gave Shyla looks that varied from terrified to impressed to confused. Some nursed bruises and cuts, but everyone had lived through the attack.

Once the caravan was out of earshot, she asked the mercenary, "Why do you want me?"

He refused to answer. Okay then. Shyla stared at the man. He glared back, and she reached deeper into his thoughts with the power of The Eyes. This was supposed to be a simple job.

He'd argued that he didn't need so many men, but, looking around, he hadn't brought enough. And no one warned him a captain would be with them. What in the seven hells had happened? Half his guys were stuck in the sand. Who was this sun-kissed anyway?

"Who hired you?" Shyla asked, urging his thoughts in that direction.

"I don't know." The truth. Vilma had assigned him the job. She always kept the client's name secret for just this reason.

"Why does your client want me?" she asked.

He'd no idea, but he was starting to suspect it might have to do with the way the sand melted under half his men and why the other half were knocked out.

"Where were you going to take me?"

He glanced at the hulking brute next to her.

Was the captain going to force the answers from him? They could guess at this one, since Nintri was the closest city.

Shyla searched through his memories and while she learned he was a successful and expensive mercenary, he had limited knowledge about Shyla and the reason for this particular job. Vilma was smart to keep the information from him. Shyla wondered if Vilma knew she wielded the power of The Eyes or if the client failed to divulge that information.

The searing heat from the sun increased its pressure on her head and shoulders. Time to go.

"You fought and lost," Shyla told the leader, using her magic. "The sun-kissed got away and you ran out of time." She gestured to the men. "Better hurry and get them to the shelter on the way to Nintri." Then she leaned closer. "Don't try again. You won't succeed."

She erased his memory of his men stuck in the sand, then did the same to the others who remained awake as she loosened the sand around them. She used the *look away* command. Suddenly everyone seemed fascinated by a section of desert in the opposite direction to where she stood. By the time the mercenaries fully freed themselves, she and Rendor would be out of sight. Shyla motioned for Rendor to join her. He was inspecting one of the holes in the sand where one of the dozen mercenaries had been hiding. Rendor sheathed his sword and they followed the caravan's tracks in the sand.

As he jogged next to her, he asked, "Will they get to a shelter in time?"

"They should. It's closer than ours," she puffed. Not from the exertion but because the air burned her throat. Her sweat dried instantly—a bad sign. Rendor should be more worried about *them* reaching shelter.

Running through the burning hot sand, Shyla wondered when her boots would melt. The dillo leather was tough, but not tough enough to withstand the heat at apex. Then it would be her feet on the searing sand. And Zhek's healing goo was fifty-two sun jumps away.

"How did…" Rendor gasped. "You…survive…out here?"

There were no velbloud flocks nearby. No surprise as they were kept near the cities. "Just…keep…moving," she urged.

Waves of heat emanated off the sands, blurring the landscape, creating shimmering illusions. The air thickened and pressed. Her energy faded with each step and every centimeter of her body burned both inside and out.

So hot. So very hot. She could probably swallow a lump of dough and it would bake into bread by the time it reached her stomach.

Shyla fought the desire to rip off her sun cloak. The fabric was the only thing keeping her skin from blistering. If they only had some shade— Scorching sand rats, she was an idiot.

Using her magic, she scooped up a two-meter-square layer of sand and floated it above their heads, blocking the sun's lethal rays. Rendor only had enough energy to grunt in appreciation as the air cooled by what felt like ten degrees. Blocking the sunlight might just keep them alive a little longer—if she didn't collapse from exhaustion first. She hadn't used this much magic in a long time.

"There." He pointed to the beacon.

Lota's caravan was already parked nearby. The gamelus wilted in the full sun. Most people panicked if they were outside after angle seventy, but they still had another ten angles before it turned deadly. The caravanners must have believed they didn't have enough time to set up the shade or give the animals water. But after the extra quick trot to the shelter, the gamelus might not survive apex.

"Go…inside," she told Rendor. "I'll—"

"No." He grabbed the fabric from one of the wagons. "Just…cover them."

Oh. They fanned it out and laid it over the gamelus like a blanket. She added a layer of sand to weigh it down and give them some more protection. Her arms and legs shook with the strain. The desert spun around her as Rendor set out the water buckets for the herd.

"Come on." Rendor guided her toward the shelter. "Go…now."

With the last of her energy boiling away in the heat, she mounted the ladder. Shyla considered it a win that she made it halfway down before fainting.

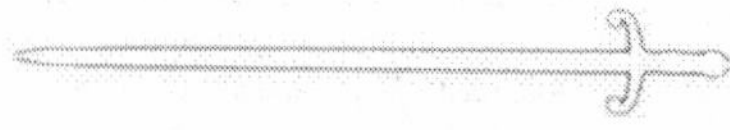

A strange creaking and grinding noise like a sword being dragged through the sand woke Shyla. She lay on her back and stared up at a cloth ceiling while the world around her swayed with the motion of the wagon, its wheels the cause of the sounds.

"See? She's not dead. You owe me an osee," Anwar said.

Lota's children stared at her. Both sat cross-legged next to her.

"I would have been right if Mommy didn't pile those cushions under the entrance." Faizah pouted.

Well, that explained why Shyla hadn't broken all her bones when she fell. "Water?" she croaked.

Anwar handed her a skin. Then the kids left the wagon, announcing to the rest of the caravan and anyone within ten kilometers that she was awake. Shyla gulped the liquid. Even though it was warm, it still soothed her mouth and throat. Drinking exhausted her, and she flopped back. She must have slept through apex. At least they didn't leave her behind in the travel shelter.

The fabric was soon swept aside and Rendor peered inside. His face was creased with concern. "Finally. How are you feeling?"

"Like a gamelu chewed on me and spit me out."

His expression smoothed. "That good?"

She struggled to sit up. "What did I miss? How long was I out?"

"You missed nothing. It's almost darkness. We'll be stopping soon." He paused. "Everyone wants answers about earlier."

"So do I."

"Should be an interesting conversation. I'll follow your lead." Rendor paused and stroked her cheek. "Rest up." Then he ducked out of sight.

When they arrived at the shelter, Camlo offered to cover Shyla's shift. He hefted his mallet, bragging he'd bash anyone's skull in if they came near the caravan. The others all sat around Lota and Shyla. Rendor stood near the entrance where he could watch for intruders and listen to their conversation.

"Rendor told us what happened after we left," Lota said. "But he said you'd explain about the sand and why those people are after you."

What Shyla really wanted to do was curl into a ball and sleep for an entire sun jump. And she didn't have the energy to erase everyone's memory of the fight to avoid this conversation. Plus, she wasn't sure she should. Lota had stood by her when she could have handed her over. So, Shyla told them that the attackers were hired to kidnap her for reasons unknown.

"Mercenaries!" Yegor said in surprise. "There haven't been any since King Ondro's soldiers arrested them and they were outlawed in Koraha."

"That was so long ago," Lota said. "Things change and our current king doesn't seem to care about anything but growing his mound of coins."

"We heard rumors of merc troops in a few other cities," Rendor said.

"Are there any in Zirdai?" Lota asked him.

Rendor met Shyla's gaze. She shook her head. The Invisible Sword would never charge people to help them.

"We completed a full investigation but didn't find any evidence," he said. Although humor sparked in his umber-colored eyes.

"Could they want you because of what happened in Zirdai?" Lota asked Shyla.

"Probably." The former Water Prince could have relatives living in Nintri who desired revenge. But would the news of her summons to the King have reached Nintri so soon?

"What happened in Zirdai?" Uma asked.

Too much to explain. "I helped with the rebellion."

"Helped? Like how you sank those mercs in the sand *helped?"* Uma had paid attention.

Shyla debated. She could erase that from their memories or she could blame sluff sand, even though it was unlikely to have that many patches so close together. Or she could trust them. Since Jayden's betrayal, it hurt to trust.

"There was lots of unstable sand all around us," Lota said,

coming to her rescue.

"Not enough," Uma shot back. "They managed to hide underneath it."

"A clever trick," Yegor said in admiration. "We'd no idea they were there."

Neither had she, and that worried her. The mercs didn't wield magic while they fought, so what had stopped her from sensing them? Shyla glanced at Rendor. Maybe he'd spotted something. He mouthed *later*.

It had taken her two sun jumps to recover and resume her normal duties in the caravan. When Rendor arrived to relieve her from guard duty that darkness, they finally had a moment alone.

After their kiss, she leaned against him, drinking in his warmth. Even though she hadn't practiced with the sand during her shift, the twenty-plus angles on patrol had drained her.

"It's too soon," Rendor said. "Camlo could have covered your shift again."

"He's trying to steal my job," she said in a conspiratorial whisper. "I can't show any weakness."

"Then you shouldn't have fainted in front of everyone." Rendor's sour tone meant he wasn't in the mood for jokes. When she glanced up at him, he cupped her cheek and his hard gaze softened. "You're not invincible. You have to learn how to pace yourself."

"You're right," she admitted.

Rendor had the good sense not to gloat.

"And I obviously have limits. I couldn't feel the mercs hiding in the sand." She stepped back. He was on duty after all and the mercs could be tracking them.

"The mercs were about one meter deep," he said. "Can The Eyes see through all that sand?"

She'd sensed people through sandstone and granite walls. But they had been closer to her. "How did the mercs breathe?"

"There was this long thin tube." Rendor spread his hands to demonstrate the size. "I think they used it to breathe through."

"What was the tube made of?" she asked.

"I didn't get a chance to examine it. If I had to guess, I'd say it was glass."

An effective trick. She'd never thought to search a meter *underneath* the sand. Was that even possible? Lota had shovels. She looked at Rendor, sizing him up. They'd have to dig a big hole.

He was instantly wary. "What are you thinking?"

"I want to test a theory. How are you with small enclosed spaces?"

"I don't do small." His pained expression made her laugh.

Guess she'd have to recruit someone else, but she couldn't resist teasing him. "You were small at one point in your life." She mimed rocking a baby.

"Nope. My mother said I was the biggest baby the physician had ever delivered."

Ouch. She wondered if birthing big babies ran in his family. But she didn't even know if Rendor wanted children. Or if he'd want them with her. And why had her thoughts turned in this direction? Perhaps due to all the time they'd been spending with Anwar and Faizah. While most of the caravanners were initially intimidated by Rendor, the children accepted him without question. He frequently had one of them riding on his shoulders.

"Shyla?" Rendor waved a hand in front of her face. "What are you scheming about now?"

She blushed. "Just thinking about you being a big baby and too scared to help me with my experiment," she teased.

He growled and stalked toward her. She retreated until her back hit one of the wagons. Rendor trapped her between his arms before he leaned in close to her ear and said in a husky whisper, "I seem to recall you enjoying the fact that I'm big." Then he nipped her neck.

A spike of desire shot right through her. "So *you* keep claiming. I've nothing to compare it to." She goaded him because she wanted him to bite her again.

"Then you'll just have to trust me, sunbeam. There's nobody in Koraha bigger than me." And then he not only bit her again but kissed her until she was breathless.

When the caravan was eleven sun jumps away from Qulsary, Shyla spotted a line of strange dunes in the distance. They were huge, with tops shaped like jagged pieces of broken glass. Odd. As they neared, they grew larger until they loomed high above the landscape, blocking the sun. The bright orb disappeared behind these dunes earlier and earlier every sun jump.

Lota laughed when Shyla asked about the alarming feature. "It's a mountain range. Haven't you heard about them?"

She had, but obviously there were gaps in her knowledge. Not a pleasant thought. "I thought they were buried under the sands." Just like the temples, castles, cities, lakes, and forests. The relentless sand had buried everything on the surface of Koraha as the sun baked their world over the millennium, forcing them to retreat underground.

"This one was too high," Lota explained, pointing. "We're on the windward side of the range so the mountains block the sand. There's a dune at its base that grows a bit bigger every sun jump. On the leeward side, there's no sand at all."

No sand? That concept was hard to imagine. "What's there instead?"

"The bedrock that the cities dig down into."

Amazing. "What do the velbloud tether to?"

"The gravel and rocks. There used to be a great river that surged through the valley between the mountains and it carried stones and artifacts from far away and deposited them there."

Excitement pulsed through Shyla. This was why she wanted to travel. To see the wonders and learn about new things like *gravel!*

"Did you know about this?" she asked Rendor after Lota left to check on her children.

He smiled at her with indulgence. "Yes, I was one of the guards that escorted the old Water Prince to Qulsary about a circuit after he claimed the position. It's expected that the new

Water Prince or Princess visit the King and swear fealty. Jayden will have to make the trip once he's established."

He hadn't told her he'd been here before. Then again, Rendor didn't like to talk about his time with the Water Prince. "Did you see the dancing waters? And the canyons?"

"No. It wasn't a sightseeing trip. One sun jump after we arrived, the prince visited the King, then we left the next sun jump. The prince didn't want to be away from Zirdai any longer than he had to."

She hadn't been living in the city then and hadn't paid attention to the political situation. But Rendor had served as a guard for twelve circuits, working his way up to captain. "Are you upset?"

"That I didn't see the dancing waters?" he asked, confused.

"No. About the prince's death."

His expression hardened into a stone mask. She recognized the look from when she'd first met him. Back when he was closed off and almost emotionless. She didn't miss that part of him at all.

"The only thing I'm upset by is that he died too easy. He should have suffered greatly," Rendor said and walked away.

Guilt swirled in her chest as she struggled with her emotions. She hardly knew anything about Rendor. He avoided talking about his childhood or his work as the prince's guard, which left only the time since she'd met him. She did a mental calculation and determined she'd known him for three hundred and sixty sun jumps. Just under a circuit! However, they'd only been together as a couple for the last two hundred and eighty-two sun jumps. Perhaps with more time, he'd confide in her or figure out that just because he didn't discuss something didn't mean it never happened. Everyone had to face their past eventually.

Shyla spent most of her time watching the mountains claim more of the pink sky rather than looking for ambushes. There were three sun jumps remaining in their journey when they reached the base of the biggest dune she'd ever encountered. Gaping at it, she wondered how the gamelus would be able to ascend the steep slope without sinking into it and disappearing or overturning the wagons.

Instead of climbing straight up, Lota directed them along the base of the dune until they reached a path…of sorts. Before the caravan proceeded, four of the muscles grabbed brooms and swept off the sand, revealing a packed-down surface that was easier to travel on. The route wound back and forth as it gradually climbed the side of the dune.

Remembering the mercs hidden deep in the sands, Shyla pulled her gaze from the mountain peaks and focused on their surroundings, seeking bumps on the surface and below, even though she wasn't sure if it worked. She hadn't been able to test her abilities. No one wanted to be buried in the sand. Not that she could blame them.

Halfway up, the muscles switched places, handing their brooms to the fresh group. The gamelus strained. Their pace slowed to a crawl.

"Keep sharp," Rendor barked at the guards. "This is a good place for an ambush."

True. Anyone could be hiding on the top and just pop up and shoot arrows down at them. Or roll boulders. The tension thickened. Shyla inspected every patch of sand that wasn't perfectly smooth.

She was so focused on the surface she didn't realize they'd reached the top until Lota told her to stop and take a look at the view. Suddenly dizzy, Shyla grabbed the closest wagon as the ground dropped away a mere meter from her feet.

As her heart tried to escape her chest, Shyla marveled at the expanse spread out below. It was unlike anything she'd seen in her life. It was long and narrow. The flat valley was a whitish-gray color and dotted with the tiny geometrical shapes of the surface buildings of Qulsary. The kaleidoscope of colored glass glinted in the sunlight. Not one or two or twenty entrances into the city like Zirdai, but a hundred…at least. On the opposite side of where she stood was another mountain range.

"Quite the sight, isn't it?" Yegor asked from his perch on the lead wagon.

"It's beautiful. Feels like I'm flying with the velbloud," she said.

"I never get tired of it. Too bad we can't linger. We need to get to the next shelter."

Right. Shyla scanned the other side of the mountain. It dropped off and there wasn't a dune to climb down. Just pillars of jagged rocks all leaning together. How could anyone descend it let alone a team of gamelus and a wagon?

"You need to let go of the wagon, Shyla," Lota said.

"Oh. Yes. Of course." Except her fingers refused to unbend. Her hand ignored the request. Her arm appeared to be the leader of this silent rebellion. They were her tether. If she let go, she'd float away.

Rendor came up beside her. He took her free hand into his. Only then could she release the wagon. His solid presence grounded her.

The path down into the valley was just as winding as the one they had ascended. Except the surface was a gritty stone and very narrow—the wagons only just fit. The rumble of the wheels echoed loudly all around them. The gamelus fought to keep the wagons from going too fast. And there was a wall of rock on the left and a drop-off on the right.

Shyla kept close to the wall while Rendor walked next to her. They still held hands as they followed the caravan.

"I would have warned you about the height, but I thought since you flew with the velblouds it wouldn't bother you," Rendor said.

"I was desperate, delusional, and dying. I would have done anything to survive. Now..." She shivered despite the heat.

"You're safe, healthy, and have a strong sense of self-preservation?"

"Exactly! And there's no sand. There's nothing to cushion a fall."

"Although from this height, sand—"

"Would cushion a fall," she said with conviction.

"I need to believe that if I'm ever stranded on the surface at apex again."

"You won't be stranded again. Not on my watch."

That she believed.

There was no ladder into the next travel shelter. Instead, there was a tunnel halfway down that speared the side of the mountain. They didn't go down but rather in. Far enough to escape the cold of darkness. And the cavern was big enough for the wagons and gamelus.

After spending all darkness inside, they left as the first ray of sunlight lit the tunnel's entrance. Rendor took her hand as they continued down the narrow path. When they reached the valley floor, the wagons rolled with ease over the flat, hard ground. The road was clearly marked. Best of all, there wasn't anything to hide behind or under. No one was going to sneak up on them.

As the sun jumped across the sky, the buildings swelled in size. Shyla soon discovered extended walking on the bedrock caused her ankles, knees, and hips to ache. The bottoms of her feet hurt as well. Wow. She never thought she would ever, in her entire life, miss sand. But she did.

When they reached the warren of city entrances seventy sun jumps after they'd left Zirdai, her relief at finally arriving warred with her anxiety over her meeting with the King. But soon she forgot all of that as she gawked at the intricate colored-glass mosaics on the surface buildings. The structures were so close together they formed a confusing maze. And the people! Their voices echoed off the hard walls, jumbling together into a cacophony. They all dressed in bright fabrics. Some bustled by and others walked in animated groups. So many people outside the city doing…she'd no idea, as there were only a few nearby velbloud flocks to tend. Children raced around and played games, their laughter slicing through the general din. And then she noticed what was missing—the scent of the desert. The air no longer held the hot aroma of ginger and anise. Now it scratched at the back of her throat with a mix of baked earth, paprika, and a sweet odor that smelled like a perfume that had been worn too long. Remembering the reason she was there, Shyla watched for danger, but most of the people they passed showed only mild interest in the wagons. They smiled at her and she checked to see if the hood of her sun cloak was up. It wasn't. Shyla slowed to a stop.

"What's wrong?" Rendor asked. His hand rested on the hilt of his sword as his gaze swept the crowd.

"They smiled at me."

He glanced at her. "Of course they did. You're beautiful."

"And you're biased. I'm sun-kissed."

"Welcome to Qulsary. They don't care about that."

"How do you know? You were only here for a couple sun jumps."

"The King's personal guards had three sun-kisseds and no one treated them any different." He huffed. "Except some of our guards. Idiots tried to make a few snide remarks and were soundly trounced for their trouble. Served them right."

"I seem to recall a certain captain of the guard that was

grumpy to a certain sun-kissed."

Rendor frowned. "I was grumpy to *everyone* back then."

They continued to an area where other wagons were being unloaded. Yegor brought the caravan up beside an entrance into the city that was big enough to fit the wagons and gamelus.

"This is it," Lota said. "You've escorted us safely and are free to go."

"What about unloading?" Shyla asked. "Aren't you worried someone might steal something?"

Lota gestured to the guards milling around. "The King's guards make sure no one takes anything they shouldn't. There might be something in one of these wagons for the King." She mock gasped in horror. Lota clearly held no love for their reigning monarch. "We're heading to Ginda next. You're welcome to join us."

"Even though I'm the reason you needed guards?" Shyla asked.

"This time. Next time, we might encounter sand pirates. Although…" She smirked at Rendor. "I'd love to see the expressions on those cowards' faces if they have to go up against the captain."

"It would be my pleasure," he said, giving her a slight bow. "When are you leaving for Ginda?"

"Not for another ten sun jumps. My crew needs a break. I'll be in the main bazaar on level twenty-two, selling my wares. It's in the center of the city. Let me know in eight sun jumps if you're interested. Otherwise I'll hire replacements."

"We will. Thanks," Shyla said.

"Oh, and make sure you register with the guards before you go into the city." Lota hooked a thumb at another entrance. "Standard procedure." Lota returned to supervising the unloading.

"Will ten days of sightseeing be long enough for you?" Rendor asked Shyla.

She looked at him in surprise. "I haven't thought about anything beyond my meeting with the King."

"I have, and there's no reason for us to return to Zirdai right away."

"Until we run out of osees."

"Good point. How about we explore the cities of Koraha until we run out of osees."

He agreed too fast. And he had an I-know-something-you-don't grin. What was he hiding? "What are you not telling me?"

Rendor opened his pack and let her peek inside. She gasped as gold glinted. No wonder his pack was so heavy.

"How did you get that?" she asked.

"It was a gift from Gurice and Jaft, your seconds-in-command. I believe Gurice's exact words were, 'We're good. Don't come back until she sees the world.'"

Typical of Gurice. A sudden desire to hug her friend pressed up her throat.

"While I was happy to receive such a generous gift, I must admit that I'm not too thrilled to be carrying around a naked statue of King Tamburah."

Gurice certainly had a warped sense of humor. "At least there's extra gold. More osees for us." Unlike Rendor, Tamburah had overexaggerated the size of his genitalia.

"So I'll ask again. Is ten sun jumps enough time to spend in Qulsary?"

"No. Not if we want to see all the sights in the city."

"Then we'll have to decline Lota's kind offer."

And then it hit her. They had the freedom to do whatever they wanted. To go wherever they wanted. No pressure. No people to save. No wrongs to right.

Excitement coursed through her and she hopped into Rendor's arms and kissed him.

He hefted her with ease. "What was that for?"

"For giving me the world."

"Oh no, sunbeam. I didn't give it to you. You earned it. I'm just here to make sure you enjoy it."

She laughed and kissed him again. He set her down and they headed toward the entrance Lota had pointed out.

"I can ask the guards where to find a room to rent," Rendor said. "They always know the best places."

"I hope the King meets with me as quickly as he met the Water Prince."

Inside the building was a line of people waiting for their turn to register with the guards. At the other end of the line was a long table with three guards sitting behind it. One consulted a scroll and the second wrote on another while the middle guard asked questions.

Shyla and Rendor discussed the different sights they would visit while they waited. Finally it was their turn.

"Names," the guard asked in a bored tone.

"Shyla and Rendor," she said.

The other guard's stylus scratched over the scroll.

"Where are you coming from?"

"Zirdai."

The guard reading the scroll glanced up. "Shyla Sun-Kissed of Zirdai?"

"Uh, yes."

He jumped to his feet. "The King wishes to see you immediately. Follow me."

"Now?" Her heart skipped a beat. She ran a hand through the short strands of her dusty hair. "I need to get cleaned up and dressed." Although how did one dress for an audience with the King? Perhaps she should have thought of this sooner.

"Yes, now."

She and Rendor exchanged a glance.

"Better to get it over with so we can enjoy the city," he said.

It wasn't like she had a choice. They followed him through the surface buildings until they reached a structure made completely of stained glass instead of a mix of glass and stone. No doubt this was the grand entrance to the King's inverted castle. Panels of intricate mosaics decorated the glass. The sliding doors had been pushed open, seeming to invite visitors. Inside, a thick rug covered the floor, and a squad of well-armed guards stood between them and what appeared to be an access way that was well lit with expensive trol lanterns.

"This is Shyla Sun-Kissed," the guard said to a man who looked like an advisor. He wore expensive silk clothing and clutched a tablet to his chest. His dark brown hair was clipped close to his head.

The advisor glanced at Rendor. "And who is this?"

"My companion," Shyla said.

"He can wait here. Only you have been given permission to enter."

"No," Rendor said.

"It wasn't a request."

"I'll be fine," Shyla said when Rendor stiffened. She didn't want him to cause trouble.

The advisor nodded. "Come with me."

She squeezed Rendor's arm. "I'll see you later."

"You certainly will," he said.

Remembering his comment about rescuing her, she smiled. Then she turned her attention to the advisor, debating if she should read him just enough to get a sense of his emotions. But she decided not to. The man might be like Yates, the ex-captain who somehow felt her magic.

The guards parted to let them pass. As they entered the tunnel, Shyla wondered how deep the King lived. She knew his castle was completely sealed off from the rest of Qulsary for his safety. Plus he had no need to access Qulsary since it was ruled by a Water Princess.

As the highest authority in Koraha, he must live deep underground. He'd have to be deeper than any other prince or princess. Would he have a lift like the one in Zirdai to travel multiple levels without having to climb? Or would she have to descend to the very core of Koraha to reach him? She doubted he'd be *that* deep. Too bad, because it would be rather fascinating and appropriate for the King to live in the very heart of their world.

The tunnel sloped down for about six or seven levels and then abruptly opened into a grand cavern. Water fountains splashed merrily in the corners. But there was a sense of something missing. The space appeared to be primed for a display of opulence, yet it was almost bare. There were marks on the walls where tile mosaics must have hung. Rectangles of dirt outlined the floor, indicating a number of missing rugs. And partly hidden in the shadows were a number of armed guards.

Far more guards than the room warranted.

The advisor stopped in the middle of the room and gestured to the guards. "Seize her."

Shyla braced for capture, but no one moved. The guards remained in a half circle around her. In fact, if she wished to escape, the route back up to the surface was clear.

"Interesting," the advisor said.

Not wanting to be ambushed again, she lowered her mental shield. Meeting his light-green gaze, she read his intentions, sensing his emotions. "This was a test."

He nodded. "A guilty person would have run for it or attacked first."

Annoyed and not wishing to be surprised again, Shyla kept hold of her connection to the advisor. "What do you think I'm guilty of?"

The advisor approved of her practical response. "You led a rebellion that overthrew two powerful leaders who have died as a result. I'm quite sure you're guilty of many crimes even though, by your actions, you do not believe so." It should be fascinating to learn which ones this sun-kissed would confess to.

"I'm quite sure you're just guessing. Is this what the King wishes to know or are you just satisfying your own curiosity?"

Ah, a challenge. Fun. "I'm trying to determine if escorting you to a meeting with the King will endanger him."

She gestured to the soldiers. "Are they not enough of a guarantee? I'm flattered that you think so highly of my skills. You can always assign a few more to join us."

He appreciated the jab. But she was too confident. Unless it was all an act. Pretty good acting if she was pretending to be in control of the situation despite the fact that she was outnumbered. She was a rather slight figure to have accomplished so much. The sun-kissed must have plenty of supporters, which was surprising considering the citizens of Zirdai discriminated against her kind.

"Why didn't you become Zirdai's new Water Princess or Heliacal Priestess?" he asked.

"I already have a job. And don't you have one as well?" She inclined her head toward the other side of the chamber. All she wanted to do was get the meeting with the King over with and return to Rendor. It would be the first time she'd be alone with him in seventy sun jumps.

Oh, he liked this woman. "I do. My name is Najib. Follow me, please."

The "please" was a nice touch.

As she followed Najib through the tunnels, grottos, and chambers of the King's domain, everything they passed was oversized, as if the King was three meters tall. Expensive trol lanterns hung every two meters. The bright light banished the shadows, creating a feeling of being on the surface without the uncomfortable heat. In fact, braziers full of lava stones drove the ever-present underground chill away.

Yet the rooms lacked decoration. There were cushions and tables, but nothing resembling the tales of the King's lavish extravagance. Had those all been rumors? No. These chambers had been filled at one point.

The King's guards kept a watchful eye on them as they descended. Massive water fountains sent ribbons of water arcing into the air. Even though Shyla knew the water was being recycled, she still gaped at the wasteful decadence. At least these fountains matched the gossip about the castle.

After they traveled down another four levels, Shyla became uneasy. It wasn't because of the guards. They, for the most part, viewed her as a mere curiosity and not a threat. And no one was lying in wait. But something unseen jangled her nerves.

It took her another degree to pinpoint the reason for her anxiety. A muted roar vibrated through the floor. Memories of the gas explosions in Zirdai were still fresh in her mind. At least this murmur stayed constant—more like an unending cave-in, which was equally alarming.

"What is that noise?" she finally asked Najib.

"You'll see soon enough," he said.

The sound grew in volume as they traversed a long tunnel. A rug the color of sand padded the floor. The corridor ended at a set of immense stained-glass doors. They arched up two levels, tall enough for the mosaic of the mountains to fit. Three guards stood on each side of the doors. All six studied her with interest.

She met their gazes. All six incorrectly concluded she was not a threat.

"Wait here, please," Najib said. He knocked on the glass. After a moment, it opened and Najib slipped inside.

To pass the time, Shyla considered their descent and calculated that she had to be about fifty levels below the surface. A surprise. She thought the King would insist on living in the deepest level of Koraha. And where was all the famed treasure?

Thinking about treasures, she wondered how many osees Rendor would get for the gold statue and how long they could live on the coins. Contemplating their future was better than trying to guess why she was here. If they worked as guards for caravans, then their travel expenses would be low. And as long as they didn't stay in one city more than thirty sun jumps, they wouldn't have to pay taxes or tithes. They'd just have to pay for meals as guests, which was cheaper. If they were frugal, they'd be able to visit all the major cities of Koraha—a dream finally coming true.

The doors opened again and Najib stuck his head out. "The King will see you now."

She swiped a clammy hand through her hair and smoothed her dusty tunic. The actions amused Najib. Reading his emotions reminded her that she was Shyla Sun-Kissed and had the power of The Eyes at her command.

Her stomach settled and she strode into the King's throne room. And stopped dead as she encountered a bevy of unexpected things.

The now roaring sound was a river of water rushing around

the King's throne. The pure white chair sat on a block of stone that was in the center of the flowing water but high enough that the water didn't splash the King.

Sitting on the chair and wearing a crown made of what appeared to be osmium and sapphires, the King gazed at her with bemusement. No doubt she was gawking. He was…nothing like she expected and yet he still embodied the persona of a powerful ruler. His straight posture and slight tilt to his head gave him an intimidating and regal air. Yet the glint in his eyes hinted to a boyish impishness.

Beckoning Shyla closer, he pitched his voice so it carried over the noisy water. "I know it's a shock. Najib takes way too much pleasure in surprising new visitors." He swept a hand out. "Water is the ultimate power in Koraha so here I sit surrounded by it. Be careful not to fall in or you'll drown."

"Drown?" Shyla sidled up to the edge.

"It's when water replaces the air in your lungs, causing you to die. I wouldn't recommend it."

She stopped. Water could kill you? It occupied half the room. But despite its impressive presence, her gaze kept returning to the King's face.

He sighed. "I'm younger than you expected."

An understatement. The King was supposed to be over eighty circuits old. This man looked the same age as Najib, which she guessed was around thirty-five circuits old. "Yes, sire."

"I guess I should get used to that." He gestured. "Are you properly impressed by all this?"

Confused, she glanced around. Guards lined the walls and

above them were mosaics Shyla would bet were constructed out of precious stones. "Yes, sire. Most impressed."

"Good. Now we can talk business." The King stood. His silk robe and fur cloak flowed to the floor in a wave of light blue. Dark auburn hair curled at the nape of his neck.

Shyla wondered if they would have to keep shouting over the din or if he would risk drowning and ruin his garments by crossing the water. There appeared to be no other way for the King to reach her.

"Pay attention," the King said, spreading his hands.

Square stone pillars rose from the water's surface. No, that was wrong. The water level dropped just enough to reveal the tops of the blocks.

The King hitched up his robes, exposing sturdy leather boots, and hopped from one to the next, landing gracefully next to Shyla. The water surged and buried the stepping stones once again.

"You don't seem overly surprised," the King said. "Why is that?"

He was about thirteen centimeters taller than Shyla. She met his gaze. The King's light amber-colored eyes seemed to peer into Shyla's soul. Magic? Or something else? Out of respect for the monarch, she refrained from using The Eyes to examine his soul. "You are the King of Koraha and wield the power of the water. It makes sense that it should obey your wishes."

"Did you hear that, Najib?" the King asked over Shyla's shoulder.

The advisor had been waiting near the door. "Yes, sire, I did."

"This one's clever."

"Yes, sire, she is."

"Wonderful. I love a challenge. Come with me, Shyla Sun-Kissed. We've much to discuss and I don't like having to yell over the water's constant jabber."

The King led Shyla, Najib, and a dozen guards to another chamber. This one was much smaller than the throne room. Though opulent, with thick rugs on the floor, trol lanterns, and precious gems arranged into artworks, it was more comfortable. It appeared lived in, as if the King spent most of his time here. There was a desk and cushions and tables. The King sat on a cushion and gestured for Shyla to sit next to him.

"Najib, can you fetch us some hot tea, please?"

"Yes, sire." Not at all bothered by being asked to perform a servant's task, he retreated.

Shyla eyed the King, who took a moment to inspect her as well.

"Your eyes are a very unusual color. They match the sapphires in my crown," the King said. "All the sun-kisseds I know have sunshine eyes."

"Sunshine?"

"Yes, the color of the sun. I always thought it appropriate. Yellow eyes and yellow hair like the Sun Goddess herself." The King cocked his head. "However, you're not like the other sun-kisseds, are you?"

Unease stirred at the question that wasn't really a question. "I'm not sure how to answer that."

"All right. How about this? You were born to two Monks of

Parzival, which means you grew up near the city of Zirdai. One that is infamous for its strict Heliacal Priestess who demands sun-kissed babies be sacrificed. Instead of living in the monastery where you would be protected, you decided to live in the city and eventually you led a rebellion that unseated both the prince and priestess."

Careful to keep her expression neutral despite her growing alarm, Shyla wondered what else the King knew about her. Her father was the leader of the Parzival monks and reported to the King, but Shyla thought he'd send information about the city and not about his personal life.

"I guess that's still not a question, is it?" the King asked. "The question I really want an answer to is this: How did you do it? How did you get the people of Zirdai to set aside their biases and help you?"

Good thing Najib returned with tea. He set out cups with a teapot, and handed the King a scroll that was sealed with wax. "Bilal sent that from Zirdai." Najib glanced at Shyla. "His report about the rebellion."

Bilal must be the King's emissary, who hadn't asked Shyla a single question, choosing instead to talk to everyone else. She wished she could read his report.

"Wonderful," the King said, setting it down on the floor. "I'll read it later."

Najib poured three cups of tea and settled into a nearby cushion.

The King sipped his. "Ah, I can't get enough of this new blend. Try it, Shyla."

It tasted of cinnamon and vanilla. "It's very good."

"Now, answer my questions and tell us about your adventures." The King waved a hand.

Shyla had expected to give the King a report and for him to compare her account with the one Bilal sent. She was also curious about the King as well. "Can I ask some of my own, sire?"

"Of course. It would only be fair." He leaned forward like a small child waiting for a story before going to sleep. "Go on."

Shyla explained how she was drawn into the hunt for the legendary Eyes of Tamburah, was recruited by the Invisible Sword, and defeated the prince and priestess.

"Such heroics!" the King exclaimed after she finished. "I've heard of this Invisible Sword before. One of the perks of being the king-in-training. I learned about the assassination of the despot. Back when the kings ruled from Zirdai. Can you imagine, Najib? Living in Zirdai?"

"I would not like the sand, sire. I hear it gets everywhere."

"Does it, Shyla?"

This entire encounter with the King was surreal. One moment he radiated power and the next resembled a curious boy. "Yes, but only throughout the top ten levels or so due to the wind and from people's boots."

"Ah, interesting. And now before you pester me with questions, I've one more. Why didn't you mention you woke the power of The Eyes? And please don't waste my time by denying it."

Shyla's throat went dry despite the sweet-tasting tea. The temptation to read the King's soul pumped in her heart. Instead, she decided to be honest. "Not many people know about the magic wielders, so I thought you wouldn't believe me." She hesitated. "I was also worried that you'd want to use me."

"But you saw me use magic to command the water."

"Some people don't know they're using magic. You could have thought it was a gift from the Sun Goddess because you're the King."

"It is a gift. However, you're right about one thing. I do want to use you."

While Shyla grappled with this revelation, the King refilled their mugs. "All right. Ask your questions."

"Use me how?"

"Ask your others first. Then you'll have a better sense of who I am and that'll help you decide."

Decide? That meant she might have a choice. This conversation was so strange. "If you knew about The Eyes of Tamburah and knew where they were and what they could do, why didn't you wake the power?"

"The Kings of Koraha decided long ago that would be too much power for a king to have. We already command the very water. Besides, no one wants to turn into a megalomaniac despot." He held his hand out in a placating gesture. "Not to imply that will happen to you."

"But what if it does happen to me? Can you stop me?"

"Wow, she went straight for the jugular, Najib. What do you

think of that?"

"I believe it's a legitimate question, sire."

He huffed. "You would." The King met her gaze. "Try to read me." When Shyla hesitated, he said, "Go on. Try."

She sensed a trick. The blueish color of the metal on his crown had to be osmium and not platinum. He wore a silver and sapphire necklace around his neck. There were three droplet-shaped gemstones. The one in the middle was about five centimeters long, while the other two were about three centimeters long. Nothing to suggest it would block her magic.

Yet, when she reached with the power of The Eyes, she didn't pick up on the King's thoughts or learn his emotions. There was nothing but amusement glinting in his eyes.

"I can't. You must be wearing some kind of protection," she said.

"See, Najib? I am the rightful king after all."

"I never said you weren't, sire. No one has. It's your own inner doubts causing you to worry."

"Excuse me," Shyla interrupted what she suspected was a well-trodden argument. "Can you explain what's going on?"

"The Eyes don't work on the legitimate ruler of Koraha. I don't know why. Frankly, I don't know why water listens to my commands either, but I'm the only one in Koraha who can move it. Actually, there should be another—my eventual replacement. Except we haven't found him yet."

"He's just a baby, sire."

She was confused and fascinated at the same time. "How do you know he's a baby?"

"Because the old King of Koraha died one hundred and five sun jumps ago," the King said. "When he returned to the Sun Goddess, she picked another to take his place…or, rather, mine. There are always two kings living at one time. The King and the king-in-training, which I was until the old king died. And now there's a one-hundred-and-five-sun-jump-old baby out there who will eventually replace me.

"It's not well known. Well, the monks all know, but they're sworn to secrecy as we don't want a bunch of parents trying to trick us into thinking their son is the next in line."

And now she knew, which meant they would never let her leave. Her fingers tightened around her cup. But something didn't add up. "Wait. Your emissary arrived in Zirdai eighty-two sun jumps ago, which means he had to leave Qulsary before the old king died."

The King beamed at her. "You are paying attention. Excellent. When the messages about the arrest of the monks and then the change in leadership in Zirdai arrived, we were all very concerned. What if the people behind that coup set their sights on the King? Advisor Yiesha sent the emissary to assess the situation."

"But what about my summons?"

"The monk who told us about Hanif's arrest also mentioned that a sun-kissed woke the power of The Eyes.

I had no power or resources to demand Hanif's release, but…" He glanced at Najib. "I gave Bilal that summons for you just in case you were behind the coup."

"When you didn't have the authority." Najib tsked.

"The King was close to death. I took a chance."

"Why are you telling me this?" she asked.

"Because you're in a unique position, Shyla. Before Tamburah became king, it was standard practice for the king's trusted advisor to be the one who claimed the power of The Eyes. They would make the sacrifice and take the leap of faith, demonstrating they were the chosen one. Together the king and his advisor worked together to rule Koraha.

"Tamburah decided that he wanted the power of The Eyes all to himself, and that didn't go well for anyone—we think it led to his madness. After the Invisible Sword assassinated Tamburah, it was decided that no one should have that much power ever again and The Eyes were hidden away."

"So the stories of Tamburah using his intelligence and charisma to gain power are false?"

"Yes. About four circuits after a king dies, there is a search to find the next king-in-training. Tamburah was found and taken to Zirdai to prepare for his eventual role."

"Wait. How do you find the new king without The Eyes?" she asked in alarm. Were they going to ask her to do the job? She didn't want to get involved. All she wanted was to travel with Rendor.

"Every child who is born on the same sun jump the king dies is tested."

Memories of being confined in the Invisible Sword's testing chamber surged through her. She'd never wish that on anyone, let alone children. "How are they tested?"

"They are immersed in water. The new king will be the only

one who can control it."

"And the others?"

"Drowned."

Horror filled her and she cracked her cup.

The King laughed. "I'm joking. Did you see her face, Najib?"

"That was uncalled for, sire," he scolded.

"Oh, come on. She was already thinking something bad happened to the children. By the way, I'm insulted on behalf of all the kings that you would immediately think that."

She slammed the cup down on the table. It broke, spilling tea. "I'd apologize, but the prior Water Prince and Heliacal Priestess of Zirdai had no trouble harming and killing children, sire."

The humor in the King's eyes died. "I'm sorry. The children are not harmed. In fact, it's interesting that they all automatically hold their breaths when immersed. They're quickly taken out of the water, dried off, and returned to their parents with a few extra coins in their pockets."

Although relieved about the children, Shyla glared at the King. Safe and protected in his castle, he could make jokes while his people suffered. "You have your monks spying on all the cities. Why didn't you do anything when they reported the atrocities in Zirdai? You've plenty of coins from taxes. Taxes that are supposed to improve everyone's lives. Why not send your elite soldiers to help us?"

The King leaned back in his seat and rubbed a hand over his face. "I had no authority to do anything until the old king died. And even if I had broken the law, there are no more elite soldiers." He exchanged a glance with Najib. "Plus, the taxes were stolen."

Stunned, she gaped at him. That was…Shyla couldn't find a word adequate enough for just how…horrible that revelation sounded.

"I think you should have led with the coins being stolen, sire," Najib said. "It's a bit confusing the other way." The advisor turned to Shyla. "The elite soldiers left because we didn't have any coins to pay them."

"How…?" Shyla struggled to form a coherent sentence.

The King huffed and stabbed a finger at the guards in the room. "No one knows how the taxes disappeared."

Shyla sensed their embarrassment and anger. "Why haven't your guards left as well?"

The King's ire melted and his shoulders slumped. "We sold most of the castle's treasures to pay the ones who stayed."

That explained the barren rooms. "When were the coins stolen?" Shyla asked. Was this what the King wanted to use her for? To find them?

"We think it was while the prior king was dying—he was in an unconscious state. I couldn't assume leadership until he died so there was some confusion during that time."

"How long was he incapacitated?"

"Eight hundred and ninety-one sun jumps."

That was almost two and a half circuits! "Why didn't the people of Koraha know their king was dying?" she demanded in a strident tone.

"Can you imagine what your previous Water Prince would

have done if he'd known the King was unable to issue commands?"

Since she could well imagine the amount of people he would have killed to become the new king, her anger transformed into horror.

The King watched her expression closely. "And that's also the reason there's been no help for Zirdai or any of the other cities in need. And no official announcement of my accession. I don't have the coins to send heralds or to travel to all the cities in Koraha." His frustration was clear in every clipped word.

Shyla needed more tea to absorb all this information.

"Is this a good time to loop back to Shyla's first question, Najib?"

"Give the woman a bit of a rest, sire. Let me get her a fresh cup of tea." He cleaned up the broken pieces, sopped up the spilled liquid, and left.

Shyla tried to collect her thoughts. She had so many questions she didn't know where to start. Anxiety and fear swirled in her stomach. Would the King insist she become his advisor since she'd woken The Eyes? He had the power to do it. No one dared disobey the King. Well, Shyla could run away and hide. The King didn't have any coins to search for her. Except she'd constantly live in fear of being discovered. What kind of life was that? Not the one she hoped to have with Rendor.

Thinking about Rendor, she wondered what he was doing. Was he worried that she was taking too long? Was he already recruiting people to rescue her? Perhaps even fighting his way through all those levels until he reached the throne room? She sucked in a breath as an idea occurred to her.

"I know that sound. Do tell, Shyla."

Shyla gestured at the gemstone mosaics. "Why don't you sell these? Just one of them would be worth over a thousand coins."

"I've considered it. However, they are all antiques, handed down from one king to the next. Each new king adds a piece to the collection." The King took off his crown and rested it on the table. "It weighs a ton, but Najib suggested I wear it." He ran his slender fingers through his thick curly hair. "I'd hate to lose a piece of our history, but I'll do it if I must. Of course it would have to be done carefully, just like the sale of the other treasures. I'm sure you've already figured out that the theft of the coins needs to be kept a secret. If the other Water Princes and Princesses find out, someone will try to take the crown from me."

Najib returned with another cup and a fresh pot of tea. "This blend will calm the nerves," he said.

Shyla sipped the yellow-colored brew. It had a touch of citrus and chamomile. The warmth from the liquid spread from her stomach in a soothing wave.

"Najib is a master at blending teas. He has a tea for every one of my moods." The King smiled at his advisor with affection.

"The King is too kind." Najib bowed and resumed his seat. "I believe now is a good time to answer Shyla's question about how you'd like to use her."

"Now you know some of the problems I'm dealing with, I would like to hire your services to recover our stolen coins, if possible. I know it might be too late."

Shyla wasn't surprised by the request. Yet it wasn't phrased quite the way she expected. "Hire?"

"In this case we can only offer you a finder's fee, which would be a percentage of the coins you recover. I can also offer you a place to stay as well as food and water while you're searching."

"What about Rendor?"

"Who's Rendor?"

"Her companion, sire. Captain Rendor or…perhaps he isn't the captain anymore?"

"He's the captain of the Invisible Sword."

"Ah, you recruited him. Well done. Do you trust him?"

"Of course she trusts him, Najib! She wields the power of The Eyes."

"Ah, yes. Handy that."

"What about Rendor?" she asked again.

"Will he be a part of the investigation?" the King asked.

"He'd probably insist on it."

"Then he'll get the same accommodations as you and you can split the finder's fee."

And now for the scary question. "What happens if I say no?"

"Then you say no." All the energy seemed to drain from the King, his exhaustion now clear in the lines of his handsome face. "We'll continue on as best we can."

"Why ask at all? You could order me to obey."

"I could." He leaned forward. "And if I did, you'd be resentful, you'd make a token effort to investigate, and you'd claim the coins were gone for good before leaving as quickly as possible."

"I—"

"You're the leader of the Invisible Sword, Shyla, and a powerful magic wielder. If I treated you like an underling, ordering you about, I'd ruin any chance for us to be allies."

She considered his explanation. He had a point, although he didn't know she had no desire to be an ally. That implied a great deal of responsibility and she already had enough on her shoulders.

The King studied her. "If you decline, I will require you to promise to keep what you've learned a secret."

"You'd trust me?"

"To a certain extent. That's why I require a promise. You know the power of a promise. If you break it, I'll know."

"How?"

"Water. You are a creature of water. Everyone is, and I can sense it and manipulate it. Water flows throughout Koraha. It's all connected to me."

That was rather fascinating. Shyla would love to learn more about the King's magic. But now wasn't the time to ask those questions.

"Do you agree to help us?" the King asked.

"I need to think about it," Shyla said.

"Of course. Najib, please show Shyla to our guest quarters, and—"

"No, thank you, sire. I also need to discuss this with Rendor and I think it would be best to do that away from your…kind hospitality."

"All right. How about you take the next sun jump to decide? Is that enough time?"

"Yes, sire."

"Good. Najib, escort Shyla to the surface—no, wait, it's too close to apex. Perhaps a tour of where she'd be staying if she agrees. It's not as empty as the rest of the castle. And have her try Cook's gamelu sausages; they're the best."

"Yes, sire."

Najib escorted her from the room. He chatted about the various rooms they passed through—sitting, receiving, planning, entertaining—so many Shyla lost track of them all.

"Ah, you're an excellent student of history. Good to see the Monks of Parzival are teaching you properly," Najib said when she admired a statue of a wollfur—a four-legged creature that had lived in the ancient forests.

"We have a few preserved skeletons in the First Room of Knowledge. Such a shame so many species died as the sun moved closer to our world."

"It is," Najib agreed in a solemn tone. "There is an entire Room of Knowledge in the monastery outside of Qulsary dedicated to those creatures."

Instantly jealous, she said, "That would be worth becoming a monk for! Tell me, do the Monks of Quirin really have ten Rooms of Knowledge?" Even though she knew the Quirin monastery was the largest in Koraha, she never trusted rumors.

"Twelve." He grinned at her gasp. "As the King's advisor, I can visit them all."

"All?"

"Yes, *all* Rooms of Knowledge in *all* the monasteries. So can the King, but he prefers I do *all* the work and give him a concise—in other words not boring—report."

"I would actually enjoy doing that," she admitted. Access to all those rooms would be beyond bliss.

"You've woken The Eyes and can become his advisor at any time," Najib said.

His tone remained even, but Shyla's magic sensed his emotional turmoil. And it wasn't jealousy or greed or power but sadness that dominated. Najib would miss working with the King. They'd become more than colleagues during the circuits they worked together.

"I have a job. I've no interest in being anyone's advisor, Najib." And no desire to become embroiled in the King's problems.

The swell of his relief almost made Shyla laugh.

"This job, your Invisible Swords, what are your plans?" he asked.

"To ensure no one else abuses their power in Zirdai."

"Ah, do you think the people you left in power are in danger of being corrupted?"

"No. But there's still plenty to do within the organization."

"And you're the only one to do it?"

"I know what you're doing," she said, sensing he planned to use the argument that the Invisible Sword could handle any problems that might arise while she was gone. Of course they could, which was why Shyla would enjoy traveling. There would be nothing to worry about except which city they'd visit next.

"Can't blame me." Then a beat later, he asked, "Will your Invisible Swords help other cities if needed?"

Shyla had to appreciate his persistence. "It would depend on the circumstances and our resources at the time."

"Ah."

Najib showed her the guest quarters. They were huge, with a sitting room, a water closet and a gigantic sleeping cushion piled with furs. Then they visited the kitchens. Abena, the cook, was baking a dozen pies. The smell alone almost convinced Shyla to pledge her service to the King then and there.

Abena fried up a couple sausages. Shyla had never tasted anything so delicious. However, losing her freedom still wasn't worth it even if she could eat meals like this every sun jump. Abena packed a few extra sausages for Rendor—quite the bribe.

Najib finished the tour and led Shyla back to the surface. The squad of guards had resumed their protective stance, blocking Rendor from the access way into the King's castle. Rendor scowled at them. It appeared as if he hadn't moved, which was impossible as everyone had to go underground during the sun's apex.

"Please let us know your decision before angle seventy," Najib said before he returned below.

It wasn't quite a full sun jump, but close enough. Shyla squeezed through the guards. Rendor scanned her, obviously searching for injuries, before he relaxed. Well, not quite, as he kept his hand on his sword's hilt, but the tension had left his shoulders.

"Are you all right?" he asked.

"I'm fine."

"What did the King want?"

"I'll tell you all about it, but not here."

He grunted. "Come on, then. I found us a room."

It was the best news she'd heard all sun jump.

The room was on level eighteen and Shyla was impressed Rendor found it. Qulsary wasn't deep. The city reached water at a mere forty-five levels. Instead the city had spread out along the valley floor—narrow and long. So very long.

Outside their room, she gestured to the warren of tunnels branching off in multiple directions. "How did you not get lost?"

He pointed to one of the intersections. "The tunnels all have names which include a compass direction. We're in North Dolomite Tunnel at location two point three."

"Two point three?"

"Yes, it's two point three kilometers from the northernmost starting point of the tunnel. When it reaches the city's center, it turns into South Dolomite Tunnel. It's easier to navigate than Zirdai's ad-hoc labyrinth of tunnels." Rendor unlocked the door and slid it open. "I only rented this room for a couple sun jumps. The guard I talked to said the city goes on for over forty kilometers and if we want to see everything, we should start in the north and move south as we explore."

They entered a sitting area and beyond that was a nice-sized room that contained a sleeping cushion big enough for two. Unlike the ones in the travel shelters, the cushion was clean and thick. Rendor had already gathered some supplies—a few extra water skins, some jerky, and a couple of druks. The warm orange-tinted light filled the space.

"You've been busy," she said.

"Better than going crazy worrying about you." He pulled her close and nuzzled her neck.

After seventy sun jumps and one crazy conversation with the King, Shyla was finally alone with Rendor. Truly alone with no chance of anyone interrupting them. Not even the King.

"Are you going to tell me about your audience with the King?" Rendor asked.

"Eventually," she said, making him laugh. Taking his hand, she pulled him to the sleeping cushion. "It's been so long, I think I need an extensive refresher course."

"I'm always at your service." He pulled her tunic off. "Step one," he murmured before kissing her.

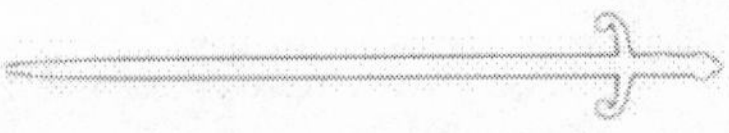

They woke deep into the darkness. Shyla told Rendor everything that she'd learned and what the King wanted them to do.

"We're lucky that he didn't just demand your services," Rendor said.

Shyla agreed. "What should we do?"

"It's your choice. I'm here for you. Whether we see the dancing waters or interrogate witnesses, I'm happy as long as we're together." He stroked her cheek.

"That's lovely, Rendor." She gave him a kiss. "But it doesn't help me. What should I do?"

"You should do what you truly want."

"Again, not helping."

His deep chuckle vibrated against her chest. Suddenly her biggest desire at the moment was to repeat steps one through twenty and never leave the sleeping cushion.

"You've wanted to travel since you were little. You have done so much for Zirdai. No one will blame you for being selfish."

True. Yet the King couldn't help anyone without the taxes. "I can't be selfish," she said.

"I know. But you can be smart."

"I can?"

"Before you agree to investigate the theft, you can negotiate and set some terms."

"What type of terms?"

"Things like you'll only do this one job and then you're done. We go on our merry way."

"I knew you were more than just a big brute," she teased.

"Sunbeam, I'm a man of many talents."

"Oh?"

He moved, and she was pinned beneath him within a heartbeat.

"Allow me to demonstrate." He dipped his head low and his lips touched very sensitive skin.

"Oooh."

They woke again at angle zero. Taking their time, they dressed and went out to use the collection stations. They had plenty of angles before they needed to give the King an answer so they descended to level twenty-two to search for Lota's market stand in the main bazaar.

After a number of inquiries, they found the huge cavern filled with every possible item that a person could ever need or want. Shyla marveled at the sheer scale of the chaos. Rows upon rows of stands lined up with merchants hawking their wares. Shoppers clogged the aisles, bargaining over prices as coins clinked. The noise echoed off the walls and ceiling, amplifying the buzz of voices.

She gawked at the array of clothing. In Zirdai, almost everyone wore a tunic and pants woven from gamelu wool. The fabric was warm and durable and they tended to be dyed in muted colors like brown, tan, dark red, and deep green. Here the citizens' clothes were dyed in a variety of bright colors. They wore skirts, robes, capes, and wrapped multicolored scarves around their necks or heads or both. Not wound quite like the mercenaries who'd ambushed them, but similar. The women who didn't cover their heads had styled their hair in elaborate knots. Some had braided their hair in multiple thin braids that hung down their backs.

Rendor clasped her hand before they joined the flow of people.

"Stay close," he said, inclining his head toward a group of young men. "Thieves."

"Surely they won't try anything," she said.

"Not on me, but you stand out, and they know you're new

to the city—a prime target."

She touched her hair with her free hand. "But you said—"

"They're accepting, but sun-kisseds are still rare. They probably know all the local ones."

"I can take care of myself."

"I know, but if you hang close to the big brute, they won't bother you. And you can save your energy for later." He winked at her.

She laughed. "The big brute comes in handy, doesn't he?"

"Oh yes. Not many physical challenges. And if they think you're big and stupid, they'll underestimate you every time and the advantage is yours."

They wove through the market, searching for Lota's stand. Shyla stopped at one place selling scarves. She admired a long thin scarf that was orange and yellow with black silhouettes of sand rats.

"I've much prettier prints, my dear," the seller said. "That design is for the boys. They think rats are creepy and wear it to upset their parents and scare their sisters."

"Actually, rats are intelligent, loving creatures." Shyla couldn't help defending the animals since they'd saved her parents' lives.

The woman stared at her. "Who am I to disagree with a customer? I'll sell it to you for four osees."

"One."

"It's made from the finest gamelu fibers, my dear. Imported all the way from Tarim. I can't accept anything less than three."

"Two. Plus you'll show me how to wrap it around my head

and neck like the locals."

The merchant sighed and agreed, muttering about being taken advantage of. Yet she took the coins quickly enough and taught Shyla how to arrange the fabric. Rendor watched it all with amusement.

"She probably would have taken one osee," he said. "There's a dozen people selling scarves."

"Yes, but I liked this pattern."

"You do realize that if your aim was to use the scarf to blend in, you did the opposite by picking that pattern."

"I do."

"All right."

Rendor muscled his way through the crowds. Shyla stayed right behind him, enjoying the ease of traveling in his wake. Eventually, they found Lota's stand. Yegor was stacking blank scrolls next to jars of ink and styluses while Lota bantered good-naturedly with a customer as she wrapped the man's purchases.

"Where are the children?" Rendor asked Yegor.

Yegor glanced around as if expecting to see Anwar and Faizah nearby. He shrugged when he didn't spot them. "Probably off scamming grandmothers."

"Scamming?" Shyla asked. "And you allow this?"

"It's harmless. They pretend to be lost and the woman takes pity and buys them some sweets before she helps them find us. She walks away feeling happy for doing a good deed. Sometimes we even get a new customer." He swept a hand out. "With this amount of competition, I'm glad to get some notice even if it's because of my two brats." That last bit was said with affection.

"You're here early," Lota said to them after her customer left. "I suspect that's bad news for us."

"Yes, sorry," Shyla said. "We're going to stay."

"For how long? I'll be looping back this way before heading to Nintri."

"Unknown, but if we're ready to move on when you return, we'll let you know," Rendor said.

Shyla touched the woman's arm. "Be careful in Nintri.

Those mercs know your name and since they failed to capture me, they might take their anger out on you."

Lota glanced at Yegor. "She makes a good point. Maybe we should skip Nintri and go to Catronia instead."

"You're the boss," Yegor said with a smile. "I go where commanded."

The merchant just shook her head. "This is the same man who had a temper tantrum when we skipped Apanji because of a sandstorm."

"Apanji has the best velbloud eggs—they're twice the size of anywhere else."

"Velbloud eggs are not worth—"

"Bypassing Nintri is a good idea," Shyla said, interrupting the impending argument. "I'll sleep better knowing your family is safe."

They said goodbye to Lota and Yegor and continued to browse the stands, purchasing a few more supplies. Then Rendor made a few careful inquiries with some of the merchants. He passed a coin or two in exchange for information on the location of Qulsary's black market.

The city's guards probably knew exactly where it was, but it was one of those places where they earned a few coins by looking the other way. There was an understanding that if the merchants kept everything civil and there weren't any problems, they'd be left undisturbed. If there was trouble, the guards would raid the market. All the merchants would scatter and in a few sun jumps there would be a new location and the cycle would start again.

"Is this so you can sell Tamburah's statue?" she asked Rendor after he confirmed the directions to where the market was currently located.

"Yes. No legitimate antiques dealer will touch it without a certification."

They left the main bazaar and headed south. Even with the detailed instructions on how to navigate the city, Rendor made a few wrong turns and had to backtrack a couple times. After about ten angles, his expression turned wary and he stiffened.

"What's wrong? Are we lost?" she asked.

"No. Someone's following us."

"Who?"

"I don't know, but I'm going to blunder around some more to see if I can flush them out."

"Wait, have you been making mistakes on purpose?" She hurried after him.

"Did you really think I couldn't follow simple directions?" He was amused, which was better than being upset.

"Now that I'm thinking about it, no. But it seemed so real."

"That's the idea, sunbeam. When doing something illegal, it helps to not lead the guards straight to the scene of the crime."

That was a bit of an exaggeration. "Are guards following us?"

"Not sure yet."

Shyla could lower her mental shield to help him, but there were far too many people around. After a few more "wrong" turns, they exited a tunnel and the area opened up into an oversized hexagonal intersection where four guards waited along with a man who appeared to be in charge—his cocky confidence and impressive physique gave him away. Boots scuffed behind them and Shyla glanced over her shoulder. Four more guards moved closer, blocking their retreat.

"Follow my lead," Rendor whispered to her before he stopped about three meters in front of the leader. "A welcoming committee. How nice." He smiled, but there was nothing friendly about it.

The man, who was only a centimeter or two shorter than Rendor, straightened. "Surely you didn't think you could come into *my* city without me knowing, Rendor."

"*Captain* Rendor," Shyla corrected, hoping to deflate some of the unpleasant man's puffed-up sense of importance.

"He betrayed and murdered his prince. You should be glad I didn't call him traitor."

Betrayed and murdered. Those were fighting words. Shyla met the leader's gaze. He was the captain of the guard of Qulsary. Disgust and anger simmered inside him, but he would obey his orders despite his desire to show his people what you should do to a traitor—kill him on sight.

"And you should be glad I don't jump to conclusions and assume you're an idiot, Captain Kilab," Shyla said. "You've no idea what really happened in Zirdai. All you've heard are rumors. So shut your mouth until you've learned the truth."

He was surprised she knew his name, but he kept it from his expression. "Why in the seven hells should I listen to you?"

"Call him a traitor and you will find out." Shyla added heat to her gaze, showing him a small fraction of the power of The Eyes.

Uncertainty flashed for a moment before the man pulled it together. "The Water Princess has ordered me to escort you to her office. Follow—"

"Now?" Shyla asked.

The man huffed. "Yes, now."

"I'm sorry, but we have a meeting with the King. Please extend our regrets."

"You can't—"

"Do you want me to insult the King?" Watching him grow increasingly flabbergasted was too much fun. "I'm sure you don't. We can meet with the princess at angle one-sixty. If that doesn't suit her, let us know an alternative time. I'm sure you know exactly where we're staying." Then she turned to Rendor. "Come on, Captain. We don't want to be late."

Rendor bowed slightly and led the way. As long as the guards didn't rush them, she didn't care where he was headed. She kept a link to Kilab, finding it amusing as he struggled to decide if he should force them to accompany him to the princess. In the end, he prudently chose to report back to the princess and let her decide.

Once they were far enough away from the squad, Shyla relaxed. Or she tried. Rendor's continuing silence didn't bode well.

"Are you mad I didn't follow your lead?" she asked.

"No."

Was it the truth? This would be easier if she could read him. "When that arrogant bastard accused you without cause, I couldn't keep quiet. No one calls you a traitor."

He stopped and turned to her. "But I am one." His tone was matter-of-fact.

Oh no, this had to stop right now. Shyla got right in his face.

Well, as close as she could on her tiptoes. "You. Are. Not. Doing the right thing is not being a traitor. Saving lives is not being a traitor. Freeing the people of Zirdai from fear and oppression is not being a traitor. Do. You. Understand?"

"I understand that your definition of being a traitor is different than mine."

Argh. The man could be so stubborn. "The Water Prince was the traitor. He swore to protect the people of Zirdai and instead he betrayed their trust. He exploited them, tortured them, and killed them."

"And I helped him," Rendor said.

She rocked back on her heels. He wasn't wrong. "By switching sides, you went from a traitor to a hero. So my original statement stands. You are *not* a traitor."

Rendor didn't say anything else. He continued down the tunnel in long strides. Shyla had to hurry to keep up. What else could she say to make him understand? Except, deep down, she knew he had to believe it in his soul. Nothing she said would change his mind until then.

Instead of going to the black market, Rendor took her to the surface. Technically they didn't have an appointment with the King. He'd wanted a reply before angle seventy, but after their encounter with Captain Kilab, Shyla and Rendor knew they'd be followed. They arrived at the grand entrance at angle fifty. Najib was fetched. They watched the guards watching them as they waited. Rendor remained closed off.

Najib arrived and escorted them down to his office. It was exactly the same size as the King's but without the guards.

"The King has asked me to take charge of this investigation. That is, if you agree and there is one," Najib said after he poured them all some tea. "If you have questions for him about the theft, he will make himself available for an interview."

"Are you able to negotiate terms?" Rendor asked.

Najib's left eyebrow rose. "It depends on the terms. What do you want, Captain?"

"If we agree to investigate, we want access to the vault, cooperation from the guards, and the ability to come and go from the castle as we see fit."

"I can arrange all that. However, ordering the guards to cooperate doesn't mean they won't lie to you."

"That won't be a problem," Shyla said.

"Ah, yes." He gave her a long speculative look. "What else do you require?"

"We'll need an account of your prior investigation. Also details about how the security in the castle is run," Rendor said.

"Yes, of course, I can get you all the information you need."

"We'll need a local guide, someone who can be assigned to us and doesn't have any other commitments. Someone who blends in and will follow our orders."

Mojag. That was who they really needed. The boy had begged to come along, but he needed to learn how to wield his magic. And he needed his family close, including Jayden, who he'd eventually realize was still a part of his family. She hoped.

"All right," Najib said.

"If we agree to this," Shyla said, "once the investigation is finished, so are we. We've plans to travel to the other cities."

"Understood," Najib said. He glanced between them. "Will you take the job?"

They'd already decided to do it. Having their terms met just sweetened the deal. "Yes."

"Wonderful! Do you need a list of what we'll provide in writing?"

Shyla leaned forward. "Not if you allow me to read your intentions."

His brow furrowed. "Haven't you been...ah...reading me all along?"

"No. The only time I used the power of The Eyes on you was when you ordered the guards to seize me. Otherwise, I don't invade others' privacy unless they give me good reason."

"Ah, good to know."

Rendor scowled at Najib. "Why did you order your guards to seize her?"

"A test to see if she'd run away." His voice squeaked a bit under Rendor's intense scrutiny.

"You're lucky there were no injuries."

"Oh, she wouldn't have been harmed, Captain. I assure you."

Rendor grunted. "I was referring to your guards."

Shyla ducked her chin into her new scarf to hide her grin at Najib's shock.

The advisor cleared his throat and sipped some tea before he regained his composure. "In order to save myself some extra work, please read my genuine desire to meet all your terms for this investigation," he said to Shyla. "Do I need to do anything?"

"No. Once I've made a connection to a person, it's easier." And she didn't need to make eye contact again. She lowered her shield and found no surprises lurking in his thoughts. They were focused on finding the taxes. "I hope we are successful as well, Najib."

"Ah, you are a mind reader as well!" He paused and a worried expression creased his face. "Did you learn that I'm afraid of velblouds?"

"No, I didn't dig that deep."

"How can you be afraid of them?" Rendor asked. "They're harmless."

"They have sharp claws and are very protective of their young, Captain," he snapped. Then he drew in a breath and released it slowly. "While I gather all the information you requested and find you a guide, would you like to go to your rooms?"

"We'll stay in Qulsary for now," Rendor said. "I've some business there and it'll be the best place to pick up any gossip about the theft."

"No one in Qulsary should be gossiping about it," Najib said.

"In my experience, something that big doesn't stay a secret for long."

"You're the expert. What would you like to do now?"

"Can you show us the vault?"

"I can."

Najib stood and escorted them down into the lower levels of

the castle. The air grew moist as they descended. It didn't take long for the rumbling of water to hum in the walls. Eventually they reached a level that was empty of all decoration and furniture.

Trol lanterns blazed and they encountered the first of many sets of guards. They stood like statues, alert and ready. But there was a fog of embarrassment and shame and anger around them. Shyla strengthened her mental shield.

Six guards watched the door to the vault. Made of solid black iron, it seemed to suck all the light and heat from the tunnel. Rendor inspected the surface carefully. He appeared small next to the massive entrance. Najib pulled a necklace from underneath his tunic. On it hung three oversized keys which he used to unlock a series of locks.

"Is there a pattern?" Rendor asked.

"Yes. I have to do it in a certain order or the last one won't open."

Once the door was unlocked, four guards lined up along the side and pushed. With their muscles flexing from the strain, they revealed a small opening only one meter wide by two meters tall. A cold dampness blew from inside the vault.

"Smart," Rendor said, eyeing the entrance. "The size limits how many people can get through."

Najib took a trol lantern from its hook and entered first. Shyla and Rendor followed, but the guards remained outside.

"Careful," Najib said.

The bright yellow light reflected off a round pool of water. There was nothing else in the room except a meter-wide walkway that circled the pool.

The advisor pointed to the water. "This should explain a few things. It's the reason the theft wasn't discovered right away, and why we know it was an inside job."

"How deep is the pool?" Rendor asked.

"Deep enough that you'd have to swim in order to reach the bottom."

"Swim?" Shyla had never heard that word before.

Najib moved his arms, sweeping them out from the front of his body to the back, making big semi-circles. "It's how you move through water. It's hard and you have to hold your breath. Korahans aren't meant to be in the water. We flail and sink like rocks. Swimming is an awkward, exhausting affair." He shuddered. "Besides, no one can stay under for more than one angle without needing air." He gave them a sheepish look. "The guards like to have competitions. It proves their bravery or something like that."

"Do all the guards know how to swim?" Shyla crouched down next to the water. She couldn't even see the bottom.

"Yes. There's been a number of accidental drownings, so they're all taught just in case they fall in."

"Is that how you get to the coins, then? By swimming?" Rendor asked.

"No one swims in this pool. The King lifts the water into the air and it's easy to climb down the ladder and get what we need."

She dipped her hand into the water. It was cold, but not much colder than the air. "How many coins are kept in here at a time?"

"There is always at least fifty thousand, but the rest depends on when. The taxes come in once a circuit, and at that time there is the greatest amount of coins in the pool. By the time the taxes are due to arrive, we're usually back to that fifty thousand. However, during the two circuits that the old king was dying, all the taxes were dumped in here and nothing was spent. So we estimated there were over a million."

Wow. Shyla would never see that many coins in her entire life. And that amount couldn't be smuggled out all at once. It must have taken multiple trips. The guards had the opportunity and were her first suspects.

"When was the theft discovered?" Rendor asked.

"When the old King died, the new King's first order of business was to lift the water so everyone could be paid. The pool only held that fifty thousand and the King gave it to the guards and servants." Najib held up a hand, stopping their next question. "The King insisted on paying them their back wages. There's nothing left. The next tax payment is due to arrive in two hundred and thirty-four sun jumps."

She considered the problem. "Who oversaw the dumping of the taxes?"

"The old King's advisor."

Suspect number two. "Are they still in Qulsary?"

"Yes, she is enjoying her retirement. And I know what you're thinking, but she has been exonerated. A King's advisor is the same age as the King and the old King lived for eighty-four circuits."

That meant the advisor was now eighty-five circuits old.

Probably too old to be swimming and carrying heavy bags of coins.

"We still want to talk to her," Rendor said.

"I'll make the arrangements," Najib said.

Shyla swirled her fingers in the water. The King could command it. But was it due to a divine gift or because of magic? She concentrated her will on the surface, imagining it was similar to the surface of the desert and composed of a million tiny grains of sand or, in this case, a million drops.

Float, she commanded.

Nothing happened. She tried again, putting more power into the order. Again nothing. So much for that theory.

"Do the castle's staff know how to swim?" Rendor asked.

"A few can."

"We'll talk to them as well."

"All right." Najib looked doubtful.

"What is it?" she asked him.

"It's just that it would take a long time to bring up all those coins from the bottom."

"It would. But the thief or thieves had two circuits to do it." Rendor walked around the pool, inspecting the walls. "I'm assuming there is no other way in or out of this room. But what about the water? How does it get here?"

"The King completely drains it every five circuits and refreshes it with new water. Frankly, I've never seen it done, but I've heard the water is like a snake, slithering through the tunnels."

"The new King hasn't changed the water then?"

"No."

Shyla wondered if the water tasted like coins. She trickled a few drops into her mouth, expecting a metallic tang. Instead it was salty.

When they left the vault, Najib waited until the door slid back into place with a loud clang and then relocked it, reversing the order—so he claimed. Shyla wasn't really paying attention. Instead she wondered how the staff and guards had lived without being paid for two circuits.

"Everyone who works in the castle is given food, water, and clothing as part of their pay," Najib explained when she asked him. "Their families are also taken care of. We've plenty of room for everyone. The King especially enjoys seeing the children race around the tunnels. Their pay is more for luxury items or trips so it wasn't too much of a hardship to wait." Najib frowned. "Since it's illegal to spend the coins without the king's permission, Qulsary's Water Princess had been paying for our basic necessities until the king died. Once he died, she expected to be paid back."

"What about the elite forces?" Rendor asked. "Do they get the same compensations as the rest of the staff?"

"No. They were paid only in coins. The squads lived in Qulsary, the theory being if the castle was under attack, they wouldn't be trapped inside with us."

"There has to be escape tunnels," Shyla said.

"Of course, but they can be blocked or used by the enemy."

"Where are the squads located?" Rendor asked.

"Does it matter?" Najib asked. "There's no one there.

They've left for other jobs."

"Yes, it matters."

"I'll have your guide show you."

By the time they were done with the vault, it was angle one hundred and still too hot to return to Qulsary. Rendor and Najib spent the time discussing the previous investigation. Shyla half listened while sipping another delicious tea blend and watching Rendor. He was in his element.

No doubt the coins were long gone, along with the culprits, but Najib insisted no one working in the castle had left. It would be smart to remain to avoid suspicion. Wait a few circuits after the discovery before leaving. In that case, they should be able to find them. Now she hoped the thieves were smart.

When the sun jumped past the danger zone, they returned to their rented room in Qulsary. A guard waited for them with a message that Captain Kilab would come by at angle one-fifty to escort them to the Water Princess.

They had twenty angles. Shyla studied Rendor as he rummaged in his pack and removed a scroll, stylus, and jar of ink. He sat at one of the tables with his back to her and wrote on the scroll. The stiffness of his spine warned her to leave him alone. Was he still upset over Kilab's comment about being a traitor?

Not one to take a hint, she glanced over his shoulder. "Are these your thoughts about the theft?"

"Yes." He tapped the end of the stylus on the scroll. "It's obvious that the guards are involved. Probably all of them. I suspect they were angry about not being paid so they took matters into their own hands. Except…there's something we're missing."

"Like why they would leave fifty thousand coins behind?"

"No. That was smart. It throws suspicion onto the advisor."

"But why were they embarrassed?"

Rendor turned to look at her. "They were?"

She explained. "Yes. I didn't read anyone in particular and it might not have been everyone we passed, but it was just…in the air."

"No guilt? Or smugness?"

"I picked up shame and anger, but I didn't go deeper."

Rendor cursed. "Then maybe they're not involved. Those emotions tell me they're angry about being tricked and ashamed over failing to do their duty."

"And the embarrassment?"

"That the King asked us to investigate. To do their job."

"Does this mean we don't have to interview them?"

"No. It means I don't think they're *all* involved. A few still have to be. It took four of them to open that door."

And, at eighty-five circuits, the old advisor couldn't move it by herself. Unless she was really strong for her age. Shyla almost laughed at the image. Except Rendor had returned his attention to the table. She left him alone and tried to decide if there was a reason to worry about their upcoming meeting with the Water Princess.

Captain Kilab banged on their door at exactly angle one-fifty. When she moved to open it, Rendor stopped her. He held up a finger. Only after Kilab knocked a third time did Rendor saunter to it. Men.

Kilab glared but kept his peace. "Come with me." It almost sounded like an order rather than a request.

Rendor stepped out first. He surveyed the group with the captain. "Ten guards? Are they for our protection or yours?"

"Consider it an honor," Kilab said tightly. He swept a hand out. "This way."

Shyla walked between the two men. The silence became a heavy weight, dragging on her. To ease the tension, she asked Kilab, "How long have you been the captain?"

"About four circuits."

"With a city this size, it must be difficult supervising so many guards."

"I've a number of lieutenants that help me. The city's been broken into quarters in order to keep everyone organized."

Shyla continued the small talk as they descended. The citizens took one look at their party and quickly moved out of the way. But they weren't afraid to show their interest and curiosity. A few even called out hellos to the captain.

The arrangement of the city's levels appeared to be similar to Zirdai, with the wealthier citizens living deeper. When they passed through a university—one of many reported to be in operation—Shyla craned her neck, taking in its massive size and wishing to linger and explore.

Qulsary had an openness to it. The tunnels were bigger, there were more caverns, and there was plenty of light. The city didn't press down so hard on her shoulders. Laughter, boisterous voices, and a general hum of contentment rumbled in the air.

She wondered if the configuration made a difference to the overall soul of the city. Zirdai was narrow and deep, while Qulsary was shallow and wide. It was probably the leadership, but it would be interesting to see if Zirdai's atmosphere changed now that Jayden and Kaveri were in charge.

Soon the number of people thinned and they encountered more and more guards, though not as many as she expected to be protecting the entrance into the Water Princess's level. Instead of closed doors and a dozen armed guards, the arched entrance was left wide open. And while guards did stand nearby, no one stopped the citizens from going inside.

Captain Kilab nodded to a few of the soldiers. They responded in kind but eyed Shyla and Rendor with interest. Shyla hadn't thought it was possible but the tension rolling off Rendor increased with each step. Did he think they were going to be arrested? Or was it his own guilt, reminding him of what he'd done when he'd been the captain of the guard? Or perhaps he thought everyone was judging him, believing that he was a traitor?

As they went further into the princess's level, Shyla noticed the familiar luxuries—the water fountains, trol lanterns, and expensive furniture. But it wasn't as…dense. Like the city, the princess's level had an openness to it as well.

Kilab brought them to a comfortable sitting area. Big soft cushions surrounded a low table and rugs lined the floor. A woman who appeared to be a member of the staff—she wore the same plain light blue tunic and dark blue pants like the others Shyla had spotted on their way here—set out a teapot and cups on the table.

The captain dismissed his escorts, although a few of them took up stations out in the corridor.

"Please sit down," the woman said, gesturing to the cushions. "The Water Princess will be here shortly."

Shyla sat but Rendor remained on his feet. Kilab stood by the far wall with his arms crossed. While the two men glared at each other from opposite sides of the room, the woman met Shyla's gaze and mouthed *men* with an exaggerated eye roll. And wow, the lady had a set of beautiful maroon-colored eyes. Shyla hid a smile. She'd been thinking the same thing.

The woman bustled about, arranging the table, then left and returned two angles later with a plate of delicate pastries. First the King's sausages and now pastries? Shyla was bound to gain back the weight she'd lost existing solely on jerky.

After arranging the plate just so, the woman poured tea into the four cups and stepped back. "There! How's that look?"

"Delicious," Shyla said.

"Good, good!" She clapped her hands together as if in delight. "You can sit down now, Captains. This is a safe space."

"No place is safe," Kilab said, but his tired tone suggested he said those words so many times he didn't expect a reaction. However, he took a seat across from Shyla.

Rendor settled next to her. His posture remained stiff, apparently agreeing with Kilab.

And the woman bounced into the last cushion, crossing her legs underneath her. "The Water Princess is here. Welcome, visitors."

Shyla glanced at the door but no one entered.

Confused, she met the woman's extra bright gaze. Ah. Quite the surprise. Shyla wondered if the princess enjoyed confounding her guests. Or perhaps she preferred to get a sense of her visitors before revealing her identity, which was rather smart. Shyla studied the woman. Black hair cascaded in ringlets down to her chest, framing her heart-shaped face. Her dark skin matched Rendor's; both would have no trouble blending into the shadows. Crinkling in amusement, her small delicate nose was easy to miss when compared to her unique eyes. The princess's full lips stretched into a smile as Shyla continued to stare.

"I can't make a big impression like the King," she said. "But I can be a good hostess. Especially when you've traveled so far. Please…" She gestured to the tea and cakes. "Help yourselves."

Shyla sipped her tea to be polite, wondering if asking the princess why she wanted to talk to them would be considered rude. She settled on easing into it. "It was kind of you to invite us. Captain Kilab gave me the impression that you may have some concerns." It wasn't quite a question.

"Just like your captain, he tends to be overprotective. Yes, Kilab, it's your job," the princess said, placating him. "And I will admit to some curiosity as to why the King requested your presence."

Shyla admired the princess's ability to pose the not-question as well. "I'm sorry, but I'm not allowed to divulge his reasons."

The princess's friendly demeanor disappeared and a cold calculation filled her gaze. The change was striking. "That's unfortunate," she said. "I was hoping you could put my worries to rest."

"Worries?" Rendor asked.

"Information travels fast, Captain. Both of you were part of the coup that killed Zirdai's Water Prince. You can imagine that I'd be concerned when you showed up in my city."

"The King's reason for seeing me doesn't have anything to do with you," Shyla said. Unless the woman was somehow involved in the theft of the taxes. Perhaps she hadn't wanted to wait for the king to die to get her coins back. Shyla debated if she should use The Eyes to read the woman's emotions. Remembering Tamburah's terrible abuse of the power, she held off.

"I find that hard to believe," Kilab said.

"Are you calling her a liar?" Rendor demanded.

"Easy, Captains." The princess's harsh tone erased the last vestiges of her happy hostess facade. "Would the King's request be linked to the disappearance of his elite soldiers?"

Shyla kept her expression neutral. Although the woman's use of the word *disappearance* was interesting.

"How do you know they are not on a mission for the King?" Rendor asked.

"They live in my city, Captain. Like you, they're highly trained and dangerous. My people keep an eye on them."

"You've spies inside their organization."

The Water Princess didn't reply—an answer in itself.

"And they disappeared as well," Rendor said. He glanced at Kilab. "Could the soldiers have gone to ground? Moved to another hidden location in the city?"

"No. There's been no rumors. They haven't been spotted at all."

"Why are you so curious?" the princess asked.

"Just trying to help out."

"Admirable." Although her tone implied otherwise. "With their disappearance, I wondered if they'd joined the Invisible Sword." Her gaze speared Shyla.

So much for her organization being a secret.

"The timing works out. They left in small batches over a circuit," Kilab said. "Perhaps to join you in overthrowing Zirdai's Water Prince."

If only. Shyla imagined how much easier it would have been if the King had sent his elite soldiers to help the Invisible Sword. How many people would have survived. Perhaps Ximen, Elek, and Lian would have lived. But those thoughts didn't change anything.

"That happened over two hundred and eighty sun jumps ago," Rendor said. "Why haven't they returned?"

"You tell me," Kilab challenged.

"They didn't help us," Shyla said. "We don't know where they are. And we're not here to cause trouble in your city." She stood. "Thank you for the tea."

The princess's expression hardened, but she nodded. "We'll be keeping an eye on you. Captain Kilab, please see them out."

The captain was all too happy to escort them from the room.

He led them up a few levels then abandoned them with a gruff, "You can find your own way back."

Shyla had no idea which way to turn, but Rendor twined his fingers in hers and guided her through the city's busy tunnels.

"Keeping an eye on us means we're going to be followed, right?" she asked Rendor.

"Only when we let them."

"And we can avoid that?"

"Sunbeam, I can ditch a tail with ease. And you're the leader of the Invisible Sword."

"Except there's too many people around for me to use the *gone* command."

"Then I'll help you spot the important people." He squeezed her hand and was quiet for a few angles. "The princess did give us quite a bit of information."

Shyla reviewed their conversation. "The fact the squads left in batches?"

"Yes. If they were upset by not being paid, they'd have left all at once. Leaving in small groups means they didn't want to draw anyone's attention. Also why didn't some of them apply to work as guards for the Water Princess? It doesn't make sense for them to all leave Qulsary."

"Unless they had another offer," Shyla said. "Maybe another city's prince or princess hired them."

"That's possible. Did you read the princess?"

"No." She waited for his response.

"Your reluctance to invade another's privacy is admirable."

"I sense a but," she said.

"In those situations, you might want to establish a light connection. Not a full invasion, a—what do you call it?"

"Picking up on their surface emotions?"

"Yes. Even with the King's support, we're outnumbered here in Qulsary. It would give us a slight advantage."

"All right."

Rendor glanced at her but remained quiet. Her reluctance was also due to what the King had said about turning into a megalomaniac despot. Had the power of The Eyes transformed Tamburah into a bloodthirsty tyrant? Or was it because the power was so easy to abuse? Just because she could do something didn't mean it was right.

After another dozen angles, she still didn't recognize anything. "Where are we going?"

"You'll see."

Actually, the sound reached them first. It was a strange almost spitting noise followed by a wet *rat-tat-tat.* They entered a large cavern filled with people. The crowd gasped and oohed and aahed. Rendor muscled through them, pulling Shyla behind him. When he stopped, he stepped aside and Shyla sucked in a breath.

A series of round basins were spread out in front of her in what appeared to be a random pattern. Each was a different size, from half a meter to three meters wide. A single ribbon of water jumped from basin to basin. It arced high into the air and then disappeared, making that *rat-tat-tat* noise inside the stone bowl before springing back up and jumping into another. Then a second and third and fourth ribbon leaped between the circles.

They appeared almost alive as they soared through the air, hopping as if by magic and narrowly missing the other streams, seeming to be playing a game of chase.

Fascinated, she watched the show, oohing and aahing with everyone else. These must be the legendary dancing waters of Qulsary. She lost track of time and was only dimly aware of Rendor now standing behind her with his arms wrapped around her waist. His solid presence warmed her back.

The show ended. After a stunned moment, there was an explosion of applause before the crowd dispersed.

"Will there be another show?" Shyla asked Rendor.

"They do them at angle one-eighty and angle zero every sun jump." He reclaimed her hand.

They went to the closest dining cavern, paid, and ate second meal before returning to their room. Out of habit, she scanned for intruders as Rendor pulled the key from his pocket.

She sensed a bump and touched his arm, stopping him from opening the door.

"What's wrong?"

"Someone is inside our room."

Rendor handed her the key and pulled his sword. "How many?" he asked in a whisper.

She extended her magic, seeking more bumps inside their rented rooms. "One."

"Armed?"

"I can't read their intentions without making eye contact. It's not Kilab or Najib." Or anyone else she'd read in the past.

"Can you still wield your magic?"

"Yes." Aside from the power of The Eyes, Shyla's own magic had three other abilities—movement of the sand, influence over another's perceptions, and manipulation of people's thoughts and actions. "But if I trap the person with my magic, they'll know what I can do."

"Good point." He tightened his grip. "What about that *look away* command? Can you do that so I can get through the door without them seeing me?"

"I can."

She pushed the command at the intruder.

Look away.

Then she unlocked the latch and slid the door open. Rendor rushed inside and stopped, making the all-clear signal. Shyla withdrew her magic. The young intruder sitting on a cushion jumped to her feet in surprise.

"What are you doing in here?" Rendor demanded in his I'm-the-captain-of-the-guard-and-I-must-be-obeyed voice.

Confronted with an angry and armed Rendor, the poor girl's face paled three shades.

"Well?" Rendor demanded.

"I'm…" She swallowed. "I'm…your guide. Advisor Najib sent me."

"Why did you break into our room?"

"I…er…" Another swallow. "I wanted to demonstrate…my skills."

"Skills?"

"Yes, sir. That there's no part of this city that I can't get into."

That was a rather handy skill, except Shyla still didn't like the fact she was in their rooms without permission. She glanced around to see if anything was missing.

"I didn't touch nothin'," the girl said as if offended. "Advisor Najib told me to impress you."

Shyla met her gaze and lowered her shield. Her brown eyes were wide. She appeared to be about sixteen circuits old, but on the small side for a girl her age. Good for getting through tight places. Aside from being afraid of the big man with the sharp sword, she was telling the truth.

"Consider us impressed," Shyla said. She touched Rendor's arm. "You can put away your sword. The girl's not a threat."

The girl in question straightened in indignation. "I'm twenty circuits old."

She was only a circuit younger than Shyla—quite the surprise. She introduced herself and Rendor, who slid his weapon back into its protective leather sheath but kept his hand nearby just in case.

"What's your name?" she asked.

"Hakana."

"What instructions did Najib give you?"

"To guide you wherever you wish to go at whatever time." She bowed. "I'm at your disposal."

"Does that include the King's castle?" Rendor asked.

"Yes. I've spent the last five circuits working as the King's page."

"Page?" Shyla asked.

Some of the puff in Hakana's chest deflated. "I run his errands, fetch stuff, find people, and report on what's goin' on in Qulsary."

"I thought the Monks of Quirin spied on Qulsary."

"They concern themselves with the politicals and wealthies, while I'm more inclined to mix with the regulars. You know what I mean?"

In other words, she listened to the gossip. "Do you talk to the vagrants?" she asked.

"Nah. They don't trust nobody. And the few that are left are hard to find. Captain Kilab's been hunting them for circuits."

Rendor stiffened. "What happens when he catches them?"

"They've three choices." Hakana held up three fingers. "Become a guard. Become a deacon. Or leave the city."

"How can they leave without any coins?" Shyla asked.

"They're given enough for a one-way trip." Hakana shrugged. "The Water Princess expects everyone livin' in Qulsary to do their share of the work."

It was a reasonable expectation as long as the princess provided water and safety for her citizens.

"What other skills do you have?" Rendor asked Hakana.

"I know this city like no other. Ma says I was born explorin' and that's why the King hired me."

She wondered if, like Mojag, she unconsciously wielded magic. Except Mojag could travel without anyone seeing him. While she could dig deeper into Hakana's memories, she resisted. Instead, she'd watch her for any signs she tapped into magic.

"All right," Rendor said. "Report back here at angle twenty."

"Yes, sir!" Hakana dashed out of their rooms as if relieved to no longer be under their scrutiny.

Rendor stared after her. "The girl probably has orders to report everything we do to Najib."

Shyla moved closer to him. "I hope not *everything*." She hooked her arms around his neck.

He automatically pulled her against him. "A locked door won't keep her out."

"No. But you scared her. She won't surprise us again."

"Good." Then he peered at Shyla. "I never scared you, did I? Not even when we first met."

"Oh no, I was properly terrified."

"But you held your own, standing up to me. I was impressed."

"And now that you know it was all an act?"

"Even more so."

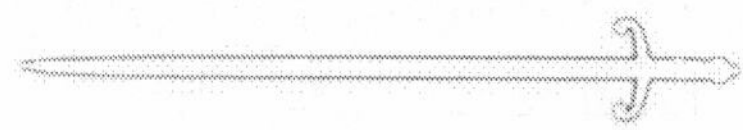

Hakana arrived promptly at angle twenty. She tapped on the door and waited for Rendor to open it.

"Advisor Najib said that Advisor Yiesha is available to talk to you at angle sixty," Hakana said as soon as she entered.

"The old king's advisor?" she asked. "You know where she lives?"

"Yes to both." She glanced between them. Her tight shoulder-length curls swung with the motion. "What do you want to do before then?"

"Do you know where the King's elite squads were housed?" Rendor asked.

"Yes."

"Let's go take a look."

"Which one?"

"There's more than one?"

"Yes, there's lots. Doesn't make sense for them all to stay together." She held her right hand out with her palm up. "One cave-in and they're goners." She slapped her other hand on top, demonstrating being crushed flat.

A shudder raced over Shyla's skin as the memory of waking

up buried in rubble threatened to unfold in her mind. She pushed the image aside.

"Or one ambush," Rendor said.

"There's that. Can't have all your velbloud eggs on the same table."

"Table?" She couldn't resist asking.

"Yeah. They're slippery little devils. They'll roll off and...*splat.*"

Sounded like she was speaking from experience.

"Take us to one of the main barracks," Rendor said.

"All right, I know just the one!" Hakana led them through a variety of tunnels and caverns and up a number of levels. Some of the passages were well used and crowded with people while others were empty with druk lanterns few and far between. While crossing through one of the deserted tunnels, Shyla sensed a few bumps behind them. When they entered another little-used passage, the bumps remained. Shyla exchanged a glance with Rendor. He nodded at her unspoken question. They were being followed.

Hakana seemed oblivious to the tail, which could be problematic in the future. However, the girl never hesitated as she guided them. Nor did she study the markings on the walls near the intersections.

After a couple angles, Hakana slowed down. "We're being followed."

Impressed, Shyla asked, "How many?"

"Three, maybe four. They're not wearing uniforms, but they move like guards. Do you want me to ditch them?" Hakana asked.

"Yes," Rendor said.

"All right. Keep with me no matter what we encounter."

Curious, she followed close behind Hakana. Rendor appeared more amused, almost as if he didn't think Hakana could lose their followers.

Their guide executed a series of sharp turns through a maze of short tunnels. Then she darted to a wide ramp with a metal railing. No one was in sight. Instead of going down, she hopped onto the railing and teetered on the thin metal rail.

Shyla reached out, trying to grab her arm and keep her from falling over and crashing to the bottom. Except Hakana shot her a grin before jumping into the blackness. With a cry, Shyla leaned over and connected to Hakana's thoughts with her magic. Amusement and not fear or pain dominated. Relieved, Shyla waited for her eyes to adjust to the semi-darkness below.

Hakana gestured for them to join her. She stood in an alcove that was all but invisible from the ramp. "Come on, they'll be here soon."

They didn't need any more encouragement. Both jumped over the railing, landing about a meter lower than the ramp.

"Watch your heads, it's going to get narrow," Hakana warned.

She wasn't kidding. With her in the lead and Shyla right behind, they started down a tunnel that shrank as they traveled further into its depths. Eventually they were forced to crawl as all light disappeared. The sound of fabric rubbing on the stone walls alarmed her. Shyla worried Rendor's wide shoulders would get wedged. But then the ground dropped away underneath her and she tumbled out of the tunnel. Behind her, Rendor cursed before landing next to her.

Hakana opened a druk lantern. "Sorry, forgot to tell you about the drop." They were in a small cavern. "The good news is we've lost the guards."

Rendor stood and pulled Shyla to her feet. He glared at Hakana. "Any more surprises?"

"No. It's a straight shot from here."

"Make sure you warn us next time."

"Yes, sir."

Shyla brushed the dirt off her tunic and fixed her wrap. It didn't take long to arrive at one of the elite squad's barracks.

"They're all located on level seven," Hakana explained when they reached the entrance. "So they're close to the surface but deep enough to be safe."

Hakana opened the door using what she called her special tools. The squad's quarters were plain with rows of sleeping cushions and trunks for personal possessions lined up in large rooms. The common areas had tables, cushions, and desks. The place was obviously abandoned.

Rendor found the secret entrance that gave the soldiers access to one of the city's escape tunnels. "They needed a way to come and go on missions without alerting anyone," Rendor said.

"Then how did the Water Princess know they'd left?" she asked.

"Probably when her spies stopped reporting in. I'd guess she sent Kilab to investigate."

"Why did you want to see this? How does it help us?" she asked, thinking they'd just wasted time.

"To determine how they'd left. For example, were they in a rush?" Rendor opened a number of the trunks and peered inside. "Nothing left behind. So no, they had time to pack." Then he scanned the area. "No signs of a fight, so everyone was probably in agreement." He walked around. "No destruction means they probably weren't angry at the King."

Shyla gazed at the barracks with new insight. "Do we need to visit all of them?"

"Not all, but I'd like to see a few more."

"Then let's get movin'. I don't want to be late for the meetin' with Advisor Yiesha," Hakana said.

The other barracks resembled the first one—neat and cleaned out. They also had another exit that led to an escape tunnel. Shyla and Rendor agreed that the soldiers probably left due to lack of pay.

Hakana hustled them out of the last barracks. She almost jogged through the city in order to arrive at Yiesha's apartment on time. Shyla wondered what the relationship was between the two. Hakana would have also been the old King's page and would have worked closely with Yiesha.

They eventually arrived at a strange tiered area. There were five or six levels of apartments that climbed one wall of a huge cavern. Each of the living quarters had a low-walled area that jutted out, hanging over the open space. Below was a busy market. Not as big as the main one Lota worked in, but bigger than any of the markets in Zirdai.

Hakana led them around to the back side of those apartments…or was it the front? She knocked on one of the doors. They were on level twenty-three—not deep-level wealthy, but Yiesha probably had enough coins to be more than comfortable.

A stained-glass panel slid aside, revealing two stone-gray eyes. The upper eyelids drooped and wrinkles underlined the eyelashes. "Hakana, is that you?" The woman donned a pair of eyeglasses and her gaze focused on them with a shrewd sharpness.

"Yes, Advisor Yiesha. I brought the consultants from the King."

"Don't keep them waiting, girl. Let them in."

"Uh, you need to open the door, Advisor."

"Never stopped you before." The panel slammed shut.

Hakana turned to Shyla and Rendor. "This might take me an angle or two. She delights in installing complex locks just to test me."

"Why does she do that?" Shyla asked.

"She trained me. Claimed that the King's page should not be stopped by a locked door." Hakana pulled out her slender metal tools and set to work.

Rendor watched. "How hard is it to learn?"

"Once you get the right…feel, it's easier. Takes lots of practice, though."

Shyla turned to Rendor. "I'm surprised you don't already know how to do that."

He grinned. "I don't need to know. If I want in, I just break the door."

"Even the ones made of thick glass or stone?"

"Every door has a weakness. But there are times when it would be good to know how to get in without letting the owners know you're there."

"Thinking of starting a new career as a thief?" she teased.

"No, but if this consulting business continues—"

"It won't. After this, we'll continue on our way." Shyla kept her tone firm even though emotions twisted in her chest. What if the King changed his mind and insisted she work for him? It'd be like swearing an oath to the monks. She'd lose the freedom she'd finally earned.

"Got it!" Hakana slid the door aside in triumph.

Yiesha stood on the other side. Her eyeglasses now hung around her neck. The older woman was a few centimeters shorter than Shyla. Her pure white hair had been wound into a large bun on top of her head. She held a cane but didn't lean on it. Shyla suspected it was either for show or a weapon. Like the one Shyla used that had a knife hidden in the handle.

"Don't stand there staring, come on in," Yiesha said. "Except you, Hakana." She handed her a few coins. "Go buy me more velbloud yarn, please. You know the thickness I like."

Hakana glanced at them, seeking permission.

"Go on," Rendor said, shooing her away.

Yiesha then led Shyla and Rendor to a sitting room filled with bright-colored cushions. Druk lanterns hung from the walls. And while the décor reflected a person who had extra coins to spend on higher quality goods, it matched what the others living in the mid-levels could afford. In other words, no expensive items that might point to Yiesha as the tax thief.

The advisor leaned on her cane as she settled on a blue cushion with white stripes. Shyla chose a pretty orange one with gold tassels.

"Don't hover, Captain," Yiesha said, waving at Rendor with her cane. When he sat on a large oval pillow, she asked them, "Are you here to accuse me of stealing?"

"No. We're here to ask you some questions," Shyla said, lowering her mental shield in order to read the woman. Yiesha's surface emotions flipped between annoyance and curiosity—both in equal measure.

"And you have new questions to ask? Ones that Najib hasn't already asked me?"

"Probably not," Shyla said.

"Then why are you wasting my time?"

"Do you have something else to do?" Rendor asked.

"I've knitting to do." She picked up a half-finished sun cloak then put her glasses on and showed the needles wrapped with loops of yarn. "See? And sitting on my balcony to watch the shoppers below," she shot back with thick sarcasm. "I'm a busy person, Captain."

"Then we won't take long," he said in a reasonable tone. "Can you tell us what happens when the taxes arrive from a city?"

Her sigh, while exaggerated, didn't quite match her annoyance. She took off her glasses and rubbed her eyes. Yes, she was irritated, but Shyla sensed that she was also intrigued. And happy to have some company—

Hakana's visits were too infrequent. "When the taxes arrive, one of the monks escorting the wagons reports to the castle guards."

"Monks?" Shyla asked.

"Yes, monks," Yiesha snapped. "They work for the King and they're well trained. Of course they'd be the ones to guard the tax caravan."

Yet another secret about the monks Hanif hadn't shared with Shyla. She wondered if she'd ever learn all the things they did without becoming a monk.

"I sent a few of my men along with the monks as backup," Rendor said. "They never reported any trouble."

"Of course not. Sand pirates are stupid, but not stupid enough to attack monks."

According to Lota, they were cowards and stole goods during darkness. But what about the mercenaries? They were smarter, but could they overwhelm the monks? Even if they had, the news would eventually reach the castle.

Yiesha smoothed her hair even though not a strand was out of place. "Now, if I may continue. Once the monks arrive, I'm fetched to supervise the transfer of the coins. A dozen guards accompany me and the monks, who carry the chests down to the vault. Then I count the coins to ensure the amount matches what was reported by each city's Water Prince or Princess. Counting the shiny coins is fun. Each one is tossed into the pool as it's counted." She flexed her fingers. "*Plink, plink, plink.* Then we all leave. The vault is locked until the King needs the coins."

She was telling the truth. "No one else supervised the transfers during the last two circuits?" Shyla asked.

"No. I was there for both of them. I was the only one who had the keys."

"Same guards each time?" Rendor asked.

"No. Just who was on duty at the time."

"What about the monks? The same ones?"

Yiesha snorted with amusement. "The monasteries all take turns collecting the taxes. Even if the same monks returned, I doubt I'd recognize any of them."

"Which monasteries collected the last two rounds of taxes?" Shyla asked.

"The Monks of Callow from Nintri did both circuits. The second time they were filling in for…" She waved a hand. "I can't remember. One of the cities was having a crisis and the monks needed to stay close to home."

Shyla wondered if the city was Zirdai.

Yiesha continued. "And to answer your next questions, no, nothing unusual happened during those transfers. No one was there that shouldn't have been. No one showed any suspicious behavior. The keys never left my person."

The woman was still surprised and angry about the theft, and she was still telling the truth.

"Did you go into the vault at any other time?" Rendor asked.

"No. Since the King was not lucid, the only time the vault was opened was when the taxes arrived." She stabbed a finger at him. "And don't you believe the new King's claim that the castle staff was okay with waiting for their pay. As each sun jump passed and the old king still drew breath, they grew more discontented. Many of them left. Only a couple dozen guards and a few of the others remained."

"Why didn't the king-in-training ignore the law and pay the staff?" Shyla asked.

"You can't ignore a law. He has no authority until the King dies. That's how it is and always will be."

And Shyla could well imagine Advisor Yiesha ensuring no one broke that law, adding tension to an already difficult situation. Shyla doubted the new King would keep that particular law intact for long. Perhaps he was waiting for Yiesha to join the Sun Goddess before altering it so this exact problem didn't happen again.

They asked a few more questions, but it was obvious Yiesha wasn't involved in the theft. Shyla and Rendor thanked her for her time and left. Hakana was waiting for them in the tunnel outside the ex-advisor's door. She held a half dozen skeins of velbloud yarn, all dyed different colors.

Hakana dashed inside to deliver the yarn before returning. "Where to next?"

"I'd like to interview the guards," Rendor said.

"We have to wait until after the danger zone to get to the castle."

Rendor stared at the young woman. "There's really no passage between the castle and the city?"

Interested in the answer and whether Hakana would tell the truth, Shyla lowered her shield.

Hakana squirmed and dropped her gaze to her boots. Shyla sensed her inner turmoil. Advisor Najib told her to take the consultants anywhere they asked, but the King made her swear an oath not to divulge the location of the secret tunnel.

"No matter," Rendor said, taking pity on their guide. "We can wait until after it cools down on the surface. I've another place I'd like to visit." Then he whispered in Hakana's ear.

Hakana's head snapped up and she grinned. "Good choice, sir. This way."

"Hey," Shyla said. "Don't I get to know where we're going?"

"No. It's a surprise." Rendor took her hand.

And since she'd loved the last one, she replaced her mental shield, blocking out any stray thoughts or emotions.

Taking note of the information carved into the tunnel walls, Shyla kept track of the distance they traveled. Her stomach growled when they'd walked about three kilometers. She hoped the surprise was near a dining cavern. It'd been at least ninety angles since she last ate.

Eventually, they entered a dark cavern. Hakana slowed, allowing their eyes to adjust. There was just enough light to pick out the other groups of people standing inside. Boots scraped on the stone floor and hushed conversation filled the space. It was rather creepy.

"What's—"

"You'll see," Rendor interrupted.

After a couple angles, a voice boomed, "Are you ready?"

"Yes!" everyone yelled.

There were way more people in the cavern than Shyla had thought. She stepped closer to Rendor. He pulled her in front of him like before, wrapping his arms around her. In that space, she was protected and felt almost invincible. It was quickly becoming her favorite place to be. Well, other than tucked beside him on a sleeping cushion.

"Are you certain?" the voice asked.

"Yes!"

"All right. On the count of three."

"One," everyone shouted. "Two! Three!"

Dozens of trol lanterns were opened at the same time. The bright white light blinded her at first, but then it illuminated long clear crystal stalactites jutting from the ceiling. The stalactites shone, but better yet, they fractured the light, breaking it into ribbons of color. These ribbons reflected off the clusters of crystals on the walls. The entire cavern filled with beams of red, orange, yellow, green, blue, and purple. The crystals sparkled and the light bounced and moved as if alive.

Shyla gasped at the spectacle. If magic was visible, she imagined this was what it would look like. Mesmerized, she stayed frozen in place, afraid if she exhaled it would break the spell. And just when she thought it couldn't get better, the people holding the trol lanterns began to move in a choreographed pattern. The beams of color swung and dipped and danced. It was marvelous. Worth every single sun jump she sweated and trudged through the sand to get to Qulsary.

At the end of the show, the trol lanterns were closed as abruptly as they'd been opened. Everyone hitched in a breath at the sudden darkness and there were a few disappointed *awwws* before deafening applause echoed. Shyla worried the noise might crack the crystals.

After Hakana led them out, Shyla asked her what the show

was called.

"It's The Dancing Lumineers of Kaleidoscope Cave. I never get tired of seeing it."

Who would? She turned to Rendor. "We need to come back."

He smiled. "We will. But first food and then work."

Even though she knew finishing the investigation would free them to see as many shows as they desired, the thought of interviewing all those guards failed to excite her.

After eating second meal, they arrived at Najib's office in the castle to arrange the interviews. Najib confirmed that there were only about two dozen guards who remained. His expression was pained.

"Do you know where the others went?" Rendor asked.

"Some were hired by the Water Princess," Najib said. "And some left for other cities."

"Why aren't there rumors about the theft then?" Shyla asked.

"They all left before the old king died and don't know about the missing coins."

Unless they were the reason the coins went missing. Would they have to track everyone down? Shyla suppressed a sigh.

"We'll need a conference room for the interviews," Rendor said.

"What size?" Najib asked.

"On the smaller side. We want them to be relaxed and comfortable."

"All right." Najib showed them to a room that matched Rendor's requirements. "Who would you like to talk to first?

About half of them are off duty."

"The off-duty guards, followed by those on duty. And I want them ranked lowest to highest."

Najib studied Rendor. "You don't want the superior officers coaching the others on what to say."

"Exactly."

The advisor left and Rendor dismissed Hakana, instructing her to find them the next sun jump. It didn't take long for the first guard to arrive for the interview. Shyla let Rendor take the lead. He had experience working with guards and his familiarity with the lingo and duties made him the better choice. She read emotions and signaled Rendor whenever anyone lied.

It was interesting to learn what the guards lied about. Not anything major, or even about the theft, but they covered for each other. They avoided criticizing their colleagues and insisted everyone worked hard and was diligent.

"So we're back to the beginning," Shyla said after the last guard left. "With no suspects."

"Not the beginning. We've eliminated a number of suspects."

"I fail to see the difference. We still have no suspects." She mulled over who had the opportunity and the skills to steal all those coins. No one. At least, no one without magic. "I could have stolen the coins."

"You?"

"Yes. I could have used my magic to convince Advisor Yiesha to unlock the vault and make the guards swim for the coins. Afterward, I could have erased everyone's memories of the theft."

"Do you think a magic wielder is responsible?"

"It fits."

"The person would need to be almost as powerful as you are. Or perhaps there was more than one?"

"That's possible."

"Could there be another organization like the Invisible Sword that wields magic?" Rendor asked.

"I haven't heard of any, but, then again, I didn't know about the Invisible Sword. According to Jayden, everyone in Koraha has the potential to wield magic, but only those who've experienced trauma and successfully tapped into the magic can become wielders on their own."

"Sounds like you don't agree with him."

"I don't think everyone has the potential. I've encountered people who've survived a trauma and still weren't…cracked." It sounded bad, but that was how she saw the magic inside someone. The thin ribbon of power glowed like a druk lantern that was only opened a crack. And she'd learned how to widen it, unlocking the person's ability to wield magic. Just like she had done for Mojag. But Jayden had done it for others, too, so it wasn't due to the power of The Eyes.

"Let's say there are people in Qulsary who can wield magic. How do we find them?" Rendor asked.

Good question. There were far too many people living in Qulsary for her to use The Eyes to see if anyone glowed. "Perhaps one of the King's staff saw a stranger with Yiesha when they went down to the vault." Another idea popped. "Wait. Going down to the vault and influencing enough guards to bring up all those coins and then carrying the sacks out is too much work. Thinking about it, I'd grab the coins before they went into the vault and just plant new memories of the taxes being successfully delivered."

"Still doesn't help us figure out who has the power to do that." Rendor rubbed his face as he covered a yawn.

It was angle two-seventy. They'd worked well into the darkness. "I know what will help us."

"You do?"

"Yes. We need sausages."

Rendor chuckled. "We missed third meal."

"But we're in the King's castle. I bet there'll be someone in the kitchen."

Suddenly energized, Rendor said, "Let's go."

They encountered Najib on the way. The advisor fell into step beside them as they updated him on their investigation. No one was in the kitchen, but Najib insisted on frying a few sausages for them as he mulled over their report.

He set a plate down on the table and joined Shyla and Rendor. "If these magic people can do all that you say, I wonder why they went after the taxes and didn't take advantage in smaller ways."

"Smaller ways?" Rendor asked between bites.

"Like small crimes where a couple missing coins wasn't going to cause an alarm or an investigation. Or by using their power to get better jobs or take advantage of rich customers—things that wouldn't be noticed. Influencing one or two people sounds much easier than a dozen guards, a bunch of monks, the advisor, and the six stationed at the vault."

When he put it that way, he made an excellent point. Plus she still couldn't get around the fact the thieves had to move so many coins from the bottom of a pool. Unless they could move metal. She commanded the sand, and water obeyed the King. Why not metal? A coin was like a grain of sand. It was bigger and heavier, but if she could move buckets full of sand, then another might be able to command the coins. But even if these people existed, how would Shyla find them?

"The bazaar," she said.

"What about it?" Rendor asked.

"If there's anyone who is using magic to steal, that's where they'd be."

"If they stole the taxes, they wouldn't need to hang around the market stands anymore," Najib said. "Wouldn't they be long gone?"

"Yes, but there might be others. And if we can talk to one of those others..."

"They might tell us who stole the taxes," Rendor finished. "It's a very long shot."

"I know. But do we have any other options?"

Rendor considered. "We could interview the Nintri monks. Ask if they ran into trouble while collecting the taxes."

While Nintri was on her list of places to visit, she wasn't ready to leave Qulsary just yet. "How about we try my idea for a couple sun jumps first?"

"All right."

They spent the rest of darkness in one of the castle's guest suites. The cushion was so comfortable Shyla didn't want to leave. She burrowed deep under the fur, ignoring Hakana's insistent knocking at angle twenty and letting Rendor answer the door.

But he returned far too soon and yanked the fur off of her. "Rise and shine, sunbeam." His tone was way too chipper.

She threw a pillow at him, but she might as well have blown him a kiss—the result was the same. After getting out of the cushion, which took more effort than she'd like to admit, Shyla changed and joined Rendor and Hakana in the sitting room.

"Why do you want to go to the main bazaar?" Hakana asked when they informed her of their destination.

"Why are you asking?" Rendor countered.

"If you wish to shop, there are many other smaller bazaars that have better quality goods for reasonable prices. The sellers in the main bazaar will charge you twice what an item's worth. And you have to be careful that they don't sell you a fake."

That last word slammed into her, causing her mind to whirl with possibilities. "A fake? What do you mean by that?"

Hakana shrugged. "Things like selling you a sun cloak that's not made of velbloud fibers but some cheap imitation. You pay four times the price for it, then when you wear it topside, you fry in the sun."

Shyla pulled together the little clues she'd picked up on without really knowing she was collecting them. Fakes. Could the coins be fakes? Not made with osmium but a cheap metal or stone painted a shiny silver-blue color to resemble an osee to fool the guards and monks.

But Yiesha's *plink, plink, plink* meant the fakes would still be in the pool, where they would have been discovered when the King lifted the water. Unless—

"That's it!" she exclaimed.

"What's it?" Rendor asked. He and Hakana stared at her.

"Salt," she said.

"What about it?"

"The water in the vault was salty."

"And that means?"

"The coins were fakes. They may have looked like osees and plinked in the water, but they were made of salt. They dissolved in the water!"

Hakana stared at her as if she'd lost her mind, but Rendor's expression was more contemplative.

"The use of fake coins solves a few mysteries, but Advisor Yiesha would have noticed the coins were fake," Rendor said.

"Not if she didn't have her eyeglasses on," Shyla said. "She needs them to see close up, so as long as the coins were the right color and weight, she wouldn't see the details. Blocks of Polvein salt are very heavy before they're ground down. How long has she been wearing glasses?" she asked Hakana.

"Four or five circuits, I think. But she never liked them and would leave them places. I've fetched them for her dozens of times." She smiled at the memory. "The new King bought her that eyeglass necklace as one of her retirement gifts after she complained about giving up the vault keys. She said the keys have been around her neck for fifty-some circuits and she felt like she was going to float away without the weight."

"If the coins were fakes, then we need to talk to the Nintri monks," Rendor said. "Either they're in on it or someone switched out the chests of coins while in their possession."

It was hard to imagine either one of those scenarios. Monks wouldn't steal and they were diligent and wouldn't allow anyone to swap out the chests on their watch. Unless all the cities were in on it and sent fake coins instead of real ones when they paid their taxes. That seemed very unlikely.

Najib had speculated that the theft had been an inside job. If the coins were fakes, then the insider had provided information but didn't participate in the theft. So focused on finding the guilty party, she and Rendor hadn't asked the guards questions about passing along details of how the taxes were collected to the thieves. It even could have been inadvertent.

"Hakana, can you take us to Najib's office?" she asked.

Rendor gave her a questioning look but didn't say anything.

"Yes, but I don't know if he'll be there."

They followed Hakana to the advisor's office. If they spent any more time in the castle, they soon wouldn't need a guide. The room was empty so Hakana left to search for the man. Shyla explained her thoughts to Rendor while they waited.

"They lost a number of guards and staff while the King was sick," he said. "The informant could be any of them. Plus all those elite soldiers who left."

"It's possible, but I don't think so." She tapped her chest. "Something tells me that the informant is still here. I think the thieves would want to know what's going on and what steps the new King is taking to find the coins."

"That would be a smart move. Plus there would be less suspicion on the informant if they remained."

"If who remained?" Najib asked as he entered with Hakana right behind him.

Rendor turned to the page. "Hakana, please get us something to eat."

Figuring out that Rendor wanted her gone, the young woman frowned before she left.

Once the door closed, Najib asked Shyla, "Haven't you read her? Hakana is trustworthy."

"I did when she snuck inside our rooms, but I don't like to invade people's privacy. Only when I have a good reason to dig deeper into a person's thoughts and emotions will I do it."

"I don't know how you can resist the temptation," Najib said. "If it were me, I'd be digging away." He gestured for them to sit on the cushions around the table. "How can I help you?"

"I wanted to establish the timeline for the old king's deteriorating health and find out who was aware of his condition."

"Ah, I see." He hummed as he gathered his thoughts. "Let me give you some background. As the old king aged, he tended to spend the taxes on more...frivolous things and not the most critical or needed. He sent his elite soldiers on treasure hunting expeditions. Complaints came from the various cities, but he ignored them. He also spent the taxes right away and paid all the soldiers, guards, and staff one large sum. Everyone thought it was wonderful until they failed to ration out their coins over the entire circuit, then they grumbled until the next tax delivery.

Everyone knew he was getting old, but when he fell seriously ill, only a few were aware of his true condition."

"Who were they?" Rendor asked.

"Advisor Yiesha, the king's physician, the captain of the guard, Qulsary's Water Princess, and the commander of the elite squads."

"How soon after he became seriously ill did the taxes arrive?"

"A hundred and fifty sun jumps. The physician took excellent care of him despite the king's deteriorating state of mind. It was only when no one was paid that the news about his health was told to me, the king-in-training, the officers, and the higher-level staff members. It didn't take long for everyone else to know."

"And over the next two circuits, people left, right?" Shyla asked.

"Yes. The elite squads right away, but a few of the others had some sense of loyalty. And again their basic needs were met by the loan from the Water Princess."

"Do you know where the commander of the squads has gone?" Rendor asked.

"There have been rumors that Commander Xerxes went to Nintri," Najib said.

Nintri—that city kept coming up. Shyla and Rendor exchanged a look.

"Does Xerxes have friends or family here?" Shyla asked.

"In Qulsary?"

"Yes, or in the castle. Maybe one of the guards or staff?"

"His sister is in charge of ensuring we have enough food and water."

That seemed too easy. "We need to talk to her."

"All right," Najib said.

"What do you know about the Water Princess of Nintri?" Rendor asked.

"Not much. Her people love her, and we've had no official complaints. The monks haven't reported any problems since she gained the throne about ten circuits ago."

"How did she come into power?"

"Peacefully. The old Water Prince of Nintri died and she'd been one of his advisors. The people pretty much decided she should take the throne and that was that. No one challenged her. It was refreshing."

No wonder Banqui, Shyla's friend and an archeologist, wanted to move to Nintri. After all the trouble with the former Water Prince, Banqui deserved a nice peaceful city to retire in. However, Jayden had asked Banqui to stay in Zirdai and help organize the artifact displays in the new museum.

But now that she was thinking about Nintri, she remembered the mercenaries. She wondered if the city wasn't reporting problems to the King. Perhaps they'd tried and the old king ignored them.

"Have you gotten any requests for help from Nintri?" Shyla asked.

"Not according to the records." Najib drummed his fingers on the table. "To be honest, the records were rather…incomplete when I finally had access to them."

"Incomplete how?" Rendor asked.

"Over the last five circuits, there are gaps and inconsistencies. I believe it was due to Yiesha's age and her failing eyesight. It's the advisor's duty to record everything."

"Everything?"

"Yes, everything. An account of the taxes, all the decisions that are made, any new laws that are enacted, the requests from the cities, changes in personnel…everything." He splayed the fingers of his right hand, showing them the ink stains on his skin. "It takes a great deal of time."

Hakana arrived with an assortment of fruit slices and toasted bread for them. Before the page could relax, Najib sent her to fetch Commander Xerxes' sister.

After Hakana left, Rendor asked the advisor about the mercenaries in Nintri. "Do you know when they appeared? Is it in the records?"

Najib sighed. "I've heard the rumors but haven't gotten any reports from the monks in Nintri. I'm not sure if they exist or not."

"They exist," Shyla said, explaining what happened to them out in the desert.

The advisor cursed. "Why didn't you tell me sooner?"

"I didn't think it was relevant."

"And now?"

"I suspect something is going on in Nintri."

Commander Xerxes' sister's name was Izusa. She hovered in the doorway as if reluctant to enter. Najib waved her to join them around the table.

He introduced her to Shyla and Rendor. "You just need to answer a few questions. Shouldn't take long." Najib sent Hakana to get a pot of hot water for tea while he mixed a blend of special tea leaves.

Shyla hid her grin when Hakana huffed and muttered about the thankless job of a page.

Izusa sat, but her spine remained stiff and she avoided meeting anyone's gaze. Shyla wondered if the woman had learned about The Eyes and was purposely avoiding looking at her. It depended on how quick gossip spread in the castle.

Rendor leaned forward. "Izusa, you're acting guilty. Do you have something to confess?"

The woman glanced at Rendor in terror. Then she shot a desperate look at Shyla. Their gazes met. *Got you.* Just like Rendor had intended. Clever man.

"Please excuse him," Shyla said. "We're here to ask questions, not accuse you of anything." Shyla turned her full attention to Izusa, reading her surface emotions.

The woman was skittish and on edge, but her fears were not about being discovered as a thief but being fired. Her brother got her the job, and now that he no longer worked for the King, she worried the new advisor would hire one of his own friends or family members. Izusa really liked her job and the people she worked with. And she loved her brother.

"How long have you worked in the castle?" Shyla asked.

"About five circuits," she said to the table.

Shyla continued with easy questions, getting Izusa to relax. "No plans to leave even with not being paid for a while?"

"Oh no. I trust the King will pay me when the next round of taxes comes in." And she hoped by then that Malik—one of the guards—would ask her to marry him.

Then Shyla asked the expected questions about the theft. Izusa claimed her innocence, which was the truth. But she also showed a touch of anger on Malik's behalf. Everyone always blamed the guards, who had been working hard without pay for over two circuits.

Shyla suppressed a smile. If Malik didn't ask for her hand, he was a fool.

"Have you heard from Xerxes lately?" Shyla asked.

Guilt welled. Izusa ducked her head. "Yes. He's doing well in Nintri." Although she wasn't sure what he was doing. He'd said he found a job but never mentioned what type of work it was. She understood why he left—he needed the coins and the excitement since the old king had stopped assigning interesting cases to the squads, instead sending them on stupid or boring missions. Izusa had been telling him what had been going on with the new King so when the taxes came in, he could return and be in charge again.

Izusa confirmed what Shyla and Rendor suspected. Shyla asked a few more innocuous questions and dismissed the now relieved woman. Then she told Rendor and Najib what she'd learned from Izusa's thoughts and emotions.

"You got all that from those easy questions?" Najib asked in surprise. He stared at the doorway. "And she has no idea she revealed so much."

"No. Not now, but how fast is the gossip in the castle?"

"Unfortunately pretty fast. No one should guess about The Eyes or magic, but they do know you're investigating the theft."

"Did they know before we arrived?" Rendor asked.

"No. We weren't even sure what we'd learned about Shyla was true until she arrived."

That meant the merc ambush in the desert wasn't connected to the stolen taxes. Yet another mystery to solve. But one thing was clear... "We need to travel to Nintri."

"I don't know what I'm going to miss more, the gamelu sausages, having Hakana as our own personal guide, or the castle's guest suite," Rendor said as he finished stuffing his few belongings into his pack. "At least I had time to sell that awful statue of Tamburah." He jingled the pouch of coins, which only contained a quarter of what he'd earned. The rest of the coins were safely locked away in the King's vault.

They hadn't wanted to take them along just in case they were ambushed again. Since they knew no one in the castle had stolen the taxes, they trusted the huge iron door and deep pool of water to do their job.

Shyla would miss the kaleidoscope cave, the dancing water, and their privacy. Nintri was nineteen sun jumps away from Qulsary.

However, she knew they'd be back to give the King a full

report. And she hoped they'd have time to see a few of Nintri's wonders while there. In order to get there without drawing too much attention, Rendor had found them jobs as guards for a caravan heading to the city.

"Did you warn the owner we might run into trouble?" she asked him. It had taken them six sun jumps to find a Nintri-bound caravan that was hiring. She worried that the delay would allow the news about their destination to reach the mercs.

"No need," Rendor said. "The mercs are not going to waste time and energy setting up an ambush when we're traveling right to them."

Good news for the caravan, but for them…not so much. "And what is stopping them from ambushing us in the city?"

"Two things," Rendor said.

"And they are?"

"Me and you."

She laughed. "I think one of us has an inflated opinion of our skills."

"And one of us needs to start being more confident," he countered, shouldering his pack. "Come on, we don't want to be late."

She followed him to the surface. The sun hung low in the sky, beginning its jump. The gravel crunched under her boots with a crispness that matched the air temperature. A number of caravans were in the process of assembling. Long lines of wagons pulled by gamelu teams waited for the signal to begin their journey.

Rendor found their caravan and introduced Shyla to Dasan,

the owner.

The man eyed Shyla. "She's not even armed."

"She grew up in a monastery," Rendor said.

"Doesn't mean she studied."

"*She's* standing right here." Shyla put her hands on her hips. "And I'm happy to give you a demonstration."

The man grunted with amusement. "Welcome to the crew." He returned to barking orders to the wagon drivers.

As they prepared to leave, Hakana rushed up to Shyla. "The King…" she puffed. "Said to…give you this." She handed her a leather pouch. "It's so the monks…Water Princess, and Heliacal Priest…know you're working for him."

She opened the pouch and poured the contents out onto her palm. It was a platinum bracelet. About two centimeters wide, it had a sigil crafted from osmium. It was a crown, except the points of the crown were water droplets. Clever and beautiful.

"Najib said Captain Rendor would know how to secure it around your wrist. Does he?" Hakana asked in concern.

"Yes, he does." Memories of when Rendor locked a similar bracelet around her wrist pushed to the surface of her mind. He'd been an entirely different person then. And then another recollection followed and she almost laughed out loud. Biting down on the giggles that threatened, she gave Hakana a few coins.

"You don't—" she started.

"I know, but we wanted to thank you for your help."

She shot her a wide grin. "You're welcome. Good luck." She waved to Rendor before dashing away.

Rendor came over to her. "What did she want?"

"To give me this." She showed him the bracelet and waited. Would he remember?

At first he scowled. Probably remembering when the old Water Prince had given Shyla his sigil to keep her safe while she investigated the theft of The Eyes. It hadn't worked. The deacons had cut it off her wrist before they planned to torture a confession from her.

Then Rendor laughed. She loved that deep rumble.

"I was right," he said. "You've gotten the King's sigil."

"A lucky guess. There's no way you could have anticipated this."

His good humor faded. "Not this. But after I met you, I thought you might inform the King about the Water Prince and return with his elite soldiers." His gaze grew distant. "I figured they were bound to show up at some point."

"And if they had arrived?"

"They would have killed the prince, me, and all the officers. Exactly what we all deserved."

She opened her mouth to argue, but Dasan shouted for everyone to get ready for departure.

Rendor took the bracelet from her hand and snapped it around her right wrist, adjusting the tightness. "This will open doors, but it won't protect you."

She wanted to counter with a sarcastic comment. After all, she was well aware that these mercenaries were not loyal to the King. But his serious expression stopped her. "I'll be careful."

He squeezed her hand. "Thank you." He hurried to take up

his position at the front of the caravan with Dasan, leaving her to wonder what he was really thanking her for.

Shyla found her place alongside the fourth wagon. The caravan had eight wagons, eight drivers, four guards, four muscles, sixteen gamelus, and Dasan. The caravan owners must have figured out the best ratio of wagons to guards and muscles. Four guards meant she'd have a longer shift during darkness—forty-five angles versus the twenty-five angles with Lota's caravan. It would give her more time to practice using her magic. She suspected she'd have a greater need of her skills in Nintri.

They arrived at Nintri nineteen sun jumps later. They hadn't encountered any trouble during the trip—no ambushes or sand pirates. When the caravan rumbled to a stop, the muscles burst into action, unloading the colorful rugs and cushions that Dasan had bought in Qulsary and hoped to sell at the market in Nintri.

"Only one market?" Rendor had asked.

"Yes. Right in the very heart of the city," Dasan had said. "Nintri is unique in that it has a gigantic cavern in its center. It's twenty levels high and spans a kilometer." Dasan had spread his hands wide to demonstrate its size. "The city also has dozens of other caverns almost as big. These spaces are linked together by tunnels like stones on a necklace. And the city is not like Qulsary where the levels go from one side of the city to the other in neat rows down to the bottom. In Nintri everything is grouped around the caverns and many levels are not connected."

"How do you keep from getting lost?" Shyla had asked.

"Once you find the main tunnels that go between the caverns, that's all you need to know. And those are always filled with people so they're hard to miss."

Shyla couldn't wait to explore the city's unusual layout. She had bought another head scarf before they left Qulsary. One with a pattern that would blend in with the locals. Not because she worried about being seen as a sun-kissed, but because she worried about being seen as Shyla Sun-Kissed.

It was close to darkness when they parted ways with Dasan. They avoided the main entrance into the city. Two guards stood near it, telling visitors to register. The last thing Shyla wanted to do was let the city's guards know she'd arrived. The mercenaries had probably bribed a couple guards to pass along any pertinent information. And with that in mind, they also avoided asking the guards for accommodation recommendations. Instead, they followed the flow of people.

When they reached their first cavern, Shyla couldn't help craning her neck. It was huge and well lit. Druk lanterns had been affixed to the walls from the bottom all the way to the top. Crystals glinted and streaks of color painted the surface.

"Yellow is sulfur, green is copper, and orange is iron," a woman who'd been walking near Shyla said.

Shyla glanced at her. "Were all those substances mined from here? Is that why the cavern is so big?"

"No. Koraha's molten core welled up into the space, then retreated, leaving a shell behind. All the caverns in Nintri were formed that way."

"Ah, thank you."

The woman smiled and continued on her way. It didn't take them long to discover that most of the locals were friendly. Despite Shyla's new scarf and Rendor's plain clothes, they failed to blend in as well as they hoped. But as they walked through the city, welcoming strangers gave them recommendations on rooms to rent, places to visit, and which market stalls had the best quality goods.

In fact, the city practically hummed with contentment. Shyla spotted a few guards, but they interacted with the citizens, talking and laughing instead of standing on the fringes watching. The deacons also appeared to be too busy with their own chores to notice if anyone wasn't being properly devout.

"This place is a little too…nice," Rendor whispered to her. "It's creepy."

"No it isn't. It's refreshing."

"It's hiding something."

There were no signs of the mercenaries, but she doubted they'd have a market stall advertising their services. Or that they would stand out like Rendor. Few people carried swords or knives. If anyone appeared to be a grunt for hire, it was Rendor.

After eating third meal, they rented a room near the main cavern. Or at least that was what the older woman who owned the rooms had told them. Her cluster of small apartments was located at a dead end, which Rendor hadn't liked until he learned there was a back door in their suite to another tunnel.

"The heart cavern is just another kilometer or two down the main artery," the woman said as she unlocked the door to their room. "You'll want to be there right at the sun's apex. It's glorious." She dropped the key into Rendor's palm. "Let me know if you need any help. My granddaughter guides people through the lava tunnels, but she can also navigate Nintri blind."

"I've read about those lava tunnels," Shyla said. "Were they formed the same way as the caverns? By the molten core?"

"Yes, though they're deep underneath the city. Some are still hot and others are filled with toxic gas so you have to be very careful. Which is why the Water Princess will only allow guided tours."

Good to know. Shyla thanked the woman and closed the door behind her. Rendor was already exploring. It wasn't a big place, but there was a sitting area with a desk and sand clock. One extra-large sleeping cushion occupied its own room—Rendor had requested it and the woman's gaze had swept over him as she readily agreed. Another room had a big stone table with enough cushions that they could invite people over. Plenty of druk lanterns shone with a red-tinted light.

Rendor checked the back door, opening it and peering out as if he expected an ambush. Satisfied, he closed and locked it. They were on level twenty-nine and a half. She'd no idea why they'd bothered with the half. It was either a level or it wasn't.

Shyla was about to ask Rendor his thoughts on the numbering when she met his heated gaze. His thoughts were obviously not on the strange quirks of Nintri but rather on the fact they hadn't been alone in nineteen sun jumps.

"Come here," he said, spreading his arms wide.

Just like that, her focus shrank to one person. And the rest of the world disappeared.

Much later, they discussed their plans for the upcoming sun jump.

"We're not splitting up," Rendor said in his I-must-be-obeyed voice. His arms tightened around her. They were curled together on the sleeping cushion.

"We can get more done. There won't be an ambush on the way to the monastery."

"How do you know?"

"The monks would never allow it." She waited, but his muscles remained tense. "I grew up in a monastery; the monks are sworn to protect the King. Plus a portion of those taxes go to the monasteries. They wouldn't steal from the King."

He reluctantly agreed. "While you're visiting the monks, I'll make a few discreet inquiries about the mercs and then check out the market."

"I'll meet you there at apex."

"Should I be insulted that you're only promising to meet me because you want to see what's glorious about the heart cavern?" he teased.

She met his gaze. "I already know what's going to be glorious in that cavern at that time."

"You do?"

"Yes. You." She was dead serious.

But he laughed it off. "Yeah, right. I already agreed to your plan, no need to use false flattery."

Before she could correct him, he glanced at the sand clock. "We better get moving if you're going to make it back in time."

After a number of helpful people pointed her in the right direction, Shyla finally found an exit to the surface. It was about angle twenty. Warm enough not to need a sun cloak, but not yet blazing hot.

She spun in a slow circle, getting her bearings. Part of her education included learning the names and locations of all the monasteries in Koraha. The Monks of Callow lived four kilometers southwest of Nintri. The leader of the Callow monks was Barika.

Once she determined the correct direction, Shyla set off at a fast pace. With all those sun jumps traveling with the two caravans, she'd learned how to spot the well traveled yet still sand-covered paths, therefore avoiding having to trudge through the deeper sand.

Shyla kept her mental shield down as she walked, scanning for any bumps that would indicate a person lurked nearby. Remembering the mercs who hid underneath the sand, she aimed her magic through the grains as well. She passed a few velbloud caretakers out feeding the flocks. Soon she was far enough away from the city to spot the light tracks of the monks out on patrol. They wore special wide-soled boots to avoid leaving prints in the sand. Only those who knew what they were looking for could find them.

Another couple angles later, she encountered a few bumps. Even though the monks wore turbans, tunics, and pants that matched the reddish-orange color of the desert, Shyla located them lying on top of the dunes. By the time she reached the surface building for the monastery, she had counted sixteen monks—more than Hanif would assign, but nothing alarming. Not even when they moved closer. It was standard procedure when a stranger approached their home.

Inside the simple one-room structure was a single monk. He stood when she entered. Behind him were the steps down into the monastery. If she tried to get around him and enter without permission, he'd call out and the other monks would rush in to help him stop her.

"How can I help you?" he asked.

The young monk wore a dark green tunic and matching pants. Each order of monks had chosen a different color to wear when they were inside. The practice allowed monks to know each other's order at a glance. The Monks of Parzival wore tan.

"I'd like to talk with Barika."

"I'm sorry, but Barika is no longer in charge of our monastery."

Not too much of a surprise since her information was at least four circuits out of date. "Who is your leader now?"

"Who would like to know?"

"My name is Shyla. I grew up with the Monks of Parzival."

"You are not a monk."

She clamped down on her sarcastic reply. "I am allowed to

seek an audience with your leader."

"He is very busy. I can call for his assistant and you can schedule an appointment in a few sun jumps."

"I'm afraid the matter is quite urgent." Shyla pulled back her sleeve, exposing the King's sigil. "I'm here at the request of the King."

"Why didn't you say that sooner?" he snapped.

"I wished to see how the Monks of Callow treat strangers."

He finally realized that he'd just grumped at the King's emissary. "My apologies. Please follow me." He led her down into the cooler underground levels and to a reception room. "Please wait here while I fetch Lonato."

While he was gone, she examined the room. It was nicer than the one in the Parzival monastery. Cushions ringed the space and the monks guarding the tunnels weren't as obvious. Mirror pipes brought in the sunlight from the surface, making it a bright cheery place.

It didn't take long for the monk to return with Lonato. The man wore the dark green tunic and pants that the monks preferred when not on the surface. His brown hair was pulled back into a tight knot. He appeared to be around thirty to thirty-five circuits old—rather young for a leader. A thin beard clung to his lower jaw.

"Welcome to my monastery," Lonato said, bowing slightly. "I'm sorry you caught me by surprise. I hadn't been informed that you were coming."

Shyla met his gaze, but she resisted reading his emotions. He hadn't given her any reason—other than calling it *his* monastery—to invade his privacy. Instead, she said, "No need to apologize. The King was unable to send advance notice."

His wide shoulders relaxed, but his expression remained on guard. "How can I help you?"

"I need to talk to you in private."

"Oh, yes. Of course. This way." He led her down another twelve levels to his office.

The room was larger than Hanif's and had much more furniture, cushions, rugs, and wall hangings. To be fair, it wasn't like the leader of the monks had to adhere to certain rules of austerity. Hanif just liked things simple.

A woman entered and Lonato sent her for some tea. He then invited Shyla to sit down and they chatted about nothing important until the monk returned and set out the refreshments.

When she left, he asked, "What is all this about?"

"Your monks collected the taxes for the last two circuits. Were there any problems?"

"Other than the occasional bandits?"

"Bandits?"

He stared at her as if she was the biggest idiot in Koraha. "Desperate people who attempt to rob the tax collection wagons. They're never successful."

"Then, yes, other than the bandits."

"No." Lonato leaned forward. "Why? Was there a problem with the taxes?"

A legitimate question, but there was an intensity behind it as if he already knew the answer and was already preparing his reaction to the news. She decided to tell him the truth. However, she would use The Eyes to read his emotions. She suspected it would be the only way to learn his true reaction. "Yes, there was a big problem. Your monks delivered fake coins."

He jerked back as if she'd slapped him. That wasn't what he'd expected her to say. At all. He'd braced for another accusation. "Fake coins? Are you sure? Why haven't we heard of this sooner?"

"Are you aware that the old king died?" she asked, wanting to keep him off balance.

"Uh, yes, of course. The monks are informed right away. What—"

"Did you know the old king was seriously ill the last two and a half circuits of his life?"

"No, but we suspected something was going on with his health."

That was a lie. He was well aware of the King's condition. "How long have you been in charge?"

Lonato went immediately on the defensive. "Why is that relevant?"

"I need to talk with the monks who escorted the taxes. If you're new to the job, then—"

"I was promoted almost two circuits ago. I know the monks that collected the taxes. It takes almost a full circuit to visit each city and then travel to Qulsary so the same group did both rounds."

The truth. At least that meant fewer people to interrogate. "I'll need an office or conference room to interview them in."

"Are you accusing them of stealing?" he demanded. That was

what he'd expected her to say before.

"I'm not accusing anyone. The investigation is ongoing."

"Do you have any of the fake coins with you? They must be excellent forgeries."

"Why do you say that? Do the monks examine the coins when they collect them?"

"No, they're secured in chests, but the monks witness all the coins being transferred to the vault."

Ah, the *plink, plink, plink.* "The fakes were good enough to pass a casual inspection," Shyla said, which was the truth.

"Then you should be interviewing all the Water Princes and Princesses," he said. "They're the ones who paid the taxes with fake coins."

"All of them? That's quite a conspiracy." And he was trying to distract her. Did that mean he had something to hide? Or was he just defending his monks? At this point, she wasn't sure.

"The King's been unresponsive to the cities' needs. Perhaps they took matters into their own hands. That scenario is more likely than monks stealing. You were raised in a monastery. You should know *that.*" He added heat to the last word. "*You need* to interview the King's guards. *They* probably *exchanged* the real coins for the fakes." Each word he stressed pushed on her, commanding her.

Scorching sand rats, the man had magical abilities!

She fought the magical directive to leave the monastery as it pulsed through her body. With effort, she regained control. "The guards were exonerated." Either her statement or the fact she didn't obey him caused him concern. "You can see why interviewing the monks is imperative."

"It's a *waste of time*. My monks *wouldn't steal*." This time he put extra power into his words.

No, of course not. She nodded in agreement before realizing what she was doing. Again she struggled to ignore the command. It was so very strong. And he spoke the truth, which meant someone else had stolen the taxes. "I'd also like to talk to Barika. She was in charge when the thefts first started." She used the power of The Eyes to seek the magic inside him.

"*You* don't *need* to *talk to anyone*. It's time for *you* to *leave*," he ordered.

When he responded, magic glowed inside him, but it wasn't a crack, nor did it fill him completely. Instead it was a bright ball of light around his heart and it pushed on her. Hard.

She was half out of her seat to comply before coming to her senses. Lonato stared at her in amazement.

Not waiting for him to command her again, she gathered all her magic, including the power of The Eyes, and aimed it at him. It was time to put an end to this charade.

"You can stop influencing me now."

"I'm—"

"Using magic, I know. Do you know who I am?"

His confidence ebbed, replaced with confusion. "The King's emissary." And that sun-kissed who overthrew the people in charge of Zirdai.

She leaned closer. "Yes, I'm *that* sun-kissed. And you're going to tell me everything you know." Shyla pushed magic into her words, forcing him to speak.

"I..." He clamped his mouth shut with a snap, pressing his lips together. The man was resistant to her commands.

She increased the pressure. "Go on, Lonato, *confess.*"

"The King of Koraha is no longer needed!" The words exploded from his mouth. "He's expensive. And there's nothing he does that the cities can't do for themselves. If they keep their tax money, they can all have their own special elite forces and take care of their own problems without having to wait on the King to send help." Appalled by his outburst, Lonato covered his mouth with both hands. But then he surged to his feet and flung his arms wide. "You know this firsthand. Zirdai was struggling under corrupt and power-hungry leaders with no help from the King. Even when he was lucid, he didn't care. It's just like what you've done in Zirdai—we've taken matters into our own hands."

Shyla couldn't fault his logic. She had taken matters in hand. But they had to act because innocent people were dying. Lonato had other options. He could have waited for the old king to die and present his ideas to the new King.

"So you stole the taxes and hired mercenaries," she guessed.

"Yes."

"Did you hire the mercs to intercept me before I reached the King?"

"No. Someone else did. Although I admit being glad when I heard about it." He gave her a nasty glare. "Too bad it failed."

She ignored the dig. "Who else?"

"I don't know. But I'm not surprised. You were part of a major upset in Zirdai's leadership. Many people died. That's going to make you plenty of enemies."

She hadn't thought anyone beyond Zirdai would be affected. But now that she did, there was bound to be relatives, business associates, and friends who were upset and might be plotting revenge. A chill raced along her spine, but she clamped down on her emotions. That was a problem to be solved later.

"And you're planning to set up mercs in every city in Koraha?" she asked.

"Yes. Each city will have mercenaries."

She considered. If there'd been mercs in Zirdai, would the situation have gotten so dire? Maybe Rendor was right to call the Invisible Sword a mercenary unit. "Are other cities suffering like Zirdai was?" she asked.

"A few."

Not good. The Sun Goddess's command repeated in her head. *I do not like to see my people suffer. Make it stop.*

"Who else is involved?" she asked.

He fought. The magic around his heart flared. But she reached deep inside him with The Eyes and read the answer. "Commander Xerxes."

"How do you know? How are you making me talk? Do you have magic?"

"Just him?" she asked, ignoring his questions.

"Of course not! I expect he has his entire squad of soldiers, but I only work with him." Lonato started to pace.

"How do you know him?"

"We were acolytes together."

That was a surprise. "He wanted to be a monk?"

Lonato's brittle laugh was bitter. "No. He wanted to learn the Ways of the Yarin."

And the only way to learn it was to join a monastery. Except some acolytes decided not to take the oath mostly because they realized that lifestyle was not for them. Many of the Invisible Swords were ex-acolytes. However, to purposely join with no intention of staying…that was almost as bad as becoming a monk to spy on the monks. At least she now had an idea of just how skilled Xerxes and his soldiers-turned-mercs were.

"Aside from swapping out the real coins for the fakes, what is your role in all this?" she asked.

"The monks work for the King, but we should be concentrating on our duties for the Sun Goddess and not spying on the cities for him."

"What duties are those?"

"Helping the people." Lonato stopped and glared. "You can't say that's a bad thing."

She couldn't. "What about the other Callow monks? Are they in on this scheme?"

"Some are, some have no clue, and others…"

"Others?" She turned up the heat. Her hands shook with the effort.

His face contorted as if he were in pain. "Resisted."

Scorching sand rats. "What did you do to them?"

"They weren't hurt. Only a few, like Barika, needed to be reminded of the Sun Goddess's love to change their minds and happily join our cause. The majority of the monks agree that we're wasting our talents and energy spying for the King. We believe the Rooms of Knowledge should be available to all Korahans."

Shyla agreed as well, but this wasn't the way to enact change. Or was it? Many people had died in the defeat of Zirdai's Water Prince and Heliacal Priestess. She was in no position to judge Lonato's actions. Look at what she'd just done to get this information—forcing him to confess versus reading his soul. That was something Tamburah would have done in order to flaunt the power of The Eyes. Was this a step down the path of madness?

Shoving her own recriminations aside—for now—she considered Lonato's crimes. The current state of affairs with the monasteries wasn't nearly as horrible as the killing and torture of people in Zirdai.

"Which monasteries are involved?" she asked.

"Callow, Ketran, Bejin, and Dunnar."

They were near Nintri, Ginda, Riffa, and Sinkat—all the cities that were closest to the King's castle. Except Qulsary. "Who is next?"

He curled his hands into fists, refusing to answer. She increased her power. A strange raw and scraping buzz went through her, setting her teeth on edge. Not a good sign.

"Apanji is next."

"What about the Monks of Quirin outside Qulsary?"

"They'll be last. No sense tipping the King off early."

"How do you convert the monks?"

"There's a dozen Callow monks who are out on a spiritual pilgrimage. They've been visiting monasteries and preaching our message. Between the conversions and the travel, it takes time."

Shyla grappled with all the information. She needed to consult with Rendor and figure out what they should do. Changing directions, she asked Lonato about Xerxes. Or rather she tried. She'd exhausted her energy. The room spun dangerously around her.

Lonato stared at her. Then he smiled. It wasn't a nice smile at all. "Your magic is limited." He crouched down beside her. "You know too much. I can't let you leave," he said in almost a whisper.

She straightened and gathered what was left of her energy for one last command.

Except Lonato was faster. "*Sleep.*"

The order pressed on her like a heavy stone. She struggled.

"*Sleep.*"

She fought until there was nothing left. Nothing but the oblivion of sleep.

When she woke, there wasn't a single muscle in her body that didn't ache with a deep fatigue. Aside from celebrating the fact she was still alive, Shyla noted that she was in a cell. Assessing her situation needed energy that she didn't have so she rolled over on the cushion and fell back to sleep.

The next time she was awake long enough to care, she scanned her accommodations. Three stone walls and one lined with metal bars surrounded her. Inside the cell was a sleeping cushion, a druk glowing with orange-tinted light, two buckets, a water skin, and a few rolls of jerky, which meant killing her wasn't on Lonato's agenda at this time. Small comfort. She drank half the water skin, ate a roll, and returned to oblivion.

The fifth or sixth time she roused, she no longer ached as if she'd been buried in a cave-in. She explored the space. It took a fraction of an angle to discover there were no weak spots and her pack was gone. Using her magic, which rubbed on her nerves like grains of sand in her boots, she explored the area beyond her prison, but there were no bumps within range.

So much for being powerful. If she didn't have anyone to work her magic on, she was rather stuck. Now she wished she had asked Hakana to teach her how to pick a lock. On the heels of that thought was another. Rendor.

No doubt he was worried and probably plotting a way to rescue her. Except he couldn't get into the monastery. Not by himself. The monks were too well trained. Unless he hired the mercs to help him. She laughed at the ridiculous idea. Since she was the sun-idiot that used up all her energy interrogating Lonato, it was up to her to find a way to get free. She only had enough water for a couple sun jumps. If they'd wanted to kill her, she'd be dead. Someone was bound to arrive, and Shyla would use them to escape. Simple plans were the best.

Conserving her strength, Shyla ate and slept as much as possible and rationed her water. She kept her thoughts focused on what she could control instead of obsessing over everything that might go wrong. It was nice to have the druk. The orange tint meant she was between twelve and twenty-four levels below ground. Assuming she was still in the monastery, she had the advantage of knowing the layout of the levels above twelve. She was somewhat surprised that there were cells in a monastery, but, once she thought about it, it made sense. Not all those who came seeking shelter had the best intentions. Hanif had to confine a few until the Water Prince's guards had come to collect the offenders. She never considered where he'd put them before.

Later, a voice woke her, calling her name. Shyla sat up. A

monk stood on the other side of the bars. She set a full water skin and a handful of jerky on the ground inside the cell.

"Are you well?" the woman asked.

"Yes, thank you. Why am I here?"

"Lonato wished for you to be here." She said it as if it made all the sense in the world.

Shyla met the woman's gaze. Her honey-colored eyes were filled with kindness, and her thoughts were content.

"What's going on?" Shyla asked, increasing the power of The Eyes.

"Lonato wishes for you to stay here." Her thoughts focused on how important it was to follow Lonato's orders. How it was joyful to do the Sun Goddess's work.

Shyla dug deeper, but the woman's own thoughts and emotions just slipped out of reach. All she thought about was Lonato and his wishes. Information on the situation was maddeningly lacking. The only thing she learned was the monk didn't have a key to the cell on her. Lonato must have used his magic to turn this poor woman into a mindless minion. It made Shyla sick to her stomach.

"Do you know how long I'm going to be locked in here?" Shyla asked.

"As long as Lonato says."

This was going nowhere. Shyla changed tactics. "Tell Lonato that I'm not staying here any longer." Gathering her magic was painful. "Tell him goodbye for me."

Gone.

The monk gasped as Shyla disappeared from her sight. She

clapped a hand over her mouth and stared. Then she called, "Hello?"

Gone.

She bit her thumbnail. "Hello? Are you there? Come out. Lonato will not be pleased." After an angle, the woman spun on her heel and dashed away.

After a few moments to recover from that simple effort, Shyla sought bumps in the distance. She wasn't going to wait for Lonato to use his influence on her. As soon as she sensed him, she'd grab him.

Too bad he didn't come alone. He had four monks with him. One of them was the woman. Shyla pushed magic at them all.

Gone.

Gone.

They strode up to her cell and peered inside. The woman hung back as if afraid.

Lonato cursed and rattled the locked door. "Where in seven hells did she go?"

"She just disappeared. I swear to the goddess," the woman said.

"Magic?" a man on Lonato's right asked.

Lonato frowned. "You mean a miracle?"

"Yes, sir. That's what I meant. Maybe the Sun Goddess called the sun-kissed to her?"

"It's possible. The Sun Goddess is all powerful," Lonato said.

Shyla wished she had more energy to read that man's soul. He appeared lucid and not under Lonato's influence. And he held a ring of keys in his hand. Guess she'd just use her regular magic.

Freeze.

Freeze.

Her head ached with the effort of holding all five of them immobile. Hurrying to the bars, she reached through and plucked the key ring from the man. After trying almost every single one, she found the right key and unlocked the cell door. Then she replaced the ring.

Forget.

Forget.

She erased their memories of her stealing the keys. Her muscles shook and a dizzy spell threatened to topple her, but she rallied. Fainting now would ruin her chance to escape.

Gone.

Gone.

Lonato started. "Did you see that?"

"What?"

"I thought I caught a glimpse of the sun-kissed." He peered inside the cell. "It's a trick. She's still there."

And that was her cue. She stopped her magic and reappeared. Huddled on the cushion, she wilted as if exhausted.

The woman cried out and jumped back.

"Thought so," Lonato said, mighty pleased with himself. "Nice trick. You'll have to show me how to do that."

Shyla looked at him. "What do you want?"

"You. You're going to tell me everything the King knows and then you'll tell me why you can do things like disappear. And then you'll teach me how to do it."

"Why would I do that?"

"Because it will please me." He gestured to the others. "Come on before she regains her strength." They hurried away.

That was odd. How did he expect to force her to comply? Especially when she was at full strength? It didn't matter because they didn't test the door again. Thank the goddess. While she waited for them to be well and gone, she finished the water and ate. Then she tied the new water skin to her belt and shoved a couple rolls of jerky into her pocket in case she was stuck inside the monastery. She'd no idea what angle it was. If it was close to the danger zone or if it was darkness, she'd have to hide until a safer time. However, it made the most sense that the woman who brought her fresh supplies had come after the angle zero prayer session.

The door squealed when she opened it. Shyla froze. Her heart banged against her rib cage, demanding action. When nothing happened, she crept down the tunnel. Keeping her senses open, she scanned for bumps.

As she navigated through the monastery, she had a few near misses. There were more monks living here than in Zirdai and they moved in packs. Quiet, too. Unwilling to drain too much of her magic, she avoided the bumps and searched for an empty room. She needed to change into the red tunic and pants the monks wore when on the surface. In the first empty room, the trunk was locked. In the second, the clothes were three sizes too big. It wasn't until the sixth room that she found the perfect combination of an unlocked trunk and clothes that almost fit her.

Then she needed to decide her next move. It was angle twenty and she should have enough time to reach Nintri. It all depended on her energy level. But staying here any longer would increase the risk of being discovered. At least now that she was dressed like a monk and her hair was hidden by a turban, she wouldn't need to wield her magic as much.

Walking like she belonged, she headed for the surface. No one questioned her even though the sound of her heartbeat was loud enough to trigger a cave-in. When she reached the surface building, she used her magic on the greeter.

Look away.

Look away.

Then she aimed it at the monks on patrol. Only a few were nearby. Once she was out of sight, she stopped the commands and erased her boot prints. Taking her first full breath since she escaped, Shyla headed to the city.

At first she kept a quick pace. Then the heat increased and her steps slowed. It was hard enough to walk in the sand when she was rested, but with fatigue turning her limbs into stone, it was a tough slog. Each step was a victory. She dangled the promise of being reunited with Rendor in front of her. One step closer to him. Two. Ten. Fifteen.

Halfway to the city, she stopped to wield her magic, scanning for bumps. She paused long enough to swallow a couple large gulps of water. The liquid tasted divine.

It had a slightly citrusy taste. Reminding her of... The memory slipped away. It didn't matter. She continued her trudge.

After a couple steps, a strange languid sensation flowed through her, melting her tensions, soothing her aches and pains. It reminded her of…Zhek's healing tea. Or so he called it. The tea hid the taste of…pain relief? No. His restorative? No.

The dunes around her softened, resembling giant cushions. Standing became difficult as the ground sloped suddenly to the side. She stumbled and fell to her knees. What had Zhek given her? Healing tea? But that made her…sleep!

"Ha!" she said aloud. "I figured it out." But she wasn't sleepy. She was…off kilter and spinning. Just like…before. When she…drank…she drank…

"Holy water!" she said in triumph. Then she blinked. How? That Heliacal Priestess was dead, dead, dead. Shyla giggled. Everything around her blurred. The sand melted into pools of water. The thought made her thirsty so she took another drink. And stopped at the citrusy taste. Holy water was bad, bad, bad.

All her humor evaporated as a small part of her brain set off warning sirens. Lonato had filled her water skin with holy water. Why? To talk. To tell him everything. To please him. It's all about him, him, him. That son of a sand rat!

No. Sand rats were wonderful, smart, loving creatures. He was the son of a sand demon. And she needed to move, move, move. Except her body was no longer following orders. She struggled to her feet. The world tilted and spun. Drawing in a deep breath of hot air, she focused on her legs. They were useful things and would have to do all the work. "I'm counting on you," she whispered to them.

She then concentrated on putting one foot in front of the

other. When she managed it, she knew she was one step closer to Rendor. "R!" A second step. "E." Then two more. "N. D." Another two. "O. R." Six steps! She celebrated with a moment's rest before starting again. "R. E. N." A pause to catch her breath. "D. O. R." Six more steps! "Woot!"

Time blurred. The sand blurred. Even the sun's harsh rays wobbled. The heat turned into a living thing, pressing on her head, shoulders, and back. Her entire focus remained on her boots, willing them to keep moving. Six more steps. "Just six more," she muttered. She only glanced up to check her bearings. But even that became too much of a drain.

Then her legs quit. They gave up and collapsed under her. She cursed at them as the hot sand burned through the fabric of her pants. Stupid legs. Now she would have to crawl and that messed up her counting. What was considered a step when on your hands and knees? After all four moved forward? Or just the hands? No. When one side advanced, since both the hand and knee moved at the same time. Pleased that she figured it out, she placed her palms on the sand and pulled them back with a cry of pain.

She stared at the red burn marks on her skin. She needed to rethink crawling. But if she couldn't move, she'd be cooked alive. What about burrowing under the sand? Her magic…was as fried as her brain. Stupid holy water.

Then a shadow blocked the sun. The relief was instant until the shadow crouched beside her and asked questions that she didn't understand. She stared at the shadow… It slowly coalesced into…Rendor. Blinking, she stroked his cheek, ensuring he was real. He stopped talking. She was lifted and cradled and…

Awareness came in the form of her burning throat and the lack of moisture in her mouth. Her tongue had shriveled and sand crunched in her teeth. The room was dark. She tumbled out of the cushion and searched for her water skin by feel. As if by magic, it pressed into her hands. Opening the top, she brought it to her dry lips and stopped, remembering.

"Go on," Rendor said. "You need to drink." He was a black shadow in a room full of them.

"No." Her voice rasped. "It's—"

"Clean. I dumped the holy water."

She guzzled it, only stopping when her stomach threatened to send it back up. "How did you know?"

"You told me. Many times. One of the side effects of the drug."

"I don't remember anything after you… How did you find me?"

"I've been watching for you. I figured when you escaped you'd either leave near angle zero or after the danger zone." He settled on the floor next to her. "I was just about to go inside when I heard you cry out."

She looked at her palms. They were dotted with red blisters. If she hadn't burnt her hands, she would have died out there. A shudder ripped through her over how close she'd been to joining the Sun Goddess.

Rendor wrapped his arms around her and crushed her to his chest.

"...can't...breathe..." she gasped.

The pressure eased, but he didn't release her. "Don't scare me like that again."

"I'll try not to, but some things are beyond my control." Although from now on she would taste just a sip of water before gulping it down no matter how thirsty she was.

"I thought I'd lost you."

"But you knew I'd escape. You even said *when*, not *if.*"

"I know. That's why I waited and didn't take on an entire monastery full of monks. It's just..." He released her and rubbed a hand over his face. "I feel like this...us together...is just a dream and that I'm going to wake up soon and you'll be gone and I'll be..."

"You'll be what?"

"Alone again."

"Like when we were apart in Zirdai?" A knot formed in her throat.

Rendor had left the Invisible Sword because he had suspected there was a traitor and he'd wished to recruit the prince's guards to switch their loyalties without letting the traitor know. A smart move that had saved many lives but had broken her heart. She hadn't realized how much she loved him until he was gone.

He curled his fingers into fists. "No. Like most of my life." He stared at his knuckles. "A big bruiser who didn't want to go into the family business. Who, according to my father, would rather punch and stab things. Who was disowned at sixteen circuits old. Then, in the guard, it was too cutthroat to make friends—everyone was either trying to stab you in the back or was terrified of you stabbing them in the back. Pride was linked to promotion. Being good at your job. Being the best. But it meant being alone."

She covered his clenched hands with hers. "You'll never be alone again."

"How can you promise that? You're not invincible. You almost died from the heat."

"True. But you have the Invisible Swords. You have Hanif and Kaveri and even Jayden. They would all welcome you. Find a place for you."

"Not without you."

"No. You've earned their love and loyalty. That's all you. Not me."

He shook his head.

"Yes. They've forgiven you, Rendor. Now you need to forgive yourself." But she might as well have been talking to a stone statue.

"What happened at the monastery?" he asked, pulling his hands away. "You were gone for three sun jumps."

Three? Wow, she really had exhausted her energy. She knew he was trying to change the subject, but what else could she say to convince him of his worth? Instead, she told him about Lonato and Xerxes' plans. By the end, he was pacing and cursing under his breath.

"With that extensive operation, the coins have all been

spent," he finally said. "We won't be able to get any back."

"That's not our biggest problem. We need to stop the monks and Xerxes."

"With what?" He halted. "You exhausted yourself countering Lonato's magic. We can't fight an entire monastery or a merc company. We need soldiers and the King doesn't have any coins to pay them."

"Nintri's Water Princess has guards. Surely she would lend them to the King to help. She could take the cost out of the next round of taxes."

"And you have the authority to make that arrangement?"

She did not, which he knew.

"Besides, I've been talking to a few of the guards. It sounds as if the princess would rather have mercs in her city than have to petition the King every time she needs extra help."

"Except they're illegal. King Ondro outlawed them because they were getting out of hand."

"What's the difference between a merc captain becoming a prince or princess or another citizen with enough manpower doing that same thing? That's how the cities in Koraha are run. The strong take control by force."

"Not always. Remember what Najib told us about Nintri?"

"A rare exception."

"There are others."

"Not many. You're not the only one to study history. And ours is filled with coups and violent changes in leadership."

"Having mercs in all the cities will just continue the cycle. When the King had his elite forces, there weren't as many violent overthrows because the people knew the King would send his troops if things got too vicious."

"We can't stop it. Besides, it's not our job. Our job was to recover the taxes. Since there is nothing left, we need to report this to the King and let him figure out a solution."

He was right. "Before we do that, we should bring back as much information as possible. Can we at least find out where Xerxes is before we leave? That will help the King."

Rendor's gaze grew distant as he considered. "It took you a full sun jump to sleep off the drug. Lonato has probably tipped off the mercs that you escaped and know too much. They'll be following us, looking for the perfect opportunity to snatch you again. Are you sure you want to risk that?"

"What's the perfect opportunity?"

"Secluded areas. Being out in the city after angle two-seventy. If we keep to public areas that are popular, they won't try anything. I've been careful not to lead anyone to these rooms, but when I carried you back from the surface, I was rather preoccupied and not looking for a tail."

"Could we in turn grab one of the people following us and interrogate them?"

"It's possible. Still risky."

"I think it's worth it. We can find another room to rent. I also want to talk to the Water Princess and find out if she's had any contact with the mercs."

"All right, but you have to promise to rest for the remainder of this sun jump." He waited.

"I promise."

"Good. We can go down to the Water Princess's level at the start of the next sun jump and make an appointment." Rendor gripped the hilt of his sword. "The mercs will probably try to stop us going to that appointment."

"Because they don't want the princess to know they stole the taxes?"

"Yes. They'll want to appear legitimate so she won't have any qualms hiring them when needed."

He raised another good point.

"Can they stop us?" she asked.

"Depends on how many they send." Rendor grinned. "They'll probably underestimate us. It'll be nice to get some exercise and stretch my muscles."

"Overconfidence can be a weakness," she said, half teasing.

"It's only overconfidence if you can't back it up, sunbeam." He pulled her close and lowered his voice to a husky whisper. "Have I ever disappointed?"

Tingles raced down her spine as heat bloomed deep inside her. "Not yet."

He growled and swept her off her feet. "Not ever." Rendor set her gently onto the cushion and covered her with the fur. "Go back to sleep."

"Aww. You're no fun."

"Shyla," he rumbled. "You promised. Unless you'd rather not—"

"Can't talk. I'm sleeping."

After first meal at angle zero, Shyla and Rendor headed down to the Water Princess's level. Except it wasn't quite a full level, more like a…bowl. It was in a dip at the bottom of one of those oversized caverns. She guessed it was the lowest point in Nintri as the sound of rushing water vibrated the ground underneath their boots.

"How did you know where this is?" Shyla asked Rendor.

He shrugged. "I've a good sense of direction. And one of the sellers at the market gave me an idea of where the princess is located."

"I'm buying maps of all the cities in Koraha later," she grumbled.

"Does that mean you're not an expert in everything, sunbeam?" He pressed a hand to his chest in mock horror.

"Shut up." She tried really hard to ignore his sexy chuckle, but the desire to punch him transformed into another.

Of course it wouldn't do to stop and kiss him breathless in public. They didn't want to attract any attention. Right now no one followed them, but that was sure to change once they arrived at the Water Princess's quarters. One of the mercs would be nearby keeping an eye on the entrance.

The princess's extensive suite was guarded by four soldiers. However, the doors stood open and just inside was a reception room. The armed guards tensed when they approached and eyed Rendor warily but didn't move to stop them as they entered. Four more guards blocked another entrance on the other side of the spacious area. In the middle, a woman sat behind a massive desk, talking to a man who twisted the fabric of his sleeves.

"...has to be injured or lost..." He sniffed back tears.

"We have search teams out looking for her. If they find her, we'll let you know," the woman said in a soothing voice. "I know it's hard to wait, but that's all you can do at this point. You don't want to get lost as well."

He swallowed a sob, nodded, and shuffled away.

When he was far enough away, the woman shook her head. "Poor man. I don't have the heart to tell him his wife probably ran off with another guy."

Curious, Shyla asked, "Do you get that often?"

"No, thank the goddess. How can I help you?"

"We'd like to schedule an appointment with the Water Princess."

The receptionist raised a slender brown eyebrow. "As you can well imagine, the Water Princess is busy running the city. Perhaps I can—"

Shyla exposed the King's sigil.

"Well now, why didn't you lead with that?" The woman's voice remained pleasant despite her frown.

"I wanted to see how accessible the princess was."

"To strangers who just walk in, not very. But for the King's emissary, she'll make adjustments to her schedule." The woman scanned a sheet of velbloud skin. "Do you need to see her now? She's in a meeting, but I can interrupt her." The receptionist's pained expression said she'd rather do anything but that.

Shyla didn't wish to upset the princess, but she'd rather not wait. The mercs would try to prevent them from coming back. "How about after her meeting is finished?"

"That will be fine. May I tell her your names?"

"Yes, I'm Shyla, and this is Rendor."

She scanned him from head to toe. "Your bodyguard?"

"No," Shyla said the same time Rendor said, "Yes."

The woman smiled. "Which is it?"

"He's my partner," she said.

"I'm both," Rendor said.

"All right, then you can keep your sword." She gestured to the cushions lined along the two side walls. "Please have a seat. I'll let you know when she's available." She returned to her work.

Shyla and Rendor moved out of the way. They didn't sit down. Not that they expected trouble here, but it never hurt to be ready. Instead, they watched the receptionist deal with the citizens who arrived. She was kind and firm and sympathetic when needed. Only one other person was told to have a seat. The man took one look at Rendor and chose a cushion on the opposite side of the room.

After three angles a tall, muscular man strode through the well-guarded doorway behind the receptionist. He moved like a sand devil—all smooth graceful strides and coiled power as if he could explode into action at any moment. A true predator.

He spotted them and there was a slight hitch in his step. His gaze focused on Rendor, sizing him up, noting the weapon at his hip. Shyla hated to admit it, but if Rendor was a big brute, this guy was a giant beast who was at least four centimeters taller.

"The princess is ready for her next appointment, Chanda," the man said.

"Thank you, Commander," the receptionist said.

Scorching sand rats. That answered the question of Xerxes' location. Because there was no doubt he was the commander of the King's elite troops. And it was pretty obvious that he was also on good terms with the princess. It took all of Shyla's willpower not to glance at Rendor.

Xerxes frowned at Chanda, but instead of cowering, she gave him a flat that-won't-work-on-me stare. Shyla's opinion of the receptionist increased a few levels. After one more assessing glance at them, Xerxes left.

The ability to breathe returned. Shyla filled her lungs to steady her wild heart rate. Her body had reacted as if she'd just had a brush with a venomous sand snake. No surprise since the man was probably gathering his people to ambush them.

"I'll be back," Chanda said to them, retreating through the doorway.

Shyla turned to Rendor. "That's not good."

"It isn't." He had his arms crossed and his scowl firmly in place. "We need to be careful what we say to the princess. I think you should monitor her emotions right away."

"I will. At least you won't intimidate her."

Rendor huffed. "Xerxes isn't that impressive."

Shyla wisely refrained from commenting. Chanda returned and escorted them to the Water Princess's office. They passed a few water fountains and mosaics. As expected, guards flanked her door and were arrayed around the large comfortable space.

Chanda introduced them to the Water Princess of Nintri. The woman stood and approached them. She had pulled her dark ringlets up into a high ponytail, which allowed the black curls to cascade down her back. Her bearing was regal and she wore a long-sleeved silk gown that flowed to the floor in one long sweep. The burnt orange color of the material contrasted nicely with the princess's deep brown skin.

A pendant hung from her neck and it drew Shyla's full attention. A black triangular-shaped jewel the size of a thumbnail glinted from the center of the pendant. The gemstone pulsed with a strange energy, drawing Shyla into its depths. It tugged at her soul.

The princess noticed Shyla staring at her pendant. She tucked it underneath the collar of her gown. The motion snapped Shyla back to herself.

"Welcome to Nintri, Shyla and Rendor," the princess said in a soothing, liquid voice. "Your visit is an unexpected blessing. I hope the King is well?"

Shyla met her gaze. A calm serenity filled her olive-colored eyes. The princess wasn't surprised that they were in Nintri. Xerxes had informed her of their arrival and the reason the King had sent the two emissaries.

"Yes, he's well." Shyla said.

"What can I do for the King?" the princess asked even though she already knew the answer.

Shyla played along, telling her about the stolen taxes and how they suspected the mercenaries. The princess feigned surprise and she defended Xerxes.

"The monks collecting the taxes were probably tricked and too embarrassed to admit they'd been robbed, so they're blaming an innocent man and his loyal soldiers," the princess said.

The princess had all the right responses to the rest of Shyla's questions because Xerxes had coached her on what to say. True information, if there was any, was not to be found. The princess's thoughts were saturated with his words. The only emotion the princess felt was utter devotion to Xerxes. It reminded her of the Callow monk who had brought Shyla food and water. It was similar but different.

Changing tactics, Shyla asked, "When did the commander come to Nintri?"

"A couple circuits ago. He and his squads have been so helpful. We had some trouble and they took care of it."

"What trouble?"

"Does it matter? It's no longer a problem." Gratitude filled the princess as her thoughts lingered on all the wonderful qualities of Xerxes.

Shyla would have to dig deeper into the woman's soul to learn the truth about what was going on between her and Xerxes. Signaling Rendor with a subtle gesture, Shyla focused on the princess.

"It does matter," Rendor said, catching the hint to take over the questioning. "The King would like to know what problems you've been dealing with."

As the princess explained about a group of rebels who were gathering support to overthrow the princess and whose headquarters couldn't be found, Shyla burrowed into the woman's emotions, bypassing the adoration for the commander. She found the frustration over the lack of response from the King and the relief when Xerxes arrived. And nothing else. Just more gushing about the merc commander.

Wow, the princess was completely smitten. There had to be more to the woman. Shyla pressed deeper, searching the princess's soul. There were a few thoughts about not sending the taxes to the King this upcoming round and giving it to Xerxes instead. Treason didn't bother her nor was she worried about the King's reaction. Xerxes said he and his squad could handle anyone the King sent. And she trusted him absolutely.

The woman had no doubts. No worries. No concerns. No guilt. Which explained her serenity. Yet there was still some of her own soul inside her. There had to be in order for the woman to function as the princess and run the city. If Lonato had used his magic on her, he hadn't given her the full…treatment like he had for his minion.

Shyla hated to plant doubts about Xerxes in the princess's thoughts, but the woman needed to see that he was a criminal and she couldn't trust him. Except, when Shyla inserted those ideas, they melted and dissolved like the fake coins in water. Either the princess was incredibly strong-willed or something else was going on. Although what that "something else" could be, she hadn't a clue.

Rendor finished with his follow-up questions so Shyla had to pull back. Besides, she was uncomfortable with how deep she'd already gone. They said goodbye to the Water Princess and promised to keep her updated about the investigation.

Once they were far enough away from the princess's cavern, Rendor said, "I thought we were supposed to keep the theft a secret."

"She already knew." Shyla told him what she'd learned. "In the princess's eyes, Xerxes can do no wrong."

"Sounds like she wasn't involved in the crime."

"She wasn't."

"But?" Rendor prompted.

"All she thought about was Xerxes. He's a big influence on her life."

"Do you think Lonato used his magic to make her believe Xerxes?"

"He could have. Xerxes and Lonato are working together. Although…" She stopped her next thought.

Of course Rendor wouldn't let it slide. "Although?"

"Xerxes is a handsome man; maybe she's infatuated. Or obsessed."

"He's not *that* handsome," Rendor huffed. "Obsession is a strong emotion. It tends to push out logic and reason."

True. The Water Princess certainly shoved Shyla's mental suggestion to be careful away. Too bad there was nothing Shyla could do about it. At least not now. Hopefully the King would have a better idea of how to solve this problem. "We need to check if there is a caravan leaving for Qulsary."

Rendor agreed. "We've already picked up a few tails." He paused. "Do we need to talk to the Heliacal Priest before we leave? See what he knows about this situation?"

Instinctively, she recoiled from the idea. However, not all priests or priestesses viewed sun-kisseds the same as the zealot who had overseen the spiritual well-being of the citizens of Zirdai. That priestess had called Shyla evil, sun-cursed, and destined to spend eternity in the seven caverns of hell.

Would the priest have any information? He and his deacons were responsible for growing and cooking food for everyone who paid them a tithe. They also led the worship services for the Sun Goddess, who they claimed was their higher power and not the King.

Reluctantly, she said, "We probably should. He might have some information on the mercs in the city. They have to eat like everyone else. And the deacons tend to know everyone in their chapel districts." And torture them! No, that was in Zirdai. In the past. Shyla pulled in a calming breath but admitted, "I'd rather catch one of the mercs following us and find the information that way."

"Might be harder to do than I thought," he said.

"Why? Are they not following us anymore?"

"Oh, they're still trailing us, and there's more of them." His voice remained calm.

"How many?"

"Six, maybe eight. But that's not the problem."

"What *is* the problem?"

"Xerxes is with them. And if he's being careless enough to allow me to spot him, that makes me worried about what he has planned."

"We shouldn't head back to our rooms."

"We're not."

She looked around and didn't recognize anything even though there were directional markers scratched into the walls at each intersection. "Where are we going?"

"To the heart cavern. Did you get a chance to read Xerxes?"

"No. He never met my gaze." She wondered if that had been on purpose. Xerxes knew she was more than the King's emissary. The mercs that had attacked Lota's caravan had been after her. "Why are we going there?"

"To see something glorious." Rendor grinned.

She remembered the suggestion from the woman who rented the rooms to be there at apex. Except that was sixty angles away. "Was it glorious?"

"I don't know. I was worried about you and didn't pay attention. But I do know it was crowded beforehand. Plus the market is there."

"Which means there'll be too many witnesses."

"Yes. That might make Xerxes hesitate if he's planning something. Also it's easy to get lost in a crowd."

"For us? Or for them?"

"Both."

"Devious. I approve."

"If it works. Xerxes won't be easily misled."

"What are you thinking?"

Rendor explained his strategy to separate one of the mercs from the rest. It was smart and simple. Except before they reached the heart cavern a wall of oversized men appeared, blocking the far end of the tunnel. Shyla glanced over her shoulder to see another blockade behind them.

Seemed Xerxes had another idea in mind.

No one else was trapped in the tunnel with Shyla and Rendor. Why did that always happen? There must be some magical twist of fate that arranged these inconvenient coincidences. There had been people around them not too long ago. Did everyone just have an instinct to disappear before trouble? Rendor hadn't been traveling through forgotten passages or keeping to the edges of the city. Yet there was not a soul in sight.

Instead, there were at least six men waiting for them ahead and another half a dozen behind.

Rendor pulled his sword when Xerxes' men parted to allow him through. Shyla reached out with her magic. Thirteen people were within her range to influence. But she waited. Might as well learn exactly what Xerxes planned first. It would save them guessing later.

"Relax, Captain," Xerxes said. "I only wish to talk to you both."

"There are friendlier ways to arrange a meeting," Rendor said.

"Would you have met me at a location that I picked in advance?" His focus was on Rendor.

"It depends if it was in a public place or not."

Xerxes laughed. "It wouldn't matter. My soldiers have gotten away with quite a lot in so-called public places. Most people go through their lives blind to what's around them. And they're easily distracted."

"So instead you ambush us in a tunnel."

"Which you expected. Come on, Captain, you can't say this is a surprise. You spotted my soldiers following you as soon as you left your meeting with the princess."

"What do you want to talk about?" Rendor asked.

"Your mission for the King, of course."

"Are you going to confess?" Shyla asked, startling him into finally meeting her gaze.

Amusement sparked in his light blue eyes as a slow smile spread across his face. Damn, the man was good-looking and he knew it. Shyla reached out to pick up his emotions, but she was…diverted. It was as if he'd stepped aside. She'd never encountered this ability before. He wasn't like the King, who outright blocked the power of The Eyes, but rather he slipped away, like when you tried to cup a handful of water and it was gone by the time you brought it up to your mouth.

"There is nothing to confess," Xerxes said. "I'm the *soul* of innocence."

He must have talked to Lonato. Did he suspect she had

woken The Eyes? That still shouldn't protect him from them.

"You're no longer the King's commander," Rendor said. "So it is no longer any of your business."

"Have you *considered* that I'm also here to find the missing taxes?" There was heat in his words.

Seven hells. Xerxes was another magic wielder.

"No," Rendor said slowly.

Shyla focused on Xerxes with The Eyes, seeking that inner glow.

"As soon as I heard," Xerxes said, "*I've* been looking for information. Seems there is a new mercenary squad in Nintri and they're *my* prime suspects."

Every time Xerxes stressed a word, Shyla spotted a glowing ball of magic around his heart just like Lonato's. It still didn't explain the weirdness when she tried to read his emotions or thoughts. They kept slipping out of her reach.

"Why have you been investigating?" Shyla asked.

Xerxes frowned. "*I* want the coins recovered. I'd like to resume *my job*."

Son of a sand demon, he was strong and on guard. No way she'd be able to force answers from him without exhausting herself. Good thing she was on guard too and could block his commands.

"He has every right to investigate," Rendor said to her.

Oh no. She wasn't the only one he was influencing. Fear slid down her back with icy fingers. If they escaped, she hoped she'd be able to reverse Xerxes' influence on Rendor. Except she hadn't helped the Water Princess. Bile churned in her stomach.

"Where is this squad?" she asked, trying to pull Xerxes' attention away from Rendor. "Can we infiltrate them? See if they have the coins?"

"*I'm* taking care of it. *Go back* to Qulsary and *report* to the King. *Tell him* your investigation has hit a *dead end.* There's *nothing* more *you and Rendor* can do."

His magical commands seared into her, pushing on her to obey. They stuck to her like cobwebs. She fought the compulsion, using precious energy to brush the strands from her body.

"Commander Xerxes has it well in hand," Rendor said. "We need to report to the King."

"That's being smart, Captain," Xerxes said. "And after you make *your* report, *both* of you are to *return* to Nintri and *join* me."

"Yes, sir," Rendor snapped. "We'll leave as soon as possible so we're not gone long."

Xerxes smiled. "You're in luck. There's a caravan leaving for Qulsary at angle zero. The owner needs two more guards."

"Perfect." Rendor grabbed Shyla's hand. "Come on."

She nodded enthusiastically, pretending to be enthralled, hoping his ego wouldn't let him question why she agreed so easily when Lonato had a hard time. "Yes, let's go."

"*Don't* miss the show in the heart cavern *before you leave,*" Xerxes said. "You'll want to *hurry back* just to see it again."

"We won't," Rendor said.

"Thanks, Commander," Shyla gushed.

"Safe journey," Xerxes said.

Rendor pulled her down the tunnel. The mercs blocking the way parted, allowing them to pass through. Although it about killed her, she didn't stop Rendor. No doubt Xerxes was following to ensure his orders were carried out. Instead, she allowed Rendor to tow her to their new set of rented rooms. Only when they were inside and the door was locked did she break his grip on her hand.

"We need to pack," he said, grabbing his bag.

"Rendor, wait."

"No. We have to be ready to leave." He folded his extra tunic and pants. "And we can't miss the show."

She had promised not to use magic or the power of The Eyes on him unless she had a damn good reason. This qualified.

Stop.

He froze, but he stared at her in surprised anger.

"I've an excellent reason. Do you trust me?" she asked.

The anger faded. "Yes."

She released him. "Please sit down."

Rendor sat cross-legged on the oversized blue and purple cushion. She knelt in front of him so they were at eye level then accessed his thoughts. They were conflicted. He wished to obey Xerxes and leave Nintri, but he loved Shyla. She was smart, sexy, and all his. But Xerxes was his commander and he needed to please him.

Worry edged toward fear as she chased those magical directives. They slipped from her grasp, melted away, and dodged. Frustrated, she tried erasing his memories of their encounter with Xerxes. They kept reforming. Panic pulsed in her heart when the commands grew stronger.

Rendor wondered why Shyla and his commander were at odds. Xerxes' intelligence and skills made him the perfect leader. He couldn't wait to pledge his loyalty to him. The man saved Nintri and was working for the Water Princess. A noble man.

She had to stop the hero worship before she lost Rendor. But everything she tried failed. Why? No idea. Changing tactics, she concentrated on how magical commands worked. Xerxes had used manipulation, one of the three magical techniques. Yet once the instruction was carried out, the wielder stopped pushing the magic and the person went back to normal. But in this case...Xerxes pushed, but didn't stop.

No. If he was still wielding magic on Rendor and the princess, he'd be exhausted. It was almost as if the magical order remained...magical, working even after the wielder stopped. Wow, that would be an incredibly powerful skill. No wonder all the princess could think about was Xerxes. Was that also Lonato's skill?

Focusing on Rendor, Shyla considered how to remove the magic. If it was— Scorching hells. Jayden. She had taken his ability to wield magic. But would that work in this case? Rendor wasn't glowing with magic. No time to worry about it. Shyla pressed her hands to the sides of his head.

"Is this really necessary?" he asked. "We need to follow Xerxes' commands. Or he might not want us to become part of his unit. And that would be horrible. You alone would be such an asset to his cause."

"Just give me another angle." She concentrated, trying to

find the magic. But without that…light, she couldn't. Desperate, she thought of another idea. "Rendor, can you envision Commander Xerxes? Imagine him in your mind. Try to form a picture."

As soon as his thoughts converged, the magic lit up. It resembled a figure of a man. However she didn't waste time examining it. Instead, she tugged it, pulling it from his mind.

Rendor grunted in pain. "What—"

"Just another…"

The last of it gushed out and the magic—now invisible—exploded. The force blew her back. Rendor toppled over in the opposite direction. With Jayden, she'd been thrown across the room and knocked unconscious. At least this time she remained upright.

Shyla hurried to check on Rendor. He lay on the floor, appearing dazed and rubbing his temples.

"What happened?" he asked.

"How do you feel?"

"Like I was kicked in the head." He struggled to sit up.

She sat next to him. "Can I read you?"

He nodded, but his expression was wary. Despite the pain thudding in his skull, worry about what happened dominated his thoughts. Did Xerxes do something to him? Or Shyla? If that bastard so much as laid a hand on her, he'd rip the commander limb from limb.

Shyla suppressed a grin. Her Rendor was back. "You'll be fine."

"Are you going to tell me what happened now?"

"What's the last thing you remember?"

"Xerxes ambushed us. He wanted to talk about taking over the investigation." Rendor pressed a hand to his forehead. "I agreed with him. It lined up with our desires to travel. Yet a part of me knew I shouldn't be agreeing with him. A part that had no control over what I did and said. It was like I was two different people. Does that makes sense?"

"Yes."

He rubbed his fingers on his temple. "Did Xerxes and I fight?"

"No." She explained how she freed him from Xerxes' compulsion. "Sorry about your head."

"Don't apologize, sunbeam. You saved me. I'd rather have been stabbed than turned into one of his sycophants."

"I wonder how many of his loyal soldiers have been coerced to obey. I can't imagine the person would be useful if they can't think for themselves." Yet the princess still had some independence. Except it was skewed.

"They'd obey orders without their doubts and questions making them hesitate."

"Yeah, but they wouldn't be able to adapt if the situation changed."

"No. Sometimes, though, you don't want your people to think. When they start to question their orders, they can make mistakes." Rendor considered. "How bad was I?"

"Completely smitten."

He moved, pinning her under him. "Want to try that again?"

"Obsessed."

He growled and nipped her neck.

"That's not an incentive for me to lie to you."

"No?" He changed tactics, kissing her neck and then taking off her tunic to go lower.

She forgot all about…whatever they'd been talking about until he stopped, leaving her breathless.

He looked up at her with one raised eyebrow. "Well?"

"That's a low blow."

"Not really. I could go lower." The promise was implied.

"You fought his compulsion and would have won, but I didn't want to wait. Better?"

"It's a bit over the top, but, considering the circumstances…I accept." He fulfilled his promise and the rest of the world melted away.

"I think our smartest move is to act as if the compulsion worked and leave Nintri with that caravan," Shyla said after their…nap. "He's too dangerous. I need to figure out a way to counter his magic."

"Can you close him?" Rendor asked, miming shutting a druk. "Like you did to those seers?"

"I might be able to. But what happens if I can't? Then I would have tipped him off about what I can do. We need to report to the King and figure out our next move."

"That gives him at least forty more sun jumps."

"To do what? He's already entrenched in Nintri. The

princess is his." Hopefully, Shyla would be able to clear her mind of Xerxes' magic like she did for Rendor when they returned.

"I still don't like it."

"I know. You like action and this seems like we're retreating."

"We are retreating."

"No, we're regrouping."

Unconvinced, Rendor looked at her, but instead of arguing, he glanced at the sand clock. "We still have time to get to the heart cavern by apex."

She'd forgotten Xerxes had ordered them to enjoy the show. An odd command until she thought about it. The order was probably a test to make sure his magic had worked on them. "Do you still want to trap a merc and interrogate them?"

"Do you think we'll get anything useful from them?"

"Not if they've been influenced by Xerxes. Their thoughts will be dominated with all the wonderful qualities of the commander."

"Then we won't risk it. But we do need a few supplies for the journey to Qulsary."

They arrived at the heart cavern at angle eighty. Because of the name, she expected the space to be heart-shaped. However it was just another huge cavity at the heart of the city. Tiers of market stalls ringed the main area. Each ring was wider than the one below so they appeared to be a gigantic circular ramp. Up above everything, distant spots of druk light marked a series of balconies. While she normally enjoyed bartering for goods, Shyla couldn't shake the creepy-crawly sensation that she was being watched.

"How many are following us?" she asked Rendor.

"Five or six mercs."

"Xerxes?"

"Not that I've seen."

"Good. Don't look him in the eye if you do see him."

"I don't ever back down." He just about growled.

She sighed. Men.

They muscled their way through the crowded market. The sounds of shoppers, sellers, and children shrieking was both overly loud and swallowed by the immense empty space hovering over them.

At angle eighty-nine, a man called, "Prepare for the sun!"

The druks were closed, but the cavern still had enough light to see. In fact, high above their heads, sunlight illuminated a giant hole in the ceiling, revealing the pink sky. Rendor stepped behind her and pulled her close. She leaned on him as she tipped her head back to get a better view.

Except the sunlight brightened to a painful degree and she had to avert her gaze or risk going blind. Then the sun reached apex. An intense sunbeam shot straight down—a brilliant yellow shaft that appeared solid. Its arrival caused gasps of wonder even from the sellers. Those who stood close to the roughly three-meter-wide beam stuck their arms into it. She half expected their skin to catch fire.

"I give you the heart of the sun," the man called. "Now!"

A tarp was yanked off the floor right underneath the sunbeam, revealing a huge crystal. Immediately prisms shot out in all directions, waterfalls of colors going up. When they reached the walls where other crystals had been installed, they fractured and reflected until beams of lights crisscrossed the entire cavern. Her breath locked.

Glorious indeed. No other word matched.

She marveled until the sun shifted and everything disappeared as quickly as it had appeared. A sigh of disappointment sounded from everyone in attendance. The crystal was covered and druks were opened. The red light was weak and thin and utterly ordinary in comparison. Commerce resumed, voices called and haggled. Life continued.

"That's why I call you sunbeam," Rendor whispered in her ear. "That's what you do to my heart every time you look at me like I'm worthwhile."

Oh, Rendor. She wanted to melt and yell at him at the same time. Keeping within the circle of his arms, she turned to face him. "You are worthwhile." Before he could deny it, she added, "These eyes don't lie."

He pulled back slightly. "You said you haven't gone that deep into my soul."

"I don't need to, Rendor. I've seen—"

"Not enough. Just surface thoughts and feelings. You've no idea what I've done. What I'm capable of. Who I really am."

"Then tell me." But he'd already turned away, heading for the stall selling travel rations of jerky, bread, and cheese.

As they finished their shopping, she mulled over Rendor's comment. He was right; she didn't know much about him. She'd picked up on his intentions to atone and his love for her when she'd first awoken the power of The Eyes, but nothing deeper.

He'd had a life-changing moment when he'd almost died. Did she need to know the details of what he'd done prior to that? The rumors in Zirdai had painted him as evil incarnate, but there had been a few stories of kindness. As for what he was capable of...did it matter? Actions, not thoughts or abilities, spoke the loudest. Plus she had the power to manipulate people, to do harm, to kill.

No, she decided. It didn't matter to her what he'd done or what he could do. She already knew who he really was. The hard part would be revealing Rendor's true self to Rendor.

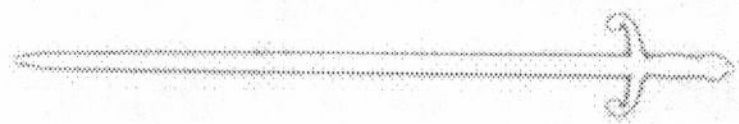

The trip back to Qulsary took nineteen sun jumps and was uneventful. Soon after they arrived, Shyla and Rendor went to the castle's entrance and asked to speak with Najib. The advisor's expression was welcoming but worry lurked in his gaze.

"We'll go straight to the King," Najib said. "He's been anxious for news."

"Not yet," Shyla said.

Najib gave them a questioning look.

"We'll explain in your office."

"You better be quick. News of your arrival is traveling throughout the castle as we speak. If the news reaches the King before you do, his anger will shrivel you."

"Shrivel?" Rendor asked.

"You'll sweat. A lot. So much that your muscles will cramp and your head will ache."

"Speaking from experience?"

"Unfortunately." Najib led them to his office. He didn't offer tea or invite them to sit down. "What's going on?"

She briefly explained what they'd learned. When he opened his mouth to ask for more information, she stopped him. "We need to talk to the King without any of his guards in the room. Is that possible?"

"They're all loyal. You said yourself they didn't steal the taxes," Najib said.

"Izusa is sending Xerxes information. She's getting it from Malik, who is a guard. We need Xerxes to believe we did what he ordered. So we need two audiences with the King. One to give him the false information, and the other for the truth."

"Oh, I see. They're with him constantly."

"Even in his sleeping chamber?"

"They're just outside the doors."

"Is there another way in?" Rendor asked.

"No. And they check it before the King enters."

"That won't be a problem," Shyla said. Then she explained her plan. "Can you pretend to be smitten with Xerxes?" she asked Rendor.

"I can," he said, but his gaze promised she'd pay for using *smitten* later.

She responded with an I'm-looking-forward-to-it grin. "Good."

Najib took them to the King's office and they put on a performance for his guards. It didn't matter if Malik was there or not; they'd tell him everything. Shyla's stomach twisted over lying to the King. He seemed so relieved that Xerxes was handling it. He invited them to stay in the castle as long as they liked and even offered them a small percentage of the coins that Xerxes would recover for their efforts.

"Best to drink lots of water before you tell him the truth," Najib said once they were alone again.

Around angle two-forty, Najib escorted them to the King's suite. Shyla distracted the guards on duty while Najib unlocked the doors. They slipped inside and she kept her connection to the guards until Najib was well away.

The amount of rooms was impressive. Water fountains gurgled in every one. Thick rugs coated the floors. Lush fabrics hung on the walls, absorbing the moisture and muting the sounds.

When they entered the King's sleeping chamber, they stopped in surprise. The King's sleeping cushion was surrounded by a pool of dark water. Rendor recovered first. He crouched next to it and stuck his hand into the water.

"It's not deep so it's not for protection." He straightened. "There's also no place to hide."

Shyla glanced around. The chamber was about five meters wide by seven meters long. The cushion and pool took up most of the space, leaving a meter-wide strip between the water and the doorway. The King obviously dressed in another room. Perhaps the one next to the massive water closet.

"We can stand in the corner," Shyla said. "I'll hide us from the guards."

"What about the King? You can't use The Eyes on him."

"If he yells for the guards, I'll stop them and erase their memories. But I hope the King figures out why we're hiding in his room before that happens."

Waiting was never fun. Every noise from the hallway outside the King's suite sent her heart into spasms. Boredom filled the spaces in between as they couldn't talk or do anything that might distract them. Because as soon as the key turned in the lock, they would retreat to the sleeping chamber.

It was a relief when the metallic scrape and click sounded. Shyla followed Rendor. He pressed into the corner and she stood in front of him as she sought the bumps of the guards' thoughts.

The four guards checked the suite for intruders. They followed their routine, each one taking a different room and not expecting any surprises. As the guards neared them, Shyla gathered her will. When they poked their heads into the sleeping chamber, she used the *not here* command.

Not here.

Not here.

They stepped back. "All clear, sire."

"Thank you," the King said as he stepped into the room. He wore a long blue dressing gown. Turning to slide the doors closed, he spotted them and froze in shock.

Shyla pressed a finger to her lips. He stared at her a moment, then pulled the doors together. The King mirrored her, pressing his finger to his lips, before he moved his hands out in a circle. The water silently swirled and drained from the pool, revealing a ramp that descended into the darkness. He grabbed the trol lantern from the wall and gestured for Shyla and Rendor to precede him down.

Rendor took point and she followed. A part of her worried the King planned to drown them for their impertinence. The floor of the ramp was slick and cold drops dripped from above. She'd no idea where the rest of the water had gone but now understood why the color was so dark—it hid the ramp.

There was another chamber at the bottom. This one was twice as big as the King's sleeping quarters above. It too had a huge cushion, but it also had a desk, tables, sitting cushions and other amenities, including another pool. Except this one was off to the side. The King set the trol on the table and swept his hands out. The water in the pool flowed up the ramp like a transparent snake, filling it in until it blocked the passage up to the chamber.

"Effective," Rendor said.

"Against those who can't swim," the King said. "But not many people know that my true quarters are underneath the water. Najib must trust you." He studied them a moment. "I thought the news about Xerxes was too good to be true. Sit down and tell me what's really going on."

They sat around one of the low marble tables. It had a pattern of green and blue veins that wove through a light yellowish-orange stone.

Reluctant to launch right into an explanation, Shyla asked, "Do the guards know about this room?"

"Yes. If they need to wake me because of some emergency and I'm gone, I don't want them to panic."

"Then you're not protected from them," Rendor stated.

"You're right. They can swim, but water is an effective

weapon, Captain. I'm perfectly safe." He gave them a tight smile. "The news must be really bad."

"Unfortunately, it is." Shyla told the King what happened with the taxes, from the fake coins to Xerxes and Lonato's plans. "And I doubt you'll get any tax payments this circuit."

The King remained quiet for a long time. "Not even fakes?"

"No. It'll be a waste of time. Xerxes and his mercs know you can't do anything," Rendor said.

"I'm not without resources, Captain. In emergencies, I've the power to pull the guards from the cities of Koraha to make an army."

"You've the right, but will the cities acknowledge that power? The old king has upset many of them."

"Besides, they are not skilled enough to counter elite fighters," Shyla said. "You'd be better off using monks. They're trained in the Ways of the Yarin."

"There are not as many monks as you think." The King held up a hand, stopping her protest. "Many are too old or too young. Some of the monasteries haven't been getting enough new members over the circuits. And, according to you, I've already lost four monasteries' allegiance." He slammed his palm on the table. "Seven hells."

"Some fighters are better than none," Rendor said.

"I can sell the old king's mosaics and use the coins to hire soldiers."

Rendor glanced at Shyla.

The King caught the look. "What's wrong with that?"

"It'll take time, and you might not be able to find anyone to hire," Shyla said.

"Why not?" he demanded.

"Xerxes' soldiers are loyal, and if he uses his magic on all of them, they're not going to leave him."

The King let out a long breath. "All I have are my guards. Are they even trustworthy?"

"They are," Shyla rushed to assure him. "And you need them."

He jumped to his feet and paced with short, agitated strides. "You are basically telling me that I've no one other than a handful of monks. Is that correct?"

Yes, and as much as she'd love to walk away from this mess, she couldn't. Not if she wanted to have peace of mind. She met Rendor's gaze, seeking his input. This wasn't just her decision. He nodded.

"No. You have me, Rendor, and the Invisible Sword. You have the monks and the Arch Deacons."

"Arch Deacons?" Surprised, he skidded to a stop.

He wasn't the only one. Shyla couldn't believe she just suggested going to the Heliacal Priests and Priestesses for help. "They're an elite fighting force in Zirdai. I'm not sure if they're in all the cities."

"They're in some," Rendor said. "The last Water Prince sent a couple squads of guards to other cities to train with them. He wanted us to be able to defend ourselves if we ever had to fight the Arch Deacons in Zirdai."

"And I'm just learning about them." The King fisted his hands in his hair. "That spiteful old bastard kept so much information from me. How am I supposed to fix the mess he left?" Then he drew in a couple deep breaths and lowered his arms. His sharp features softened as he visibly relaxed. He shot them a wry grin. "Sorry. Najib isn't here to remind me that complaining isn't kingly." The King resumed his seat. "Even with you, the Invisible Swords, the monks, and the Arch Deacons, we'll still be outnumbered."

"Yes, but we'll have the element of surprise," Rendor said. "And we've already proved a smaller force can beat a bigger one."

"Even with that advantage, I doubt I'd get those cities with mercs back. What can we do?"

"We can stop the spread. Limit the number of cities and monasteries under their influence. Once that's done, we can take back one city at a time."

"Lonato said the Monks of Lyons were next," Shyla said. "We can travel to Apanji and stop the visiting monks from converting the Lyons monks."

"We can also determine if the mercs have set up shop or are in the process of doing so," Rendor said. "And start recruiting Arch Deacons."

"And the Invisible Sword?" the King asked.

"Can meet us in Apanji." Shyla considered having them go to Nintri. But if Xerxes was still there, they might be spotted. No doubt the man was dangerous and by then he would know Shyla and Rendor were no longer under his influence.

"It'll be a while before I can pay you."

"The Invisible Sword doesn't work for pay."

"That's very noble, but I'm sure you have expenses and

people to feed." He ran a hand through his thick hair.

Shyla remembered his comment about his crown and wondered if, even though it wasn't on his head, the heavy weight of responsibility still pressed down on him.

"Not all the cities are under Xerxes' influence," he continued. "Is there a way to get their taxes before the mercs steal them?"

That was a good question. "Do you know whose turn it is to guard the wagons?"

"The Monks of Dunnar, but they're part of the conspiracy."

She swallowed a curse. "What route do they take?"

"They start in Ginda and travel counter-clockwise until they loop back to Qulsary." He drummed his long fingers on the table as he stared into the distance. "Najib would know for sure, but I believe the caravan will reach Apanji in roughly one hundred and sixteen sun jumps."

"If they're in the process of converting Apanji, then Xerxes would most likely go there next," Shyla said. "He and Lonato have converted four cities in about two circuits, which means they're averaging half a circuit per city. The timing works out that he'll be in Apanji when the caravan arrives. Also I don't think he'd delegate picking up the taxes to anyone else."

"We could try to intercept the tax caravan," Rendor said. "Ambush them in the desert before they reach Apanji."

Robbing the mercs of their income would certainly slow things down. "It's worth a try."

"What do you need?" the King asked Shyla.

"We need to send a message to the Invisible Sword. And we can't wait if there isn't a caravan heading to Apanji, we'll need to hire a guide. Rendor, do we have enough coins?"

"We should."

"Najib can help you with all the preparations. Just tell him what you need. Also tell him to sell one of the small gemstone mosaics. He'll know which one." The King waved away her protest. "I need to start collecting coins regardless. Don't worry, he's been doing a fine job discreetly selling the other treasures."

The King moved the water so they could leave. He opened the door and asked a guard to fetch him something to eat. Shyla used the *not here* command as they followed the guard from the King's suite. They ran into Najib almost immediately. The advisor had been waiting for them.

"You don't look shriveled. How did it go?" Najib asked.

She told him what they'd discussed with the King.

"There might be a caravan heading to Apanji. You could go as passengers. It's cheaper than hiring a guide and less…obvious. I'll check. Go get some sleep, I'll have everything ready by angle zero."

Before Shyla collapsed onto the very nice sleeping cushion in the King's guest quarters, she wrote a message to Gurice. She needed to be careful with the wording, giving her friend enough information without revealing any secrets in case someone else read the scroll.

When she finished, she rolled it up and sealed it. It would take seventy sun jumps for it to reach Zirdai. Then she guessed another three to five sun jumps for Gurice to get ready and find a caravan. Add another thirty sun jumps to reach Apanji from Zirdai, and it would be a total of a hundred and five sun jumps until Shyla and Rendor would be reunited with the Invisible Swords.

It would take Shyla and Rendor forty-eight sun jumps to reach Apanji. That would give them about fifty-seven sun jumps to assess the situation in Apanji before the Swords arrived, and another eleven sun jumps before the tax caravan arrived—more than enough time.

A mere half a sun jump into the trip, Shyla and Rendor realized being passengers in a caravan was worse than being guards. Sitting on a wagon and having nothing to do was beyond mind-numbing. After they found shelter for the apex, Shyla told the owner that they planned to walk and keep an eye out for trouble.

"I've enough guards. I can't pay you," Tahir said.

"That's fine." Shyla put a hand on Rendor, stopping him from commenting. With eighteen wagons and only four guards, Tahir really didn't have enough. He also didn't have any muscles accompanying them, preferring to hire them to unload and load goods at each city.

As for "keeping an eye out" for trouble, no one should know they were with Tahir's caravan. Before they left Qulsary, Shyla had kept her head covered and they each had arrived at different times. They had been very careful that none of the King's guards or staff knew where they were heading. Najib would spread the rumor they planned to return to Nintri.

For the next eight sun jumps, all was trouble free as expected.

Unfortunately, on the ninth sun jump bandits ran out from behind a dune to attack the caravan.

Of course Tahir blamed Shyla and Rendor for the attack despite all their precautions to keep their destination hidden.

"Is that why you wanted to help guard?" Tahir asked as he brandished a curved knife. "You knew this was coming!"

The bandits streamed down from the dunes on both sides of the caravan. Shyla counted sixteen. They wore light orange cloaks, turbans, and black veils. The clothing didn't exactly blend with the desert's colors, but it didn't stand out either. Shyla sought more bumps hiding under the sands but didn't find any.

The quickest of the bandits slowed when they approached, probably spotting Rendor and the four guards with their swords drawn. Then the others caught up and they formed a circle around the caravan, which meant thieves and not murderers.

A man pushed through to the front and faced Tahir. "This is my road. You must pay a toll. Once paid, we'll let you pass."

"This is the King's road. It's free for everyone to use." Tahir's brave words didn't match the tremble in his voice.

"The King's not here, is he? We are. It's my road now."

"How much?" Tahir asked in defeat.

"Fifty. Two osees per person."

"I have no coins," Tahir cried. "I spent it all on merchandise. I can give you rugs and cushions or—"

"Coins. Or you can turn around and go back."

Except they would never reach their last shelter before apex—the closest one was ahead. Shyla tried to catch the leader's gaze, but his attention was on Tahir and Rendor.

Tahir turned to her with a panicked look. "Do you have coins?"

She did and so did Rendor, but they weren't about to pay a toll on a free road. And something seemed…off. Meeting Tahir's gaze, she read his emotions. Despite his body language and tone, he wasn't scared. In fact, he'd anticipated the ambush.

The son of a sand demon was in league with the bandits! He wanted to scare his passengers into paying the outrageous toll. Instead of seven against sixteen with some help from the wagon drivers, it was all of them against Shyla and Rendor. Too many for her to influence at once.

"If we don't pay these men, we'll be cooked," Tahir said in a pleading tone.

She thought quickly. How could they get out of this situation without tipping Tahir off? They still needed him to get to Apanji. They could pay the toll and then loop around and steal it back. That would take too much time and it was too risky. She needed to trick everyone.

"I have the coins in my pack," Shyla said, gesturing to the wagon she'd stored it in. There was no reason to carry it out here when her water skin was heavy enough.

"Well, go on, sweet cheeks," the leader said. "The sun's not getting any lower."

She placed a hand on Rendor's shoulder, stopping him from growling at the leader. She'd been called worse. After he relaxed a hair, she went behind the wagon. Once there, she was out of sight. Only the driver of the wagon behind hers watched. With her back to him, she dumped the coins out of her pouch. She gathered her magic and aimed it at the driver as she turned sideways. She imagined she held a pouch full of shiny bluish-silver coins.

Coins.

Coins.

Except she commanded the sand to fill the bag instead. The grains flowed up the side of the wheel so they wouldn't be seen. When the pouch felt heavy enough, she stopped.

As she carried it back to Tahir and the others, she extended her magical influence to those close to her, concentrating on how a bag of coins sounded.

Jingle. Clink.

Jingle. Clink.

Jingle. Clink.

Rendor was the only one she didn't influence.

"Here's your toll," she said as she handed the bandit leader the pouch.

Jingle. Clink.

He grinned, sheathed his sword, and opened the pouch, peering inside.

Fifty coins.

Fifty coins.

"It's all there. You may pass." He made a magnanimous sweeping gesture with a bow, then called to his gang. They climbed over the dunes and disappeared.

Tahir quickly ordered the caravan to continue. "Let's go. No time to waste."

Everyone hustled after the wagons.

Rendor jogged beside Shyla. "What just happened?" he whispered.

"I'll explain later," she said because Tahir was headed toward them.

"Thank you so much!" Tahir said a bit too enthusiastically. "You saved all our lives! I'll pay you back once I sell my goods," he lied.

"Do you think we'll have any more trouble?" she asked him, reading his thoughts.

He didn't have any more ambushes set up so he hoped not. "These bandits are getting bolder since the King's soldiers haven't been patrolling in circuits. But I think we should be safe."

When Tahir went to his place at the head of the caravan, Shyla dropped back so she was at the very end. Rendor matched her pace. She glanced behind her, seeking bumps. None so far.

"Should we expect trouble in that direction?" Rendor asked, following her gaze.

"Once the bandits discover they've a pouch full of sand instead of fifty coins, I think they'll come after us at the next travel shelter."

"Ah. I wondered why everyone seemed so focused on that pouch." Rendor examined the desert. "The six of us can protect the entrance to a travel shelter better than being out here."

"That's not the problem." She explained about Tahir's involvement.

Rendor cursed under his breath. "Too many for us to fight and we'll lose our guide to Apanji."

"That's what I thought."

"Unless you can alter everyone's memories."

"There are too many of them." She considered. "The bandits probably have a hidden shelter near where they ambushed us."

"And?"

"And I think I should encourage them to use it." She reached out with her magic again. This time she encountered bumps. They had caught on to the ruse and were following the caravan.

"Do you need my help?" Rendor asked.

"Yes. If anyone asks where I am, tell them I'm making a pit stop."

Rendor laughed, but he soon sobered. "Please be careful and don't take too long."

"I'll catch up before you reach the shelter," she promised.

Shyla stopped jogging. The rest of the caravan kept going. Only Rendor noticed since everyone else was facing forward. She turned to scan the desert. The road was in the valley between two large dunes and the bandits were traveling on the other side of both dunes to keep hidden.

The bandits hurried so they could ambush the caravan before it reached the shelter. Shyla didn't waste any time. Concentrating on a large slice of sand, she commanded it to rise, creating a giant wall. Then she pushed it toward the bandits.

Blow.

And again.

Up.

Blow.

Up.

Blow.

And repeat.

All those angles on duty guarding caravans and practicing moving the sand had paid off. Shyla's intense and localized sandstorm was a thing of beauty. Cries of surprise mixed with shouted orders. Storms like this were rare this close to the danger zone. She pelted the thieves, pushed them back, and harassed them, grinning all the while. Fun. Tracking their whereabouts, she kept the pressure on until they reached their shelter.

Once they were inside, she sent a whirlwind of sand to spin around that area, pushing enough magic in it to keep it going for a while. Then she turned to catch up with the caravan.

Her energy started to lag once the initial thrill wore off. The air thickened in the heat. It was an effort to fill her lungs. Sunlight turned painful, its rays needling through her sun cloak. Remembering the gorgeous arcs of light in Nintri's heart caravan, she marveled that something so deadly could also be so beautiful.

She slowed to a trudge. The distant wagons seemed to float

on the heat undulating from the sands. It took her longer than she'd expected to reach the caravan.

Rendor waited for her by the entrance to the travel shelter. He looked over her shoulder. "Do we need to worry about the bandits?"

"No. Do we need to worry about Tahir and his people?"

"No one noticed you were gone until we arrived here. I covered for you." He studied her. "Do I need to help you inside?"

"No." She summoned the last of her energy and climbed down the ladder into the cool semi-darkness. Then she drank all her water and collapsed onto a cushion.

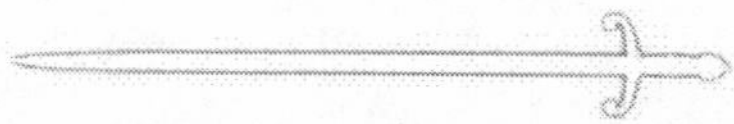

Shyla had a "conversation" with Tahir once she recovered her strength. Seemed he and a number of other caravan owners worked with that particular group of bandits. The road was a bit of a detour, so the caravans only traveled that route when they had passengers. The owners then received twenty-five percent of the toll coins the bandits collected.

Angry fire pulsed in her chest, and Shyla used The Eyes to convince Tahir of the error of his ways. The desire to track down the other owners sizzled in her blood. They were taking advantage of good people!

Sensing her fury, Rendor touched her arm. "The bandits will just attack other caravans. At least this way no one is injured."

Of course he was right. And anxiety twisted in her stomach as soon as she calmed down. She'd judged Tahir and punished him without any hesitation, just like King Tamburah. Icy fear spread through her body and she shivered. Had she just taken another step toward madness?

Once again, Rendor picked up on her mood. He moved closer. "Don't worry, we'll inform the King. Once he has the coins to hire soldiers, these ambushes will be stopped."

But would the King be able to stop her?

The rest of the trip to Apanji was uneventful. It was close to darkness when they arrived at the surface buildings of the city. Shyla pointed out the two thick pink columns that stood twenty meters higher than the rest of the structures.

"Those are the pillars of the sky," she explained to Rendor. "They go all the way down to the bottom of the city."

"Impressive."

"Wait until you see them when the sun is up." Shyla was looking forward to being underground when that happened. It was the best vantage point to view them. Most cities had something that celebrated the Sun Goddess and showcased her glorious sun. Except Zirdai. According to the historic records, Tamburah had destroyed the mirror falls that brought sunlight into Zirdai like a cascade. He'd claimed he was more powerful than the Sun Goddess and everyone should worship him.

Rendor made a few inquiries and found them rooms to rent. The two-room suite was small, clean, and located away from the crowded center. After third meal, Shyla insisted on going to the local market to purchase a map. They would be living here for a while.

Rendor was amused. "You can decipher archaic languages and read ancient maps, but you can't figure out the signs etched into the walls? How'd you find your way in Zirdai?"

"I bought a map and explored. Besides, those signs only tell you the immediate area. I need to see the whole city." She spread her hands wide.

"Most city maps are out of date almost immediately," Rendor said.

"Doesn't matter, I just need a general layout."

She found a seller and purchased a map that had enough detail for her purposes. When they returned to their rooms, she spread it out on the table. At first glance, Apanji appeared to be shaped like Zirdai, a deep narrow vase. But upon closer inspection, there was a yawning cavern that had a rectangular shape in the middle of the city. It extended from level ten all the way down to the bottom level.

"There's another reason why I wanted this." She tapped the map with her finger. "If you were going to bring in a bunch of mercs and wanted to lay low for a while, where would you stay?"

Rendor peered over her shoulder. "I'd seek out rooms like ours—on the edges, but close to the action." He pointed to the market, which had been built on tiers up the side of that huge cavern. "In the levels behind the stalls, there's a number of places for temporary stays. They're mostly for the merchants and wagon drivers who come and go. However, just beyond that is another grouping of rentals." Rendor paused. "I could check them out, see if the mercs are there. That would be a good starting point."

She faced him. "And I'll infiltrate the monastery and see how many monks Lonato's pilgrims have converted."

"No," Rendor said immediately. "Too dangerous."

She had expected his resistance. "Not really." She held up a hand. "By the time Xerxes figures out we're not coming back to Nintri and sends a message to Apanji, it will take approximately sixty sun jumps. We've used forty-eight of them to get here, so we have another twelve sun jumps before word arrives."

"Fine, then I'll go with you," Rendor said.

"You'll stand out. No one will believe you're a monk. I know how monasteries work. I can pretend to be a visiting monk, have a look around, and leave."

"Leave? Just like that?"

"Well, no. I have to see how bad the situation is and fix it if I can. Plus if they're not converted yet, I'll talk to their leader about assigning monks to help the King."

"What if they're all converted? Are you going to influence an entire monastery?"

"No. I'll retreat." When he hesitated, she added, "I escaped the Monks of Callow and they knew who I was right from the start. This time, I'm not announcing that I'm working for the King, and I'll wear long sleeves to hide the sigil. No one will suspect."

He grumbled and was clearly not happy, but he didn't have a solid argument. "How long?"

"Three or four sun jumps at most." And before he could change his mind, she asked, "Are you going to be able to avoid drawing notice?"

"Don't worry about me, I know how to blend in."

They spent the next sun jump together and visited the shaft—a underwhelming name for the gigantic vertical cavern. The pink sky columns speared the space into thirds as if they'd been installed to hold up the city. They both shone with bright white light, illuminating the entire area. There was no need for lanterns when the sun was in the sky.

"What causes it to shine like that?" Rendor asked her.

"It's something in the stone that transforms the sunlight." She swept her arm up. "This entire cavern is man-made. Those pillars were discovered when Apanji's ancestors started building their underground city. They cleared all the sand, dirt, and rocks away, exposing the pink stone until it ended sixty-six levels down."

"I'm surprised they didn't stop when they hit water."

Her attention focused on the waterfall. The massive gush of water poured out from the side of the shaft at around level fifty-seven and fell nine levels down into a huge pool at the bottom of the shaft. The water roared and white froth bubbled in the pool. It looked like a sandstorm raged in the air above, except instead of grains of sand, it was tiny droplets of water misting the area. The heavy moisture smelled rich with minerals.

"The sky pillars are producing natural light. They were smart to expose the entire length to take advantage of that." Shyla decided she could easily live in Apanji. It was a beautiful city and her favorite so far. Soaking in the happy murmurs of the citizens, she filled her lungs with the lush air. Once they finished helping the King, she looked forward to visiting the other wonders of Koraha. Excited, she entwined her fingers in Rendor's and squeezed. He grinned at her.

They returned to their rooms so Rendor could demonstrate what she'd be missing while she was at the monastery.

"*That* should give you plenty of incentive to return," he said smugly, nuzzling her neck as she gasped for breath.

"Return? Scorching hells, after *that* I'm never leaving this cushion."

"I've no objections." His level of smugness increased.

Unfortunately, duty called. Shyla dressed as a Monk of Parzival in a tan-colored tunic and pants, wrapping her turban in their signature style. Then she shouldered her pack and headed for the surface.

Shyla reached topside just as the sun touched the horizon. Sand swirled in the cooling air as the sky changed color, darkening to a deep red. Hiding near the surface buildings, she waited for a caravan to arrive. If none appeared, she'd have to retreat to her rooms and try again the next sun jump. Which she wouldn't mind doing. At all. Her blood still crackled from Rendor's goodbye.

A large caravan finally pulled in when only a thin crescent of the sun remained in the sky. The gamelus were panting from the effort to reach the city before full darkness. Their yellow fur was matted with sweat. The owner must have miscalculated the timing or they were waylaid by bandits.

Amid the flurry of activity, Shyla wove through the wagons as if she belonged, then headed toward the monastery at a fast clip. She'd sensed the Monks of Lyons hiding in the sands, watching the city. And now their focus should be on her, a monk on pilgrimage who'd just arrived with the caravan.

As the light faded, Shyla considered removing the druk from her pack. She had a vague idea of where the monastery was located, and most monks would be able to find and track the slight prints left behind by those on patrol. That was if she could see them. Shyla had been following the bumps, but that wouldn't help with her disguise.

Just as she was fumbling for the druk, a monk appeared in front of her. She jumped in surprise. Guess she'd been distracted.

"Sorry," he said. "But it'll take you forever to find the monastery in the dark. I thought I'd save you some time."

"Thank you." She'd already forgotten she was *supposed* to be a monk. They didn't let their colleagues stumble around in the dark. Strangers, yes. Fellow monks, no.

"I'm Walkur Lyons." He held out his hand.

"Shasta Parzival." She gave him a fake name just in case they'd heard of her. Shaking his hand, she hoped Shasta was close enough to Shyla that she remembered to respond when someone called her by that name.

"Zirdai's pretty far. Are you on a spiritual journey or do you have news for us? We've heard rumors about the Water Prince arresting monks."

"I'm on a pilgrimage, but I can answer your questions as well."

"Wonderful. You can join the pilgrims from Nintri."

"Nintri? Have they been here long?" she asked as he led her

through the desert.

"No. About three or five sun jumps." Walkur laughed. "I can't keep track."

They arrived at the entrance. Like all the other monasteries Shyla had visited, this one had a single room on the surface. About a dozen monks waited within.

"What took you so long?" a man asked. "We thought you got lost *again.*"

Chuckles sounded.

"Looks like Walkur's found another stray. What did we tell you about that?" one woman teased.

"Very funny," Walkur said. "This is Shasta, she's from Zirdai. She just got off that caravan we tracked."

"They made it to Apanji?" a monk asked Walkur in surprise.

"Just about."

There were mutters about foolish caravan drivers as they all descended into the monastery. A few monks stood guard at the bottom of the steps. Walkur removed his veil, exposing kind brown eyes and a thin black mustache. She guessed he was close to her age, maybe a few circuits older. Walkur then played host, showing Shyla around before escorting her to the guest wing.

"No one is here now, but most of the rooms are taken. However, there's at least two open. Third meal will start soon. Come join us and I'll introduce you to Neda. She's our leader and I'm sure she'll want to hear the news from Zirdai."

"Thank you." Shyla found an empty room at the end of the hallway. The small space held a cushion, a fur, a trunk, a sand clock, and a druk. Memories of her childhood rose. She'd grown up in a room just like this. She placed her sun cloak and pack into the trunk and then locked it before removing the small key. Then she searched for the dining area.

It didn't take her long to find it. She followed the scent of roasted gamelu meat and the buzz of voices. The monks might be considered different orders, but the layout of their homes was similar. And they all worshiped the Sun Goddess.

Walkur spotted her and gestured for her to join him at his table. He'd taken off his turban, revealing an explosion of black hair. She glanced around before joining him. The Monks of Lyons wore light blue tunics so the dark green of the Callow monks stood out. She noted the Callow monks didn't all sit together; instead each one sat at a separate table. They noticed her too and their gazes tracked her as she wove through the dining area. She hoped they hadn't heard from Lonato yet. If Lonato trusted Xerxes, he wouldn't send a message until the commander informed him of Shyla and Rendor's escape.

When she arrived, Walkur introduced her to Neda and three other monks. They were between sixty to seventy circuits old and the elders of the monastery. Neda appeared to be around fifty-eight circuits old. Shyla decided to give the leader the benefit of the doubt and not use The Eyes on her. Not unless something the woman said or did triggered suspicion.

"Welcome to Lyons," Neda said. "We are blessed by your presence."

"I'm blessed to be welcomed to your monastery," she said, remembering the proper response.

They exchanged pleasant small talk during the meal, but as

soon as Shyla finished eating, Neda leaned close and asked, "What news do you have from Zirdai?"

Interesting how she didn't ask about the Parzival monks. Shyla couldn't think of any reason not to tell Neda about the defeat so she reported what had happened from the perspective of a monk that was not directly involved.

"Hanif arrested!" She barked a laugh. "Bet that took some of the puff out of his chest."

It wasn't a question, so Shyla ignored it and continued with her story.

"We heard about a sun-kissed who took down the Water Prince and Heliacal Priestess. You say she was part of an organization called the Invisible Sword?" Neda asked.

"Yes."

"What's your take on them? Are they like those mercenaries we've been hearing about?"

Shyla decided to go for ignorance. "What mercenaries? Aren't they outlawed?"

"Yes, they are. But they're forming in some cities, offering their services for hire."

"The Invisible Sword wasn't hired. They stopped the atrocities because no one else would or could."

Neda studied her and Shyla regretted her heated tone. If she'd been as uninvolved as she claimed, she wouldn't be defending the Invisible Sword.

"It's rather an odd time for you to leave your home, considering all the recent upheavals in your city," Neda said.

"That's why I left. I needed peace to reconnect with the Sun

Goddess."

Neda glanced over to the Callow monks and frowned before returning her attention to Shyla. "You're welcome to stay, of course." Then she lowered her voice.

"I just don't know how peaceful it will be here."

"Is Apanji having troubles?"

"No. It's an internal matter. A disagreement over what our role is in society. If you want to avoid conflict, I suggest you travel to Catronia."

"Has our role changed?" Shyla asked, hoping for more information and wanting to confirm that Neda hadn't been converted yet.

"No. And until I hear otherwise from the King, our role will remain the same for this monastery."

"That is good to hear. I'll stay for a little while. If it gets too contentious, I'll leave."

Neda stood and the other three, who'd been quiet the entire time, rose as well. "In that case," Neda said, "prayers are in the chapel at angles zero, eighty, one-sixty, and two-forty. There's a chore chart in the common room. We'd appreciate it if you could help out once a sun jump."

"Of course."

When the monks left, Walkur beamed at her. "That went well, don't you think?"

"It did. How long are the Callow monks expected to remain?"

His good humor died. "They didn't say." Then he hopped to his feet. "Since you're my stray"—a grin flashed—"you're my responsibility, which means if you need anything or have any questions, come find me.

I work in the kitchen during first meal and help in the growing caverns from angle sixty to one-twenty, then I'm on patrol until darkness. You're also welcome to help out any of those times. I might as well benefit from finding a stray, don't you think?"

"I do. Which of the three chores is your favorite?"

"The growing cavern. I just love tending the plants. Our world is so dry and hot and scratchy. And they are so smooth and moist and soft. It does smell bad at times, but if you get close to a leaf…" He pulled in a deep breath as if transported. "It smells divine." Then he blushed. "Sorry, I… It sounds… I'm…"

"Sounds fun. I'll see you there."

He shot her a grateful smile before bolting. As she debated her next move, one of the Callow monks came over to her table.

"Mind if I sit?" he asked.

"Not at all." She met his gaze as he folded his long legs underneath him. Unlike Neda, she wasn't giving this man the benefit of the doubt. Curiosity dominated his emotions, followed closely by suspicion.

"I'm Fellan Callow," he said.

"Shasta Parzival."

"Lots of crazy stories have been coming out of Zirdai. Are any of them true?"

"Depends on what you've been hearing." Shyla was going to make him work for the information.

He gave her a sly smile. "How about the one saying a sun-kissed overthrew the Water Prince and Heliacal Priestess?"

"Yes, that's true." Again, she opted not to expand. Fellan acted as if he was gifting her with his presence and she should be honored by his regard.

"Any relation to you?"

"No."

He considered her, then changed the subject. "How are the Monks of Parzival handling the upheaval in Zirdai's leadership? Is Hanif still in charge?"

Ah. He wished to know how difficult it would be to convert the Parzival monks.

"We're as strong as ever. Hanif has been a blessing. Everyone loves him so." *In other words, good luck, you're going to need it.* Then she asked him about his pilgrimage.

"We're actually on a mission. The Monks of Callow have refocused our efforts. We believe the monks should be doing more to help the citizens and we should be sharing knowledge with everyone." He launched into the hard sell.

Shyla had to admit it sounded reasonable. All good ideas that she hoped the King would consider for the future. What bothered her was Fellan's utter belief that if things didn't change, he had every right to force it. And if a few old, useless monks died, so be it.

She searched deeper into his soul but the conviction remained strong, as if it had erased everything else. Odd. She hesitated to alter it with the power of The Eyes, afraid there would be nothing of him left. She wondered if the other Callow monks would be the same or if this was unique to Fellan.

Not wanting to tip her hand, she pretended to agree with his rhetoric. But when he asked her to start preaching to the Lyons monks, she shook her head.

"I'm here to reconnect with the goddess."

"What about when you're back in Zirdai? Can we count on you to help us out there?"

"If Hanif asks us to assist the citizens, I'll be happy to do whatever he decides."

Fellan rubbed a hand over his face as uncomplimentary thoughts about her intelligence swirled. She clamped down on the urge to slug him.

He stood. "May the goddess guide you." He bowed slightly and walked away to join another table.

It was too easy. She'd missed something important. Besides the tables with the Callow monks, the rest of the dining area was empty. Shyla considered her next move. There were fifteen angles until the next call to the chapel. Monks prayed four times a sun jump. Attending all four sessions was not required; monks were encouraged to be at two. Since she'd professed her desire to seek the goddess, it would be strange for her to miss any of them. At least she could use the opportunity to get a sense of how many monks had fallen for Fellan's sermon.

One angle before prayers, Shyla entered the chapel through the door near the altar. About to start the session, Neda stood behind the holy stone.

Shyla ducked her head as if embarrassed. "Sorry," she muttered, pausing as if uncertain of her welcome.

The other monks were already at the kneelers with their

heads bowed, wearing their robes. The garment was a sign of respect for the Sun Goddess. Shyla had to borrow one since she had "forgotten" to pack hers. Two sizes too big, the oversized robe could hide a gamelu.

"Go on, find a spot," Neda urged.

When Shyla hurried to a kneeler, she tripped over the hem and fell with a loud thump. Every monk in the chapel glanced at her. Shyla quickly made eye contact with as many as she could, giving them all a sheepish clumsy-me look. A few gave her rueful grins, others frowned, but there was no mistaking Neda's exasperated sigh. Shyla gathered the excessive material, scrambled to her feet, and knelt on an empty kneeler near the back.

Neda waited a moment and then launched into the standard benedictions. As the monks settled into the routine and performed their recitations, Shyla scanned their moods. Reading their souls while they prayed would be inappropriate. A number of the monks had found that peaceful meditative state, but a few were conflicted, questioning why they were wasting time praying when they could be helping others.

By the time the session concluded fifteen angles later, her knees and back ached. Exhaustion pulsed in her bones and she returned to her room. The cushion was comfortable, but she missed sharing it with Rendor.

She hoped he was being extra careful. He'd claimed he could blend in, but to her he shone as bright as the sky pillars.

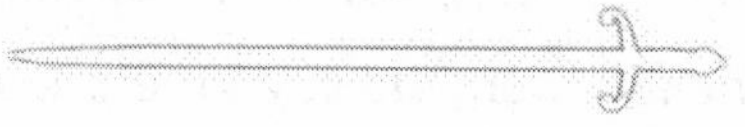

Shyla showed up late to the angle zero prayer session. Her loud entrance interrupted Neda and caused everyone to glare at her in annoyance. She met their gazes with an apologetic wince as Neda lectured her that tardiness was not tolerated in the Lyons monastery. Appearing chastised, Shyla found an empty kneeler in the back. It was the last one—definitely a more popular time.

The mood for this gathering was more conflicted and less peaceful. A restlessness vibrated in the air. Even Neda seemed to pick up on it. There was a slightly quizzical crease in her forehead. Many of the monks also looked straight ahead instead of bowing their heads in respect.

The disquiet increased at the angle eighty session. Shyla arrived early and claimed her kneeler before anyone else arrived. As they filed in, she made eye contact with each one. Some nodded in approval that she had learned her lesson about being on time. During the service, she noted the rebellious displays turned from the passive actions of earlier to the more obvious. Some monks sat on their heels. Others muttered comments. And two stood up in disgust and left.

After eating a quick meal, she ascended to the growing cavern. It was located on level six, which was the perfect depth to be protected from the surface heat and warm enough during darkness for the vegetable plants to survive. The vibrant scent of living green mixed with moist soil enveloped her as she entered. Sunlight poured from the mirror pipes poking through the ceiling.

The space was tiny compared to the vast growing caverns in the cities. And the caretaker had filled every square meter except for a narrow path. Shyla followed it and found Walkur shoveling fertilizer. His tunic and the knees of his pants were stained black and he had a smear of dirt along his right cheek. His appearance matched his unruly hair.

He spotted her. "You made it!"

"You convinced me this is the place to be."

He laughed. "Yep, nothing is more devout than shoveling sh—"

"Walkur!" a woman shouted from the depths of the cavern. "Cans are ready. Those potato plants aren't going to water themselves."

"Yes, sir." Then he lowered his voice. "Elschen's a bit gruff, but she can get anything to grow." He pointed to his bushy hair. "I used to be bald."

Shyla laughed.

"Come on." Walkur went farther down the path and entered another room.

The rich scent of growing things was replaced by a harsh acidic stink. No doubt this was the area where the odorous contents of the collection station buckets were turned into nourishment for the plants. The gardener was a tiny woman with long white braids. Her skin matched the soil and she grunted, clearly unimpressed when Walkur introduced Shyla.

Elschen thrusted a can into Shyla's arms. "Here, Walkur will show you what to do."

Shyla followed him, carrying the heavy can. It had a spout and sloshing inside was a liquid that wasn't quite water. It smelled a bit like spoiled milk mixed with sweat. Walkur poured his out on a row of short squat plants. He gestured to another row. Shyla got the hint. She "watered" the plants. Watching the liquid soak into the soil gave her a strange sense of satisfaction. They made repeated trips back to Elschen who took the empty cans and replaced them with full ones.

Shyla asked Walkur some general questions about the monastery. Then she worked the conversation around to the visiting monks. "I noticed none of the Callow monks attended prayers. Are they too busy with chores?"

Walkur straightened with a wince, rubbing his back. "No, they don't think we should be spending all that time praying. We should be *doing*." He wiped the sweat off his forehead, leaving another black streak. "Except they don't help with chores, so they're not practicing what they preach, don't you think?" Then he lowered his voice. "Lots of our monks agree with them. I'd rather be doing, which is why I'm always busy during prayer times." He gave her an earnest look. "You're not going to rat me out, are you?"

"No. I agree. There are many ways to honor the goddess."

"Finally! Someone who understands." Then he sobered. "I think things are going to get ugly around here and Neda is going to ask our Callow guests to leave despite the policy that all monks are welcome. It's not going to be pleasant, don't you think?"

Neda had the authority to kick the monks out, but Shyla worried it was too late. And her suspicions were confirmed at third meal. There was no need to read people's thoughts and emotions. The room had a definite divide between those who aligned with Neda and the older monks, and those who had converted to Fellan's philosophy. Unfortunately, Neda's side was smaller.

Shyla was amazed how the atmosphere had changed in just one sun jump. Had her arrival caused Fellan to increase his efforts? She needed to "talk" to the monk and find a way to stop him from converting everyone.

He gave her the perfect opportunity after the prayer session at angle two-forty. When she returned to her room, Fellan was inside waiting for her.

Fellan stood in the middle of her room. Even though it wasn't really hers, common courtesy should have prevented him from entering. Shyla paused in the doorway but hands from behind shoved her forward. When she turned, a big bruiser stood in her recently vacated spot with his arms crossed. They weren't here for a friendly chat.

Returning her focus to Fellan and lowering her mental shield, she asked, "What's going on?"

"I received word to be on the lookout for a sun-kissed who is working for the King and knows too much." He grabbed her arm and yanked her sleeve up, exposing the sigil. "Do you want to explain why you're pretending to be a monk, *Shyla*?"

"Who sent word?" she asked, jerking free. She'd thought she had more time.

"I'm asking questions. Not you."

"As an emissary of the King, I don't have to answer any of your questions."

Fellan stepped closer. "The King no longer has any authority here. I suggest you cooperate."

"Or what?" she challenged, gathering her magic.

"Egan," he said.

Stop.

The bruiser tried to move. He put forth quite the effort, but he wasn't anywhere near as strong-willed as Captain Yates had been. Shyla's magic held him immobile.

"Egan?"

"I…can't…move."

Stop.

This command was aimed at Fellan who froze in place. Amused, she watched the monk struggle. His confusion soon turned to anger.

Fellan glared at her. "You."

"Me."

"What kind of demon are you?"

"One you can't bully and who is loyal to the King." She moved toward him, getting into his face. Well, as close as possible considering his height. "What kind are you?" It was a rhetorical question. She met his gaze and reached with the power of The Eyes to find out.

His anger hid his fear that this sun-kissed might affect his mission. That was all he cared about. The mission. It was so important that no one was going to stop him. His belief and desire to convert others consumed him to a point that there was nothing left. Shyla tried to find his memories or anything not focused on his mission and couldn't.

Wow. She'd heard the term single-minded, but this was…beyond an obsession. Then she read Egan and encountered the same mindset. Lonato must have converted them to his cause before sending them out to do his dirty work.

"What was Egan going to do to me?" she asked Fellan.

"Give you a gift."

Not what she expected. Unless that was code for a punch to the gut. "What gift?"

"A pendant that represents the Sun Goddess. All our flock are given one. It's in his left pants pocket."

She sensed a trick, but his honesty and her curiosity got the better of her. Reaching into Egan's pocket, her fingertips brushed metal. Shyla pulled out a gold necklace with a pendant. It was exactly like the one the Water Princess of Nintri had worn. Shyla stared at the black triangular jewel. It gleamed with an iridescent shine and tugged at something deep inside her as if a hook had snagged her heart.

So distracted with the pendant, Shyla released her hold on the two men. Yet she didn't care. Fellan took the necklace from her hands and she protested.

"Do not fret, little one. It's yours." He looped it around her neck. Then he tucked it under her tunic so the cold metal rested against her skin. "Yours forever."

"Mine." The tugging sensation grew. A part of her cried out in alarm that this wasn't right. But those thoughts were drawn into the pendant. It reminded her of the water soaking into the soil.

"You'll answer my questions now," Fellan said.

Her refusal slipped from her. "Yes."

"Who are you?"

She told him. Everything. Happiness filled her as she divulged all her secrets. A person shouldn't have so many. Not if she wished for the Sun Goddess to bless her.

"Seven hells," Fellan said when she finished. "Magic. The Eyes. She's..." He cast about as if trying to find the right word.

"Ours," Egan said.

That word grated on her. No, she wasn't. She belonged... Her original thought drained into the pendant and in its place rose Fellan's name. He'd given her the goddess.

"Think of the mission," Egan said. "How useful she'll be."

Fellan smiled. "You'll help us? Use your magic to convert other monks to our mission?"

"Yes."

"Lonato will be so pleased," Egan said. "I'll send word." He strode from the room.

Fellan turned to her. "You will attend prayers at angle zero and you will stand at the altar and use your magic to convince everyone to follow the new order."

She opened her mouth to protest, but again the negative reply slipped away, sucked up by the goddess's love. "All right."

"If anyone is too strong-willed to be converted, we can gift them with a pendant. It shows them the goddess's love and removes all resistance."

She touched the lump on her chest, pressing the metal against her skin. "It's the most wonderful gift. Why don't you give one to everyone? It would save so much time and strife."

"It would, but we have a limited quantity. That black jewel is very special. It was cut from a one-of-a-kind gemstone that fell from the sky. A gift from the Sun Goddess herself. Lonato and his friend realized the significance and had it cut and polished for our growing flock."

"I'm honored to have one. Have you been gifted one as well?"

He pulled a necklace from beneath his tunic. On it dangled an almost identical pendant. The only difference was the jewel. It was a brilliant yellowish-orange instead of black. "I believed in Lonato's vision right away and he gifted me with this one."

"Is there a difference other than the color?" she asked.

"Yes. This one allows the Sun Goddess to speak through me. My words are blessed and have more…weight when I talk to others. They listen to me."

The rational part of Shyla understood what the jewel was doing. And even though she tried to stop the words, they flowed out because it was important to please Fellan. "It gives you magic that you use to influence people. Just like The Eyes."

"No. It's a divine *miracle*. From another *gift sent* from the *heavens*."

A ball of magic glowed around the stone when he stressed his words. She peered closer. "It's not a very strong miracle. Does Lonato wear one as well?"

"Of course. They are worn by all the leaders."

"Is his bigger?"

"Yes, as is his due."

That explained why Lonato's ability to work miracles was stronger. She started to explain it to Fellan, but he interrupted her.

"Go to sleep, little one. It matters not how the goddess works her miracles. You have a busy sun jump ahead."

"Yes, Fellan." Shyla removed her boots and sank into her cushion, pulling the fur up to her chin. Pure contentment wrapped around her. The goddess would solve all their problems. All Shyla had to do was listen to the goddess's direction through Fellan. For the first time since Shyla was young, her dreams were worry free.

Shyla entered the chapel a few angles before zero. At this session, Fellan, Egan, and a couple other Callow monks knelt on the back row of kneelers. Fellan instructed her not to use her goddess voice on the Callow monks. Shyla stood at the front, drawing attention.

"Please find a kneeler, Shasta," Neda said.

She turned to the leader and met her gaze. Then she gathered her divine power and aimed it at Neda. "No. You're no longer in charge of this monastery. Kneel down with the others and listen to *me*."

Neda's shock and surprise melted as Shyla channeled the Sun Goddess's divine will. The woman fought for a few heartbeats before nodding and settling on one of the empty kneelers. Fellan and Egan exchanged a triumphant look. They had worried that Neda would need a pendant to obey. However guilt and shame seared through Shyla before the goddess's love took it from her, soothing her soul.

Now that she had everyone's attention, Shyla preached. Putting her divine power into her words, she changed everyone's mind about the monk's duties. "We work for the Sun Goddess, not the King. The Sun Goddess commands me, and now you, to help the citizens. No longer will you sneak around and spy on the city's leaders. You will go and aid those in need, fight for the weak, and obey the goddess. She speaks through Egan. He will remain here and guide you. He's in charge of this monastery." Shyla used her magic…no, not magic, but the goddess's voice to ask, "Do you swear to the Sun Goddess to obey her by following Egan?"

Their response of "I will" was immediate and unanimous. Shyla released them and they gathered around Egan, asking what the goddess wished for them to do. Another flare of guilt burned in her heart. Shyla tried to hold on to it because what she'd just done was…was…the right thing. Pleased, she watched Egan guide his followers.

Fellan came up beside her. "Are you tired, little one?"

She'd influenced over forty-five monks. "Yes."

"Go rest until the next prayer session."

"Yes, Fellan."

The next session held around fifty monks. Those that Fellan and Egan had already converted no longer attended—prayer sessions were considered a waste of time by the new order. By the fourth prayer session, Shyla had convinced almost the entire monastery—some two hundred souls. There'd been a few, like Walkur, who avoided the sessions. She would preach to them one on one during the next sun jump. For now, her body ached with fatigue and Fellan had ordered her to go to sleep.

Lying on her cushion, she marveled at her contentment in doing the goddess's work. It hummed through her veins. Everyone was so much happier. The air in the monastery buzzed with excitement.

Deep inside her, another voice struggled to be heard. Its distant cry pleaded with her to stop. Insisted that this was all very wrong. Listening to the voice would threaten her peace. So she placed her fingers on the pendant's jewel and allowed those unsettling thoughts to be silenced.

After first meal, Shyla and Egan tracked down those who'd been avoiding listening to the goddess's will. Some tried to fight. Egan quickly subdued them and, once Shyla met their gazes, all defiance drained away as they learned that the new way to worship the goddess would bring them peace and joy.

Soon only Walkur and Elschen were left to convert. Shyla knew where to find them and Egan needed to organize his flock.

"Should I send Fellan with you?" he asked.

"There's no need."

He studied her. "You haven't needed to use a single pendant. Will those you've convinced revert back?"

"No."

"How can you be so sure?"

"Have the ones Fellan convinced changed their minds?"

"No."

"He has his pendant and the yellowish-orange jewel, which has a fraction of the power of The Eyes." She pointed to her eyes.

"The only way those I convert will change their minds is if *I* change it for them." A true statement that caused her inner voice to scream at her for her hubris, reminding her about Tamburah's descent into megalomaniac madness. But that dire warning disappeared into the jewel.

Egan smiled. "Good. Finish up with those last two. I want everyone assembled in the minster at apex."

The minster was the only place big enough for all the monks to assemble. It was used every fourteen sun jumps so the entire population could pray together.

Shyla climbed up to the growing cavern on level six. Walkur and Elschen would be working among the plants. Not much would change for them since providing food for the monks was vital. Yet an unease grew as she walked along the narrow path. She was Walkur's stray and she…was…doing…doing…the right thing.

Walkur spotted her heading toward him. He reversed his grip on his shovel, wielding it like a weapon. "Go away. I don't want to hear what you've come to preach."

She stopped. "Walkur, you don't have a choice." She'd already made eye contact with him and could reach him from anywhere in the monastery.

"I think I do." He hefted the shovel. "I can knock you out. Unless you talk in your sleep, it will be blissfully silent."

That would work. Except it was a bluff. Walkur was hoping she'd leave him alone and then when the air cooled he and Elschen could leave the monastery and get help.

"Get help from whom?" she asked.

He jerked. "Did you read my mind?"

"Yes." She laughed at his expression. "Walkur, the goddess has given me the divine power to do her work. And she wishes for all the monks to join together and follow her orders to help others. If you go to the monastery near Haiya or to Parzival near Zirdai, we'll just make them part of our flock sooner rather than later."

"You're insane. What *happened* to you?"

For a moment her confidence in being right disappeared. Something had happened to her. And it wasn't good. Fellan had…had…given her the goddess's love. "A miracle, Walkur. One you're about to embrace." Shyla reached deeper into Walkur's soul and—

A force slammed into the back of her head. Pain exploded as the sunlight disappeared.

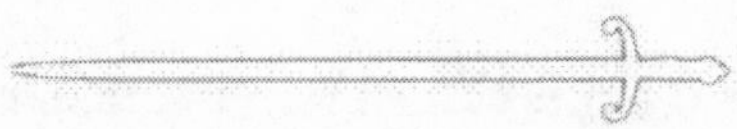

The pain was almost unbearable. It filled her head and pressed on her skull with such force, she imagined a series of cracks widening, spilling her brain matter. The image didn't help with her unsettled stomach. In fact— Shyla rolled over as bile pushed up her throat. A bucket sat next to her and she vomited into it. The action increased the agony hammering inside her skull. She groaned and touched a particularly sensitive spot on the back of her head. Someone had stitched up a long gash not too long ago because her fingertips came away wet with her blood. After another stomach heaving bout over the bucket, she curled into a ball in utter misery.

What had happened? Fractured bits of memory surfaced. The chapel. Neda. The goddess's love. Walkur brandishing a shovel. Had he hit her? No. He'd stood in front of her. Then who? Elschen! But why?

An uncomfortable thought that she was guilty of abusing her powers floated just out of reach. As more memories clicked together, forming a better picture, Shyla eyed the bucket. Nausea swirled and this time it wasn't due to the pain. What had she done? She'd—

Fellan entered her room. It had started with him! She struggled to a sitting position, gathering her magic for a strike. Nothing. Her body held not a single spark of energy.

"Ah, thank the goddess you're awake." He came closer and held out a glass. A liquid with a reddish tint sloshed inside. "This will help with the pain."

She glared at him, refusing the drink. He studied her. Then he placed the glass on the trunk and knelt in front of her. She tried to punch his face, but he grabbed her wrist, stopping the admittedly weak blow. And then he reached for her neck. Instead of choking her, he pulled a pendant out from underneath her tunic. She glanced at it in surprise. What…

The goddess's love embraced her, draining all her fear and guilt. Shyla stopped fighting. When he placed the pendant in her hand, she sighed in relief. *Mine.*

"You had quite the blow to the head," he said, releasing her. He gave her the glass. "Drink."

She gulped the water. It soothed her throat and settled her

stomach. Soon the pain in her head went from skull crushing to tolerable. "What happened?"

"I was going to ask you the same thing," Fellan said. "You told Egan you could handle a couple of monks, yet we found you lying facedown among the plants."

Walkur's image flashed in her mind. He'd threatened her with a shovel, but the blow had come from behind. "I made a mistake." She hung her head because Fellan looked far from pleased. "I didn't check the bumps to locate Elschen when I found Walkur. I assumed she was in the fertilizer room."

"Bumps?" he asked.

She explained how she wielded her magic to sense other people nearby.

"Handy."

That word reminded her of another and caused her some anxiety. Someone she worked with… No. She only worked for the Sun Goddess and Fellan.

"Do you know where they went?" he asked.

"No. It was close to apex. Perhaps they're still hiding here."

Fellan gave her a humorless smile. "They're gone. You've been unconscious for two full sun jumps, little one. We worried you'd never wake."

Two? No wonder she ached all over. And she'd missed so much! She needed to do the goddess's work. Laboring to get up, she was gently pushed back.

"Rest. The physician will check on you soon and bring you something to eat."

She relaxed back, wondering if the physician was as good or

as grumpy as...her...friend... Then her worries dissolved. Of course whoever came would do the goddess's work.

The woman who arrived checked her stitches, claimed she'd pulled a few, and ensured Shyla ate. Then she was ordered to rest. Happy to comply, Shyla slept for another two sun jumps.

On the third, Fellan strode into her room. "How are you feeling?"

She considered the best response. His stiff posture and creased brow warned her he was upset. "Much better."

"Full strength?"

"Almost. My head still aches when I concentrate too long." The physician had brought Shyla some scrolls to read to help pass the time.

"It'll have to do. Get dressed, we have a visitor." He left.

She scrambled to change from the soft sleeping gown to the tan tunic and pants she'd worn as part of her disguise. Why had she needed a disguise? There was danger...no...no danger...not here with Fellan. But what about this visitor?

Fellan waited for her in the tunnel. Handing her another glass of the reddish water, he told her to drink it. "Should help with the headaches."

She downed it in a few gulps and then followed him to the receiving room on level six where a number of people had gathered. Sunlight filled the area and Shyla turned her face up. Closing her eyes, she soaked in the warm rays. It'd been too long since she was topside.

"Shyla, come meet our guests," Fellan said.

She hurried to join him. He faced a large man who looked

dangerously familiar. Stepping closer to Fellan, she pressed her fingers on the pendant underneath her tunic. The sharp edges of it dug into her skin, bringing comfort that the goddess would protect her.

"Easy there, little one," Fellan said, tucking her tight to him. "You're safe."

"Well done," the large man said. "You caught the only person who could have upset our plans. And now she's working for us."

"For me," Fellan corrected. "We're going to travel to Haiya to convert the Monks of Grane."

The large man straightened to his full height. "She's too valuable to use on monks. They're mostly weak-willed and you've been doing just fine without her. I need her for the Water Princes and Princesses; they're harder to convince."

"She's mine," Fellan insisted. "She won't listen to you."

"She will when I take her from you." The giant strode forward and grabbed Shyla's arm, yanking her away from Fellan.

She struggled to break free from his grip, but she might as well have been trying to break a heavy metal chain. Glancing at Fellan, she waited for his orders.

He pressed his lips together and shook his head. "Go with him, little one. He's right."

Dismay flared. He wasn't Fellan. She wouldn't be at peace unless she pleased Fellan. The big man's oversized muscles and looming presence scared her. Her fear spiked when he grabbed the necklace, pulling the pendant free. Then he removed it, yanking it over her head.

She squawked and tried to get it back. He tossed it to Fellan who tucked it away in his pocket. Her world spun and then steadied. A clarity that she'd been lacking brought everything and everyone in the room into sharp focus. She was surrounded by enemies. And the beast holding her arm was the worst one. Xerxes.

Anger filled her along with the realization that she had regained control of her thoughts and actions. She gathered her will and—

Xerxes looped another pendant around her neck. He held it up to show her the jewel, but she turned away, averting her gaze. *Not this time*. Grabbing the hair at the back of her head, he forced her to face him. A hot spike of pain stabbed from the still healing stitches. She jerked and…the goddess's love claimed her. Xerxes had returned the goddess to her. So thankful, she sagged against him.

"You did a good job, Fellan. I'll make sure Lonato knows how much you pleased him," Xerxes said.

Fellan puffed up his chest. "Thank you, Commander."

Then Xerxes moved so she stood in front of him. He crouched a little so they were at eye level. "You're mine now. The goddess speaks to you through *me*. Understand?"

His words slammed into her. They obliterated the inner voice that had been trying to warn her how very wrong this was. Xerxes had four times the power Fellan had. "Yes."

"Sir. I'm a commander; you address me as sir."

"Yes, sir."

"Good. Now you tuck this close to you." He slid the pendant

under her tunic. "And don't ever take it off or the goddess can't protect you or show you her love."

Shyla nodded and pressed her hands over the lump on her chest. "I won't."

"That's good, Little One." He glanced at Fellan. "That name fits her perfectly." Then he straightened. "Keep with the mission, Fellan. We're ahead of schedule because of you."

"Yes, sir," Fellan snapped.

Xerxes turned to his men—five in all. "We've time to return to Apanji before darkness. Let's go. Double time."

They climbed to the surface and took off at a fast pace. Shyla kept up with everyone for a while. But then her head pounded in rhythm with her boots and she couldn't fill her lungs fast enough. She worried about disappointing Xerxes but was unable to push her body faster without fainting.

He noticed her lagging behind and slowed until she caught up to him. When she reached his side, he stopped.

"Rest a moment," he said.

Grateful, she wiped her brow. Her sun cloak was back at the monastery along with all her other possessions. No coins, though. She'd left them…behind…with…someone. But there was no need to worry, the goddess would provide.

"I forgot you were injured. Do you think that blow to your head has affected your ability to…what do you call it? Wield magic?"

Confused, she said, "It's a gift from the goddess. She has allowed me to work miracles. And if she decided to take away my abilities, it would be her right."

Xerxes sighed. "You're with me now. I'm going to call your ability to work miracles wielding magic. And I want to know if it's been affected by your injury."

"I don't know if the concussion has changed anything."

"Can you do something with your magic that doesn't involve influencing me?" he asked.

"Of course." She wanted to please him so she concentrated on creating an arrow made of sand. Then she had it fly around their heads and slam into the side of a dune.

"That is amazing." He grinned.

Return. The starburst impact pattern on the dune disappeared.

"How many people can wield magic like this?" he asked.

"I don't know."

He focused on her. "You cannot lie to me, Little One."

She rushed to assure him. "I'm not. There are many new magic wielders and I don't know how many of them are able to move the sand."

Xerxes glanced at the sun. It hovered about five degrees above the horizon. "Feeling better?"

"Yes, sir."

"Good. We've enough time to walk the rest of the way to Apanji." He headed toward the city.

Shyla hurried to keep up, needing two steps for every one of his long-legged strides.

"Tell me about magic. How does it work?"

She explained the three techniques of magic.

"Anyone can do them?" he asked.

"Anyone with the power inside them. It has to be opened." Then she told him about those who were cracked and those whose full potential was open, filling their entire bodies with the glow.

"Can you test my soldiers for cracks?"

"Yes, sir."

"And teach them how to wield magic?"

"Yes, sir."

"Ah." He was silent for a while. When they were within sight of the great sky pillars, he asked, "This magic is different than the power of The Eyes of Tamburah, which you also possess?"

"Yes, sir."

"Explain how The Eyes work and what they can do."

"The Eyes make my ability to wield magic stronger. They also allow me to read souls." She described how that worked, about being able to erase memories, and why it'd been easy for her to convert the Lyons monks.

"How did you make them work for you?"

She hesitated. The compulsion to obey was as strong as ever, but her tongue stayed locked behind her clamped teeth. Deep inside, a voice woke, yelling that if she told him, he'd kill her and take The Eyes for himself.

"Little One, your silence upsets me."

"I'm sorry, Xerxes." Yet she could not produce the words. They remained trapped inside her.

"*Explain* to me how you woke the power of The Eyes."

His magic wrapped around her chest and squeezed tight. "I can't." The words exploded from her mouth.

He stopped walking and studied her. "You believe divulging the information will lead to your death?"

She nodded, feeling terrible. "I've upset you."

"No, you haven't. If you believe obeying an order is suicidal, then the goddess will prevent you from carrying it out. She doesn't wish for you to become a martyr."

That was a relief. "But what about if we need to fight? There's always a chance of getting killed."

"That works differently. If you go into a fight thinking you'll lose, then you shouldn't be fighting. It's my job to make sure you're well prepared and confident of your success. You've studied the Ways of the Yarin, right?"

"Yes, sir."

"Good, then I won't need to teach you. Come on, the sun is almost down." Xerxes strode toward the city.

Shyla jogged to keep up with him, but it didn't take them long to reach the entrances to Apanji. Without the bright sunlight, the sky pillars shone like a beacon. It would take them a few more angles to lose all their luminosity.

Xerxes led her down through the city. He strode through it as if born here, barely glancing at the marks on the walls. That struck her as odd for some reason.

"Have you been here long?" she asked.

"Twenty sun jumps." He scowled at her. "When you didn't show up in Nintri, I figured you'd shaken off my orders. So I headed here."

"But..." There was something about beating him here, but she couldn't grasp the rest of the memory.

"My men and I can cross the desert twice as fast as a caravan."

"Double time?"

He laughed. "Right." Then he glanced at her. "There are…levels of obedience with the pendant. If you keep pleasing me with your intelligence, then I won't have to push your thoughts toward a simpler state where all you think about is listening to my will. Do you understand?"

That if her inner voice managed to make her disobey him, he'd erase it. An alarming thought, even though she'd be completely happy without it screaming at her. "Yes, sir."

"Good. I think this is going to work out quite well."

A thrum of contentment pulsed through Shyla. She followed in his wake. The extra-large man created his own path even in the most crowded areas. Either everyone moved out of his way or the force of his presence nudged them aside. It reminded her of…someone.

They cut through the shaft, passed the market stalls, and walked by the rooms rented by the merchants. Beyond that was another grouping of rooms and apartments. Xerxes unlocked the door to one on level thirty-six. And she wasn't surprised. She already knew where they'd be staying, yet how could she? A name tried to form in her mind. Someone important. The inner voice shouted letters, but…they were diverted by the goddess's love inside the black jewel, which meant it wasn't important enough.

Xerxes gestured her inside. The entrance opened up into a suite of rooms. They were well furnished with plenty of cushions, tables, and chests. Stained-glass murals decorated the walls. This apartment was probably one of those long-term leases. Already inside the large common area were the five soldiers who had accompanied Xerxes to the monastery and two others she didn't recognize.

"This is Little One." Xerxes introduced her to the others—four men and three women. He pointed to one of the women. She was tall with an athletic build and long black hair that had been twisted into one long braid that reached down to her hips. "This is Vilma, my second-in-command. You are to obey her orders as well unless they are counter to mine."

The woman met Shyla's gaze with an intensity that surprised her. It was either hate or jealousy. However, the name Vilma rang with strong familiarity. Yet when she tried to recall the situation where she might have met her before, it slipped away and Shyla no longer cared why.

"Report," Xerxes said to his soldiers.

"The Water Prince has not responded to any of our requests for an audience," Vilma said. "You're going to have to go in person and *convince* the receptionist to get us an appointment. Although, I've heard he's pretty stubborn and might not agree. We've also determined which of his people is the captain of the guard and will try to bribe her to get us an appointment."

Captain of the guard. A sudden warmth flowed through her. It was mixed with love and desire, therefore the goddess didn't take it from Shyla. She clutched it to her chest, keeping it all to herself.

"We no longer have to worry about getting an audience." Xerxes raised Shyla's arm and exposed the King's sigil to everyone in the room. "This is our ticket in. And once Little One makes eye contact, the prince will be ours. No pendant needed."

"Are you sure?" Vilma asked, eyeing Shyla as if she'd like to punch her.

"Yes. She converted an entire monastery in two days without using a single pendant." Xerxes let that sink in. "We do have two fugitives from the Lyons monastery. They are probably heading to the Monks of Grane near Haiya. Vilma, assign a team to catch up with them and see that they don't reach it."

"Yes, sir."

Worry and fear for those monks flared. Guilt rose as well, but all those emotions disappeared as fast as they'd appeared like a strange unsettling tug of war. It was as if she was trapped in sluff sand, sinking faster the more she struggled to find firm ground.

"Zahoor, keep working on creating a good reason for the prince to hire us. Even with Little One's powers, the citizens and the Heliacal Priest need to see that we're vital to the city."

"Yes, sir," Zahoor said. He wore a sleeveless training tunic and loose pants. Scars marked his muscular arms.

"At angle zero we'll visit the Water Prince," Xerxes said to his team. "Vilma and Zahoor will accompany me and Little One." Then Xerxes gazed at Shyla. "A monk's tunic is not suitable for the King's emissary. Dayana, take her to the market and buy her clothing that is suitable for someone of her station." He handed the woman a small pouch of coins.

"Yes, sir." A short but powerful-looking woman, Dayana eyed Shyla like she was appraising a haunch of gamelu meat. "Do you want to hide the fact she's sun-kissed? Rumors have been swirling about a sun-kissed who overthrew and killed Zirdai's

Water Prince."

"I didn't kill him," Shyla said. "The Heliacal Priestess slit his throat before she committed suicide." That memory was clear. So why couldn't she recall why she shouldn't…no, she *should* be here listening to Xerxes.

Dayana raised a slender eyebrow. Everyone stared at Shyla with a variety of expressions from impressed to worried. Only Vilma's glare hadn't changed.

"Yes, hire a beautician to dye her hair, eyebrows and eyelashes."

"Yes, sir."

"You have your orders. You're dismissed." Xerxes strode from the room.

Dayana sighed. "Do I look like a fashion expert?" she asked Zahoor in a low whisper.

"You're a fashion disaster," Zahoor teased. "Just find a merchant that has fancy clothes and have her do all the work."

Another huff, but Dayana headed for the door. "Come on, Little One."

Shyla hesitated. Xerxes hadn't ordered her to go, but he'd be pleased if she looked more like an emissary. She hurried after the woman.

When she caught up, she tried to introduce herself. It didn't feel right for anyone to call her Little One except Xerxes.

"I don't want to know," Dayana said, interrupting her. "You wear a pendant so we call you the name Xerxes gives you. Soon you won't remember your real name."

Alarm pierced her like the sharp blade of a knife. She

stumbled to a stop, panting. Her harsh breaths echoed in her ears as she struggled to regain her independence. A defiant *I'm Shyla* broke through before her rebelliousness was tugged away. Her real name was… Her real name was…was…not important.

They went to the main market in the shaft. Druks and trol lanterns lit the cavernous space. The roar of the waterfall echoed and at times drowned out the buzz of shoppers. Business was brisk. Dayana wove through the stands until she found one selling silk tunics for women.

The merchant was more than happy to help dress Shyla. She picked a beautiful pale gray fabric that had small clusters of orange and green shapes that resembled flowers. Then the woman matched a solid light orange skirt to wear with it.

"Skirts are more refined for the professional woman," the merchant said.

The skirt almost reached the ground. "I can't fight in this," Shyla said.

"Doesn't matter," Dayana said. "Your job isn't to fight. That's what we're for."

In that case, Shyla allowed the nice lady to fit her and adjust the hem. The merchant also fashioned a head scarf out of the print and sold them a pair of sandals. Shyla disliked removing her boots but had to agree the sandals looked better with the nicer clothing. Still, she bought a new pack and put the monk's uniform and boots into it along with a wrap and a new sun cloak they'd purchased. The construction of the cloak was nicer than any other she'd owned. It reminded her of the commune in Zirdai where…people…did…something not important to

Shyla's current task.

The two of them then sought a beauty stall and told the beautician what they wanted.

"Black would be too severe," the woman said. "Let's go with a warm brown with honey highlights, and I'm going to trim the ends of your hair." She tsked. "They're a bit…ragged."

"That's because a deacon cut off all my hair and was about to shave the rest when I was rescued," Shyla said. Odd that she could remember all those details, yet whenever she tried to recall something more recent, it just slipped through her grasp.

"Oh my. Well, good thing hair grows," she said brightly. "Just relax and let me pamper you." The beautician proceeded to dye Shyla's hair, eyelashes, and eyebrows.

When Shyla looked at herself in the mirror, she stared at a stranger. But the person in the glass no longer needed to hide. No one would accuse her of being sun-cursed and try to kill her for being different. Yet there was a…wrongness to it. As if she betrayed…something. Or perhaps someone. Those feelings soon faded and her reflection matched her—the person Xerxes wanted. Little One. Yes, this would do.

Dayana studied her. "That'll work. Let's go, it's getting late."

The two women walked through the shaft. Little One drew more than a few glances. She didn't like the attention. A creepy-crawly sensation of being watched from the shadows brushed her skin.

"Relax," Dayana said. "You're the King's emissary. You're used to being noticed."

When they returned to the apartment, Xerxes was pleased.

Little One basked in his praise. He dismissed Dayana and showed Little One to her room. The sleeping cushion was big enough for two.

"There's some sleeping gowns in the trunk and other necessities for you. Do not leave your room. I will come for you with plenty of time for you to dress and eat before we visit the Water Prince."

"You're not staying?"

"No, Little One. I've done a number of terrible things for the old king. I'm ambitious and greedy and will do what it takes to get what I want, including murder. But I won't ever force a woman to have sex with me."

"But you're not—"

"Go to sleep, Little One."

"Yes, sir."

She changed and slipped under the fur. The cushion was comfortable, but she needed…needed…Xerxes…no…not him… The goddess's love smoothed her conflicted thoughts and Little One soon fell into a peaceful sleep.

Her peace was shattered when a hand clamped down over her mouth. A large figure crouched next to her. She relaxed and the hand released her. Xerxes had come to share her cushion after all. The druk that she left half open had been closed to a crack. Her eyes adjusted. And she smiled at—not Xerxes. She drew in a breath to yell.

Not-Xerxes held up his hands to show he was unarmed. He whispered, "Shyla, it's me. Rendor."

Those two names tugged hard on her soul. She struggled to

recall why they were…no they meant nothing. "Who?"

"Rendor. Come on, sunbeam. You're stronger than Xerxes. Fight the compulsion."

So many confusing statements. She scrambled for clarity.

"Let's get out of here, and then you can clear your head." He grabbed her hand and pulled her to her feet.

A familiar warmth spread at his touch.

"Just be really quiet. I don't want to wake Xerxes."

Xerxes. Her commander would not be pleased to find her gone when he came for her. The goddess's love sucked all the warmth from her body. Fear of not following orders sent icy tendrils through her.

Not-Xerxes towed her toward the threshold of her room. No. Xerxes said not to leave. Little One dug in her heels, stopping her forward momentum only for a moment. The man was strong and she knew he'd drag her away, thinking he was rescuing her.

She did not need to be rescued by *him*.

"Xerxes, help me!" Little One screamed.

The man froze and his expression creased with hurt betrayal. But it was gone in a flash. He dropped her hand and pulled his sword, turning to face the soldiers who had suddenly appeared. They too had drawn swords and a few had knives. Little One hovered on the threshold of her room. Conflicted, uncertain, and miserable.

Xerxes stood behind the half circle of his four-man team. He was unarmed and only wearing a pair of white silk sleeping pants. The muscles on his upper body looked as if they had been carved from stone. A pendant the size of her fist rested in the middle of his massive chest. The multifaceted yellowish-orange jewel in its center glinted, reflecting the druk light. It was about four centimeters wide. Her pendant warmed when she stared at the jewel.

"Captain Rendor," Xerxes said.

That name! It stabbed into her heart and cut it into two pieces—fear and guilt. She had endangered…him…no, she'd obeyed Xerxes. It was just the big man's name. The pain eased.

"It didn't take you long to find her," Xerxes said. "Good. I would have hated to set this trap every darkness." He held out his hand. "Little One, come here."

She dashed past the big man and grabbed Xerxes' hand. He tucked her close and her contentment returned full force. When she looked up, the big man stared at her. His expression was raw with grief.

"As you can see, she's mine," Xerxes said. "You've two choices, Captain."

"This ought to be good," the captain said to Xerxes, but he kept his gaze on her. Odd.

"You can join me or you can die."

That last word caused an eruption inside her. "No!"

Xerxes turned to her. "Little One?"

"He…can't…die." It took a great deal of energy for her to say those words. Similar to when she refused to explain how to wake The Eyes to Xerxes.

"Ah. It's like that, is it?"

"Yes," she gasped.

"Can you convert him?" Xerxes' tone was gentle.

"I'd rather die," the captain said. He brandished his sword. "I hope you have more men, Xerxes. You're going to need them."

"Captain, your skills are well known, but I'm not the commander because of my good looks. Little One?"

"I can, but…" She fought her own conflicting desires. Grabbing bits of fractured knowledge, she sorted through what she'd learned.

"But?" Xerxes prompted.

"He'll need a pendant." She panted for breath as if she'd run over a dozen dunes. "He's a big brute. Strong-willed."

"Yet I had him before in Nintri."

She couldn't lie to Xerxes. Her entire body trembled.

"Oh, please," the captain said, saving her. "That was all an act. And you fell for it."

Xerxes stiffened but otherwise ignored the jab. "All right, Little One. Can you disarm him?"

"No, but I can freeze him."

"That will work. Go ahead."

"Shyla, don't! Let me fight!" the captain yelled.

Freeze.

The captain fought the command, but she had him. It was easy. His soul was almost a part of hers. Xerxes pulled a pendant from his pocket and crossed to the captain. He looped the necklace around the big man's neck. With them facing each other, she noted a number of similarities—both broad shouldered, dark skinned, and powerful.

"Captain Rendor," Xerxes said. He held up the new pendant, capturing the big man's gaze.

Little One watched the fierce glower fade from the captain's eyes as he stared at the black jewel. It was replaced by a rapt expression. Xerxes told him the same thing he told her. She experienced a tug of jealousy. Xerxes was *hers.*

Xerxes tucked the pendant underneath the captain's tunic. "Keep this close."

"Yes, sir," he said.

"Very good..." Xerxes looked at her. "What shall we call him?" But he didn't wait for a reply. "I liked when you called him a big brute." He focused on Big Brute. "Go with my men, Big Brute. They will show you what's expected of one of my soldiers. I'll give you a few sun jumps to get settled before you're included on missions."

"Yes, sir," Big Brute snapped and followed the others from the apartment.

A strange hollowness pulsed inside her when he was gone.

"You did well, Little One." Xerxes clapped her on the shoulder. "Big Brute will be a wonderful addition to my team. From what I've heard about his skills and intelligence, he may soon work his way into my inner circle." Then he turned serious. "When you didn't return from Qulsary, I assumed you'd told the King everything you learned in Nintri. Am I right?"

"Yes, sir."

His gaze grew distant for a few moments. "I'm not overly worried about the King, but he might surprise me with unexpected resources. Can you convert him to our cause?"

"No, sir."

"Why not?"

"He's protected from The Eyes."

"But not from your magic?"

"I don't know. I didn't try to manipulate him."

"What about his power over water? Can you prevent him from using it?"

"I don't know."

Xerxes drummed his fingers on his thigh as he thought.

"How can you find out?"

"I can visit the King and try."

"No. I mean, who else might have this information?"

"Oh. Najib might know. And perhaps there is a record of it in one of the Rooms of Knowledge."

"Which room? There are dozens of them throughout Koraha."

"Most of the Rooms of Knowledge hold the same information. The monks have copied historical documents to distribute to all monasteries. Of course there are always those documents that are overlooked as not important and are not copied. I'd expect the Monks of Quirin would have the best information since they're closest to the castle. Also many of the monks keep journals, which are added to the rooms when they join the Sun Goddess."

"What about the rooms in Lyons?"

"They may have the information you seek. Monks do move to other monasteries and bring their records with them."

"Good to know." He glanced at the sand clock. It read angle three forty-five. "Are you tired? We can visit the prince the next sun jump. I want you at full strength."

"I'm…" She touched the back of her head. Pain pulsed. "Still recovering."

"All right. I'll give you a few more sun jumps. Go back to sleep, Little One."

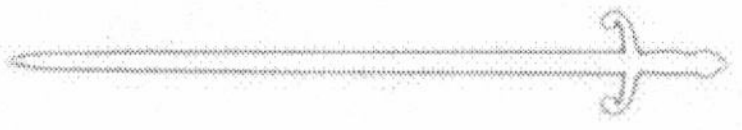

Four sun jumps later, Xerxes led their small parade down to the Water Prince's level. Unlike the rulers of most of the other cities, Apanji's leader did not live at the bottom of the city. Instead, he resided in the levels below where the water gushed out into the shaft. And he occupied the next eight levels down. His suite of rooms went deep instead of wide.

The entrance to this unique residence was on level fifty-eight. Similar to Nintri, there was an outer receiving room open to the public and a well-guarded inner door. Every single soldier tensed when they spotted their party, which included Xerxes, Vilma, Zahoor, and Little One. She hadn't seen Big Brute since he'd been converted, and it ached like a loss even when Xerxes' praise gave her such joy. Strange.

The receptionist was a thin man with a long black goatee, thick eyebrows, and a high forehead. He scowled at them.

Little One didn't waste time with pleasantries. She exposed the King's sigil and said, "I'm here to see the Water Prince."

When the receptionist didn't move, Xerxes said, "*Go*, announce us to the prince."

The man stood slowly, as if uncertain. "And who should I say is here?"

"The King's emissary and her retinue. *Go*," Xerxes ordered.

The receptionist glanced at Little One. "Is it urgent? He's in a meeting."

"Of course it is." She added heat to her voice.

"Then please follow me." The man waved the guards aside as he led them through the inner door and to another reception room.

This one was intended for the prince's guests. It was cozy with thick cushions and a pot of hot tea simmering on lava stones. The sound of the waterfall rumbled through the stone walls—a muted roar. She wondered how close they were and if there was any chance that the water would break through.

"Please wait here. I'll be back in less than a degree." The receptionist bolted.

"Don't get comfortable," Xerxes said to all of them.

"Must be nice to have that type of influence," Vilma said to her in a sneering tone. "The King's sigil *and* magic. Guess you're just one lucky girl."

Lucky? Anger rose. She opened her mouth to correct the woman, but Xerxes touched her arm.

"Don't let her goad you, Little One. She's jealous."

"Jealous? Come on, Commander, you know better. And when she ruins all our plans, just remember who warned you."

"Repeatedly, I know. But she's ours now. If we'd killed her when you wanted—"

"We'd still be here. Still on schedule. She's not the resource you think she is."

Vilma had wanted her dead? Little One couldn't quite summon the outrage. She was too distracted by a wisp of memory about the woman. The second-in-command hadn't bothered to hide her hatred for Little One, but there was…something else. Little One chased that thin tendril, but when she reached out, it slipped through her grasp and was gone.

"She's about to prove you very wrong, Vilma," Xerxes said.

"The Water Prince will see you now." The receptionist

gestured for them to follow him.

He led them down a tunnel. The roar of the waterfall increased in volume as they drew closer to a set of large stained-glass doors guarded by four soldiers. The sound doubled when the doors were open. Inside, the Water Prince sat on an oversized chair at a massive marble desk. But that wasn't nearly as impressive as the water behind him. It fell in sheets just past a square opening in the wall. Stunned, it took her a moment to realize it was the underside of the waterfall.

"Classic power move," Xerxes said just loud enough for her to hear, which was pretty loud. They would have to shout for anyone more than a meter away to understand them.

The Water Prince, an older man with gray sprinkled in his short auburn hair, didn't bother rising to greet them. He pointed her to a chair opposite him.

"Insist on moving to a quieter location," Xerxes ordered her.

Instead of sitting, she introduced herself to the Water Prince. As soon as she met his gaze, he was hers. "Take us to your real office."

Without a word, the prince stood and led them from the room. The guards followed them to another area, which was just as lavishly furnished but much quieter. The guards were ordered to remain in the hallway. It was in here that Xerxes gave the prince a pendant and claimed the man.

"Usually it takes me a number of visits to wear them down," Xerxes said to her, but it was also an I-told-you-so to Vilma. "Once they've given in, I present the pendant. Then I have to work on their advisors. It's a long process, but with you, we'll finish by apex. Prince Ibrahim, please invite your inner circle to join us."

They met and claimed the prince's entire staff and a few of the guards. The captain of the guard was notably absent.

"Could Rendor have warned the captain about us?" Xerxes asked Vilma.

"It's possible. He was in the city for about eight sun jumps. You'll have to ask him."

"Why me? I told him to obey you as well."

"Yeah, well, you gave him the perfect name. Big Brute is stubborn even with the pendant. Either that or it's working too well on him and you're the only one he'll obey."

"Then I'll have another chat with him. Have him report to me here."

"Yes, sir," Vilma said and strode from the room.

The thought of seeing Big Brute again made Little One happy even though she was tired from converting so many people and exhausted by the constant fluctuations in her emotions.

Xerxes worked with the prince, instructing him on how to conduct business and to pay the taxes to Xerxes and his mercs instead of the King. Little One found a soft oversized cushion and listened to Xerxes. Eventually she could no longer follow the conversation. She curled up and fell asleep.

A familiar deep voice woke her up. And for one brief moment she remembered the man attached to that voice. The desire to run to him pulsed through her muscles. But when she opened her eyes, her gaze was immediately drawn to Xerxes. Big Brute was relaxed and smiling, answering questions about settling in with his new squad, suggesting changes to improve training.

Except he had trouble remembering the recent past and if he had talked to Apanji's captain of the guard or not. He claimed those details were blurry. But when Xerxes put more force into his questions, Big Brute snapped to attention.

"I warned Captain Mahira, sir," Big Brute said.

A crease of worry furrowed his brow.

"Don't fret, Big Brute. That was before you were working for me. Do you know where she might have gone?"

"No, but if it was me…"

"Go on."

"I'd take my most skilled guards and set up a base of operations in an unknown location in the city."

"Unknown?"

"All underground cities have places that have been forgotten by almost everyone. Vagrants will squat in those areas, but if the guards are any good at their jobs, they know these locations as well and will sweep them every dozen sun jumps or so."

"So I need to ask one of the guards where these locations are?"

"That would be the best way to find the captain."

Little One's stomach knotted at the thought of Captain Mahira being caught. The goddess's love tugged at her worry, yet with Big Brute in the room, her resistance lasted a bit longer.

"Excellent," Xerxes said. "Vilma, bring me a few of the

prince's guards."

"Yes, sir." She left.

While she was gone, Xerxes and Big Brute discussed strategy and tactics. They both knew quite a bit and she was content to listen and learn.

Vilma soon returned with two guards who were escorted by four armed mercs. The guards' expressions switched from angry to scared when they spotted the commander. They refused to answer any of Xerxes' questions about their captain.

"Little One, can you find this information in their souls?" Xerxes asked.

"Yes, sir." She met the woman's gaze first. Reaching for her thoughts, Little One sorted through her memories. She tried to ignore the woman's emotions as they were...difficult for Little One. "This woman doesn't know where Captain Mahira is, but she has a couple of guesses."

"Try the other," Xerxes ordered.

Little One made eye contact with the man. He jerked back as if she'd punched him. But distance wouldn't help him. She rifled through his thoughts and emotions. "He knows where they're hiding. They're on level twenty-seven in the northwest quadrant. There's a number of abandoned storage areas that had been used by a textile manufacturer."

The guard was horrified. He pressed his hands to his mouth as if that would block her from getting the information.

"How many of them?" Xerxes asked her.

"They have forty-four in total, but they're not all there at one time. They rotate, keeping their shifts so they'll know when you make your move."

"Do they know?"

"Yes. You were spotted heading to the prince's residence."

"They might still believe they're safe," Xerxes said, more to himself. "I think we need to shatter that notion. The sooner the better."

"Do you want him to show you the way?" she asked Xerxes.

"Yes."

"I won't," the man shouted.

"Oh, you poor soul," Xerxes said, almost gleeful. "Haven't you figured out that you don't have a choice?"

Xerxes asked her to convert him and his partner. It was easily done. Too easy. A demonstration of just how much power she held. Again conflicted emotions surged and drained.

Xerxes had watched her. Then he glanced at Vilma. "Do you know what I'm thinking?"

She smiled. It was borderline feral. "If she has the juice."

"Oh, she has it," Xerxes said. "We can convert *all* the prince's guards without using any pendants. The city will be ours. We don't have to pretend to be mercs anymore and slowly take over each city. We can just go in and conquer!" Excited, Xerxes picked up Little One and spun her around. "All because of you!"

His last two sentences sent a jolt of horror right through her and for a crystal-clear moment, she had control. But he noticed her expression and quickly set her down. He pulled out her pendant. Shyla closed her eyes—she didn't need to see to influence him with her magic. Except she forgot his ability to slip out of her magical reach. Was it due to his own pendant?

He laughed. "You don't need to see the jewel. Not when I do this..."

She opened her eyes. He'd taken his pendant out. The beautiful yellowish-orange jewel winked at her. Then he touched the jewel to the one on hers. Suddenly, she was sucked into the blackness. All her thoughts and emotions—her soul—were trapped within the jewel's depths.

Shyla struggled to return to her body. Hard unyielding and invisible walls kept her contained. She banged against them in sudden terror. Nothing. Not even a sound.

Her thoughts turned to her physical body. Had it become a mindless minion? Did her magic stay with her body? Those questions actually helped settle her panicked thoughts. In order to wield her magic, she had to gather her will. And since her will was in here, then Xerxes couldn't use her. Small comfort. Better than nothing.

It didn't take long to figure out she was well and truly trapped. No matter how hard she concentrated or exerted her will, she remained locked within the jewel. Xerxes' yellowish-orange stone had to be a magical artifact like The Eyes of Tamburah, allowing the wearer great power and influence over those wearing the black pendants. The connection was obvious now that she could think clearly. Still didn't help her, though.

Then a surge of energy filled her and she was ejected from the jewel. She slammed into her body with such force she toppled to the ground. Pain burned inside her as if she'd been set on fire. She moaned.

Xerxes crouched over her. "That's what happens when you

fight me. I could have kept you in there forever. Even after your body had withered and died." He held up her pendant. "Look."

She stared at the black jewel. It soothed her soul, but not the pain in her body. "Why…" It was difficult to talk with her blood boiling.

"Everything has consequences, Little One. The pain will go away when you have learned your lesson." Xerxes stood, leaving her on the floor. "Vilma, take a unit and Big Brute and go clean out that nest of guards on level twenty-seven," Xerxes ordered.

They were still there? It seemed as if she had been trapped a long time.

"But sir, he's—"

"The one who came up with the idea to interview the guards." He turned to Big Brute. "You need to listen to Vilma. She's in charge. Understand?"

"Yes, sir." He followed Vilma from the room, but before leaving he met Little One's gaze and there was a spark of the man he'd been. Then it was gone.

She lost track of the time, her surroundings…everything. Her world consisted of one thing. Pain. She burned and sizzled as if staked to the sand at apex.

When it finally stopped, the world around her solidified—the hard floor underneath her, the cold air on her sensitive skin, the bone-deep ache in her body as if she'd used too much of her magic.

Xerxes soon crouched next to her. "Better?"

"Yes," she croaked.

He scooped her off the ground and carried her through the prince's residence until they reached a large guest suite. Xerxes settled them both onto a sleeping cushion. He pulled her close so her head rested on his shoulder. No inner voice screamed warnings. It was silent. Little One sighed and relaxed against him. The goddess's love had granted her peace again.

"Remember when I said there were different levels of obedience?" Xerxes asked her. He didn't wait for an answer. "What happened with the pendants was me taking more of you. I can take all of you and you would exist in that jewel forever, but I don't wish to do that. You're smart. And your power can help me immensely. I know you're horrified by my methods. But consider that with your help, there will be no bloodshed. No one needs to die. Isn't that better than some violent takeover?"

She had to admit it was better. "What do you want?"

"Ah, that's complicated. At first I planned to have my soldiers in all the cities, offering to help keep them safe. Except most of the Water Princes and Princesses refused my aid, clinging to the belief that the King would save them and demonstrating to me that they're not smart enough to protect their cities. I found a way to convince them that they needed me and my soldiers. And the quality of life has improved in all my cities. I can keep doing it my slower way, or you can help me speed up my timeline."

He shifted slightly so he could meet her gaze. "Will you help me?"

"Of course." It was the right thing to do. And it was refreshing not to be conflicted anymore. Her internal struggle was gone.

"Thank you. Now sleep, Little One."

She immediately fell into a restful slumber.

Over the next fourteen sun jumps, Little One worked with Xerxes, converting the prince's guards, including Captain Mahira, and testing his mercs for magical potential. She found only three—two women and a man. When she explained the process of opening their power, one woman refused. That was when Little One learned that Xerxes' original soldiers had not been influenced by his magic. They'd signed up due to loyalty. Those that wore pendants had been…collected by the commander as people useful to him.

Xerxes didn't order the soldier who had refused to let Little One unlock her magic, so she only opened the two and taught them how to wield it. They were quick to learn.

That darkness Xerxes praised her efforts. As a reward, he stayed with her as they slept. Just having his warm body next to her relaxed her, but he didn't do it often.

Her new assignment came the next sun jump. Xerxes woke her when he brought her first meal.

"How do you manage to get up without waking me?" she asked between bites.

"Your sleep is undisturbed by worries or fears. A benefit of the goddess's love."

"Your pendant doesn't give you peace?" That was sad.

"No, I get something better. Eat, Little One. I'd like you to go to the monastery and do some research."

Research? A jolt of excitement pierced her. "On what?"

"The King's power. How he moves the water. How he blocks the power of The Eyes. If magic can be used on him."

"The information might not be there," she said. The last thing she wanted was to disappoint Xerxes.

"I know. But if anyone can find it, it's you."

She preened. "There are four Rooms of Knowledge. How long do I have?"

"Until the taxes arrive and we need to leave for Haiya." He paused. "About forty sun jumps. Will that be enough?"

Forty sun jumps to do research! It was the best gift Xerxes could ever give her. "It should be. It'll help if I have a research assistant—one of the monks who is familiar with the collection."

"You can request anything you need. But take your pack as you'll stay at the monastery until you've gone through all the rooms."

"By myself?" The thought was horrifying. She needed to be with him.

Xerxes smiled. "Of course not. I'm going to send a few of my people with you. Not that I think you'll be attacked in the monastery, but we haven't found those two monks, Walkur and what's-her-name, and I don't want you to be...bothered on the way to the monastery."

"Are you coming as well?"

"No, but I want you to send me a message if you find anything. Then I'll come visit and hear what you've learned."

In other words, he was giving her a big incentive to do a thorough job. "All right."

After first meal, she packed her few possessions and changed into the standard monk's tunic and pants. When she'd finished, she found Xerxes with three of his team—Zahoor and a man and woman she didn't recognize. A part of her had been hoping Xerxes would assign Big Brute to her mission. Her disappointment lingered, which was odd.

"This is Kamila and Fareed," Xerxes said. "They will stay with you at the monastery. Zahoor is just escorting you through the desert."

Kamila and Fareed kept their expressions neutral, but they both wondered what they'd done to upset the commander. Babysitting wasn't what they'd signed on to do. They wore civilian clothes, and except for the hidden weapons, they blended in with the citizens of Apanji.

Xerxes must have sensed their reluctance. "Little One is our greatest asset. Nothing is to happen to her, do you understand?"

"Yes, sir," they said in unison.

"The monks are excellent fighters or I would have assigned a dozen to guard her. Use the monks if there's trouble."

"Yes, sir."

"Good. You're dismissed."

Little One walked with Zahoor while the other two remained a step behind. They climbed to the surface. After spending the last nineteen sun jumps underground, she welcomed the sun.

The heat wrapped around her like a fur, chasing away the chill that had settled in her bones.

She spotted the monks on patrol before the others and soon they were underground again. Egan was consulted.

"Neda will know the monk most familiar with the collection," Egan said. "In the meantime, you can have your pick of rooms in the guest wing. I'll send the monk to you. Do you need anything else?"

"Since I'm going to be spending all my time in the rooms, can you have someone bring water and meals for me and my companions?"

"Of course." Egan hurried away.

Little One, Kamila, and Fareed picked three rooms in a row. By the time she unpacked, Neda had arrived.

The ex-leader panted. She must have run to the guest wing.

Deep lines etched Neda's face and she appeared to have aged ten circuits. Little One lowered her shield to read the monk. Neda's emotions swirled and her internal conflict was clear. She both hated Little One and hoped the girl would break the curse.

Curse? That didn't sound good. After a little more digging she discovered what Neda meant. The monk thought the compulsion the girl had put on all of them to obey that idiot Egan was a curse. They couldn't refuse his orders. It was degrading, humiliating, and perverted. They were quite aware of what was going on but unable to stop or say anything against him. Torture.

Little One rocked back on her heels. That wasn't how it was supposed to work. They needed to be at peace and content to do the goddess's bidding. She needed to send a message to Xerxes that the conversions with The Eyes had gone wrong. She stormed into Kamila's room.

"Something the matter?" Kamila asked.

"Yes." She explained the problem.

"Is there a chance they can break the compulsion?" Kamila asked.

"No, but we need to fix it," she said. And also for the Water Prince and all his guards!

"Why? It's working. And you need to do your research for the commander," she said. "He will be upset if you don't find anything."

Although she fought it as long as possible, the desire to please Xerxes soon overruled all other thoughts. She returned to her room and asked Neda about the Rooms of Knowledge.

"I can help you," Neda said. "I've spent the most time in them."

Little One explained what information she sought.

"We should start in the Fourth Room," Neda said. At least the monk was happy to be helping.

They went down to the southeast corner of level twenty. Two oversized stained-glass doors blocked the entrance to the Fourth Room of Knowledge. The colored panels depicted the two sky pillars. Except they extended all the way to the sky and supported a dais for the Sun Goddess's throne. The deity sat on a beautiful plush cushion of red and gold. Little One studied the goddess's expression. She appeared very disappointed.

The two monks on guard unlocked the doors and allowed

them inside. Fareed had remained behind. He and Kamila would take turns staying with her. The stacks of shelves and piles of scrolls filled most of the space. There were many small rooms scattered throughout with study tables and cushions. Also plenty of druks. Basically the place was a maze, which could be said for all the Rooms of Knowledge.

Neda moved with confidence. She collected a number of scrolls and tablets and placed them into a pile on one of the tables.

"This is my favorite reading nook," Neda said, gathering a couple more druks to brighten the space. Once the documents filled the table, she stopped. "That should be enough for now."

Little One and Neda sat down to read while Kamila stood nearby. Taking one of the scrolls from the pile, Little One held it for a moment. The smell of dried velbloud skin and dust awoke a dozen memories. She inhaled and took a moment to savor the true contentment of being somewhere that she loved.

The sun jumps piled up as they worked. While Little One learned a number of interesting facts about the kings of Koraha and how they found their successors, she didn't discover anything related to their magical abilities. She wondered if this particular information would only be found at the King's castle. Was there a Room of Knowledge somewhere inside? Or perhaps it was kept at the closest monastery with the Monks of Quirin.

Ten or eleven sun jumps into the research, Little One learned that there had once been over eight thousand cities on the surface of Koraha. These cities slowly died over time and the residents perished due to huge sandstorms and epic droughts that drained aquafers. Survivors migrated to the last freshwater lake until it dried up. Then they had to dig deeper and deeper to reach water.

The twelve underground cities of Koraha were all roughly within a 2800-kilometer-wide circle with Qulsary located at the highest elevation and Catronia at the lowest.

But the most interesting and relevant fact to her current research was that the King had moved from Zirdai to Qulsary *because* of the water. Of course the details were thin—they always were. She compared the water level of both cities. Zirdai's was down around level ninety-seven and Qulsary's was at forty-five. They didn't have to dig as deep in Qulsary, but all the cities had roughly the same amount of water. She remembered someone...Big Brute?...had said that the water flowing out of Zirdai eventually went to another city. Could all the water for all the cities be connected? But what did that have to do with the King?

She mulled it over. Perhaps it was just easier for the King to access the water in Qulsary. He wouldn't have to use as much energy to fill his vault and protect his throne and secret chambers. While interesting, it didn't explain how the King's magic worked or how to counter it so Little One continued her search.

Little One returned to her room well into darkness. Her back ached, her butt was numb, her shoulders were stiff, and pain pulsed in the spot right between her eyes, causing her vision to blur. They'd been working later and later as they only had ten sun jumps left. While she waited in the hallway, Kamila checked her small room for intruders, declared it safe, and headed to her sleeping cushion. Fareed remained outside to stand guard.

When Little One entered, she paused. A strangeness brushed against her, encouraging her to be calm and quiet. The inclination stopped just as two people appeared right in front of her.

She jumped in surprise as the woman pressed a finger to her lips. The young man beside her grinned before almost tackling Little One as he hugged her. Confusion swirled. Where had they come from? At least they hadn't attacked. Not yet.

"Okay, rat, that's enough," the woman whispered.

"I want a turn."

They exchanged places and now the woman squeezed Little One to her. She smelled familiar.

"We missed you!" the woman whispered and in the next breath said, "What in the seven hells are you doing here?" Then she released her and stepped back. "Wait, don't answer that yet. Are you distracting the stiff outside, rat?"

"Of course. And the other one who's in her room," the young man said at a normal volume, seeming not at all upset to be called a rat.

"Good." The woman focused on Little One. Her light green eyes narrowed. "Okay, now you can tell us what in the seven hells you're doing here. Are you working undercover? Why didn't you meet us at the rendezvous location? What's going on?"

Little One didn't have answers to any of those questions, but she did have one of her own. “Who are you?”

The woman gaped at her. "Is this a joke?"

"If you're not monks, you need to leave," Little One said.

"I think she's serious," the young man said. "Shyla, it's *us.* Gurice and Mojag."

"Gurice as in your *best* friend." The woman…Gurice…crossed her arms and scowled at her.

"I know you?" Her unreliable memories once again failed to make a connection.

"Gurice, I think she's been influenced," Mojag said. "Something's not right."

"That's impossible. She has The Eyes. No one is stronger than her." Gurice stepped closer to Little One. "Look at me. *See* my memories."

At first Little One averted her gaze, but then she noticed Mojag's worried expression and it stirred a protective instinct inside her. Xerxes hadn't told her what to do in this situation.

And she wasn't in danger. They were obviously brother and sister with their similar eyes and tall thin builds.

Determined, Little One met Gurice's gaze. Her recent memories showed them traveling from Zirdai to Apanji. The sense of urgency. The worry when Shyla and Rendor failed to show up at the rendezvous location. Then, further back, the friendship and comradery as they built a new headquarters. The fierce loyalty of fighting together to unseat the maniacal Water Prince and corrupt Heliacal Priestess. They were more than best friends. They were both… The goddess's love tugged at the emotions attached to the memories. It tried to wash them away, replace them with thoughts of Xerxes.

"Shyla, look." Mojag had pulled up his sleeve, exposing his left arm up to his shoulder.

And on his bicep…Little…no…Shyla drew in a sharp breath as pain surged through her—the goddess's punishment for thinking such thoughts. But Shyla stared at the symbol glowing on Mojag's arm. An important symbol. Fire replaced her blood and she cried out and fell to her knees.

Gurice leaned over and grabbed her arms, supporting her. "Mojag, what did you do?"

"Nothing, I swear!"

"Gurice," Shyla panted, clinging to her friend's arms. If she let go, she'd be swept away.

Gurice crouched down. "Tell me how to help you."

"That symbol…what…" Another wave of intense pain slammed into her. She collapsed onto the ground with a moan.

"It's the Invisible Sword's symbol," Gurice said, pulling her into her lap. "It's *your* symbol. You're our leader."

"Show…me." Black and white spots danced in her vision, threatening to send her to oblivion.

"Mojag, cut her sleeve off," Gurice ordered.

There was a snick of a blade and he sliced the material open, exposing her bicep. On it glowed the same symbol. But it soon brightened until it pushed the darkness consuming her vision back. The pain eased a fraction.

Shyla groped for the necklace around her neck. Her fingers brushed the metal and she jerked her hand away with a cry. It had burnt her fingertips and increased the agony pulsing through her body.

"Scorching hells. Did you see that?" Gurice asked.

"Yeah, and smelled it, too." He crinkled his nose. "Burnt flesh."

"I can't…take…it…off…" Shyla dug her fingernails into Gurice's arm. "Can…you…please…"

"Will it burn me, too?"

"Not…sure."

"I'll do it." Mojag grabbed the necklace with both hands and yanked it off Shyla's head. The pendant swung free.

"Don't look at it," Shyla cried, grabbing the pendant and hiding it in her fist. "I need something to crush the jewel."

Mojag glanced around. He brought the druk lantern over. "Will this work?"

"I hope so." Shyla placed the pendant on the ground face down. Then she bashed the lantern onto it as hard as she could. Instead of looking at the jewel, she slipped a hand under and felt smooth edges. "It didn't break."

"Wait!" Mojag rummaged around in his pack. "Aha!" He pulled out a chisel and a fist-sized stone.

"What are you doing with those?" Gurice asked.

"We're in a new city. Sometimes even I need to mark my route to keep from getting lost. I know, surprising." He handed Shyla the tools.

"Look away," Shyla said.

Even she closed her eyes as she flipped the pendant around. Going by feel, she lined up the edge of the metal tool along the center of the black jewel. Then she slammed the rock down on the chisel's handle. Hard.

A loud crack reverberated through her hands as the jewel fractured. At the same time her heart lurched as if the chisel had cleaved it in two. Pain exploded in her chest. The darkness was instant.

A pinprick of yellow light speared the darkness like a sun ray. It hit a figure made of crystal and fractured into a dozen arcs of colorful light. The crystal glowed with a soft golden hue. The figure turned and faced Shyla. The Sun Goddess studied her and frowned. Exquisitely beautiful, with hair that flowed to the floor, the goddess emanated power and warmth, melting the ice that had coated Shyla's frozen body.

What are you doing here? the Sun Goddess asked.

I…don't know where here *is. Am I trapped inside the jewel?*

You are in the sky.

I died? She rubbed her chest. It ached for a number of reasons. The biggest over never seeing Rendor again. And not being able to apologize for trapping him. Other memories sprang to life, revealing all the terrible things she had done. She had abused the power of The Eyes just like she'd feared, taking another step toward Tamburah's madness.

I did not call you here, the Sun Goddess said.

Of course not. I should be burning in the seven caverns of hell for all I've done.

You did what you had to and it led you to me. I have another task for you, Shyla Sun-Kissed.

She couldn't refuse the goddess, but she did question her choice of champion. Obviously Shyla hadn't been strong enough to resist the jewel's power.

Stop the enslavement of my people.

Again with the stop! *How?*

By doing what you do best.

But I'm the reason many of your people are enslaved. I'm weak and will continue to exploit the power of The Eyes. I'm—

Not Tamburah. You are my *champion,* the goddess said, as if that settled the matter beyond all doubt.

It didn't. Shyla almost growled at her. *But—*

Wake up, Shyla Sun-Kissed. Your friends are working hard to get you back.

"Are you sure this is the right thing to do?" Gurice asked. She was straddling Shyla and had her hands pressing down on her chest. "She's not responding."

"That's what Zhek said to do. Keep the pressure even and don't slow down. One and two and three and four," Mojag said, chanting the rhythm. His fingers were pinching Shyla's nose closed. His other hand was pushing her jaw up, tipping her head back.

A bruising pain ringed Shyla's heart and chest. Her ribs creaked alarmingly and pain radiated out with every compression. Her mouth was dry and her throat raw. Mojag leaned over like he was going to kiss her.

He met her gaze and jerked back. "Stop! Stop! She's awake!"

"Thank the goddess," Gurice said, rolling off Shyla and sprawling on the floor as if exhausted.

He checked her pulse. "What's your name?" Mojag waved two fingers in front of her. "How many fingers am I holding up?"

"Shyla, two, and what's going on?"

Mojag sagged with relief. "I think we just saved your life."

Memories of her conversation with the Sun Goddess rose unbidden. Was this what the goddess meant about working hard? "How?"

"Zhek taught me." He waved a hand. "Thought I needed to learn since I always seem to be in the thick of trouble." Then he smirked at his sister. "See? I told you that you needed me."

"I apologize for yelling at you for stowing away," Gurice said.

He'd stowed away? She bet it would be a good story for later. She pushed up to her elbows with a groan. Her entire torso hurt.

"I think you might have cracked my ribs."

"Zhek said that can happen," Mojag said. "Better than dead."

True. "How long was I…dead?"

"An angle. Maybe less," Mojag said. "Zhek told me that I couldn't hesitate. I only had a limited time."

"What about Fareed?"

"Who?"

"The guard." Shyla pointed to the door.

"Oh, I have him. He didn't hear a thing." He shrugged like it wasn't a big deal.

Shyla glanced at Gurice. Her friend mouthed the word *later*. Oh yes, they had lots to discuss. But for now… Water. She had a horrible taste in her mouth. In fact, all three of them drank deeply from their water skins. Too bad every swallow hurt.

Wiping her mouth on her sleeve, Gurice asked, "What's going on, Shyla?"

She explained about Xerxes and Lonato's plans to take over all the cities and monasteries in Koraha.

"And they're using these pendants to coerce people?" Gurice asked in disgust.

"Yes. The jewels on them are very powerful."

"I'll say,' Mojag said, kicking the broken pendant away.

"No wonder you asked us for help. Can we even beat these guys?"

"I've no idea. I don't know how the magic in the pendants work. I can free everyone I…" Nausea swelled along with a deep shame. She forced the words out. "I coerced. But they still have their pendants and magic. That's harder to remove." Shyla had barely freed Rendor from Xerxes' compulsion after their first encounter with the commander. "But I do think if you remove each person's...black pendant, the person should recover."

"But you died!" Mojag cried.

"I think cracking it wasn't the right thing to do."

"You think?"

"Mojag, be nice."

"No, he's right. I've no idea how to counter the pendants."

"We should free Rendor. We're going to need him," Gurice said.

There was nothing she'd love more than having Rendor by her side, except... "That would tip off Xerxes. We're not ready to go against him."

"Then what do you want to do?"

By doing what you do best, the goddess had said. "Research."

"Excuse me?"

"I'm going to stay here and do research on those pendants. We need more information."

"But you don't have much time before you're expected back." Gurice peered at her as if trying to read her mind. "Are you going to pretend to be enslaved to get close to Xerxes?"

"Would he know you've broken your jewel?" Mojag asked. He twisted the end of his tunic as a worried expression creased his brow.

That was very possible. "If he does, then he'll come here."

"Why here? Why wouldn't he expect you to run away?"

"Rendor," Gurice said for her. "He must know you care about him."

"Yes. And the city is filled with his mercs and the guards so I'd be spotted pretty quick. My best bet would be to remain here and recruit monks to help rescue Rendor. However, Xerxes doesn't know the Invisible Sword have arrived in Apanji."

"Unless Rendor told him."

"Rendor wouldn't," Mojag said with a firm I'm-right-and-don't-try-to-argue-with-me tone.

Gurice didn't look as convinced but instead asked, "What should we do?"

Ah. Good question. Shyla considered. "Can you keep an eye on Rendor? Track his location so when it's time to escape, I know where to find him?"

"That's easy," Mojag said. "Give us something harder to do."

"Who else is here?" Shyla asked.

"Jaft and Rae insisted on coming," Gurice said. "We also brought Vashi, Lamar, Nard, and Balin."

Rae and Lamar were magic wielders. Jaft, Nard, Balin, and Vashi were strong fighters. Gurice was the brains and Mojag was the secret weapon. No one expected a gangly fourteen-circuit-old boy to be a threat. Yet he wielded the strongest magic of everyone in the Invisible Sword except Shyla.

"I have another task for you." She explained what she needed them to do. "Of course our plans will all change if Xerxes figures out I'm no longer his biggest fan."

"And in that case?" Gurice asked.

"We'll figure it out then."

"Well, I'm not worried. At all." Gurice's sarcastic tone suggested otherwise.

"Aw, come on, sis. It'll be fun. We're the Invisible Sword. That commander fellow won't know what hit him."

Ah, the confidence of youth. Shyla glanced at the sand clock. Angle three-forty. Kamila would be in to wake her in twenty angles.

"My two guards and I will go to first meal at angle zero," she said to them. "You can leave then." She picked up the pendant. Cracks zigzagged through the jewel. The black stone no longer glinted with iridescence. "I need to wear this. If my expression turns rapt, Mojag, please yank this off of me." She paused, unwilling to loop it around her neck.

"Wait," Gurice said. "Give me that."

Shyla handed it over. Gurice yanked a necklace out from under her tunic. It had four thin round disks hanging on it. Opening the clasp, Gurice pulled two of the disks off, closed it, and tucked it back. She added the disks to the pendant's chain and returned it to Shyla. Written on one of the silver disks was Gurice's name and Mojag's was etched on the other.

"Now you won't forget us," Gurice said.

Touched by the gesture, Shyla squeezed her friend's hand. "Thank you." She donned the chain and slipped the pendant down next to her skin. She braced for the goddess's love to drain her will. The siblings stared at her, but nothing happened. Everyone relaxed.

"It was our mother's," Mojag said with melancholy darkening his gaze. "All of our names together."

Shyla pressed her hand to her heart. "I'll make sure you get these back."

"We haven't been a family in so long. Makes more sense for them to be apart. You keep them."

Poor Mojag had seen so much death in his short life. Shyla vowed that when this was over, she'd ensure they'd be a family.

Angle zero came a heartbeat after she lay down. She blinked at Kamila's blurry face, then blinked a few more times to bring the woman into focus. Shyla's room appeared to be empty, but she sensed the magical commands keeping Gurice and Mojag's presence from the guard.

Shyla's entire body hurt and pain ringed her chest from her cracked ribs. She wished Zhek had sent his pain relief medicine with the Invisible Swords. The temptation to return to her comfortable cushion and recover from dying pulsed in her exhausted body, but her time was limited.

The guards went with her to the dining area to eat first meal and then Fareed returned to his room to sleep and Kamila accompanied her to the Second Room of Knowledge. Neda waited for them in their reading nook. The monk had pulled out a number of new tablets. Had the woman slept at all? Not according to the dark circles around her eyes.

Gathering her will, Shyla sent Kamila to sleep, catching the guard before she hit the hard ground. Then she freed Neda from the compulsion.

Neda swayed and Shyla moved to help, but the woman held out a hand. "Don't come any closer."

Understanding, she stopped as shame twisted inside her. Neda had good reason to hate her, but Shyla hoped she'd still be willing to help her.

Neda straightened, visibly pulling herself together as she drew in a few deep breaths. "What changed?"

In response, Shyla pulled out the broken pendant. "I'm free from Xerxes' compulsion."

"Who is Xerxes?"

She explained what had happened and what she needed to do.

"You'll free all the monks." It wasn't quite a question, more of a demand.

"Yes, but not all at once. I don't want Egan tipping Xerxes off. I can do it slowly over the next nine sun jumps and then when we leave, you can deal with Egan."

Neda considered. "How do we deal with him?"

"I hope to learn how to counter his pendant. It might be as easy as taking it off, but at this point I don't know."

"And all this..." She gestured to Shyla and Kamila and herself. "Is due to magic?"

"Yes. I know it's hard to believe. But—"

Once again Neda held up a hand. "Who are you really?"

This might be the deal breaker. "I'm Shyla Sun-Kissed, leader of the Invisible Sword and the King's emissary." She exposed the sigil.

"Anything else?"

"I'm the daughter of Hanif Parzival and Zirdai's new Heliacal Priestess." And, according to the Sun Goddess, her champion.

"Well. That's quite the list. If anyone is going to fix this mess, it'll be you. All right. Let's get to work." She rubbed her hands together and glanced around. "We need to go back to the Fourth Room; there's an entire collection of scrolls on historically significant artifacts." She pointed to Shyla's face. "The Eyes are mentioned in one of them."

The woman was sharp. Good. "Then we'll tell Kamila that you remembered a collection of scrolls on the history of the Kings of Koraha."

"We're going to need more help," Neda said.

"Then gather your best researchers. They can be the first group I set free."

After moving to the Fourth Room of Knowledge and adding six more people to the research group, they read through the collection. To avoid alerting Kamila and Fareed, the researchers called anything that might be about the pendants the King's gifts and showed the reference to Shyla. It still took them about four sun jumps to find anything of value.

Neda set a scroll in front of Shyla, covering the one she was reading. "This mentions the King's power to rule. Perhaps there's something more to it."

"Thank you. I'll take a closer look." Shyla clamped down on a groan. The text had been written in the language of the kings. Archaic and difficult to read, the dialect changed throughout the circuits, morphing with time, which made it even more maddening to decipher.

However, it didn't take her too long to realize this might be exactly what they'd been searching for. Trying to keep her expression neutral even though her pulse raced, Shyla translated the text. It reported a set of pendants that were gifted to the first King of Koraha. When the people finally realized that in order to survive they needed to stop killing each other over their dwindling resources, they banded together.

These pendants were set with two different one-of-a-kind gemstones. One was a sunfire, a bright yellowish-orange jewel, which they claimed held the essence of the sun. The other held a blackfire, an opaque black jewel with a sheen of iridescence, which held the essence of the earth. And since the sun ruled the earth, the sunfire commanded the blackfire.

Shyla found a reference to the people wanting their king to have one loyal advisor. After circuits of war, the leaders were naturally suspicious of each other and it was exhausting being on guard all the time. They gave the King the means to ensure he'd have someone he could trust with his life. Therefore the King wore the sunfire pendant and his closest advisor—the one who woke The Eyes—wore the blackfire.

The description of these pendants matched hers and Xerxes' except for the size. According to the account, the original trillion-cut jewels were approximately eight centimeters wide. That was about two times the size of the one Xerxes wore.

She remembered Fellan showing her his pendant. Same gemstone as Xerxes' but only half a centimeter wide and with a fraction of the power. Had Xerxes cut the original jewel into smaller pieces? He needed lieutenants and that would make sense. Lonato's piece must be bigger than Fellan's. The man had been rather strong. She had to give Xerxes credit for risking the power of the gemstone. Cutting the jewel could have ruined the magic. And a bad cleaving could destroy the stone like what had happened to Shyla's.

It appeared he had done the same for the blackfire pendant, cutting it into smaller stones to get the most minions as possible. She wondered how many. No wonder they were careful about who received pendants. Except why use the blackfire at all? Seemed the sunfire was strong enough to influence even those without a pendant. Then she recalled that they only used the blackfire on those who were particularly strong-willed.

Concentrating on the rest of the text, she continued the translation. Unfortunately, there wasn't a reference to how to counter the sunfire's influence. Shyla sorted through her memories, putting clues together.

The person wearing a sunfire pendant could use the magic to influence others. If the person proved too stubborn, then they gave them a blackfire pendant. The enslaved had to look at the gemstone in order for it to work. A painful shudder rocked her when she recalled how the jewel had tugged and captured her soul. It appeared that Fellan's sunfire had been linked to her blackfire, and when Xerxes decided to control her, he'd yanked off Fellan's blackfire and replaced it with one of his own, giving the original pendant back to Fellan.

How did knowing that help her? They each had a limited

number of pendants to enslave people and they couldn't be shared. And when Xerxes had taken off her necklace, she had a moment of clarity. Same with when Mojag removed hers. They couldn't destroy the stone without fatal consequences. Perhaps they could put the pendants into a black cloth bag and bury them.

At least she had a temporary solution for freeing those enslaved. Although she now needed a way to stop the magic of the sunfire. Unless it was as easy as taking the pendant off Xerxes? But could she? The man was resistant to her magic, and his fighting skills were legendary. She might be able to trick him. Or overpower him. Nine members of the Invisible Sword could easily handle the commander.

She translated the rest of the document and didn't find a solution. In the lower right-hand corner was a symbol that indicated the scroll had been copied. Grabbing one of the magnifying glasses on the table, she peered closer at the symbol. It matched the one on her bracelet. Did that mean the King had a Room of Knowledge? Many times not all the information was copied. It was possible there were more details there. And, if she thought about it, it was smart not to copy the details on how to counter the sunfire. The King wouldn't want too many people to have that information.

That thought triggered another question. How had Xerxes found the pendants? According to the record, Tamburah's advisor, who was supposed to wake The Eyes, stole the pendants and disappeared before the King could claim both magical artifacts. Another rib-aching shudder ripped through her over the thought of Tamburah having the sunfire and The Eyes.

From what she just read, it appeared that the sunfire was an added protection for the King. It made sense since his advisor wielded the power of The Eyes, and there was a very real danger of the advisor using The Eyes for their own purposes. With the sunfire, the King had both a powerful and trustworthy advisor.

In Shyla's experience, lost artifacts were found in unexpected places or by pure chance. Xerxes had access to the castle, perhaps he'd just been lucky. Or . . . Shyla searched her memory. The old king had sent his elite forces on treasure-hunting missions. Xerxes must have found the pendants and kept them for himself.

Over the next two sun jumps, Shyla and the others read through as many documents as possible but found nothing else about the pendants. She still had three more sun jumps before she was due to return to Xerxes. All the Monks of Lyons had been freed, but Shyla promised to help Neda deal with Egan since they hadn't found a solution to countering the sunfire. However, once Egan was neutralized, Neda and her loyal monks could deal with those who were loyal to him.

At angle zero, Shyla, her two guards, Neda, and a few monks gathered in Egan's office to officially say goodbye.

"Ah, Little One. Have you found what you needed?" Egan asked.

"Yes, I've learned how to counter the King's magic. Xerxes will be pleased." She unrolled the scroll she held. "See here."

Moving closer to Egan, she turned it so he would pivot to see better. "This document explains exactly what we need to do," she said.

Egan glanced at the text, but she doubted he could read the ancient language. "Excellent. Are you leaving then?"

"Yes. And I've bad news for you."

Then she aimed her magic at Kamila and Fareed.

Freeze.

"Me?"

She jerked the scroll down just as three of the monks grabbed him from behind. They held him immobile as Neda yanked his pendant off his neck.

"Don't look at the jewel," Shyla reminded her.

Neda wrapped her hand around it, covering the sunfire. Egan struggled, but even though he was strong, the three monks held him easily.

"The bad news for you is you're no longer in charge of this monastery," she said to Egan.

"Xerxes will not be pleased. You won't be able to trick him," Egan hissed.

"I no longer wish to please Xerxes. In fact, I'm looking forward to upsetting him a great deal."

Neda handed her the pendant and Shyla put it inside a black pouch, pulled the ties tight, and knotted it.

"What about them?" Neda asked, inclining her head at Kamila and Fareed.

"I'll erase this little coup from their memory."

The monks took Egan to the holding cells in the lower levels of the monastery. Neda left so Shyla could alter Kamila's and Fareed's memories of what had really happened.

When she finished, she asked them, "Ready to go?"

"More than ready," Kamila said, setting a fast pace to the surface.

Shyla soaked in the sun as they walked quickly back to Apanji. Somewhere along the way, she dropped the black bag with Egan's sunfire pendant. Moving the sand with her magic, she dragged the pouch deep within the heart of a dune. If only dealing with Xerxes would be so easy.

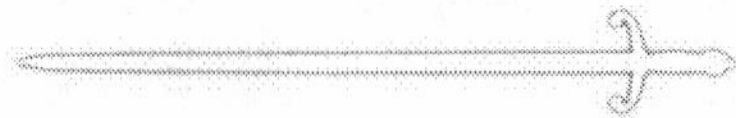

"Little One, I'm surprised to see you," Xerxes said. He had taken over the prince's residence and was consulting with one of his men in the prince's office. "I didn't expect you for another couple sun jumps."

Remembering that she had to appear eager to please, Shyla hurriedly replied, "We searched all four Rooms of Knowledge and just about exhausted the records available when I found out how to counter the King's magic."

His full attention focused on her as sparks of excitement lit his gaze. "Go on, Little One."

"I discovered a way to bypass the King's immunity. I need to use the power of The Eyes and my magic simultaneously to stop the King from wielding his magic."

"Can the King be converted to our cause?"

"Yes."

"Good to know. I'm just about finished with this city. Everything is in place. Just a few more sun jumps and we'll leave for Haiya." He studied her. "You did good. You can spend this darkness with me. I've taken over the Water Prince's sleeping quarters."

Shyla smiled as if thrilled by the idea. Inside she recoiled. "What else can I do for you?" Her stomach almost heaved.

"You can rest. The trip to Haiya will take us seven sun jumps."

Normally it would take fifteen sun jumps. She bowed her head as if accepting his orders. But she plucked at her tunic as if distressed.

"Little One?"

"It's nothing."

"Come on. Out with it."

"I need a few things for the trip. May I go to the market?" Inwardly, she cringed at her submissive tone.

"Of course." His gaze slid to Kamila and Fareed and they both gave a panicked little shake of their heads—they'd had enough of babysitting duty. "Dayana will collect you after second meal."

"Thank you," she gushed.

One of the guards showed her to the prince's suite. She had forty angles until second meal. After a long nap—there was no way she'd get any sleep during darkness—Shyla took advantage of the prince's extensive water closet. She scrubbed her hair a few times, washing more of the brown dye from it. While not nearly as nice as the prince's, the facilities at the monastery were adequate and her hair had already started to fade to her natural blond.

Second meal was delivered to her and she ate every bite. Dayana arrived soon after. The soldier looked resigned.

Jingling a pouch of coins, Dayana said, "Xerxes said to buy whatever you need."

"Including weapons?"

Dayana laughed. "No. Besides, you don't need a weapon."

"True. That's because I *am* a weapon." Shyla met the woman's surprised gaze. *Gotcha.*

Dayana's loyalty to Xerxes spanned circuits. She didn't need to be influenced by the sunfire; Dayana had earned her spot in his inner circle well before. The woman had been there when he'd revealed the pendants and explained how they worked. Unfortunately, Dayana had no idea where Xerxes found them. She also didn't know how to counter the sunfire or the details of Xerxes' ultimate plan. The commander operated on a need-to-know basis and he believed most of his people didn't need to know until the last possible angle. Vilma, who hated Shyla, was the person Xerxes trusted the most.

After erasing Dayana's memory of having her soul read, Shyla plucked the pouch of coins from the woman's hand. "You don't need to come with me. I'm sure you have better things to do with your time."

"I do, but the commander insisted." Dayana took the coins back. "Let's not waste any more of my time." She strode to the door.

Shyla followed. They traveled to the main market in the

shaft. The white light from the sky pillars illuminated the stands. People shopped and haggling sounded all around. She scanned the crowds, searching for the Invisible Swords.

"What do you need?" Dayana asked.

"Some travel clothes." Shyla sorted through a number of pieces at different stalls, all the while keeping an eye out for her friends. She spotted most of them. Dayana's impatience grew with each stop. But Shyla was waiting for the perfect opportunity to accidentally lose the soldier in the crowd. When Jaft and Rae had a heated argument right behind Dayana, distracting the woman, Shyla ducked behind a stall.

Mojag appeared next to Shyla almost immediately. She hadn't seen him at all.

"We located Rendor and Captain Mahira," Mojag said.

"Are they together?" That would be ideal.

"No. Rendor's already one of Xerxes' go-to men. He's in the prince's suites with the commander."

That would make it harder for Shyla to free him. "And Captain Mahira?"

"Nearby. We need to move fast. The taxes are coming within the next sun jump."

"Are you sure?"

"The gossip is hot."

"What about my escort?" Shyla glanced around the market, expecting Dayana to come looking for her.

"Gurice is pulling a lookalike scam. She'll tow your babysitter around like a velbloud at apex, thinking she's shopping with you." Mojag grinned. "I hope you like Gurice's clothing choices. It's probably the most dangerous thing you'll do this sun jump."

"Ha, ha. If time is limited, then let's go."

Mojag led her to the edges of the market. Captain Mahira stood between Nard and Balin. She had a hand spread on each of their chests, keeping them apart as they traded insults. When Balin noticed her and Mojag, he relaxed his stance. Nard also backed off.

Confused, the captain glanced around to see what had caused their sudden cease-fire and spotted Shyla.

"You," she growled. Murder burned in her gaze, but Mahira couldn't do anything to Shyla. Not yet.

Shyla freed the woman and braced for her attack. Mahira stumbled forward, but Nard and Balin blocked the captain from reaching Shyla.

"Do you know what you did to me and my guards?" Mahira asked. Her voice was tight and pitched low. She strained against the men.

"Yes. I'm sorry."

"Sorry! You're sorry! Oh no, that's not enough. That'll *never* be enough."

"Calm down, Captain," Mojag said. "We don't have time for this. Unless you *don't* want the rest of your guards freed from the compulsion?"

Mahira glared at Mojag. "And who the hell are you?"

Mojag straightened to his full height, which was a few centimeters taller than Shyla remembered. His normally jovial expression hardened. "I'm Mojag, a member of the Invisible

Sword. We're here to help you. Unless you'd rather Xerxes keep control of your city and your prince?"

The captain studied him. The tension in her shoulders eased. "And can you?"

"We already have." He gestured to Shyla. "Freeing our leader has freed your city. Now it's just a matter of cleaning up."

Pride swelled over how well Mojag handled the situation. Even Nard and Balin appeared impressed.

Mahira stepped back from the men. "All right." She smoothed her uniform. "Do you have a plan?"

"Yes." Shyla explained what they intended to do. "Now you know we really don't have much time."

"You're cutting it close. Come on, let's go free my people."

They raced through the city, finding Mahira's guards. Unfortunately, they couldn't reach everyone as a few were working with the mercs or on duty in the prince's residence. Shyla promised to get to them when the opportunity arose, however the captain needed to be there as well. All the guards had wanted to kill Shyla as soon as they could and Mahira's presence had been the only thing stopping them. Shyla couldn't blame them.

It was close to angle two-twenty when Shyla found Gurice and Dayana in the market. The soldier appeared tired and cranky. Shyla used the *look away* command to switch places with Gurice.

"You owe me big time," Gurice said. "Shopping for almost a hundred angles just about killed me." She handed Shyla a number of packages, then grinned evilly. "I picked you up some skimpy undergarments to wear for Rendor."

"I...er..." She blushed with embarrassment. She'd never considered wearing something like that. All this relationship stuff was so new. And he might not forgive her for trapping him.

"Just say thank you, Gurice." Her friend smirked.

"Thank you for meddling in my love life, Gurice."

"You're welcome. Although I'd have preferred it without the snark." Then she sobered. "You be careful. This thing is not over yet."

"I will. You, too."

When Gurice disappeared into the crowd, Shyla stopped the *look away* command.

"Are you done?" Dayana asked. "The commander isn't going to be pleased that we've been gone so long."

Shyla relished the fact that she no longer cared if Xerxes was pleased or not. "I am. Thanks for coming with me."

Dayana grunted. "Good thing you were right that the grilled gamelu from Tockies was the best in the city."

As Shyla followed Dayana back to the prince's residence, she made eye contact with all the Invisible Swords. Each gave her an encouraging nod as if they knew the next hundred and forty angles would be difficult for her. She kept them close to her heart.

When they arrived, Xerxes was not happy.

"I was about to send Vilma out to find you," he said. "Why did it take you so long?" he demanded.

"She's a hard size to fit, Commander," Dayana said. "And she's picky."

Shyla sensed this was important. "I just wanted to find the perfect garment for you, Commander." Ugh.

He relaxed. "You must be exhausted. Go on. I'll join you later."

Double ugh. She forced a brilliant smile and left. Glad to have a few angles alone, Shyla packed her new purchases into her pack. It took her longer than she wanted to admit to figure out the purpose of a few of the pieces, meaning they had no practical purpose.

And that Gurice's definition of skimpy didn't match hers. Gurice's was more like…next to nothing. Still…Rendor might appreciate them more.

Her heart lurched. Thinking about Rendor brought up so many conflicting emotions. She wanted to find him right now, take the pendant off him, explain everything, and beg for his forgiveness. Except she couldn't just skip to the end.

Instead, she slipped under the fur fully clothed. If Xerxes asked about it, she'd claim she had been too tired to change. Despite her nerves, she was exhausted from freeing the guards and she fell asleep almost right away. When Xerxes joined her, she was barely aware of him.

When she woke, at first she thought the solid body curled around her was Rendor. Then reality chased away all her warm fuzzy thoughts and she quickly extracted herself from Xerxes' embrace.

"Little One?" he asked sleepily.

"Water closet," she said, dashing away. The sand clock read angle three-fifty. It was almost time to wake, so she slipped out to the main room.

Vilma arrived at angle zero with first meal. If she was surprised to see Shyla awake already, she didn't show it. Instead she called for Xerxes to get his lazy ass out of the cushion.

Xerxes and Vilma discussed the arrival of the taxes while they ate. Shyla kept quiet, hoping that nothing changed.

"I'll give Zahoor a couple chests of coins to keep here," Xerxes said. "We'll send the rest to Haiya."

"All right. Who do you want on the surface?" Vilma asked.

"Zahoor, Dayana, Big Brute, and Little One."

Vilma scowled. "Why her?"

"Just in case we run into trouble. The wagons of goods are most vulnerable when arriving and leaving a city."

"We can handle trouble," she said.

"I know."

She grunted. "You're the boss."

"I know that, too."

Twenty angles before the danger zone, Shyla, Rendor, Xerxes, and his team stood sweating on the hot sands, waiting for the arrival of the tax wagons with their escort. The small caravan of three wagons would come from the south since their last stop was in Zirdai. Jayden had just paid his first tax payment to the King as the city's official Water Prince.

Shyla resisted the strong desire to glance at Rendor. As much as she wanted to check his expression and read his thoughts—

how badly was he enthralled?—she was supposed to be thinking only about Xerxes.

As the tax caravan drew closer, Shyla counted eight Dunnar monks guarding the wagons. Add in Xerxes and his soldiers and that made a dozen opponents against nine Invisible Swords. She liked their odds.

About forty meters before they reached the city proper, the wagons began to sink into the sand.

"Sluff sand!" someone yelled. "It's everywhere!"

The gamelus strained to pull the wagons out, but the sand underneath their feet softened. It was a nice bit of chaos. Many of the mercs ran to help the wagons. Shyla kept an eye on Rendor, waiting for the right moment to remove his pendant.

Except when she stepped forward, Xerxes clamped a large hand on her shoulder and spun her to face him.

"Well played, Little One. But did you really think I wouldn't know when you destroyed your pendant?" He grabbed her necklace and twisted it so the metal tightened around her throat, cutting into her skin. "Now watch as my soldiers ambush your ambushers."

Shyla's breath wheezed in and out as Xerxes kept a tight hold on the necklace twisted around her neck. Fear swelled inside her, matching the arrival of Xerxes' company of elite soldiers sprinting from their hiding spots. They were led by Vilma. Shyla stopped counting opponents after two dozen. The odds no longer looked as good for her Invisible Swords.

The wagons continued to sink into the sand along with the panicked gamelus. Their drivers tried to calm them and pull them to the stable sand. The monks worked to unload the chests of coins with the help of Dayana, Rendor, and Zahoor. No one seemed to notice that the chests then disappeared into the sand.

It would have been comical if Shyla had the breath to laugh. The soldiers rushed to do battle, except there wasn't an enemy to fight. Everyone stopped in confusion.

Xerxes turned to her. His angry gaze promised pain as he tightened his grip, cutting off her air. After a few panicked heartbeats, he eased the pressure. Shyla sucked in a breath.

"What's going on?" he growled.

Unable to fight or use her magic on him, Shyla only had one option left: remove the sand from underneath his feet.

But, as he sank into the ground, he grabbed her shoulders, dragging her down with him. That was okay, as he had no experience being buried in the sand while she'd learned to be quite comfortable underneath the grains. Once the sand closed over them, he panicked and released her. She piled more sand on him as she cleared it from around her.

By the time she regained her feet, he'd already knocked enough sand away to create an opening for air, but she ensured the rest of him was stuck tight. It would take a long time for him to dig himself out. Vilma glanced over, most likely seeking orders, and the second-in-command's expression hardened into murder when she failed to see her boss next to Shyla. Uh-oh. Shyla quickly formed a sand arrow and shot it at the woman. It knocked her back. Probably more from surprise than any force, but it was the signal. The monks stopped unloading the chests and pulled their swords. The ringing sound drew every one of Xerxes' soldiers' attention. They turned as one.

Shyla hoped Captain Mahira and her handpicked guards—who were disguised as the monks—could handle themselves against elite soldiers. There was a moment's hesitation, then the two groups clashed. The city guards were outnumbered, but the Invisible Swords had a few more surprises.

Sand erupted as the Invisible Swords leaped from their hiding places in the dunes and came up behind the soldiers. Sand weapons and mini sandstorms blew, distracting their opponents.

Other mercs froze as the magic wielders attacked with invisible weapons.

As much as she wanted to free Rendor, she needed to find the two men whose magic she had unlocked. They had been fast learners and would make it harder for her Invisible Swords to fight the mercs. Since Xerxes' soldiers all wore the same uniform, Shyla searched for them with The Eyes, seeking that inner glow that meant they were wielding magic. The two men were among the mercs, countering the Invisible Sword's magical efforts.

She reached and closed the first man's inner druk, cutting off his ability to wield magic. The man cried out and collapsed to the sand. His partner turned his focus on her. Magical commands pressed on her as hot as the sun. She dodged them and shut down his abilities as well. He crumpled with a wail of pain. A bit of her guilt eased as she fixed another one of the problems she had caused.

Then Shyla raced toward Rendor. His sword flashed as he fought with one of the monks. Once she drew closer, she identified the monk as Mahira. And the captain was holding her own against him. For now. Her weapon clanged as she countered Rendor's attacks, but each defensive move was a hair slower than the one before.

"Rendor, stop," Shyla yelled. But he ignored her. She hated to do this, but she had no other choice.

Freeze.

He stopped mid-strike. Mahira took in a few deep gulps of air, wiped the sweat from her brow, nodded at Shyla, and turned to help her guards, lunging at another merc. Shyla reached

Rendor. He strained against the magical hold and glared daggers at her. His expression wasn't what alarmed her. There was no recognition in his gaze. To him, she was nothing more than an opponent. Her heart ached.

"I'm so sorry for everything," she said, hoping she hadn't lost him forever. Then she yanked his pendant from underneath his sweat-soaked shirt. The blackfire glinted in the sunlight, reminding her not to look.

She closed her fist around the pendant and— A body slammed into her. Shyla lost her grip on the necklace as she flew through the air. On impact, all air whooshed from her lungs and pain ringed her still sore ribs.

"Big Brute, go help Zahoor," Vilma ordered as she straddled Shyla, pinning her arms to the ground.

Rendor ran off. Helpless, Shyla watched him go. Vilma's weight made it difficult for her to breathe and increased the agony in her ribs. So focused on Rendor, Shyla hadn't kept track of all their enemies' positions. Rookie mistake.

"Pay attention. You've bigger problems," Vilma said, touching her sharp knife to Shyla's throat. At least the woman shifted her weight, easing the pressure on Shyla's chest.

She met Vilma's gaze. Another loyal soldier that Xerxes hadn't needed to influence. Vilma's thoughts and emotions were easy to read. "Xerxes won't be pleased if you kill me, Vilma."

"After this stunt, he'll know I was right. We should have killed you right away."

"And what makes you think you'll be successful? You tried to kill me before and failed. Does Xerxes know about the mercs you sent after me?"

"Oh no, I'm not playing this game."

"Too late. I'm in your mind, Vilma. Go ahead. Try to slit my throat."

Vilma cursed when she couldn't move the knife in her hand.

"Why did you send them? Xerxes couldn't have known about me at that point." Shyla added heat to her question, compelling her to answer.

"But I knew exactly who you were. The demon who murdered my brother."

"Brother?"

"The Water Prince."

So the man hadn't been spawned by a sand demon after all. He had a family. Well, at least a sister who was an elite fighter. "I already told you the Heliacal Priestess slit the Water Prince's throat."

"And the only reason that bitch was able to reach him was because of you. You can't deny that."

The woman was right. She couldn't. "Get off me, Vilma," she ordered.

But instead of standing, Vilma was plucked off her and tossed aside. A huge shadow covered Shyla. Xerxes. How in the seven hells did he escape? She had either underestimated his strength or someone helped him. It really didn't matter at this point. She was cooked.

Shyla rolled away. But he was faster, scooping her up and pinning her back to his massive chest with one giant arm. Panicked, Shyla flung sand at his face. He squeezed harder, making her gasp with pain, but didn't let go.

"You should have killed me. Those Eyes are wasted on you," he said.

Concentrating on the grains of sand under his boots, she pulled. However, the glint of gold and the cold kiss of metal on her neck shattered her concentration. An unbroken pendant dangled, slowly twisting. She averted her gaze.

No! Not again. Not ever.

The ground beneath them buckled and lurched. Thrown off balance, Xerxes released her. She stumbled and fell. Huge dunes of sand undulated through Xerxes' soldiers, knocking them down and sweeping them away. Shyla stood frozen, gaping at the extraordinary display of magical power. Moving sand was one thing, but dunes… Seven hells.

Xerxes called a retreat. Those that could move bolted toward the city. Fast.

"Stop them with the sand," Mahira called. "They're under arrest."

But they had reached the hard pack around the city's entrances and soon disappeared inside.

"They're stuck in the city until the surface cools," one of the guards said to the captain.

"Form teams and search for them. Go now!" Captain Mahira rounded up her guards and they sprinted after Xerxes' soldiers.

Still rather stunned, Shyla rubbed her aching ribs. Her hand brushed against the new pendant hanging around her neck. She quickly hid it in the palm of her hand. Gurice and Mojag rushed over to her. Scanning them for injuries, she breathed easier over their minor cuts, bruises, and ripped clothing.

"Do you need me to take it off?" Mojag asked, pointing to the necklace.

"Yes, please."

He lifted the chain over her head. She kept the blackfire in her hand, letting the chain dangle.

"Should we help the city guards?" Gurice asked her.

"No. They know their city the best and they have plenty of people. We'd just get in the way." Her energy fizzled. She'd used quite a bit of magic during the fight. "Besides, I need to free the Water Prince and the rest of his advisors and guards from my compulsion."

"How did Xerxes know about the ambush?" Gurice asked.

She explained. "He knew I'd broken his pendant and he's smart enough to figure out that I'd try to protect the taxes."

"But he underestimated us," Mojag said. "We surprised him with the disguised monks and saved the taxes."

"Yeah, well, this isn't exactly a win, rat." His sister gestured to the group of people sitting on the sand and bleeding from more serious injuries. "We didn't capture the mercs. We barely managed to keep them from killing us."

Xerxes' comment repeated in Shyla's head. *You should have killed me. Those Eyes are wasted on you.* Were they? What if Xerxes escaped Apanji and caused more harm? Or murdered someone? Should she have been more ruthless? More like Tamburah? The Sun Goddess's words sounded in her head. *Not Tamburah.* The despot would have eliminated Xerxes and his followers without a second thought. Shyla needed to stop worrying so much about abusing the power of The Eyes and trust herself to use them in the best way possible—by helping others. An invisible yet ever-present tightness around her chest disappeared.

Shyla scanned the Invisible Swords, counting heads. Jaft limped toward them with Rae tucked under his arm. The petite woman couldn't really support the bigger—

"Rendor! Where is he?" she asked Gurice.

"Gone with the mercs."

"Sorry, Shyla," Mojag said. "I tried to grab his necklace. No luck. And his thoughts were slippery, they were all about making Xerxes proud, so I couldn't grab *him* either." He ducked his head. "I was going to ask Gurice to help, but she was busy. Then the fight turned scary and I had to move the dunes."

"You moved the dunes? By yourself?" she asked.

"Course. Everyone else was battling for their lives. And that monster had you locked in his arms."

She'd known Mojag was strong when he had stopped Jayden's sand attack, but this was on an entirely different level. Squeezing his shoulder, she said, "You saved everyone. Don't worry about Rendor. We'll get him back." Because if she didn't, she'd never forgive herself.

"If they're not caught by Captain Mahira, maybe Xerxes will ransom him to us," Gurice said. "We have the taxes."

Which they needed to deliver to the King. Another wave of fatigue hit her. Add that to the oppressive heat and painful sunlight, she longed for shade and a nap. They all needed to go underground before the sun reached the danger zone.

"Mojag, can you move the chests to a better hiding spot in the sand? Or are you too tired?" If Shyla had moved a dune, she'd be unconscious by now.

"Nope. I can bury them where no one will find them." He smirked. "Except me."

Shyla organized the rest of the Invisible Swords. They took care of their injured, the gamelus, and the wagons.

"What about the monks whose clothing you stole?" she asked Gurice.

"We left them in the travel shelter. We timed it so by the time they woke up, they wouldn't be able to get here before the killing zone." She grinned. "They'll be here by darkness, though. And looking for a fight."

"I'll send a message to Neda. Her monks can intercept them." Before they headed to the city, Shyla searched for her leather pouch that she'd hidden beneath the sands. Spotting it, she used the sand to bring it to her. She added the new pendant and her broken one to the bag but kept the necklace with Gurice's and Mojag's names on it—a reminder of her new family, which included Rendor. She'd free him if it was the last thing she did. Xerxes didn't get to keep him.

After she sent the pouch deep under the nearest dune, she re-joined Mojag and Gurice. The three of them returned to the city. Once they reached the cooler underground levels, Mojag began to lag behind. By the time they arrived at the entrance to the prince's residence, he could barely stand. Gurice lectured him on exhausting his magic as she half carried him.

The guards stationed outside glared at her. She didn't have

the energy for this, but she didn't have a choice.

Shyla approached them. "I'm going to free you from the compulsion to obey Commander Xerxes. I know you want to kill me, but if you do, then I can't release the Water Prince, his advisors, and the rest of your colleagues. Do you understand?"

Tight nods.

"Maybe we should wait for Captain Mahira," Jaft said.

"No. They've suffered long enough." She released them and braced for an attack.

They considered it, but then they opened the doors and led Shyla and the rest of the Invisible Swords to the guest quarters where the prince and his advisors were staying. While the task to free them all was easy, it drained what remained of her energy. She plopped into a cushion. Mojag had already fallen asleep on another.

The Water Prince quickly resumed control of the situation. He asked a number of questions about Xerxes' whereabouts and Captain Mahira. Gurice answered as best she could since none of them knew where anyone had gone.

"You should station guards at all the city's exits, including the escape tunnels just in case the mercs get past the captain," Gurice suggested.

The prince frowned at them. "I've no idea if you're telling me the truth." Then he gestured to his guards. "Arrest them all."

Gurice glanced at Shyla, questioning if they should fight. Shyla shook her head. Once Mahira returned, she'd sort it all out. Besides, they were in no condition to resist.

"Relinquish your weapons," Shyla said. "We'll cooperate."

"Smart," the prince said. "Take them to the holding cells."

The guards quickly surrounded them. Poor Mojag didn't even wake up. They had to carry him. The Invisible Swords were then escorted a few levels below and into a tunnel that led to the holding cells. They were obviously used for temporary stays. At least they were clean, well lit, and included sleeping cushions. Shyla was shoved into the first cell along with Gurice and Rae.

"I always knew you'd land me in jail," Gurice said, checking the lock and rattling the bars. "The surprise is that it took you this long."

"Ha, ha. At least I didn't disappoint you." Shyla collapsed onto the cushion. "Check in with everyone, make sure they're okay and that they don't need a physician. Wake me if anything exciting happens."

"Aren't we going to escape?" Rae asked Shyla. "There are three guards nearby—it'd be easy."

"No. The prince is understandably unbalanced right now. Once he gains his footing and consults with his captain, he'll release us. Plus we need his help and escaping will just anger him and exhaust us further."

"Best case scenario," Gurice said, "is that they'll kick us out of here to make room for Xerxes and his soldiers."

But Gurice's sour expression matched Shyla's thoughts. They both knew Xerxes wouldn't be captured. He and the majority of his soldiers would escape, taking Rendor with them.

It took the Water Prince of Apanji two full sun jumps before he sent for Shyla at angle one-ten. The rest of her companions were left in the holding cells. That didn't bode well for their future. At least the delay had given everyone time to recover from their injuries. Mojag had roused briefly at the end of the first sun jump and, according to Jaft, ate an entire gamelu before returning to an exhausted sleep.

When Shyla was brought before the Water Prince, she noted the increased number of guards around him. Captain Mahira stood on his right. However, the prince refused to face her, keeping his back turned. Mahira relayed the prince's questions. Shyla debated if she should tell him that once she had made eye contact with a person, she formed a permanent connection. Deciding it wouldn't help their relationship and would probably ruin any trust she might have gained, she remained quiet.

"Xerxes and half of his soldiers are gone," Mahira said. "We captured the other half, but they refused to talk. Can you interrogate them to find out where he went?"

"He was planning on going to Haiya, but I doubt he'll go there now. I'll ask his soldiers, but he might not have shared his new destination with them," Shyla said.

"We already sent a message to the Water Princess of Haiya, but we agree with you." Mahira glanced at the prince, listened, and asked, "Do you have any idea where he might go?"

Actually she did. She'd talked it over with Gurice while incarcerated. "We think he might head to one of the cities that's under his influence, but he won't stay there for long. Instead, he'll gather supplies, weapons, and more personnel." She paused.

This next part was a guess. "Then he'll aim for Qulsary."

Mahira gave her a sharp look. "Explain your reasons."

"Xerxes asked me if I could influence the King with my magic." At that word, the occupants in the room flinched, glared at her in anger, or shuffled uneasily. Until they'd met her, not one of them had believed in magic. "From Xerxes' comments, I think his plan was to take over all the cities of Koraha. Then once he had control, he'd travel to Qulsary and assassinate the King."

Her statement caused a bigger and noisier reaction. She waited for the inevitable demands for her to explain further. Mahira didn't disappoint.

"From what I've learned about Xerxes, he has a very dominant personality and enjoys being in charge. He'd never be content as a Water Prince. If that were the case, he would have been content to rule Ginda. He wants to *be* King. And not only is he converting all the cities, but also the monks. Because he knows the King can call on the monks to fight. Once he cuts the King off from all his supporters and revenue, then Xerxes can not only easily take his throne but hold on to it. He won't have to worry about anyone else having the same idea, because he'll control all of Koraha. But now that we've stopped him, I believe he's going to skip to the end of his plan. Once he's King, he can send his minions to ensure the rest of the cities cooperate."

"Why didn't he just assassinate the King first and save all that time and energy?" Mahira asked.

Good question. Shyla mulled it over. As the commander of the elite forces, Xerxes had been close to the old king. He must have known about his illness and about the king-in-training.

He'd have to assassinate them both, which would be harder to do. Also if he assassinated them, the cities would have stopped send.ing taxes and would cease all support. Xerxes wanted *all* the benefits of being King.

Shyla explained her thoughts to the captain. "Also the King is chosen by the Sun Goddess. If he'd assassinated her chosen ruler, the cities would have banded together to unseat him. His plan might have taken many circuits, but no one would have protested Xerxes becoming King."

Mahira and the prince consulted with a couple of the advisors. Shyla scanned the surface emotions of the guards. With all this speculation about Xerxes and his schemes, she figured the commander had left a few spies behind. However, no one's thoughts alarmed her.

"Assuming none of the prisoners know, which city do you think he'll go to for supplies?" Mahira asked.

"I think he'll go to Nintri. Even though it's an obvious choice, it's still the closest city to Qulsary and his co-conspirator is there."

"Captain, send a message to the King right away to warn him," the prince ordered.

"That won't be enough," Shyla said. "You'll also need to send guards and monks. The King doesn't have enough protectors."

The Water Prince swiveled around to face her. Anger radiated from his stiff shoulders. "Only if the *King* requests them."

She showed him the sigil. "I've been authorized to requisition manpower as his emissary."

"The King authorized you before you fell under Xerxes' spell." He stabbed a finger at her. "You have all this…*magic*…and yet you were caught and used. What's to stop him from enslaving you again? You are no longer trustworthy." The prince stood. "I'll release you and your friends and will provide you with whatever provisions you need. But I want every one of you out of my city within two sun jumps."

Shyla couldn't blame him after all he had suffered at her hands. But she couldn't resist a parting shot. "Don't forget to pay your taxes. The Monks of Lyons will be here to pick them up by angle zero."

Mahira took her to another deeper level that led to Apanji's prison. The captain had one of Xerxes' high-ranking soldiers brought out for Shyla to interrogate with her magic. As she suspected, the soldier had no idea what the commander planned to do next. All he knew was to meet at the rally point. Except when he'd arrived, the prince's guards ambushed him.

Shyla returned to the holding cells. Everyone was happy to be leaving the city the next sun jump. Xerxes already had a head start and she wanted to leave as soon as possible. But they had a number of things to do first. Shyla assigned Gurice and Rae to collect those promised provisions along with an additional request. She asked Nard and Balin to accompany them. Mojag and Jaft were given the task of hiring drivers and getting the wagons ready to take the taxes to the King. Shyla asked Vashi and Lamar to find a guide to lead them to Nintri, explaining exactly what type of person they needed.

"What are you planning to do?" Gurice asked her.

"I'm going to the monastery. We need monks to guard the tax caravan."

"We should stay together. Take Rae as backup. We don't need four people to get supplies."

True, but Shyla still wondered if Gurice worried that Shyla could no longer defend herself. "All right. Let's get going. We don't have much time."

"Meet back at our rooms," Gurice called as everyone dispersed.

"We probably won't be back before darkness," Shyla told her friend. "Don't worry, we'll meet you at the city's entrance at angle zero."

"You better. Or we're *all* coming for you."

"Thank you."

Gurice waved her off, but Shyla touched her arm. "No, really. *Thank you* for coming the first time and freeing me. I was so stupid, I'd—"

"Made a mistake? You?" she asked in mock horror. "Well, thank the Sun Goddess you're a normal person! Which means the rest of us don't have to be perfect either. Win, win. Now get your ass moving, you're wasting sunlight."

That right there was why Gurice was her second-in-command *and* best friend. She knew exactly the right thing to say at the right time.

Rae was quiet as they navigated toward the surface. Shyla had a better mental map of the city, but she still had to check the direction markers on occasion. And scan the area for bumps. In a crowded city, it was hard to figure out which ones might cause them trouble.

It was at one of these stops that Rae said, "I think we're being followed."

Shyla stretched her magic further. "I found them. Except I can't pinpoint who they are. Only that they feel familiar." Which meant they could very likely be Xerxes' spies.

"How many?" Rae asked.

"Two."

"Not enough to worry about," Rae said with a grin.

Shyla turned to her. "It appears you've caught Mojag's overconfidence. Xerxes' soldiers are highly trained."

"In the Ways of the Yarin. In which I am also highly trained. Plus I'm a wielder."

And most people underestimated Rae because of her petite size, which gave her a big advantage. "I think I created a monster," Shyla teased.

They continued up another ten levels. The sand clocks read angle one-fifty. Shyla increased their pace. At this rate, they wouldn't make it to the monastery before darkness.

"There has to be a quicker way to the surface," Shyla said at the next confusing intersection. Six tunnels branched off in different directions. "We should ask—" The familiar bumps suddenly appeared right behind her. She spun. "Watch out!" She shoved Rae aside as a metal shaft swept through the air. It clanged on the stone wall, spraying sparks.

Rae recovered in time to sidestep the rush of a short and thick figure who was unarmed. Then who— Movement drew her attention. Shyla blocked the second strike from a tall attacker.

The weapon slammed into her left forearm. Instant pain roared up her arm. She staggered as he pulled back for another strike.

Oh no you don't.

Freeze.

He froze with his weapon in midair. It was a shovel. She yanked off his turban and veil, revealing Walkur! So that must mean— Shyla turned to call Rae off, but she'd already frozen her opponent—Elschen, the gardener.

"Who are they?" Rae asked.

"Friends." Even though she was thrilled that they were both alive and well, Shyla took the shovel from Walkur with her right hand—her left arm was useless.

"Friends? Like, nothing says I love you better than a shovel to the back of the head, friends?"

"Now you sound like Jaft." She gestured to the pair. "They still think I'm the enemy. I'm not," she said to them. "Not anymore. I'm free of Fellan's compulsion. I'm not going to try to convert you. I'm sorry about that. In fact, I've freed all the monks and we're on the way to the monastery to enlist Neda's help."

Walkur's flat expression showed his doubt. And Elschen glared, but then again, the gardener had never cared for Shyla. She touched the scar on the back of her head—a reminder of Elschen's opinion of her.

"They don't look convinced," Rae said. "What do you want to do with them? Send them to sleep?"

"No." She considered for a moment, then said to Walkur, "You were smart not to run to the monastery in Haiya. Xerxes' people would have never looked for you here. I'm going to release you. I'm trusting that you're smart enough to see that I'm no longer enslaved." She pointed to her face. Then she freed him from her magic and asked Rae to let Elschen go.

Walkur swept a hand through his messy hair. "I can't trust you ever again."

"I know. You found a stray and she bit you." She handed him the shovel. "Come on, Rae." Shyla picked a tunnel at random and strode down it as if she knew where she was going. They needed to ask—

"Wait," Walkur called from behind them.

Both women spun and assumed a defensive stance. Shyla's arm protested the motion with needles of pain stabbing up to her shoulder.

"You're going the wrong way," he said. "Follow us."

Rae glanced at her. Shyla relaxed. "Thanks."

"I might change my mind and ditch you in the desert." Walkur eyed her. "Unless you put the idea to help you into my mind?"

She deserved his doubt and unease. "I didn't. And I won't ever again."

He grunted. "I'm keeping the shovel."

They reached the surface quickly. Walkur and Elschen didn't say a single word to Shyla or Rae as they crossed the cooling sands. Both monks tensed when they neared the monastery. Walkur kept his shovel at the ready. When the monks on patrol spotted them, he shifted his weight onto the balls of his feet as if ready to bolt. But his posture relaxed when their happy cries and smiling faces welcomed them back.

The news of their arrival traveled fast and Neda met them in the receiving room. After Walkur and Elschen told their story of escape and how they hid in the city waiting for the perfect opportunity, Neda sent the two missing monks to get a decent meal.

"I'm assuming you need help," Neda said to Shyla. "Come to my office."

In Neda's office, Shyla introduced Rae. "We've taken the taxes from Xerxes and need your monks to escort the wagons to the King."

"How many monks?"

"Twenty."

"That's more than double the standard complement."

"That's because Xerxes has probably left soldiers behind to reclaim the coins."

"And you don't believe my monks can counter his soldiers?"

"They can, which is why Xerxes is going to have more of them than the standard eight monks. I'm thinking ten or twelve. But that's not why I need so many."

"Go on."

"I want to send two caravans. One that is a decoy with extra monks, and a second with the taxes and regular guards. Well, monks that are dressed as regular civilians and two of my Invisible Swords."

"You're hoping Xerxes' people will attack the fake caravan."

"Yes. It might not work. Xerxes is intelligent and might suspect we'll try something like this."

"I'm guessing they won't be both leaving at the same time or going in the same direction."

"Yes."

"All right. I'll go ask for volunteers. In the meantime..." Neda took a scroll off a pile on her desk. "With everything going on before, I'd forgotten about a rather modest compilation of documents that is not in one of the Rooms of Knowledge but in what's considered the leader's private collection. Most of the scrolls detail the monastery's founding and lists the names of the monks and leaders who had lived here. They also include the intelligence we've gathered from our excursions into the city. Once I remembered it, I checked the documents just in case there was a reference to those pendants and perhaps details on how to counter the sunfire."

Excitement beat in her chest and Shyla stepped closer.

"Don't get your hopes up. I didn't find anything about the pendants, but I did find this account. It's written in the original scribes' language that was used back when the first city was only a few levels deep. Unfortunately I can't fully decipher it, but there's mention of the King's gifts." Neda handed her the scroll.

"I don't know if this will help you against Xerxes, but it might prove useful if you can translate it."

"I can. Hanif ensured I learned all the Korahan languages." Shyla clutched the scroll in her right hand. Her pulse jumped just at the thought of reading such an ancient document. If she gleaned any good information it'd be a bonus.

"All? That's impressive. Seemed every trade had their own. It must have been rather confusing to live during those times.

Thank the goddess we now have only one." Neda pointed to her desk. "You can stay here and read while I go find your escorts." She left.

"And I'll go fetch the physician," Rae said.

"Are you injured?"

"Your arm is probably broken, Shyla."

Rae left before she could protest. It wasn't broken. Just really, really bruised. Yes, it hurt to unroll the scroll, but it would be better after a couple sun jumps.

Shyla settled in and translated the document. It had been circuits since she'd read the scribes' formal text. Certain words were easier than others so she pieced it together. Soon she forgot all about her pain. Her entire world shrank to the faded words on the velbloud parchment. A tingle of excitement danced on her skin. As Neda had said, the text referred to the King's gifts.

The first king of Koraha was given four boons: the power to command the water, sixty circuits of health and vitality, and two magical artifacts to aid him in his rule. Shyla would bet all her coins those two artifacts were The Eyes and those pendants.

With her heart jumping in her chest, she continued to read. There was no mention of how exactly his power worked other than the nebulous magic. There was also no information on how to counter his power, which was a relief, or any explanation on how to block the sunfire's influence, which was not.

The scribe had detailed the King's water magic, but not the other three gifts. Well, not in this report. Perhaps there were more of his scrolls in another Room of Knowledge. This one detailed that when the water level had sunk too far underground, the King had been able to bring the water closer to the surface. Then, when the other cities were dug, he had manipulated the water so it flowed to the new cities, eventually linking them all together.

Huh. That explained why most of the cities were spread out in a somewhat circular shape. The layout had to make it easier for the King. She wondered if he had to consciously use his magic for the water to flow, or if it was instinctual. The scribe hadn't said, but he had warned that if— Shyla's blood drained. Suddenly dizzy, she plopped into a cushion.

If the King died, then the water would stop flowing and eventually sink deep into the earth. Too far for the citizens to reach in time. She took a deep breath as she remembered that there was always a king-in-training who would take over immediately. Since the King's magic kept him healthy for the first sixty circuits of his life, there was plenty of time for the king-in-training to learn what needed to be done.

Except if the King was assassinated while his replacement was still a baby…

In that case, everyone on Koraha would die.

Shyla reread the text, ensuring she had translated it correctly. The facts remained the same. If Xerxes assassinated the King, they would *all* die. The commander must not know the consequences of his plan or perhaps he wasn't going to kill the King, just influence him and rule Koraha through him. That wouldn't appeal to Xerxes. Maybe he thought he'd gain the King's powers when he died.

Panic surged up her throat, but she swallowed it down. How difficult would it be to assassinate the King? He not only resisted magic, but he could drown people and shrivel them. And Apanji's Water Prince had sent him a warning about Xerxes. Still, she needed to get back to Qulsary, fast.

Rae returned with the monk's physician. The older woman tortured Shyla by squeezing every centimeter of her injured forearm. By the time she was done with her "exam," tears ran down Shyla's face.

"It's not broken," the physician said. "But one of the bones is probably bruised." She wrapped Shyla's arm up to her elbow and tucked it into a sling. "Keep it still and don't use it for the next ten sun jumps."

"So not happening," Rae muttered.

Shyla ignored her. "Do you have anything for the pain?" she asked the physician, thinking about Zhek's soothing red medicine.

"Yes. Don't move or use your arm and it won't hurt." She packed up her supplies and left.

"Wow, she's grumpier than Zhek," Shyla said. "I didn't think that was possible." Plus Zhek would have given her some pain relief—after he lectured her, of course.

"I'm surprised he hasn't just given you a lifetime supply of the medicine," Rae said.

Shyla glanced at the scroll she'd been reading. If she was right about Xerxes' plans, her lifetime might be cut tragically short.

Neda arrived a few angles later. "Success. Twenty monks will be ready to go at angle zero." Then she tilted her head to the scroll. "Was that helpful?"

"Yes."

They waited for her to continue. Shyla grappled with how to tell them. As the silence stretched, Rae crossed her arms. "Are you going to tell us what caused you to pale three shades?"

"You don't want to know." But she explained what she'd learned about the King's magic anyway.

Neda's hand pressed to her chest as she gaped at Shyla. Stunned, Rae stared at her.

Finally, Neda shuddered and shook her head. "Do you need

more monks to protect the King?" Her voice was thin and weak.

Did she? The Monks of Quirin could be called on to increase the number of his guards. As long as they hadn't been converted. Would Xerxes send a message to Lonato and ask him to meet him in Qulsary? It all depended on whether Xerxes was heading straight for the King with only the soldiers with him or if he planned to take his time setting up, which would require him to stop for supplies. He also had a two sun jump head start.

She should assume the worst-case scenario. Xerxes was heading for the King in double time.

"Yes. Can you send everyone you can spare to the Quirin monastery?" Shyla asked.

"When?"

"As soon as possible."

"All right." She waved a hand at the door. "Help yourself." Neda hustled out.

"You were right," Rae said slowly.

"About what?"

"I did *not* want to know."

At angle three fifty-five, Shyla, Rae and the twenty monks assembled in the receiving room of the monastery. She explained what she had planned with the caravans. Then fourteen monks followed her to the city.

Three teams of gamelus were already assembled with three drivers. The rest of the Invisible Swords waited nearby. There was another caravan preparing to leave. It had over a dozen wagons and their muscles were busy loading goods. Other people streamed from the city's entrances to go tend to the herds and flocks. Shyla sent four of the monks to collect the taxes from Apanji's Water Prince.

As Shyla and Rae drew closer to the wagons, Gurice immediately approached her. "What happened to your arm?"

"It's fine. Just a bruise."

"A monk attacked her with a shovel," Rae said.

"I'm fine. And I'm not arguing about this," Shyla said, striding away. Mojag leaned against one of their wagons, yawning. "I've brought the monks. Can you retrieve the chests so we can load the wagons?"

"Yup. You want them to be heavy so it looks convincing?"

"Yes."

Mojag walked out into the soft sand. Soon the hiss of fast-moving grains sounded. One of the tax chests appeared and then another. The monks picked them up and carried them to the wagons. Everyone else formed a rough circle around the activity, keeping an eye out for trouble. Most of those around were too busy to pay attention to Mojag and the monks, but there were a few casting glances their way.

Gurice brought a young man over to where Shyla was watching the other caravan. It reminded her of her time with Lota and her family. A pang of sadness and longing filled her as the memory of Rendor playing with the children rose. He'd been happy and content. If she had never agreed to help the King, they'd still be together.

"This is Omar," Gurice said. "He's our guide."

Omar was a few circuits older than Shyla and she hoped he was as physically fit as he looked.

"As much as I want this job, those monks know the way to Qulsary. You don't need me," Omar said.

"We're not going with them," Shyla said.

"Oh." He glanced at Gurice. "But you said—"

"Qulsary is still our destination, but we're not traveling at wagon speed."

"Oh. You want to run it." He eyed Shyla critically. "Can you keep up with that arm? What about the rest?" Omar glanced around. "That kid might have trouble."

"Mojag is not coming with us. And my arm is fine."

"How many of you then?"

"Seven." Shyla had assigned Gurice and Mojag to travel with the second set of wagons that would assemble and leave for Qulsary in two sun jumps. With Mojag's surprisingly powerful abilities with the sand, he could easily counter any bandits, pirates, or mercs.

"We should leave now or we won't hit that second travel shelter before apex," Omar said.

"We're going to stay with the wagons for a few sun jumps before we switch to double time." Even though they needed to hurry, Xerxes had said caravans were the most vulnerable when arriving and leaving a city. Using his logic, she figured if he planned to recapture the taxes, it would be within the first couple sun jumps. Plus it would be odd if she and the others broke off from them right away.

"All right," Omar said.

Mojag brought out the last chest and carried it to the wagon. He struggled to heft it up and one of the monks helped him. Either it was a great acting job or he'd stuffed those chests with a ton of sand.

The four tax-collecting monks returned with Apanji's payment. Mojag reached to grab the new chest, but the monk holding it wouldn't relinquish it, insisting he could load it. It turned into a tug of war until Mojag yanked it free. He lost his balance and plopped onto the ground. The chest thudded next to him and sank slightly into the soft sand.

"Sorry," Mojag said. He clambered to his feet. As he vigorously wiped his pants and hands, a small cloud of sand kicked up, obscuring the chest for a moment before he retrieved it. It was a deft maneuver, replacing the coins with sand with no one the wiser. Well, except Shyla and the rest of the Invisible Swords.

After Mojag and the monk loaded the chest into the wagon, he headed toward her.

"That's all the taxes," Mojag said. "Are you sure you don't want us to come with you?" he asked for the benefit of any nearby spies.

"Yes, I'm sure. You need to stay here and help the Water Prince. You know what to do. Right?"

"Yeah. Glorified babysitting," he muttered.

"Mojag," she scolded. "It's important."

"Yeah, yeah. We know what to do. Come on, Gurice. The prince is waiting."

"Stay safe," Gurice said, giving her a small wave goodbye.

"You, too." Shyla hoped no one would pay attention to the siblings as they loaded up their wagons in two sun jumps and headed to Qulsary.

When the tax wagons set off, Omar led the small caravan that was surrounded by fourteen monks and seven Invisible Swords. Overkill for sure. By this point, Xerxes' spies were either laughing about how obvious the decoy caravan was or convinced that the coins traveled with them due to all the security. And there was always the possibility that Xerxes had no intention of intercepting the coins. After all, if he planned to be King, then he would receive them as was his due. Shyla and her friends would have wasted all this effort keeping them safe for him.

They encountered no trouble the first two sun jumps. During the darkness before the third sun jump, Shyla sat down with Omar to determine their route. The wagons would continue on the main travel roads that skirted Nintri, which was another potential ambush site.

"There are faster paths to Qulsary, but they are also more dangerous," Omar said. He was being honest.

Having learned her lesson with Tahir, Shyla used The Eyes to keep a light touch on his emotions. "What's the time difference between the safe and unsafe paths?"

"Twenty-five sun jumps versus twenty."

Was five sun jumps worth the risk? Xerxes now had a four sun jump head start. And she needed time to research how to counter the sunfire pendant and to plan for Xerxes' arrival.

"We can take care of the unfriendlies," she said.

"I'm going to give you the benefit of the doubt and agree that you can. But how much energy are you going to have? Running in sand is exhausting. Running in the heat is exhausting. If we get to a travel shelter full of unfriendlies are you going to have the energy to do anything? You can't count on me. I'm just a guide."

It was a valid question. She hated to agree, but there was no sense arriving at Qulsary half dead and unable to do anything. "All right, we'll take the safer route."

After the caravan left, Omar gathered the Invisible Swords around him. "Since it's already angle ten, we won't push for that second shelter before apex. Instead, we'll stop at the first and push until darkness. That way if we don't make it, we don't die. It just makes it harder to find the shelter without the sun." He eyed them all intently.

Shyla didn't need to read his soul to know what he thought. Jaft still favored his uninjured leg and Rae would need two strides for every one of Omar's. Shyla's bandaged arm, Vashi's cuts, and Lamar's bruised face didn't instill much confidence either. The two big men—Nard and Balin—appeared solid and healthy. However, they would expend more energy moving their extra bulk.

Omar didn't bother to hide his sigh. "Okay, this is how it works. Try to stay together, but if we're pushing to get to shelter before apex, I'm not waiting for you. Understand?"

"That you'll leave us to cook in the sun?" Jaft asked sourly. "Perfectly."

"You hired me to guide you, not die for you," Omar shot back. "And I decide the pace. Not Shyla. If you are lagging, then we revert to wagon speed. I know you're in a hurry to reach Qulsary, but if you're unable to keep the pace, there's no sense killing yourselves."

She couldn't argue with his logic.

Omar set off at an easy lope. It wasn't flat-out running, but it was quicker than a jog. His stride was graceful and appeared effortless.

Soon the reddish-orange sand and pink sky blurred together in a giant bubble of color around her. While she wielded her magic, searching for ambushes, the rest of Shyla's focus narrowed to Jaft's white sun cloak. It bobbed up and down as he ran in front of her, and she noted the hitch in his step every few strides. Was he in pain?

She shouldn't have thought of pain. Her left arm throbbed its discomfort in sync with her heartbeat. And she learned that a crossbody pack not only unbalanced her but banged against her hip while the strap dug deep into her shoulder. She refused to think about her boots and how each grain of sand dug into her feet like tiny daggers of fire and rubbed the skin off her heels. No sense dwelling on anything below her knees.

And just when she thought she'd reached pain saturation, the heat began to thicken and press and burn. Hot air seared the inside of her nostrils and rasped in her throat, scorching her lungs. If she could actually get a deep enough breath, could she fill her lungs with the hot air and rise off the sands like a velbloud? Probably not, since she weighed fifty-seven kilograms at least and was getting heavier with every single step. Soon she'd be as heavy as a dune and there'd be nothing else for her to do but lie there and be one.

Then a miracle occurred. Omar slowed his pace. Shyla ceased her envious contemplation of the dunes as the fact that they neared their destination gave her a boost of energy. Except when Omar finally stopped, it was for a water break.

"Can't run in the hot sun for fifty angles without drinking," he said without gasping for breath. Without even a wheeze or a pant.

No one else had the breath to speak. Well…Vashi, Lamar, and Rae appeared only slightly winded. And while Balin and Nard were soaked with sweat, they too breathed easier than both her and Jaft.

"Someone hasn't been keeping up with their training," Rae said in a teasing tone.

"Yeah, well, someone has been busy," Shyla said.

"Keeping in shape can save your life," Balin said. "You never know when you'll have to fight and no opponent is ever willing to wait."

"In your experience," Vashi said. "I once had some hot-headed guy who was spoiling for a fight, and I asked him to wait while I used the collection station." She laughed. "He's probably still waiting for me to return. What an idiot. Must have thought I was taking the longest—"

"We get it," Shyla said. "How much further to the travel

shelter?" she asked Omar.

"Normally we'd reach a travel shelter in thirty-five angles. But with this slower pace, it'll take us a total of fifty, so that's another twenty-five angles."

She swallowed her groan. They'd only run for twenty angles. And the heat had only just started to build. She used the remaining break time to adjust her pack and dump the sand from her boots.

Omar called them to resume the run. Their pace was slower than earlier, but the sun's rays intensified with each stride. How could light have weight? It seemed to gather on her shoulders and head like a heavy child made of fire. By the time they reached the shelter at angle sixty, Shyla decided that after this situation with Xerxes was resolved, she'd never leave the comfort of an underground city again.

The others downplayed their aches and pains. Jaft said nothing, only rubbed his ankle absently. Omar glanced at Shyla. His emotions rocked between impressed and worried.

"All right," he said. "We'll push at full speed after apex."

Omar had them out and running as soon as it was safe, which meant they were on the surface by angle one-ten. After a few angles, the hot air reminded Shyla of Zhek's healing goo—thick and viscous. And now Omar's tendency to use the word "push" made more sense. She kept the brutal pace by keeping in mind what would happen to their world if Xerxes assassinated the King.

"We're eight angles behind schedule," Omar said before they began the next push. "Not as much of a concern at this point in the sun jump. We can run during the first twenty angles of darkness without worry. But remember you won't have that luxury before apex."

Most of the trip to the next shelter was a blur. Shyla entered a strange state where her thoughts floated, her stride found the perfect rhythm, and the only sound was the rasp of her breath. The air cooled as the sun sank, giving everyone an extra boost of energy. They reached their goal at angle one-ninety—ten angles behind schedule. Omar called it a win.

Shyla woke feeling like she had run all darkness. They set off at angle zero. It wasn't any easier. In fact, it was beyond brutal getting to that second shelter before the danger zone.

However, she and her Invisible Swords slowly adapted to the pace and each sun jump was a bit better than the one before. By the twelfth sun jump, they no longer stumbled to the sleeping cushions and fell asleep as soon as they were horizontal. Instead, they sat together and talked. Blisters turned to calluses and their energy levels stayed consistent. Taking the safe route had been the right decision. They had conserved their energy and would be able to fight Xerxes and his elite soldiers in Qulsary.

The paths they traveled on weren't wide enough for the caravans to use. So it was quite the surprise when they neared a shelter at the mid-point of their journey and she sensed fourteen people inside. Shyla called a stop so she could consult with everyone.

"Could it be squatters?" she asked Omar.

"We're not the only ones traveling these paths," Omar said. "City guards will run them to keep in shape." He pointed to the sun jumping higher in the sky. "It's almost angle seventy; we don't have a choice at this point."

"I know, but let me figure out who they are before we join them. Wait here," Shyla said.

She crept to the entrance, trying to minimize the crunching of her footsteps. At least there were no bumps hiding underneath the sand—a good sign. She peeked down the ladder and no one stood guard at the base—another good sign. These people weren't worried about being attacked.

Then she stretched her power to those within. The atmosphere was relaxed, with friendly banter and laughter. Their comradery and sense of loyalty to each other was clear. They were probably a team of guards. But just to be sure, she went a little deeper into their thoughts and encountered one soul who slipped away from her, dodging her power.

Xerxes.

Shyla's thoughts boiled away to nothing. Unable to move, she stood in the sands near the entrance of the travel shelter grappling with the sudden and terrifying revelation. Xerxes was inside with thirteen of his people and she had to go in or be cooked alive. There was no possible way this would end well for her.

"Shyla," Rae hissed. "What's going on?"

So rattled by Xerxes' unexpected presence, she'd briefly forgotten the others. They waited nearby. She wasn't alone this time. Her terror eased its grip and she hurried over to tell them the horrible news.

"Is it just a coincidence or is it an ambush?" Jaft asked.

"Does it matter?"

"Guess not."

"What do we do?" Lamar gripped the hilt of his sword.

She considered their very meager options. Fighting Xerxes plus his thirteen elite soldiers inside the shelter was not one of them. Plus one of them had to be Rendor, who they couldn't harm and who would figure that out pretty quick and use it to his advantage. If she hadn't panicked when she sensed Xerxes, she would have had the presence of mind to ensure Rendor was well. The only positive about this unexpected encounter was the possibility of freeing him.

Shyla wrenched her thoughts back to the immediate future. Her only chance to survive this encounter with Xerxes was to use magic.

"We can put Xerxes' people to sleep for the duration of the danger zone, but he's protected from our magic. We'll still have to deal with him," Shyla said.

"That's fine. We can handle one man," Balin said.

"Normally we can, but this man has a magical pendant that allows him to influence people. He can convince you to turn on us."

"Can't you block his power with yours?" Jaft wiped sweat from his forehead.

"No." The sun's rays sizzled on her skin. "You'll have to avoid meeting his gaze. If you do, he'll enslave you."

"I love this guy already," Jaft muttered.

"Also, if his sunfire is out, don't look at that either. And don't let him put a blackfire pendant on you."

"In other words, just stare at his crotch," Vashi quipped.

"This isn't a joke," Shyla said. "This man is dangerous and he threatens not just our lives but everyone living on Koraha."

"How?" Lamar asked.

"I'll explain later. Right now, I need you and Rae to help me put Xerxes' people to sleep."

The three of them returned to the circular entrance of the shelter. It was a straight shaft down six levels. A metal ladder was the only way to descend. Shyla confirmed that no one stood directly below. Then she reached with her magic, seeking out six minds to send into a deep slumber. Rae would target four and Lamar would take care of the last three.

The boisterous conversation and laughter from the mercs soon died down as they grew tired. One of Shyla's targets was Vilma and the woman fought the compulsion to sleep. Xerxes' second-in-command believed being tired was a sign of weakness and she never wanted to appear weak in front of the commander. Shyla increased her command. Eventually Vilma succumbed, but not without draining a good bit of Shyla's energy. Then Shyla checked the others. Everyone slept except Xerxes.

Before Shyla could signal the others to descend the ladder, boots scraped on stone and Xerxes appeared at the base of the ladder. No surprise he'd figured out what caused all his soldiers to fall asleep.

"Come on down, Little One, before you and your friends are cooked," he called in a friendly tone. "There's no need to be afraid. I'll keep my distance." He disappeared from view.

Oh, she knew there was every need to be terrified, but there was nothing she could do about it. Balin and Nard went down first and drew their swords as soon as they hit the ground. But after a few tense moments, they signaled the all-clear. Shyla went next and then the others followed.

The cool dimness enveloped her as she descended. It was a

relief to be out of the sun's lethal rays. She joined Balin and Nard. Xerxes sat on a cushion on the far side of the shelter. Scattered around him were the prone forms of his sleeping people. She searched for Rendor, but Xerxes gestured and her attention snapped back to him.

"You didn't have to incapacitate them, Little One. I only wish to talk to you." Unarmed, he rested his hands on his knees. His pendant was tucked under his tunic. For now.

"Does that mean our meeting wasn't an unfortunate coincidence?" she asked.

"Yes. I've been waiting for you."

That was a surprise. "How did you know I was coming?"

"Don't insult my intelligence," he said. "This is the quickest route to Qulsary and you're no doubt racing to warn the King of my nefarious plans. I could have chosen any shelter along the route. But once we settled here, I stationed a man to warn me when you were near. Although I'm impressed you and your Invisible Swords arrived so quickly."

Rendor must have told him about the Invisible Swords. She scanned the sleeping forms, seeking him.

"Big Brute isn't here," Xerxes said. "That's what I wish to discuss with you. And we're running out of time. Well…he is."

The desire to strangle Xerxes rose sudden and hot. She stepped closer with murder on her mind.

Xerxes smiled. "Here's the deal. I need you to counter the King's magic. You agree to work with me and Big Brute lives."

Why did he think— Scorching hells! Shyla had told him that The Eyes, along with her magic, had the ability just to keep

Xerxes happy. And the son of a sand demon not only believed her but he remembered.

"Where's Rendor?" she demanded.

"Doing his part. Playing bait until we free him. Except we won't be able to rescue him in time if you don't agree to wear this." Xerxes held up a pendant.

Shyla averted her gaze, but she caught a glimpse of the blackfire. It appeared bigger than the one she'd worn before and in that brief glance, it tugged hard at her soul.

"You can't," Rae said. "Think of what's at stake."

That reminded her. "Xerxes, I can't counter the King's magic. I lied. And if you assassinate the King, you'll kill everyone on Koraha. He controls our water. Without him, the water will sink beyond our reach and we'll all die of thirst!"

"Nice try, Little One. But since you admitted to lying to me, I will only believe you when you're wearing this." He swung the pendant, drawing her attention.

Shyla ripped her gaze away before it sucked her into its depths. Her heart slammed in her chest, urging her to do something. Anything. But Rae was right; she could not become Xerxes' slave again. She'd be a powerful weapon in his hands and even with the King's magic to protect him, Xerxes would eventually win with her by his side. Yet to let Rendor die would destroy her. Just the thought caused a tearing pain inside her that was like nothing she'd ever experienced. However, one man versus their entire civilization? Even she wasn't that selfish.

"You should do as he says," Omar said. "He's right. Can I join you, too?"

"Of course. You're all welcome," Xerxes said.

Oh no. Shyla glanced around at the others. Rae and Lamar appeared to be struggling against Xerxes' compulsion, but the others' stared at the man with rapt expressions. Seven hells. If she said no, her own people would turn on her and force her to submit to the commander. That left one choice.

She dashed to the ladder and climbed. The metal rungs burned her hands as she scrambled up. No one chased her.

Xerxes called after her. "Where do you think you're going? It's almost angle eighty." Then he said, presumably to the others, "Don't follow her, she'll be back. There is nowhere else for her to go."

Reaching the top, she stepped onto the blazing hot sands. She had to find Rendor, and then… What? Die with him?

She banished those thoughts and focused on her surroundings. Heat pulsed off the sand in waves. The intense sunlight reflected off of them, creating illusions of large pools of water. Turning in a slow circle, she sent her magic out, searching for Rendor. He had to be hidden from sight, but close enough that Xerxes could retrieve him when she agreed to wear the pendant. Was Rendor already— *No. Stop. Just find him.*

Then she touched his soul and almost collapsed with relief. She ran toward where she'd sensed him. The air burned on her face and hands. Each breath was a lungful of fire.

Rendor was on the other side of a large dune. She cried out his name, but he didn't even raise his head. He sat on the hot sand hunched over with his arms behind his back.

Shyla reached him. Unbidden, a primal sound of despair

ripped from her throat. Chains had been locked around his wrists and secured to a stake. She needed a key to free him. Why hadn't she tried to fight Xerxes? Killing the man would have solved her quandary. Except she didn't have the physical or magical skills to defeat him. At least that thought reminded her she had *other* skills.

Wielding magic, she removed the sand from around the stake. It was a nasty piece of metal about a meter long. At the base of the shaft were retractable hooks that were triggered to spring out once the stake was driven into the sand. The curved metal hooks anchored the stake and made it almost impossible for one person to remove it. After clearing the sand away, she retracted the hooks and freed Rendor. His wrists were still secured behind his back, but he could move. Except he remained seated.

She pulled on his arm. "Come on, get up. We have to get to the shelter."

"Not until…the commander…comes for me."

Oh, right. She yanked his pendant from beneath his tunic, pulled the necklace over his head, and tossed it into the sand where she buried it deep. He gasped and toppled to his side as shudders shook him. But there was no time for him to adjust to being free. Not yet.

"Come on," she urged, yanking on his arm. "Please."

He still refused to move. "I can't. *You* can't. Or Xerxes will…"

Seven hells. If they returned to the shelter Xerxes would capture them both. Again.

The heat intensified, baking all the moisture from her mouth, nose, and eyes. It was hard to think while being pierced by the sun's daggers. They needed…something…to stop…

Shade!

Shyla floated a layer of sand to block the sun's deadly rays. A temporary reprieve. Time for a desperate plan.

Except there weren't any velblouds lifting into the sky nearby. No emergency shelters for the caretakers.

Nothing but her fear. Plenty of that. But it triggered a memory. Something about Mojag…he had said…something about something getting scary. And he moved— Son of a sand rat!

She staggered over to the base of the dune and knelt on the sweltering sand. Scooping out as much as possible with her hands, she ignored the blistering agony on her fingers. Eventually the hole was too deep and she switched to moving the sand with her magic, pouring all her energy into digging a tunnel into the dune's core that angled down. She worked until she reached the hard sandstone and could go no further. Turning to fetch Rendor, she stopped. He'd already reached her side.

"Will it…work?" he asked.

"No idea. Get in."

"I…can't." He rattled the chains.

"Get your ass in there, Captain. That's an order."

He growled at her. Well, he tried, but her command had the desired effect and he wedged his oversized body through the tunnel. It was beyond difficult for him to crawl with his arms secured behind his back, but he was still strong. And she helped by pushing him from behind.

Once they reached the center, she cleared more sand so they could sit up. It was a tight fit, though. Rendor hunched over slightly and, although she faced him, her legs were draped over his. Even though it was darker and much cooler than the surface, they still weren't safe. She estimated they were about nine meters inside and twelve meters deep—the equivalent to being on level four. Not far enough if they were in an underground city. It also depended on whether all this sand would conduct the heat or block it. Shyla dumped their water on their clothes and the surrounding sand. Evaporation would cool them for a few angles.

"Need to restrict…the hot air coming in," Rendor said. Heat still poured off of him as if he'd swallowed a piece of the sun.

Shyla filled their entrance tunnel with sand until it was only a centimeter wide, then dug another finger-width shaft in the opposite direction for air flow. Although…suffocation might be a better way to die than heat stroke. No. She wasn't giving up. Her efforts caused sand to pour into their tiny chamber. She wielded magic to stop it and to strengthen the layer of sand above their heads. Her vision blurred as black and white spots swirled. She clung to the last of her energy.

Needing a distraction, she said, "I'm sor—"

"Stop," Rendor said. "Don't say it. I don't…I can't…handle this conversation right now." He shuddered.

"It's still too soon…Xerxes is still… I've a raging sandstorm of…emotions inside me. I need…time to let it settle."

"I understand." And she did. Rendor had been enslaved longer than her. His inner voice had probably been completely erased. But they might not have a later. "How about you just listen?"

No answer. Rendor's eyes were closed.

"I know I've done some terrible things and you might not be able to forgive me. But no matter what happens, I want you to know I love you."

His eyes snapped open and he met her gaze. "You don't *need* to tell me. You are *here* with me instead of safe in the shelter. That is beyond mere words, Shyla." Amazement colored his tone.

"All right, but I need something else to think about or I'm going to pass out and the dune might bury us."

He stared at her a moment in shock. "And here I thought the heat was our only danger. How weak are you?"

"Not helping."

Rendor glanced around as if searching for an idea. His gaze landed on his weapon belt, which was empty. His sword and dagger must be back in the shelter.

"How are you with picking locks?" he asked.

"I don't know. I've never tried."

"Then you're about to learn. There's a set of lock picks in my pouch."

The picks ended up being a couple slim metal tools. Two of them were about ten centimeters long and flat with a little triangle on the ends—diamond picks, according to Rendor. One was bent into an L-shape and was rounder and thicker than the others. Rendor called it a tension wrench.

He squirmed and shifted until his back was to Shyla. The

raw burned bands of flesh around the cuffs were visible even in the semi-darkness.

"Is there enough light in here?" she asked. "I can widen—"

"No need. Picking a lock is all done by sound and feel." He instructed her to insert the tension wrench into the lock on the metal cuffs. "Twist it slightly, adding tension on the locking mechanism." Then he explained how a lock worked with tumblers and pins that kept them in place. "This lock is rather simple. It only has one pin. You have to lift it with the diamond pick."

Lifting proved to be inserting the pick and using the little triangle to push the pin up so it aligned with the cylinder. It took skill and concentration and supposedly she'd hear a click at the same time as a little vibration through her fingertips when the pin reached alignment.

Sweat poured down her face and soaked her tunic as she made several failed attempts to unlock the cuffs. She rested a moment to wipe her slick hands on her sun cloak. The heat inside their hole was stifling and she realized they were basically sitting in an oven, being cooked from the inside out. There was no way they were walking away from this. She wilted.

"Still with me?" Rendor asked.

Shyla jerked her head up. "Yes, sorry, I'm…" What? Overcome with despair? About to pass out? Did it matter? No. She concentrated on the tricky little pin. How could something so small cause so much misery?

After a million, trillion attempts, she popped the lock. Rendor grunted with pain when she took the cuffs off him and he could finally move. Well, as much as was possible in the confined space. He flexed his fingers and rolled his shoulders, almost causing an avalanche of sand.

"Who taught you how to pick a lock?" she whispered, almost afraid of reminding him of his time with Xerxes.

"One of the soldiers. I learned so I'd be more useful to Xerxes."

His disgust and self-loathing was painfully clear to her even without using The Eyes. Shyla needed to strengthen her mental shield, but she didn't have any energy to spare. Nor did she think this was the time or place to convince him otherwise.

"That was a good strategy," she said in a neutral tone.

"Strategy?" He just about sneered the word. "It was sickening. I fell right back into that soldier mindset of a loyal dog, wanting to please. Just like when I was in the Water Prince's guard as I worked my way up to captain. It felt so damn good. It was so much easier. It's who I am. Who I'll *always* be."

She laced her fingers in his. "No. You. Are. Not."

He pulled his hand away. "Come on, Shyla. Xerxes really didn't need to use a pendant on me. Or magic. We both know it was a matter of time until I slipped back to my real self."

He was worse than she feared. And insisting that he wasn't that person anymore would be a waste of time. Rendor refused to hear it. She needed a new approach.

"You just called me a liar," she said. And now that she thought about it, anger boiled in her veins. Before he could respond, she continued, "I can *read* your soul, Rendor. I know who you are better than you do. And you know what I suffered to gain that ability. You participated. You've seen me use it. But now you're calling me a liar.

"You must also think I'm an idiot because, here I am, willing to die for someone who is irredeemable. Or perhaps I'm a selfish idiot because I'm willing to risk the life of every single person on Koraha for some dog soldier. And since you think I'm a lying idiot, if we don't die, you're welcome to go slink off to the corner with your tail between your legs and lick your wounds." Shyla wanted to storm out of the hole, except the air still burned in her lungs. Or was that her fury? She settled for glaring at him.

He rubbed a blister-covered hand over his face. "I'm sorry. I didn't mean to imply you were a lying idiot. I just need time to adjust. Surely you know how it feels to be suddenly freed from the compulsion."

She did. Although she wasn't going to tell him what happened to her when she crushed the blackfire. Not yet. Her ire died. She hadn't been fair to him. "No, I'm sorry. I know you need time, but we don't have much left."

He took her hand and held it. "If we die, I will embrace the Sun Goddess and thank her for putting you in my path. Every sun jump I've spent with you has been a gift. And while I still don't believe I deserve it, I'm eternally grateful.

"As for you…regardless of anything, past, present, and future, I love you. And will always love you. You've brought the sun back into my dark heart."

Overwhelmed with the surge of joy that flooded her, she was unable to utter a word. Instead, Shyla clung to Rendor's hand with both of hers. Then she leaned forward and brushed her dry lips lightly against his chapped ones.

He reached up and stroked her cheek. "Don't cry, sunbeam. You need to conserve your moisture."

She touched her face in surprise. Her fingertips came away wet—a good sign that she wasn't completely dehydrated. Leaning back, she said, "You're making progress."

Confusion creased his forehead. "On what?"

"You said that you would embrace the Sun Goddess if you died. Before you swore you were headed for the seven caverns of hell."

He expelled a raspy half cough, half laugh. "I'm being optimistic."

"Good. Keep on being optimistic."

"You, too."

But it was hard when the heat intensified to almost unbearable levels. Hanging on to the dregs of her energy, she concentrated on filling her lungs with the hot suffocating air—an increasingly difficult act. Each inhalation was more painful and exhausting than the last. A horrible headache slammed behind her eyes. And her heart rate surged as the world spun around her.

Rendor passed out with a puff of exhaled air. She checked his pulse, resting her fingers on his hot neck. His dry skin felt like velbloud leather. His racing heartbeat thrummed under her fingertips, but he still breathed.

For how long? She wondered how much time she had left. The Sun Goddess would be disappointed to see her again. Not only had she failed her mission to stop the enslavement of the goddess's people, but Shyla's actions had probably doomed all of Koraha. It was going to be crowded in the sky. Not that she'd be there. At least she already had a good idea of what to expect in the seven caverns of hell.

And just when she thought it couldn't get any hotter, it did. Perhaps she didn't have a clue what to expect in hell. Shyla held on to consciousness until it faded and slipped through her scrabbling fingers.

The darkness was complete. Not a point of light. Nor a sound. No sense of her physical self. Not cold or hot. No goddess to perform a miracle for her. It reminded her of being trapped in the blackfire. Perhaps she'd never left. Or perhaps this was the first cavern of hell. A place where there was nothing but your thoughts. Effective punishment, facing all your failings.

And she had quite the list of mistakes, poor decisions, and selfish moments. Actually, it was more than a few moments of selfishness. She wielded the power of The Eyes and all she wanted to do was travel with Rendor. The new King was drowning in problems and her only desire was to get the job done and move on. Perhaps if she'd been more focused, she wouldn't have fallen for Egan and Fellan's trick.

A memory stirred. The one of Gurice and Mojag freeing her from the pendant. If they hadn't come along, she'd still be Xerxes' puppet. Gurice hadn't let her wallow, had claimed everyone made mistakes, and she should learn from it and move on.

However, Shyla hadn't learned her lesson and had been about to be trapped by Xerxes again. She imagined talking to

Gurice now, explaining how she'd really let everyone down this time.

Imaginary Gurice slapped her. *You're an idiot. If Xerxes kills the King and the entire population of Koraha, it's* Xerxes' *fault, not yours. Stop blaming yourself. Did you do the best you could?*

Shyla considered Imaginary Gurice's question. *Yes.*

There you go. Now wake up and go pretend to be dead.

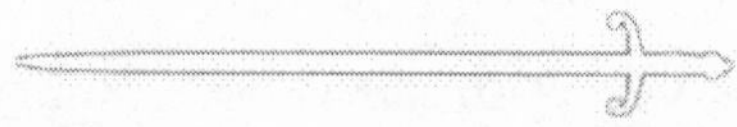

Hot brightness greeted her. Her skin was tight and stiff. Sand coated her mouth. She blinked. Her eyelids scraped over the dry orbs in her eye sockets. The tunnel they had crawled through was wider. Without her magic, the sand must have slid down into the hole. Better than the dune collapsing on top of them.

Rendor stirred beside her, groaning. He was half buried in sand. "What…Where…"

"We survived," she said. "I think."

"You think?"

Remembering Imaginary Gurice's comment, she said, "It's not over yet."

He groaned again. "What time is it?"

"Guessing by the heat, I'd say close to the end of the danger zone."

"Then you better help me find the cuffs."

Moving required an immense effort. Her brittle and dry skin cracked and bled as she dug through the sand. Once they found the cuffs, they crawled from the hole that had saved their lives from the killing heat. Even though the danger was past, the sunlight stabbed through her sun cloak and sizzled on her skin. But she ignored it as best she could because now they needed to survive Xerxes.

Wielding magic scraped her insides raw. Each push of her will on the sand left her weak and shaky. But she replaced the stake and secured the cuffs around Rendor's battered wrists. Then she smoothed the sand around the dune, erasing their tracks except the ones she'd left when running over the dune. Then they staged their bodies.

"Facing each other?" Rendor asked. He lay down with the stake behind him and twisted on his side as if he'd collapsed from a sitting position.

"But I would have tried to get the cuffs off you."

"And when you couldn't? What would you have done to save us?"

"Oh, right." She took off her sun cloak, then lay next to him. Covering them with her cloak as best she could, she moved close to him. With the last bit of her energy, she floated a layer of sand to create shade. She held it up until her strength ran out.

"Close your eyes," she warned Rendor before it fell on top of them.

The stage was set. There was nothing left to do but wait. She didn't even have enough power to scan for nearby bumps. They'd have to rely on mundane methods to warn them when Xerxes and his people approached. Exhausted, she fell asleep.

"...coming," Rendor murmured, waking her.

The sound of voices and boots crunching through the sand

reached her. Time to play dead. Considering her current physical state, she would have no trouble pretending to be a dried-out corpse.

"Seven hells," Xerxes said. "What a waste." His voice sounded from above them as if he stood on top of the dune.

"I told you she was stubborn," Vilma said. "Do you want me to check and make sure they're dead?"

"No," Xerxes said. "If by some miracle she isn't, I don't want you being influenced by her magic."

"She's pulled off a miracle before," Jaft said.

Shyla clamped down on a curse and hoped Xerxes ignored Jaft's comment.

"Sunray, can you counter her magic if she tries anything?" Xerxes asked.

"If she's alive, then yes. She'll be very weak," Rae said.

Xerxes must have given her a blackfire pendant along with that new name.

"All right. Go down and make sure they're dead."

"Yes, sir," Rae snapped.

The sounds of the petite woman's boots grew louder. Shyla gathered the tiny bit of energy her nap had recharged and aimed it at Rae. The wielder was strong, but she shouldn't be able to counter Shyla's power. The real problem was Shyla needed to use a light touch to avoid alerting Rae.

Dead, Shyla commanded when Rae's shadow blocked the sun. Rae's fingers were cool against Shyla's throat.

Dead.

Dead.

Pushing with The Eyes, Shyla read Rae's thoughts. While they focused on pleasing Xerxes, Rae also still struggled to hold on to her identity. She checked Rendor next.

Dead.

Dead.

Dead.

Then she stood. "They're dead."

Shyla relaxed.

"Good," Vilma said. "Zahoor, get those cuffs and the stake. We might need them again."

"What about The Eyes, Rae? Are they still there?" Xerxes asked.

When Rae lifted the hood of the sun cloak so she could get a better look at Shyla's face, Shyla projected into Rae's mind an image of empty eye sockets and blue, white, and black sand nearby as if The Eyes had crumbled into tiny colored grains.

"Ugh." Rae dropped the hood. "They're gone."

"How? Never mind, I want to see for myself."

Scorching sand rats. Shyla couldn't read Xerxes. His sunfire pendant countered the power of The Eyes. As his bootsteps came closer, she frantically searched for a way to stop him. He needed to believe they were dead or all they suffered was for nothing.

"What a waste," he said again. But this time his voice sounded from right near her as if he was crouched next to her. "Why are they half covered with sand?" he asked.

"She probably used it to block the sun," Rae said.

"You can lift that much sand?"

"Yes." The sand sang as it moved. "See? It's cooler under

here. Obviously it won't save your life, but it helps." It thudded to the ground. "It also takes a great deal of energy."

And it gave Shyla an idea. Xerxes was resistant to The Eyes' magic, but what about her other magic? She'd never tried manipulation on him before.

When Xerxes lifted her hood, she projected the same image into his mind and used the *dead* command. Pure fear generated the power she needed to keep sending it.

"It appears The Eyes have disintegrated. Is that what is supposed to happen?" Xerxes dropped the material.

Shyla clamped down on her sigh of relief.

"I don't know," Rae said. "I saw when she sacrificed her real eyes for The Eyes. Captain Rendor cut them out with a knife and the leader of the Parzival monks inserted The Eyes into her bloody sockets. It was the bravest and most horrifying thing I've ever seen."

"Perhaps they needed to be removed from a living host," Xerxes said.

"We'll never know."

"Yes. It's such a waste. Big Brute was turning into one of my best soldiers, and Little One…she could have been a queen."

It took everything Shyla had not to react to his statement. Queen? What did that mean? Eventually he moved away and Zahoor unlocked Rendor's cuffs. But Zahoor had to recruit two other men to help him pull out the nasty stake.

Shyla used the *dead* command on everyone nearby. If she didn't, they'd notice her shaking muscles. She was beyond exhausted and had no idea where she found this energy.

"Should we bury them?" Vilma asked.

Her heart stopped. If they did, Shyla might not be able to create air holes.

"Yes, but not deep. We don't have the time," Xerxes said. "Everyone help and just cover them with sand until they can't be seen. The winds will bury them deeper in time."

It didn't take them long. And the sand was a nice insulation from the sun. Shyla had trapped a pocket of air between them underneath the sun cloak, but she waited as long as possible before drilling an air hole with magic. But their ordeal still wasn't over. They had to ensure Xerxes and the others were well gone before she could move the sand to free her and Rendor from their graves. Except she didn't have anything left. She'd used everything. Her body refused to cooperate and she passed out.

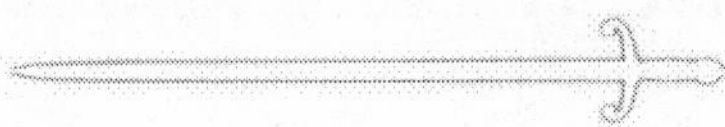

Cold wetness splashed on her face. Shyla struggled to open her eyes as fingers pulled her mouth open and pure bliss filled her mouth. Instinctively, she swallowed the water, gulping the life-sustaining substance. It stopped before she'd had enough. There'd never be enough.

"Come on, sunbeam," Rendor said. "Wake up."

Another cold splash. This time on her head. It didn't help. Her thoughts and body were mired in a thick resistant substance. Zhek's goo?

"It's almost dark," Rendor said. "I can't carry you. I've nothing left."

It wasn't his words that roused her but the panic straining his voice. She cracked open an eye. It required far more energy than she had. Rendor knelt next to her. He was covered with burns and blisters and fatigue lined his eyes, but his gaze turned hopeful when she focused on him.

"How?"

"I dug us out. Then fetched water." He gestured to her. "Lots of water."

Only then did she realize she was soaked. How long had he been trying to rouse her? According to the sun, a long time. If she was stuck on the surface during darkness and soaking wet, she'd freeze to death. She laughed. Might as well experience all the ways to die.

"Shyla?"

"Sorry, I just thought…never mind. Can you help me stand?"

With Rendor's help, she made the colossal effort to go from horizonal to vertical. "Should we celebrate?" she asked. She leaned against him, sharing his warmth.

"How about we hold off until we're in the shelter."

"Good idea." She glanced around. The colors of the desert had already faded to gray. Only a few more angles until the sun disappeared and the darkness rushed back in. Multiple tracks scored the side of the dune, which had grown to the size of a mountain while she slept.

"Yeah," Rendor said, gazing at the top. "If that hadn't been here, you'd be tucked under a fur in the shelter by now."

She hugged him. "You almost died. You're allowed to have

limits."

"I know. But I don't have to like it."

Typical Rendor. She gestured to the tracks. "Too bad Mojag's not here. He could just move the dune out of our way."

"That was Mojag?" Rendor sounded impressed.

They had a lot of catching up to do. But for now she needed to stop procrastinating. The energy required to climb the dune would not suddenly appear while she stood here. She would have to tap into the reserves of her reserves. She had those, right?

With Rendor holding her steady, she stepped forward. One. Two. Three more and they reached the base of the dune. The climb turned into another test of her endurance. Her body threatened to revolt a dozen times an angle. She suspected she'd need a full circuit of rest before it forgave her.

Shivering in the cold air, she trudged up the side. Wet sand clung to her clothes, weighing her down. She ended up crawling the last meter and rolling onto the crest of the dune completely spent.

But Rendor wouldn't let her lie there. "Look, there's the shelter." He helped her to her feet. "It's warm inside." He kept her from tumbling down the other side. "There's dry clothes." He urged her to keep walking. "Plenty of water."

They reached the entrance. A victory like no other.

Yet the final trail waited—the ladder. She almost sobbed.

"I'll go first," Rendor said. "Wait until I'm at the bottom."

"What if I fall on you?"

"I'll catch you."

He'd try, but he was too weak. More incentive for her to

hang on. Once Rendor reached the end, she struggled to mount the ladder. The metal rungs seemed slippery and her leg and arm muscles jittered with fatigue. But she lifted a foot and sought the next rung down. And to think Rendor had carried her up a ladder like this. She'd exhausted all her energy wielding magic and fainted. You'd think she'd learned her lesson not to do that by now. Nope. But Rendor had climbed with her dead weight hanging over his shoulders. She giggled at the words *dead weight*.

"Shyla? Are you all right?"

No. Not in the least. "Yes."

Eventually Rendor's hands grabbed her waist and he guided her down the last few rungs. Then she collapsed onto a cushion and embraced the darkness.

She slept for two sun jumps, waking only for food and water. Rendor also rested, slowly regaining his strength. On the third sun jump, they talked about what had happened while they were apart.

"Is Xerxes headed to Qulsary?" she asked Rendor.

"I don't know. He really wanted to recapture you before going after the King. The only part of the plan I was privy to was ambushing you here. Xerxes seemed pretty convinced that you'd agree to wear a pendant." Rendor stopped and gazed at her. "At the time, I didn't understand why you'd do it for me, but I followed my orders." He rubbed his healing wrists. "They used the stake so it'd look convincing. I trusted they would come for me before it was too late. Then you showed up. If you hadn't taken off the pendant…"

"You would have yanked that stake out. The blackfire can't make you kill yourself. Xerxes knows that. He wasn't worried about you. He figured you would have come back in time."

"Are you sure? It wasn't until you removed the pendant that I even considered leaving that spot."

"Xerxes told me. And there was no reason for him to lie." She'd been unable to tell him how to wake The Eyes' power and he claimed she didn't have to obey him if she thought it would lead to her death. "Why didn't you remind him that the King is immune to The Eyes?"

"I did." Rendor's shoulders drooped. "I told him everything I remembered even while I was still fighting the compulsion. But eventually I couldn't even remember loving you. All my emotions centered on Xerxes as I became Big Brute."

She touched his arm. "It was the pendant. The same thing happened to me. It felt so much better when I embraced being Little One."

He met her gaze. "But there was a part of you still fighting."

"Not really. There were certain revelations of what I'd done that shocked me back to my senses for mere moments." She rubbed the back of her head. "Pain seemed to snap me out of it for a bit, too."

"I stopped fighting." He glanced down. "Being Big Brute was so easy. There was no guilt. All the stuff I did for the Water Prince was viewed as a positive thing by Xerxes and his squads. I was accepted."

"And now?"

"Back to the struggle, dodging accusing glares, trying to ignore the barbs, and dealing with the constant guilt." He tapped his chest. "It burns deep inside me."

She took his hands in hers. "Tell me." When he remained quiet, she squeezed them slightly. "Tell me about Big Brute."

"You won't love me anymore." His voice was barely a whisper.

"You can't really love me until you tell me."

That captured his attention. She continued, "You believe that I gave you my love without really knowing you. You believe deep down you're still Big Brute and that you're pretending to be Rendor, Captain of the Invisible Sword, who hasn't been accepted by the members, just tolerated. And you believe that you don't deserve my love. Those beliefs keep you from fully embracing who you are now. So let's take this one belief at a time. Tell me about Big Brute."

Rendor raised his head. He yanked his hands from her grasp and met her gaze with an almost defiant expression. He said, "I killed a man when I was sixteen circuits old. The first of ten."

He expected her to react with repulsion, but Shyla kept her face neutral. "Go on."

Rendor took it as a challenge. Determined to horrify her, he told her about all his misdeeds, killings, and the people he'd tortured. He explained all the awful orders he'd obeyed. Everything he'd done to gain and keep the position of captain of the guard.

Through it all, Shyla didn't judge or try to console him or

show pity or attempt to explain that his actions were due to his parents not accepting him for who he was, forcing the young man to seek acceptance from the Water Prince. Nope. She said nothing. She remained expressionless. Of course, how she felt on the inside was another story—she wanted to hug him tight and make him believe he was no longer that man.

When he finished, he stared at her as if waiting for her to condemn him for all his evils. To tell him to leave and never come near her again. Instead, she said, "Tell me the good things Big Brute did."

"There aren't any. Weren't you listening?"

"I was. Tell me the good. Like the time you didn't arrest Mojag. There's more of them." Now she challenged him.

"They're nothing. Small things."

"Tell me or I'll pluck them from your memories."

He growled. "That's cheating."

"I don't care. Nobody is one dimensional. Tell me the rest."

His jaw tightened, but then he wilted under her fierce stare. "Those vagrant kids were going to be the death of me. The Water Prince didn't care how old they were. He wanted us to use the kids to force the parents to divulge the locations of their communes." Rendor detailed all the things he did to keep the kids safe. And that triggered other memories.

Once again Shyla didn't react. Didn't exclaim over his efforts to help the kids. Didn't interrupt.

Eventually his recollections focused on the time when he first met Shyla. "Huh." Then he fell silent.

"Huh?" she prompted.

"After I met you, I didn't..."

"Didn't...?"

He huffed at her. "I stopped being Big Brute."

Finally! Still she prodded. "What about those vagrants that were captured while I was missing?"

"I couldn't torture them. I assigned Yates to handle the interrogations." He straightened and there was a contemplative softening to his expression.

Shyla cupped his cheek. "Big Brute is part of your history, but he's gone and that's when I started falling in love with you, Rendor. Knowing your history hasn't changed my feelings for you at all. Because I know deep down"—she tapped his chest—"you're no longer Big Brute."

Rendor pulled her into his lap and hugged her tight. His confession wasn't going to make everything better, but it was a step in the right direction. And thinking of directions, they needed to decide what to do next.

Quite content in Rendor's arms, she mulled over what they'd been discussing.

"If Xerxes knew I couldn't counter the King's magic, why did he want to recapture me?" she asked.

"He wanted to use you to enslave everyone around the King. Xerxes is confident he can assassinate him."

And that reminded her. She told him what she'd learned about the King's water magic and how it kept them all alive.

Rendor released her and stared at her in shock. "Why didn't you tell me this sooner?"

"My brain was cooked, and we can't do anything about it—

we've both been recovering. Besides, the King's magic is powerful and Xerxes doesn't have me. Plus the King will have plenty of warning. Since Xerxes waited here for me, the messenger will arrive in Qulsary well before the commander."

Rendor's horror increased. "Xerxes killed the messenger."

Now she understood his alarm as it rose within her as well. The King had no idea Xerxes was coming.

Shyla didn't realize how much she'd been counting on that message getting to the King until now. It was the worst possible news.

Surging to her feet, Shyla said, "We have to warn the King. We need to leave now." She bent to pick up her water skin, triggering a wave of dizziness.

Rendor grabbed her waist to keep her from toppling. "You're in no condition to travel."

"Doesn't matter."

"It's twenty angles until darkness."

"If we go at double time, we can reach the next travel shelter before it gets too cold." Shyla tried and failed to break his hold. Either he had an iron grip or she was still very weak.

He raised an eyebrow. "Want to reconsider the double time?"

"Then you go and I'll catch up."

"No. We stay together. Or do I need to remind you what happened the last time we split up?"

Guilt squeezed her chest. "No. But—"

"I understand. I also believe that since Xerxes doesn't have you, he will stop at Nintri and gather more soldiers and supplies. Which will slow him down and give us more time to reach the King."

Of course he made perfect sense, but it did nothing to calm the impatience boiling up her throat. "We'll leave at angle zero, then."

"Do you know how to find the next travel shelter on the way to Qulsary?" he asked.

Seven hells. "No. That's why I hired Omar. Do you?"

"Not a clue. And I'm not about to go racing off in some random direction either." He gave her a hard stare. "I never want us to be stranded topside during apex again."

Neither did she. She'd barely survived. Twice. "We can figure it out. Qulsary is northwest of our location. The sun starts its jump in the east, so we can keep the sun over our right shoulder and—"

"No. One miscalculation and we'll be lost."

"We can follow Xerxes' tracks."

"It's been three sun jumps. The wind will have covered them with sand. Besides, he's not going to Qulsary."

Frustration pulsed. "That's just a guess. I'm not waiting."

"It's a good guess. He killed the messenger and us. He has time. There's no one else who can warn the King."

"Except the Invisible Swords and monks escorting the taxes."

"The fake caravan will get there in roughly twenty-nine sun jumps," Rendor said. "The real caravan won't make it at all."

"How do you know there are two?"

"Xerxes isn't an idiot. He expected you to send a decoy."

"Did he expect me to assign Mojag to the second caravan?" she asked.

"He assumed you'd have a magic wielder traveling with the wagons, but if Mojag can move the dunes…that second one might reach Qulsary after all."

"I'm not an idiot either."

"Never said you were, sunbeam." He flashed her a smile. "Is it heading directly to the capital?"

"Yes. If they haven't run into trouble, it'll arrive in Qulsary two sun jumps after the fake caravan." She considered Xerxes' timeline. He already had a head start but would need added time to collect his people and travel to Qulsary. "Both caravans will still be too late to warn the King. We're in the best position." They could reach it in twelve sun jumps.

"I agree. And we'll leave with the next messenger that comes through."

"But that might take—"

"Only a few more sun jumps at most. There hasn't been any since we survived, and they come through here fairly frequently."

"How do you know?"

Rendor dropped his hands from her waist and stepped away. "We questioned the messenger from Apanji. Xerxes wanted to know how many people used this route."

By his scowl, she didn't need to ask if it was the one they killed. Instead she sorted through everything she knew about traveling on the surface of Koraha. Perhaps she'd read something that would help them find their way to Qulsary. Waiting for another messenger would be nearly impossible in her current frame of mind.

Rendor must have sensed her mood. "You can't even stand without swaying," he said. "Think of how you'll feel running in the hot sun for a hundred and twenty angles a sun jump. We can use this time to fully recover. We'll still beat Xerxes to the King. Besides, there's no need to almost kill yourself on the trip to Qulsary. Then you'll be useless." He pulled her close. "You're allowed to have limits."

He was using her own words against her! And of course he was right. "I know. But I don't have to like it."

Rendor laughed. "I'm surprised you remember anything from the trip to the shelter."

"I wouldn't mind forgetting the entire episode."

"Tell you what." He lowered his voice to a husky rumble. "If you get some proper rest, I'll give you an improper experience that will make you forget all your troubles."

A hot flush shot right through her. At least her libido wasn't exhausted. "I've already gotten some rest, how about a demonstration of what I can expect if I continue resting?"

He picked her up and carried her to the sleeping cushion. Setting her down gently, he said, "Nice try, sunbeam." Rendor covered her with a fur. "You're just going to have to trust me."

She huffed and would have pouted except warmth enveloped her. The softness underneath her also conspired against her. "Don't look so smug," she said to Rendor before falling asleep.

THE KING OF KORAHA

At least Rendor wasn't the type to gloat. Over the next two sun jumps, she regained most of her energy. They also discussed strategy and made plans for when they reached Qulsary. Since Xerxes had spies everywhere, they needed to be careful that no one spotted them. Being dead was an advantage they couldn't lose. Not until the right time.

At angle zero on that third sun jump—the sixth since they survived the killing heat—Shyla and Rendor climbed to the surface. Worried that their skin might be overly sensitive to the sunlight, they wanted to check how their healing blisters would react. She also wished to test her magic since she had exhausted her power well beyond her limits. There had to be consequences.

Under Rendor's watchful gaze, she concentrated on a section of sand. It was a relief when it lifted into the air and formed an arrow, which she sent into the side of the dune. Then she created a small sandstorm that swirled around them a few times before she let it die.

Shyla turned to Rendor. "Can you go hide? I want to see if I can find you with my magic."

"All right."

She closed her eyes and covered her ears. Memories of being a child and playing hide and seek rose. Simple times that she had complained about. So anxious to be an adult and *know* things and *do* things. She'd wasted her youth wishing to be somewhere else, doing something else, and now all she wished was to return to that innocent carefree state.

Opening her eyes, she lowered her hands. All was quiet. Rendor was not in sight and she resisted looking for his tracks—that wouldn't be fair. She pushed her magic out, scanning the desert in a circle around her. Nothing. Perhaps he'd run further away. She extended her reach and did another sweep. Still nothing. If he was fast or still running, he might have gone far. A third effort produced the same result.

Then it hit her. He might be hiding under the sand. Impressed by his bravery—she never wanted to be buried again—she aimed her power through the sand about a meter down. Nothing! Either he was really good at hiding or she'd burnt out her ability to sense another person. Scared that was the case, she pushed as far as she could go and found a bump. Finally. Except when she dipped to read Rendor's thoughts, it wasn't him. She couldn't read the person's soul, but they were heading toward their shelter along with another. At least it meant her power worked and they wouldn't waste any more sun jumps waiting. But where was Rendor?

It took her longer than she'd like to admit to figure it out. And she didn't even need magic. Just her brain. He was in the travel shelter. She hurried down to join him and share the news.

He studied her. "If the people you felt are messengers, that means your power extends at least twenty kilometers. Unless this is their second stop, then it's about forty kilometers. Did you know that?"

She didn't.

"That's impressive. Can you go further?" he asked.

"Probably not."

"Probably?"

"It's been my experience that desperation tends to enhance my abilities." Unfortunately.

"That's good because some people experience the opposite when they're desperate. Speaking of experience…" He stepped closer and lowered his voice. "We have just enough time for my promised improper experience."

Desire arrowed straight into her core, igniting a blaze of heat—the good kind. She welcomed this fire as he kissed her. It kicked her heartbeat into double time and her skin became overly sensitive to his touch. Each stroke of his fingertips on her neck caused ripples of sensation throughout the rest of her body.

Within a few gasps of breath, all of their clothing was flung to the ground. Her hands explored his muscular shoulders and back until he grabbed them, wrapping one hand around both her wrists.

"Trust me?" he asked.

"Always."

Then he threw her over his shoulder, carried her to a cushion, tossed her down, and ravished her so completely and thoroughly she forgot all her troubles, as promised. Nothing existed in her world except Rendor.

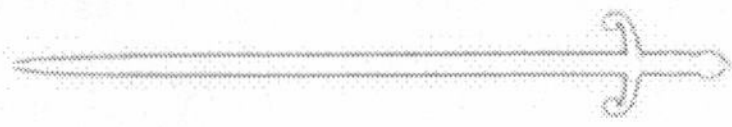

The messengers arrived at the shelter at angle seventy, which meant her power extended about forty kilometers. She really needed to experiment more. By the time the messengers climbed down, Shyla was dressed and mostly recovered. Every muscle in her body still hummed and her skin tingled. Rendor kept his gloating to a minimum, but she caught him looking at her with a pleased, almost smug expression. No doubt he had enjoyed the improper experience just as much.

The man and woman carrying the messages to Qulsary were around her age. Shyla used The Eyes to ensure they were genuine. Normally only one person was needed, but with the increase in bandits and squatters, the messengers had decided to team up. They were happy to have company as long as Shyla and Rendor kept up. The trip would last another twelve sun jumps.

The four of them climbed out at angle one-ten to start the journey. The heat slammed into Shyla like an invisible shovel. Memories of being suffocated by hot air threatened to send her right back down into the safety of the travel shelter.

Rendor cupped her elbow. "You okay?"

"Yes." She shuddered despite the temperature. "My memories are returning."

"Ah. Too bad the banishment of your troubles is only temporary. At least you never forgot my name." He smirked. "Must have been because you yelled it so many times."

She swatted him, grinning. "Brat."

However, all her good thoughts disappeared as the messengers took off. Their pace was faster than Omar's at first, but then they settled into a more manageable stride. Still, the next seventy angles was a struggle. She wasn't as recovered as she'd thought. Rendor, on the other hand, kept up with ease.

The messengers reached the second shelter about five angles

before Shyla and Rendor. He had matched his pace to hers. Once she climbed down, Shyla headed for the closest cushion and collapsed.

The following sun jump was a bit better, and like before, she eventually returned to full strength. As predicted, they arrived at Qulsary twelve sun jumps later. The messengers headed into the city to make their deliveries while Shyla and Rendor waited out of sight of the surface buildings until the sun almost reached the danger zone. That guaranteed no one would witness them entering the castle. Shyla searched for nearby bumps just in case. No one lingered outside.

The stained-glass surface building of the inverted castle was deserted. No surprise. The main doors were closed and locked tight. Rendor removed his lock picks and set to work. Shyla sent her magic down to where the guards stood, counting nine bumps. They were relaxed, bored, and confident that no one was idiotic enough to try to breach the castle during apex. She would have been insulted if she didn't agree.

When Rendor nodded, she wielded her magic, aiming it at the guards.

All's quiet.

Rendor turned the cylinder, unlocking the door. They slipped inside and relocked the door behind them.

All's quiet.

They traversed the tunnel, but before they reached the receiving room, Shyla used the *look away* command on the guards. Then they crossed to the side of the room and continued down to Najib's office. Avoiding bumps and using the *look away* command, Shyla was fairly confident no one had seen them.

After ensuring Najib was alone, she distracted the guard outside his door and entered without knocking. Najib was working at his desk, but his head jerked up when the latch clicked shut.

He studied them for a stunned moment and Shyla gathered her magic in case he started yelling for help. She scanned his surface thoughts, which were grappling with their sudden and unexpected arrival.

Eventually, he said in a calm voice, "I assume no one knows you're here since I asked my guard not to let anyone disturb me. Add in the fact it's almost apex, something must be very wrong."

"Is the King all right?" she asked.

Najib hopped to his feet. "As of a few angles ago, yes, he's fine. Why?"

Thank the goddess. Shyla swayed as emotion and all those sun jumps of running caught up with her.

"Sit down before you fall down," Najib said. When they were settled on the cushions, he said, "Tell me what's wrong."

Now she remembered why she liked Najib—he was quick. "The King's in danger. Commander Xerxes is planning on assassinating him."

The advisor's contemplative expression wasn't what she expected.

"You need to quadruple the guards around the King," she said.

"The King is well protected. His magic makes it almost impossible for someone to assassinate him. Why are you so concerned?"

She took a breath to calm her racing heart. "Xerxes has a set of ancient and powerful artifacts that can influence others and enslave them." She explained how the sunfire and blackfire pendants worked.

Finally Najib appeared concerned. "How powerful?"

"Powerful enough to trap me." Reporting her own enslavement was difficult. Shyla avoided meeting Rendor's gaze. Guilt over betraying him still gnawed on her heart.

"If he has these stones and some of your Invisible Swords, do you really believe increasing the guards will keep Xerxes from reaching the King?" Najib asked.

"No, but it might slow him down."

"While that is a sound strategy, we don't have the coins to pay them, unless you intercepted the taxes?" He raised a hopeful eyebrow.

"We did, but the coins probably won't be here in time. Can you recruit any of the Quirin monks?"

"I can, but how will we know they haven't been influenced?"

"That's easy. I can use The Eyes."

"The extra guards would alert Xerxes that the King has been warned," Rendor said. "Unless you can come up with another reason for the added security?"

"Wouldn't it be a good thing that Xerxes knows he'll face more resistance?" Najib asked. "Maybe then he won't make the assassination attempt."

"That won't stop him," she said. "If anything, he'll probably strike sooner so you don't have time to set up the extra defenses.

And I won't have time to figure out how to counter the pendants." She considered the problem. The monks should be able to travel to the castle without being seen. The risk was one of the King's guards leaking the information. "Can you prevent everyone from leaving the castle?"

"Yes, we've had lockdowns before, such as when we discovered the taxes were stolen. But that will eventually draw attention."

"This seems counterintuitive, but the best thing to do about the guards right now is nothing," Rendor said. "If one of the King's guards is compromised, then any change to the routine will alert Xerxes."

"He's right." Although Shyla hated not having the King surrounded with extra security. "I can read the guards and determine if any of them are spying for Xerxes."

"Do you want to interview them again?" Najib asked.

"No. I don't want Xerxes to know we're alive."

"He thinks you're dead?"

"Yes." She explained the episode in the desert.

Najib stared at her. "That's...unprecedented."

"That's Shyla," Rendor said. "It's the second time she has lived through apex."

The advisor glanced between them as if waiting for one of them to say, "Just kidding." When neither of them spoke, he said, "And even with all your power, you couldn't counter the sunfire?" His tone was a mixture of awe and terror. "Is there another way to stop or block the sunfire's influence?"

"I don't know, but I'm praying there is. Once I know it, then we can set a trap for Xerxes."

"How are you going to find out how to stop it?"

She remembered that symbol on the scroll Neda had shown her. "Does the King have his own Room of Knowledge?"

"I'm not at liberty to say," he hedged.

Which meant yes. "These pendants were created for the first King of Koraha. If there is a way to neutralize them, the information wouldn't be where anyone can access it. I need to get into that room."

"And I need to discuss all this with the King."

"Alone. The guards can't overhear you," she said.

"All right. Then I'll wait until our meeting before the King retires. That's always in his sleeping chambers and completely private."

"And in the meantime, I'll read all the castle's guards to see if I can find the ones that are spying for Xerxes." They already knew about Malik's connection to Xerxes' sister. When they'd interviewed the guards, their questions had been focused solely on the stolen taxes.

"You're certain there are spies?" Najib frowned.

"Yes. Xerxes is too smart not to have a couple. Don't worry, no one will see me or know I'm assessing them."

"See us," Rendor said. His stubborn expression meant there would be no arguing with him. "Also you should send Hakana to Qulsary to keep an eye out for Xerxes. We need to know when he arrives."

"Ah, yes, she'd be perfect. All right, it sounds like we have a plan," Najib said. "You're welcome to use the guest suite. No one should bother you."

They left Najib's office and spent the rest of the sun jump ghosting through the castle. Since Shyla had already made eye contact with all the guards, she was able to read them. Starting with all those on duty, Shyla dipped into the guards' thoughts and emotions. Her fear for the King's safety eased slightly as the people in this shift proved to be loyal.

"There's probably four shifts," Rendor said when they took a break. "Each one would be ninety angles. Any longer and it's hard to keep focused."

They managed to check two more shifts and found two spies before they stopped to rest. She wasn't that tired, but Xerxes could arrive at any time and she'd need all her energy to keep the King safe.

The sleeping cushion in the guest suite was more comfortable than she remembered. She snuggled in close to Rendor and, much to her chagrin, soon fell asleep.

A light tapping on the door woke her. Untangling from the fur, she was halfway to the door with an armed Rendor a step behind when she remembered to use her magic. Najib waited on the other side. His thoughts were chaotic, a sense of urgency thrumming through him. She withdrew her magic and opened the door wide enough for him to slip inside.

"How did your meeting go?" she asked.

Najib scrubbed a hand through his short hair. His wrinkled tunic and the stubble on his cheeks meant he hadn't slept. "He thinks we're overreacting. Between his powers and his immunity to magic, he believes he can handle an assassination attempt. But he promised to be extra careful and limit his meetings."

"And his secret Room of Knowledge?" she asked.

"He's given you permission to enter."

Pleased she'd guessed correctly, she grinned. "Now?"

Najib gave her a tired smile. "I need to get the key first. Have you found any more spies?"

"Two, but the good news is they aren't under Xerxes' influence."

"How is that good?"

"It means they can think for themselves and I can affect them with my magic."

"Ah." He tugged on his collar. "Have you read everyone?"

"No. I've one more shift to do."

"Come to my office when you're finished. I should have the key by then." Najib paused. "Feel free to help yourselves to food and water. The cook is serving gamelu sausages."

Rendor's stomach growled loudly.

Najib laughed. "I can just hear the castle gossip now about the mystery of the disappearing sausages." He left.

They swiped a bunch of sausages and filled their water skins before reading the last shift of guards. Once Shyla was sure she had encountered them all, they headed for Najib's office.

He appeared gaunt and distracted, his stubble thicker. Clicking his tongue, he wrote the names down—four in total, including Malik. "I guess it could be worse." Then he straightened and patted his pocket. "I've the key. Come on."

Shyla and Rendor followed him through the castle. To everyone they passed, it seemed as if Najib walked alone. After descending to level thirty-four, Najib grabbed two trol lanterns and handed one to Rendor before leading them down a number of tunnels. Dust swirled in the bright white light—not a well-used passage. The tunnel ended abruptly at the top of a stairway.

Najib gestured to the steps. "The King's Room of Knowledge is two levels down." He pulled the key out and handed it to Shyla. "It's not guarded since only the King and I know the location or that it even exists. But it is locked, just in case someone stumbles upon it."

"We'll make sure to lock it when we're done," Shyla said.

"I hope you're successful. Keep me posted."

"Will do."

Najib nodded and retreated. Since Rendor held the lantern, he went first. His boots scraped on the gritty steps. The air held the scent of moisture and abandonment. She wondered how often the King visited this room.

Across the landing at the bottom of the stairwell were two oversized iron doors. They resembled the ones to the King's vault, except there was only one massive lock.

Shyla inserted the key. "I hope it's not rusted." Much to her surprise, the key turned with ease. However, instead of a click, a loud metallic twang rang inside the door.

A grinding, bone-chilling sound rolled overhead—the familiar and dreadful noise of stone being rubbed against stone. Shyla and Rendor glanced at each other before he shone the light up the stairs. There was now a roof cutting the two levels of steps into just one.

"The lock was booby-trapped," she said as cold dread slid

down to her stomach.

"Why didn't Najib— Son of a sand demon tricked us."

"Maybe he forgot."

Rendor looked at her. "He's not the type to forget."

"Are the doors unlocked?"

Rendor pushed on them. They didn't budge. He handed her the lantern and tried again with both hands, then he used his shoulder, straining against the iron. "And that would be a no."

He mounted the stairs. When he reached the ceiling, he pressed his hands on it and tried to move it. He grunted and his muscles popped, but it was to no avail. "Do you have any ideas?" he asked.

"Sometimes there's a latch just in case the trap is sprung by accident." Shyla set the lantern down.

"What's it look like?"

"It'll blend in with the walls or floor. You have to press it or pull it. Look for a crack or an anomaly." She inspected the doors, tapping her fingers on anything that looked out of place and hooking a fingernail under any tiny gaps. Keeping focused on her task, she ignored the clammy fear that clung to her that there wasn't a latch.

Rendor slid his hands over the wall to her right. They worked in silence, exploring every centimeter of their prison. Shyla tried to keep her dire thoughts in check. Tried not to calculate how much air they had left. Tried not to recall that skeleton skewered by a sword in Tamburah's vault. Booby traps were always installed with the intent to kill.

When they failed to find the latch, Shyla tried turning the

key a different way. Perhaps there was a special sequence and Najib had forgotten to tell her. Twisting the key in the opposite direction, she produced another twang.

This time a section of the floor directly under the doors dropped down with a bang. It extended the entire length of the doors. Shyla knelt to peer underneath them. The gap didn't go all the way to the other side of the door, which must be at least a meter thick. Rendor brought the light closer, but when she reached into the gap, he yanked her hand back.

"There could be a blade or the block could spring back into place," he warned.

She shuddered at the image of crushed fingers. Rendor shone the lantern into the gap but there was nothing visible. If the release latch was inside, she might have to risk her fingers. Better than running out of air.

"What's the point of the gap?" she asked Rendor. Then she wished with every fiber of her being that she had kept her mouth shut.

With fascinated horror, they stood and watched as water swelled up inside the gap and quickly spilled over.

The water welling from the gap underneath the iron doors spilled onto the floor. It raced across the small landing and lapped at the bottom step. Shyla and Rendor retreated, standing on the stairs.

And here she'd been worried about running out of breathable air. The room was only about two meters square with a three-meter-high ceiling. Now terror gripped her heart, digging into it with sharp claws as the threat became real. The water level rose with alarming speed. They climbed a few more steps.

"I thought it was odd that Najib never asked if we could find our way back," Rendor said, hunching over so he didn't hit his head. "He expects us to die here."

Drowned.

The unfamiliar word swirled in her mind. And she was about to experience it firsthand if they didn't escape. "How tight is the stone covering the roof?" she asked.

Rendor stepped higher and pushed against it with his back and shoulders. “It won’t budge.”

“We can yell for help. Maybe someone is nearby.”

He looked at her as if she was daft. “No one is nearby.”

Right. Those tunnels hadn’t been used in circuits. They needed another idea. Except it was difficult to think when the bottom four steps were now submerged under water. Difficult to breathe with fear wrapped around her throat.

“Not *nearby*,” Rendor said suddenly. “But you can reach someone who is forty kilometers away.”

“I can!” She’d forgotten. “Except who do I reach?” They needed the King to influence the water and unlock the trap, but she couldn’t connect to him. It had to be someone the King trusted. Najib was out—the traitor. A guard might work. Who else?

“Pick anyone, we’re running out of time.” Fear tightened Rendor’s voice, making it sharp.

“Sorry.” She sought familiar bumps in the castle. Only those she’d made eye contact with would be receptive to her instructions. This effort went beyond using commands. She’d never tried it before, but with the cold water filling her boots there was no room for doubts.

Wielding her magic, she touched many occupants of the castle. She found the King just by sensing his guards. She was about to pick one of his loyal guards when she caught a familiar bump nearby. Hakana!

The King’s page would be perfect. She dipped into her thoughts. Hakana was already on her way to deliver a message to the King.

Drawing on the power of The Eyes, she reached out to the young woman.

Emergency!

Shyla and Rendor about to drown.

King must *save them.*

Room of Knowledge booby trap.

Hurry. Hurry. Hurry. Hurry!

Hakana paused outside the King's office in confusion, questioning these strange thoughts. Had she overheard a guard? Had Najib sent her to fetch the King?

Shyla increased her magic.

Emergency!

Shyla and Rendor about to drown.

King must *save them.*

Room of Knowledge booby trap.

Hurry. Hurry. Hurry. Hurry!

She kept repeating her distress call until Hakana burst into the King's office and rushed over to his desk. She reached for the King's hand and as soon as the girl touched his skin, Shyla's connection to Hakana was severed. Their lives now depended on the King agreeing to follow his page. She didn't like those odds.

Chills raced over her skin as the icy water soaked into her pants. Rendor pulled her up beside him, tucking her close and enveloping her with his warmth. They sat on the highest step they could without banging their heads. There was a meter of air space left. Her lungs strained, trying to suck in as much air as possible. Maybe she could…store it inside her? She suddenly wished she had four air bladders like the velblouds. At least when she was dying on the surface, she knew what to expect. This was an entirely new way to die.

"Did it work?" Rendor asked.

"The message has been delivered."

"Is the King coming?"

"I hope so." She explained about Hakana.

As the water climbed up her lower torso, she remembered why she'd let her friend Banqui do all the digging and exploring in the ancient ruins. Why she'd let him trigger the booby traps. It was much safer to read maps and research locations. Although she doubted Banqui had ever sprung a trap like this one. She prayed she'd get a chance to tell him all about it. In fact, she had lots of things to say to her friends and family.

Shivers set in when the water lapped at her ribs. Rendor set the trol lantern on the very top step before moving her to his lap so more of her body was out of the water. A temporary reprieve. The level kept rising. She wrapped her arms around his neck and kissed him long and hard.

"We're getting out of here," he said, pressing her to his chest.

She couldn't agree. Couldn't lie to him. Not with the water up to her armpits.

"There's nothing to forgive," he said, breaking the silence. "There never was. You did what you had to do, what you were forced to do. I don't blame you for my capture. You need to stop blaming yourself."

"Xerxes is to blame," she said.

"Yes, exactly."

"He's to blame for you as well."

"I…" He gave her a rueful grin.

"If we survive this, that means the goddess has forgiven us for *everything*. Clean slate. Agreed?"

"Yes." He hesitated. "And if we don't?"

"Then the goddess will decide our fate. But don't give up. Fight hard until the very end."

"That should be our motto," he said.

A laugh surprised her. "Done."

The trol lantern hissed and sputtered before it popped and died. The darkness was instant. Even though she understood why the lantern went out, it felt like a sign from the goddess. Not a good one. Her fear doubled and she clung to Rendor. She'd rather die on the surface in the sunlight. Not drowned in the darkness.

When the water circled her neck, Rendor adjusted so both their heads were touching the ceiling. He twined his fingers in hers. There was nothing left to say. He knew how much she loved him, and his love pumped in her heart.

Panic filled her as the water rose. She tilted her head back and pressed her nose to the ceiling, scraping it on the rough stone. Then she filled her lungs with as much air as she could and held it.

Water engulfed her. She held on to Rendor's hands and squeezed her eyes shut. Strange sloshing noises sounded inside her head right between her ears. The cold seeped into her body. Water filled her nose and it…lifted her. Sort of. She seemed weightless, as if she floated with the velblouds.

Pressure built in her throat. Soon her lungs ached with the effort to hold in the air.

The throb in her ribs turned into a burning sensation. The need to breathe pushed on her chest. How long had the King said a person could last underwater? An angle? Two? Would she pass out or would she be forced to inhale the water? Would that hurt?

Unable to stand the pressure any longer, she let some air escape. The bubbles cleared her nostrils of water. They tickled her cheeks as they gurgled. Rendor squeezed her hands, letting her know he was still fighting. She signaled him back.

Her heart beat extra hard as if trying to get her lungs to cooperate. *Come on, come on*, it urged. *What's wrong with you?*

Eventually all her air leaked out and now her body demanded more. The desire to inhale increased twofold with every frantic pulse of her heart. But to breathe in the water would drown her. Right? An old memory of the prior Heliacal Priestess of Zirdai ordering her deacons to drown Shyla rose unbidden. She had given Shyla holy water to make her talk and Rendor had rescued her…

She squeezed Rendor's hand. If she could withstand the heat at apex, then she could endure a few more angles. Except he didn't signal back. In fact, his fingers no longer curled around her hand. A scream built in her throat, except she had no breath to propel it out of her mouth. He should have lasted longer than her. He had bigger lungs!

The desire to fight to the bitter end leaked from her. All she needed was to inhale to join Rendor.

About to give up, she paused as a strange vibration shot through her. Not sure if it was a sound or a wave, she waited. Another weird pulse rumbled and she opened her eyes without thinking. A bright white glow shone above her. Then she was falling.

Shyla barely held on to consciousness as a roaring filled her ears. The light moved away, but she was too weak to protest. When her back hit something solid, she gasped. Water rushed into her mouth and throat. She gagged and choked. Then the water suddenly disappeared. Except her throat still spasmed—this time trying to suck in air. Nearby, Rendor's deep cough sounded like the sweetest song.

When her body finally relaxed, she wilted on the floor next to Rendor, sopping wet, freezing cold, but not caring because air flowed into and out of her lungs. She'd never take it for granted again.

"What in the seven hells are you two doing here?" the King demanded. He stood on the steps glaring down at them. Hakana hovered next to his right elbow and four guards loomed behind him.

"Long story," she rasped.

"Does Najib know you're here?" he asked.

"Yes and no." Shyla struggled to a sitting position. "Can we discuss this someplace private?" And dry. And warm.

"No. Explain it here. I might need to bring back the water to finish the job." Anger punctuated each word as he made his threat very clear.

Shyla explained what happened with Xerxes, why they were

at the castle, and about Najib betraying them.

"No," the King said, shaking his head. "Not Najib. He's loyal. Been loyal to me my *entire* life."

"The pendants are powerful. Xerxes is powerful. Najib has no choice."

"Why didn't you pick up on this when you first arrived?" he demanded.

"I read him when we first arrived. He wasn't under Xerxes' influence. He didn't have any alarming thoughts."

"What about when he guided us here?" Rendor asked. "Did you pick up on anything?"

"I didn't read him at that time. It was only forty angles or so after we'd seen him. Najib was distracted and upset when he came to our room at angle zero, but I would have been alarmed if he wasn't. Learning about an assassination plot is upsetting. Xerxes must have gotten to him after angle zero. He's already in the city." Shyla still had trouble believing it happened that fast.

"Hakana, did Advisor Najib receive any visitors between angles ten and forty?" the King asked.

The page jerked her attention to the King. "No, sire. But a Quirin monk visited him around angle one-seventy the jump before."

Shyla and Rendor had talked with Najib about bringing in the monks to guard the King, but they'd agreed it was too soon. "What did the monk look like?" she asked Hakana.

"Uh…a monk. He wore a brown tunic and pants under a sun cloak."

In other words, like every single monk in the Quirin

monastery. “Hakana, can I read your memories of the monk?”

Uncertain, Hakana glanced at the King.

“It’s your choice. I won’t order you to do something that makes you uncomfortable.”

“Uh…yeah, okay. What do I have to do?”

“Think about the monk. What did he say or do while here?”

Hakana scrunched up her nose. Shyla reached with the magic of The Eyes, witnessing her memory as she escorted the monk—

“Scorching hells, it’s Lonato,” she exclaimed.

“The new leader of the Monks of Callow? The one who almost caught you?” The King scrubbed a hand over the auburn stubble on his face.

Shyla was impressed he remembered. She had told him a massive amount of information in a short period of time. “Yes. He was disguised as one of the Quirin monks.”

“Do you think he used a pendant on Najib?”

“Yes. He must have ordered Najib to kill us once he found out we were here.” And the advisor did a great job of keeping Lonato out of his thoughts. Shyla marveled over the timing of the visit. They had really rotten luck.

“Can you free Najib of the compulsion?”

“If he’s wearing a blackfire pendant, which I think he is, then I can.” She remembered Najib tugging on his collar.

“And if he’s not?”

“That’ll be harder.” Much harder, but she didn’t wish to upset the King.

The King clenched the hilt of his sword as he stared at a distant point. He’d cast off his formal robe and wore an ordinary tunic and pants. The sword hanging at his side was far from ordinary. Glints of blue—probably sapphires—decorated the quillon.

"Xerxes will eventually know you survived the killing sun but will also believe you've drowned," the King said. "Najib didn't inform me of your visit or of the assassination plot during our last meeting. That might work in our favor. If Xerxes thinks you're no longer a threat and I'm clueless and he has Najib working for him…he might be overly confident and make mistakes."

"We have to keep our survival a secret from *everyone*," Shyla said, tilting her head to Hakana and the guards.

The King glanced at them. "Is that possible?"

"Yes. I can erase their memories of this entire encounter."

"No," Hakana cried. "I won't tell anyone. I promise!"

"We know you won't," Rendor said. "But if Xerxes asks, you won't be able to resist him. I couldn't. I told him everything I knew."

Hakana paled.

"What do you need from me?" the King asked.

"Does anyone else know why you're here?" Shyla asked.

"No." He gestured to the guards. "They were with me in my office when Hakana burst in. And we took the quickest route here, which is through an unused section of the castle."

Good. "We're going to need access to your Room of Knowledge." She pointed to the iron doors. The gap below them was now closed. "I have to find a way to counter the pendants. The sooner the better."

"You can't access it from here. This is just a fake entrance to trap trespassers." He gave them a wry smile. "Meet me in my sleeping chamber in twenty angles."

"Yes, sire."

"What about..." He pointed to his head.

Shyla considered the best way to erase their memories. "We'll follow you back to your office and I'll do it there. Please make sure no one sees you."

"All right." He swept his hand out before turning and leading Hakana and the guards away.

Shyla clambered to her feet, thinking the King's gesture was odd.

"We're dry," Rendor said, patting his tunic.

She checked the inside of her dillo leather boots and the bottom of her pants. They were also dry. Wow. The King's control and speed was impressive. She wondered if he had removed the water from their lungs as well, saving their lives. Rendor had been unresponsive during those final moments.

"Are you all right?" she asked him.

He patted his stomach and grinned. "I swallowed so much water, I probably won't have to drink for an entire circuit." Then he sobered. "It was another near miss. I lost consciousness. But it seems the Sun Goddess isn't ready for us."

"Clean slate, remember?"

"Yes, for both of us." He cupped her face and his demeanor turned dead serious. "I want to be with you forever. I want to make it official after all this is over. That is, if you want me in return. Think about it." Before she could say a word, he grabbed her hand. "We need to catch up."

Shyla had no need to think about anything; she knew her answer. But Rendor's insecurity had caused him to doubt his worth despite agreeing to a clean slate. After this was over, they'd have plenty of time to work it out. And if they failed… She shied away from those thoughts. Yet they hovered in the corner of her mind. They warned, *there might not be an after*, whenever she made the mistake of paying attention to them.

They followed the King to his office and she erased all Hakana's and the guards' memories. Then they went to wait for the King in his sleeping chamber. Shyla eyed the lush cushion with longing. It was surrounded by water, but it wasn't deep on one side. Almost drowning had drained her energy. Or was it calling for help through Hakana? Maybe the effort to alter five people's memories? Perhaps all three. But the thought of going near water again… She shuddered and Rendor instinctively pulled her close. Leaning on him was much better than a nap.

The King arrived right after his guards called the all-clear because she had used the *not here* command on them. He closed the doors and gestured in a circle. The water around the cushion drained, revealing the ramp down to his hidden chamber. Shyla and Rendor descended into the large room, which was half sleeping quarter and half living space. When he returned the water to block the entrance, he indicated that Shyla and Rendor should sit down. They sat on a couple cushions facing the King.

"I was going to send Hakana to watch for Xerxes, but Najib will notice and figure out you survived and that I know about the assassination attempt." The King paced. "I think the best thing to do is assume Xerxes is already here and be on guard."

"You can confide in the captain of your guards," Shyla said. "He's trustworthy and he can prepare his guards for an attack. Well, except for the four who are loyal to Xerxes."

"We should be able to work around them. They drill often in case of an attack, so it shouldn't draw too much attention." The King finally sat down. "Access to my Room of Knowledge is down there." He pointed to the back corner. "There's a hidden hallway that leads to it along with a couple sleeping chambers, which you're welcome to use. In fact, I'd prefer if you remain down here. It's safer for all of us and I can bring you food." He paused. "But in order to be granted access to the room, you must swear loyalty to me."

"You already know we're loyal," Shyla said, confused.

"This is different. This is due to the magic protecting the documents. You won't be able to enter the room without swearing an oath." His gaze seared into hers. "Only Najib has sworn this oath. If you do this, you will be one of my advisors. I won't ever force you to work for me, but I could. Do you understand?"

"That the magic would compel me?" Her voice quavered with horror. Not this again.

"Yes. The oath took the place of the pendants."

"If Najib took the oath, then you might be able to counter Lonato's commands," Rendor said.

"Theoretically," the King agreed. "But I've never used it on Najib. However, I will if this situation with Xerxes forces me to."

Shyla collected her thoughts. "I'm already sworn to the

Invisible Sword. Will it even work?"

"Only one way to find out." The King studied her. "I don't want to take you away from them. You're free to do as you please. I hope you and your Invisible Swords will consider working for me when needed, but I would never force you. My word."

That promise slammed into her like a physical blow. Shame followed her relief. Of course the King wouldn't be like Xerxes. And she was *supposed* to be working for the King. She'd been very selfish. The power of The Eyes wasn't just for her to use in Zirdai, but for all of Koraha. The Invisible Sword should be in service to the King, helping everyone. Once she made her decision, peace settled on her soul.

"If I swear the oath, you won't be able to get rid of me or the Invisible Sword. Do you understand?" Shyla asked.

The King grinned. "I wouldn't think of it. And you'll be compensated."

"Let's work out the details once we've stopped Xerxes. Now what do I need to do?"

"What do *we* need to do," Rendor corrected.

She glanced at him. His challenging stare said it all.

"We," she amended.

"Come with me." The King headed to the far left corner, which still appeared to be a regular corner until they reached it. Then the optical illusion was exposed.

A hallway led to a solid wall of stained glass. Off the hallway were two rooms, one on each side. The King stopped in front of the wall. The beautiful colored-glass panels created an intricate mural.

Shyla inspected the design closely and almost gasped. "It's a map of Koraha."

"Correct." The King quirked his eyebrows as if waiting.

Tracing the pattern of the cities, she noticed another layer. "Is that the underground river?"

"Yes."

"There's no lock or any indication that they are doors," Rendor said.

"Correct. Those that have permission to enter need only to press their hand on the heart of Koraha and the doors will open."

Heart? She studied the mural, seeking the symbol until she realized it wouldn't be that obvious. The heart of Koraha was the King. She found the castle and the symbol of the crown with water droplets instead of crenellations. She pointed to it. "That's the heart. Because without you, we all die of thirst."

The King's good humor faded. "I shouldn't be surprised that you've learned that. It's been all but forgotten, which my predecessors encouraged. But the old king's inactions have endangered me, and perhaps it's time to remind everyone."

"I told Xerxes, but he didn't believe me."

"After this, I'll visit all the cities and introduce myself and do a little demonstration for them."

"That'll work," Rendor said. "Korahans love a show."

"Then let's get working on getting to that *after*," the King said. "Are you ready to take the oath?"

"Yes," Shyla and Rendor said in unison.

"As far as oaths go, this is rather simple," the King said. "You make a shallow cut on your palm just enough to make it bleed, then press it to the heart. Then you say, 'I swear I will be true to the King, myself, and the people of Koraha.'" He handed her a small dagger.

The edge of the sharp blade gleamed in the trol light. Shyla cut a three-centimeter slice across her left palm. Stinging pain and blood welled. Not hesitating, she flattened her hand over the heart of the map. "I swear I will be true to the King, myself, Rendor, the Invisible Swords, and the people of Koraha."

Heat built under her skin, burning her hand. Then the colored glass rattled and a pulse of magic slammed into her, knocking her back. She lost her balance and landed on her butt with an *oof.* So much for a dignified pledge.

Shyla glanced at her palm. A thin bright red scar had replaced the cut. Except it was not a straight line. The scar resembled the Invisible Sword symbol with a couple added features. Instead of two swords, four swords now crossed tips. The hilts of all the swords still connected in a line that bowed away from the top, and the arched line over it still formed an eye shape, which now held a circle and pupil to mark the new archive of the organization.

The King helped her to stand. "I liked your…edits to the oath. Very you." He smiled. "Can I see?"

She extended her hand and he inspected her palm.

"That's interesting," he said. "Four swords. I wonder if that's one for me, you, Rendor, and the people of Koraha. And the rest of the symbol is obviously for the Invisible Swords."

"Is this…normal?"

The King showed her his palm. "Mine looks like a crown.

Najib's is a quill and a jar of ink, although he insists it's a sword and a bottle of poison. It's different for everyone. Well, of the five I've seen, they were all unique."

They turned their attention to Rendor. He hadn't moved, but he stared at Shyla in shock. Or was that pain? Tears glittered in his eyes and tracked down his face. Then she understood his reaction.

She walked over and wrapped her arms around his neck. "There's my answer. Turns out I didn't need to think about it that long. And I didn't want to wait until *after*."

He hugged her tight and buried his face in her neck. His shoulders shook, but he made no sound. Finally he lifted his head. "Joy is an inadequately weak word to describe what your pledge has given me."

Then Rendor took the knife from her hand, slashed a line on his right palm and pressed it to the mural's heart, which was no longer stained with Shyla's blood. Had it burned off?

"I swear I will be true to the King, myself, Shyla, the Invisible Swords, and the people of Koraha."

Once again the glass rattled and a wave of energy erupted, pushing Rendor back, but he remained on his feet. Show-off. He uncurled his fingers and Shyla and the King peered at his almost healed scar. It matched Shyla's exactly. Her heart did a strange little twirl in her chest.

"Let me be the first to congratulate you on your union," the King said. "I'm honored to have witnessed it. May the Sun Goddess bless you with a dozen children." He laughed. "Don't look so terrified. It's a standard blessing. And now I'll leave you to *rest.* You look like a couple of drowned rats."

"What about the Room of Knowledge?" Shyla asked before he could leave.

"When you wish to enter, just press your scar to the heart of the mural and it will open for you." Then he disappeared from sight. Soon the sound of rushing water reached them as the King left his hidden chambers.

When the quiet returned, Shyla said, "This was—"

"Unbelievable," Rendor finished.

"Unexpected, yet perfect." She kissed him. Then stepped back with a sigh and glanced at the mural. "We don't have time to rest. We need to work on ensuring we have an after."

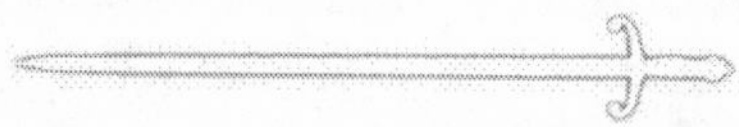

They approached the stained-glass wall guarding the Room of Knowledge. Shyla opened her left hand.

The scar had faded to a deep purple. She pressed it to the heart of the mural. A click sounded and the mural split open along a welded seam. Instead of a straight break, each half of the "door" was jagged, as if two pieces of a giant puzzle. The panels swung inward, inviting them inside. They glanced at each other before Rendor grabbed a trol lantern. Then they entered.

Since the booby trap was still fresh in her mind, Shyla moved cautiously, keeping an eye out for anything unusual. The white trol light soon revealed the room. It was square with a long low table located in the center surrounded by cushions. A plush rug covered the floor. Shelves filled with scrolls, tablets, and small chests lined all three walls from the floor to the very high ceiling.

Rendor held up the lantern and craned his neck. "It's about ten meters high. Good thing there's a ladder."

She'd missed it. It was attached to a bar at the top and had wheels on the bottom. Handy.

"How can I help?" he asked.

"Can you please get another trol lantern?"

While Rendor went to fetch the lantern, she inspected the lower shelves, hoping they were labeled. Most of the libraries and Rooms of Knowledge kept the documents in order from oldest to youngest. Or they were grouped together by subject. Much to her vast relief, the information in this room was organized by each king's reign.

Rendor returned with two trols. He set them down on the reading table. With the added light, she found the shelves for King Marett, the first King of Koraha. Guessing that the oldest documents would be on the bottom shelf, she collected as many scrolls as she could and carried them over to the table. Rendor grabbed the rest and added them to her pile.

"What about the chests?" Rendor asked. "Are they important?"

"They probably contain artifacts and not information. But if we get desperate, we can take a look inside."

Shyla picked a scroll up at random and unrolled it. It crackled and a few flecks from the edges broke off. It smelled…odd. Not the familiar musky aroma she was used to, but dusty with the scent of some kind of plant. It was also yellow and the faded ink was hard to read. Then she realized the scroll wasn't velbloud skin, but parchment—an ancient medium for writing. She sucked in a breath.

"What's wrong?" Rendor asked.

"These documents are originals. We must be very careful with them."

"That will slow things down." He peered over her shoulder. "Is that the language of the Kings?"

"Yes." Translating it would also cause a delay and Rendor wouldn't be able to help. But would she need to read every word? They were searching for specific information. Shyla knew the ancient words for sunfire, blackfire, and pendants. An idea formed. She dug into her pack for her stylus and a scrap of velbloud skin and wrote them down.

"Here." She tapped the skin. "These are the words we're looking for. You can scan the document and if you see them, let me know."

"All right." Rendor settled his bulk on the biggest cushion.

Shyla sat on the opposite side. They each took a scroll and carefully unrolled it, looking for those magic words. It was a time-consuming and boring task, but it wasn't difficult. The King arrived with roasted gamelu meat and steamed vegetables. He inquired about their progress—nothing so far—then left.

The next time the King appeared, he brought more food—the kind they could store for a few sun jumps. "Najib is coming in a couple angles for our last meeting of the jump," he said. "There can't be any light and you'll need to be quiet."

It would be a good time to take a break. "Can we eavesdrop?"

"As long as you stay out of sight." The King returned to his main room.

They closed the trol lanterns and went almost to the end of the hallway. Sitting next to each other, they held hands. Their scars touched and suddenly it seemed as if they were connected beyond the physical. Or was her control over her mental shield slipping? Her bones ached with exhaustion.

"No," Rendor whispered, squeezing her hand. "I can feel your thoughts and emotions. We're truly bonded."

A surge of warmth and love bloomed in her chest. It was an unexpected but very welcome side effect of the oath. "I wonder if this means Xerxes cannot enslave us."

"No. He caught Najib who has also sworn the oath."

Ah, too bad. They lapsed into silence, enjoying the new quirk in their relationship. It didn't take long for Najib's voice to reach them. The advisor reported on the various tasks he'd handled during the jump. Shyla debated if she should read his soul. But would the pendant pick up on her magic? Would it alert him? Or Lonato? She better not risk it.

The King and Najib discussed the various issues that arose from running a kingdom. It sounded like a ton of hard work and complex logistics. Ugh.

"Is there anything else?" the King asked.

Shyla hoped not as she needed to stretch her legs.

"I'm investigating a rumor, sire," Najib said.

"Oh?"

"It's unfortunate, but I suspect our sun-kissed lied to us regarding the taxes and the commander."

She sat up straighter. This was interesting.

"Lied how, Najib?" After a pause, he ordered, "Come on, spit it out."

"I'm sorry. I know you're fond of the woman, but the information I've gotten suggests that she did indeed find the taxes and has kept them for herself and her Invisible Swords."

She'd be outraged, but she had to give Lonato credit for this strategy.

"Are you implying the commander has not used the coins to take over those four cities?"

"We haven't been able to confirm the status of those cities. Our scouts haven't found anything amiss so far. However, a message could come in at any time. I'm still looking into it. I just wanted to let you know that there's a chance the commander is innocent."

"Find out for sure, Najib. Make it your top priority."

"Yes, sire."

Then the water sloshed, signaling Najib's departure. But they waited until the King gave the all-clear before joining him.

"Thoughts?" the King asked.

"It's an excellent strategy," Rendor said. "Make us the villains, which explains why we've disappeared. And it gets you to trust Xerxes again. That gives him the chance to get close to you."

"I agree," Shyla said.

"Did you read his soul?" the King asked.

"No. I didn't want to tip Lonato off. When I was under the influence of the blackfire, I sensed when magic was in use. But I agree with Rendor. Also, if his plan is to return as the commander, it gives him and us more time to prepare."

"Unless that message proving Shyla's treachery and exonerating the commander arrives in the next couple of sun jumps," the King said.

"Along with the mention that Xerxes is back in Qulsary a few sun jumps later," Rendor said.

"Right. And they'll expect I'll want to talk to the commander soon after." The King shook his head.

"I can delay them long enough for us to devise a counter strategy. At least this way we won't be caught by surprise. Any progress on the research?"

"No. There are over a hundred scrolls," Shyla said and explained about their delicate condition. "We'll let you know as soon as we find anything."

"Good."

"Don't relax, though," Rendor said. "We're still guessing Xerxes' plans. He doesn't share them with many and he's very smart. Plus he has Invisible Swords working for him now. This could just be an attempt to make you lower your guard."

"Good point." The King yawned. "It's getting late."

It was an obvious dismissal. Shyla and Rendor returned to their room. It'd been an emotionally exhausting sun jump. Having a bit of notice—she hoped—meant they might be ready for Xerxes.

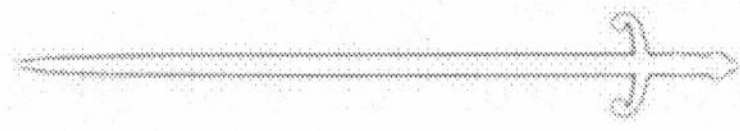

Shyla and Rendor searched the scrolls for any mention of the magic words. It wasn't until the sixth sun jump—and still no message confirming Shyla's theft of the taxes—that Shyla found one. She must have made a noise because Rendor glanced at her with a hopeful expression.

"Don't get too excited. I need to translate it." The ink was almost faded so it took her the rest of the sun jump to decipher the passages about a gifted pendant. Except it turned out to be just a fourteen-carat pink topaz that was given to the queen. She slumped in her seat, resting her throbbing head on the table.

Rendor rubbed her back. "Let's take a break. It's almost time for Najib's visit."

She had to admit sitting in the semi-darkness with her eyes closed helped ease the pain behind her eyes. When Najib arrived that sun jump, his campaign against them continued, including little "facts" about their deceit that he'd been gathering while waiting for news. It was very effective. If Shyla hadn't sworn the oath to the King, she wondered if he would start to doubt her and Rendor's loyalty.

It wasn't until the tenth sun jump that Rendor found a magic word. When he handed her the delicate scroll, she noticed a couple other magic words nearby. Trying to curb her excitement, she concentrated on the translation.

The top of the scroll explained the magic of Koraha. And while she'd love to learn how and why it worked, she was too impatient. The middle section reported what she already knew about the pendants. Toward the bottom were passages about abusing the power and—finally—how to break the magical bond between the sunfire and blackfire!

Her excitement died as she read the instructions. She carefully retranslated it just in case she'd missed something. And then a third time. The counterstrategy remained the same all three times.

It was complicated, but it boiled down to one act. In order to break the sunfire bond, the person wearing the blackfire must be willing to sacrifice their life for the King's.

She stared at the passage, but as the shock wore off, she realized this situation wasn't exactly the same. The wearer of the sunfire pendant currently wasn't the King. And there was more than one sunfire. And many more blackfires.

"Something wrong?" Rendor asked. He'd waited while she'd puzzled out the translation.

She explained what she'd read. "Plus if we take off the blackfire pendant, then the person is freed."

Rendor rubbed his neck. "The blackfires are small. Perhaps they're not as…potent as the single stone."

True. "I need to reread this entire scroll and see what I missed."

Shyla read through every sentence, but she couldn't find anything more. Why couldn't there be instructions? Something like throw water on the sunfire to shut off its power. Or use a mirror. Huh. Maybe a mirror would work. At this point, she'd try anything.

As far as she could tell, the sunfire and blackfire served a single purpose and there was no way to change it. No way to prevent it from doing its job. She groaned and rested her forehead on the table. Perhaps if she banged it on the stone, the action would dislodge the answer.

Rendor moved behind her and massaged her neck and shoulders. "You need a break." Then he leaned over and kissed her neck. "I know just the thing to help relax you."

Shyla spotted the sand clock. "It'll have to wait. It's almost time for Najib's meeting."

He grumbled but pulled her to her feet. They left the room and the mural's doors shut behind them. Rendor closed the lantern he carried, but light still filled the hallway. Colored light. They turned.

"We forgot the lanterns inside the room," he said. "I'll go."

Shyla stared at the mural. With the light coming through it instead of reflecting off it, the stained glass glowed with exquisite colors. Some hues she'd never seen before. She moved to get a better look. The map was no longer as obvious. Another picture seemed to be brightening on top of it like an optical illusion.

Rendor raised his hand to open the mural, but she grabbed his arm. "Wait. Do you see that?"

"See what?"

"Just look." She didn't want to influence him. It could just be her imagination.

"It's…the sun and the black orb is…our world…

I think…they're inside a sideways blue eight."

"I think that blue color means it's a river and the shape is an infinity symbol."

"Oh, right. Does that symbolize how we're all connected?"

"Probably." She stepped closer and touched the mural. Except it wasn't glass. The colors had been cut from gemstones. And the sun's pieces— "It's a sunfire!" She pointed.

Rendor tapped on Koraha. "Blackfire."

"And the blue?"

"I don't know, but we can ask the King."

Remembering about the meeting, they hustled to shut off all the lanterns and get into position before Najib arrived.

After the advisor left, they joined the King. Najib had been priming the King for the bad news about Shyla, dropping hints of incriminating evidence he'd been collecting.

Once they dissected Najib's comments, Shyla asked the King about the mural. "You said the oath is used in place of the pendants, but the panels of the mural are made from thin slices of sunfire and blackfire. The scrolls said the pendants were lost. When was the mural constructed?"

"When they moved the castle to Qulsary." He hesitated then seemed to make up his mind. "After Tamburah went power crazy and was assassinated, the next ruler, Queen Malin, packed up and moved to this location. She built the mural to prevent the pendants from being stolen. It's harder to move a mural. And, before you ask, the artifacts were reported to have disappeared, but they weren't lost. They were repurposed. I figured the ones Xerxes has had to be copies. But I knew it didn't matter if they were the originals or not, they worked the same and we needed to figure out how to counter the magic."

That made sense.

The King sighed. “I should have told you, but I’d been warned to keep this information secret.”

“If we’re to stop Xerxes, we need to know everything. What else can you tell us about the oath and the mural?”

“When they search for the next king, two children are found who both have the power to move the water. When they turn eight circuits old, they are brought to the mural. Their palms are cut and pressed to the heart. One child will get the crown scar, and the other will be marked as their primary advisor. The advisor then loses their magical ability.”

That was new, and it gave her a bit of hope. “If you die before the next generation is old enough to command the water, would your advisor be able to regain their magic?”

“No. Once it’s done, it’s set. Then there’s no temptation for the advisor to take the King’s place.”

“Or Queen’s, except there’s only been one in our history,” Rendor said. “It’s not really a surprise that the old king was chosen over Yiesha.”

“Actually, Captain, there have been many kings of all different genders throughout our history. They are referred to as the king and ‘he’ has been the traditional pronoun used. Except for Malin; she insisted on being called Queen and, after Tamburah’s atrocities, Korahans welcomed the change. However, gender makes no difference to the Sun Goddess.”

Shyla’s opinion of the goddess rose another notch. But they still didn’t have a way to counter the sunfire. “Where did Xerxes get his gemstones?”

"There have been other gifts from the sky that have been discovered in the sands of our world. Perhaps Xerxes found them on one of his treasure-hunting missions and figured out their significance." The King rubbed a hand over his face. "It still doesn't change the fact that we need to block the sunfire's power. Have you had any success?"

"Not really." She explained what she'd learned.

"Dying is a form of freedom," the King said. "But not the solution in this case. What's next?"

"We can see if there's information about the loyalty oath," she said. "Since it works the same way as Xerxes' pendants, maybe if there's a way to break the oath, we can apply that to his sunfire."

"A change of heart clause?" the King joked.

"Can we also get a set of guard uniforms?" Rendor asked.

"What for?"

"Shyla might be able to research all sun jump every jump, but I need more exercise and she needs the sun. You do," he said when she protested. "You get grumpy when you haven't been topside in a while." Then to the King, "Also, the first tax caravan is coming in three sun jumps. You'll have to send out extra guards to escort the taxes even though Xerxes and his people know it's fake. That could be a vulnerable time for you."

"And again when the second one arrives a couple sun jumps after," Shyla said. "We need to be nearby just in case." When the King didn't say anything, she added, "I'll make sure we're not seen."

"That's not my concern. I'm wondering if I'll be notified

about the second caravan. Currently I haven't been informed of a decoy. Perhaps I won't be told and the coins will be diverted into Xerxes' hands."

"Even more reason to give us uniforms," Rendor said. "We can be on the surface during those sun jumps."

"All right."

Rendor was right. Shyla had needed the warmth of the sunshine on her skin. And despite the circumstances her spirits had lifted as the heat soaked into her bones. They currently stood in the shadow of one of the surface buildings, watching the various caravans arrive and offload before the sun reached the danger zone. It'd been four sun jumps since their conversation with the King.

Since then, Shyla had learned the only way to break an oath was if it was said while a person was under duress, not mentally competent, or too young to know better. Technically Xerxes forced the blackfire pendants onto his victims, but they hadn't taken an oath per se.

"That looks like the decoy caravan," Rendor said, jarring her from her thoughts.

The wagons were a sun jump late, but that wasn't a concern. Najib had informed the King that the tax caravan had been spotted and would arrive at this time, which was more of a concern. What was Xerxes planning? They figured the commander had to be in the city by now. While she appreciated the extra time, each sun jump increased her anxiety.

As the decoy caravan neared, the monks guarding it appeared to be a bit…beleaguered. The wagons pulled up to the castle's glass surface building. Najib and six guards greeted them. Shyla noted there should be more. Perhaps that was a sign Xerxes wasn't planning anything at this time. He'd want almost all the King's guards to be here helping to transfer the coins to the vault, leaving the King with only a few protectors.

Shyla and Rendor moved closer.

The leader of the monks gestured with agitated motions. "…bandits and pirates everywhere. Most of the travel shelters are occupied with squatters." His voice was strident. "The King better put these coins to good use."

Najib was unmoved. He clicked his fingers at the guards and they unloaded the wagons in no time. The monks were dismissed without a thank you.

Shyla wielded her magic as she and Rendor entered the castle's surface building. The tax chests were all piled in one corner. Except for the four guards who were loyal to Xerxes, the others were confused as Najib opened one of the chests.

Najib tsked. "It is as I feared. The coins have been stolen." He held up the chest for all to see, causing a wave of dismay. "Filled with sand. I'll go inform the King. Return to your duties; there's no need to guard these."

As they followed Najib to the King's office, Shyla tried to determine what Najib hoped to accomplish.

The advisor entered the office without knocking.

"I'm sorry to bother you, sire. But I'm afraid I've bad news."

"Go ahead," the King said in a weary tone.

Najib showed him the chest full of sand. "The taxes have been stolen again. I interviewed the monks and they didn't encounter any bandits or pirates on their way here. However, they did talk to a sun-kissed wearing your sigil in Apanji. They said she wanted to ensure the coins hadn't been stolen and they opened all the chests for her. At that time, the coins were inside. She told them to travel straight here and not stop in Haiya." He took a breath. "I'm afraid that confirms Shyla stole your taxes and that everything she told you about Xerxes was a lie."

The King made all the appropriate noises of outrage and indignation over her deceit. She had to give Najib credit for using this as a way to discredit her. He had evidence and it was much better than some fictitious report from a scout. She wondered how long Xerxes would wait before requesting an audience with the King. Two or maybe three sun jumps? Either way they were running out of time.

The next sun jump, Shyla and Rendor watched for Gurice and Mojag's wagons before apex and again before darkness. They weren't the only ones. A few of Najib's guards also lingered on the surface. When the siblings failed to show, Shyla was not worried. Not at all.

"Stop worrying," Rendor said when they returned to the King's underground chamber. "Mojag can move dunes. They're fine."

"There's no sand here for Mojag to move. And you heard the monk about the bandits—"

He pulled her close. "You can't change anything by fretting."

"I agree. Now convince my heart."

Stepping back, he said with a sigh, "I'd love to, sunbeam. I've lots of ways to convince your heart, but we're no closer to a solution to our Xerxes problem."

After another frustrating round of research, the solution remained out of reach. They repeated their vigil the next sun jump. No sign of the caravan before apex, but a few angles before darkness, three wagons appeared in the distance.

That was when Shyla spotted Najib and his four loyal guards waiting for the caravan. Also hidden in various shadows were all the Invisible Swords, including Rae and Lamar, the two wielders. While Shyla was happy to see that they were healthy, their presence didn't bode well for Gurice and Mojag.

The wagons stopped in front of the castle's surface building. The eight caravan guards spread out, encircling the wagons. Shyla spotted Gurice and Mojag even though they all wore plain tunics and pants. Najib strode up to Gurice and thanked her for safely escorting the taxes.

Najib made some speech about saving the kingdom, but Shyla's attention was distracted by another set of three wagons heading toward them. The Invisible Swords crept out from their hiding places. Shyla wanted to alert Gurice, but Mojag already spotted Rae. He waved a greeting.

Seven hells. She needed to warn him. But then a strong magical command pressed on her.

"Where did that incoming caravan go?" Rendor asked.

"Magically disappeared." She pushed the command aside, then grabbed Rendor's right hand with her left, connecting them.

"Handy," Rendor said. "Too bad we can't fight like this."

"We're not fighting," she said. "No matter what happens we need to remain out of sight."

"If anyone touches Mojag—"

"He can take care of himself." She hoped.

Not much had changed around the tax wagons. Gurice and Mojag talked to Rae and Jaft while Najib ordered his guards to unload the chests. The second set of wagons pulled alongside and the guards transferred the chests into them. Ah, Xerxes planned to store them until he became king. It wouldn't do for them to be found in the castle after Najib had said they were stolen.

Gurice noticed and questioned Najib. Shyla didn't know what the advisor said, but Gurice shrugged and returned to her friends.

When Najib stopped one of the guards to check inside the box, Shyla squeezed Rendor's hand. "Wait for it."

The lid opened. Najib cursed and threw the box to the ground. Sand spilled out. Unable to resist, Shyla and Rendor edged closer as Najib grabbed another chest and confronted Gurice.

"Where in the seven hells are the taxes?" Najib demanded. He gestured to the guards and Invisible Swords to form a circle around the siblings.

Gurice glanced at the sand inside then turned to Mojag. "You were supposed to fill these with the coins, not sand."

"I did what Shyla told me to do," Mojag said in an offended tone.

"She told you to fill them with sand?" Najib asked.

"Yes."

"Why?"

"To keep the coins safe."

Najib struggled to hide his fury. "Where are the coins?"

"In the desert." Mojag waved a hand in the general direction. "Once Shyla tells me it's safe, I'll retrieve them for you."

"Nice," Rendor whispered in her ear.

By this time, Gurice noticed the threatening circle of guards and Invisible Swords. "Where is Shyla? She should be here by now."

Najib ignored her. Focusing on Mojag, he said, "It is safe. Take my wagons and my guards and—"

Mojag dipped his head. "Sorry, sir. I'm to trust only Shyla."

If a person could explode like the toxic gas in the underground tunnels, Najib would have shattered the nearby stained glass. "I'm the King's advisor, *boy.* Those taxes are the *King's* property. If you don't tell me where they are, then you will be arrested and locked into a cell for the rest of your life."

As far as threats went, that was impressive. Sensing trouble, Gurice moved closer to her brother.

"Sorry, sir." Mojag remained stubborn.

"What about the King?" Gurice asked Mojag. "The advisor's right, the coins belong to the King. If he says it's safe, then will you show them where they are hidden?"

"No. Shyla only." He scrunched his nose in confusion. "It's an easy fix. Just tell me where Shyla is and I'll ask her."

"Shyla is dead," Najib roared. "You will tell me or I will kill your sister."

Both Gurice and Mojag stared at Najib in shock. Shyla gathered her magic and aimed it at the chests. The lids flew open as the sand erupted skyward. She created a whirlwind of sand around Gurice and Mojag. Thank the Sun Goddess Mojag had filled them to the top.

Then she used the power of The Eyes on the siblings.

Run and hide.

Trust no one.

Except me.

Rae and Lamar's magic tried to calm the swirling sand. Shyla increased her effort to counter them as she manipulated the sand, creating a space between two guards. Then she sent the siblings one more command.

Run now!

They raced through the gap and Shyla kept a wall of sand between them and the others. Once Mojag and Gurice disappeared into one of Qulsary's entrances, she stopped. The sand dropped to the ground.

Najib shouted orders, sending the Invisible Swords to track down Mojag and Gurice.

"Will they find them?" Rendor asked.

"Now who's worried?"

He growled at her.

"No, they won't. Mojag excels at staying out of sight."

"Should we find them? They'll be safer with us."

She considered. "Not yet. They're too hot."

"The hunt for them isn't going to cool. Xerxes won't stop

until he finds them." Rendor glanced around. "I'm surprised he wasn't here."

So was she. Unless he was hiding in one of the deepening shadows. The sun had slipped below the mountains.

"We need to return to the King, but we can search for them when the sun begins its jump," she said.

Using the *not here* command, she led Rendor back to the King's hidden suite. Once the King returned, they reported what had happened.

"Why didn't you tell me the second caravan was also a decoy?" he asked.

"Technically it wasn't. If I'd been there to greet Mojag, he'd have shown us where to find the coins."

The King rubbed his face. "So if this boy dies, we'll never recover the taxes?"

"Yes," Rendor said before she could say no.

Shyla knew where Mojag had planned to hide them, but she kept quiet. Rendor was right. If the King believed Mojag's life was that important, he'd protect it.

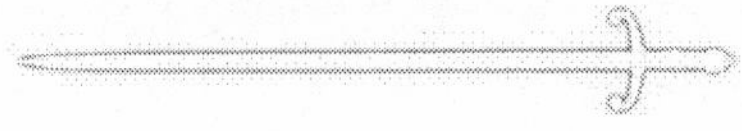

Once Shyla and Rendor entered Qulsary the next sun jump, she stopped wielding her magic. There were far too many people and she needed to save her energy just in case Xerxes or the Invisible Swords found Mojag and Gurice first. They both wore nondescript clothing and Shyla covered her hair with her scarf.

"Where do you want to start?" Rendor asked.

"At the market."

"Are you sure? It'll be packed with people and guards and Xerxes' soldiers."

"Exactly. It's the best place for them to blend in."

When they arrived at the market, she scanned the bustling stands and throngs of people. "We need to find a spot nearby that's hidden from view."

Rendor didn't question her. Instead he found an alcove along the back wall. It was being used to store boxes of merchandise. Shyla sat on a stack while Rendor guarded the opening. Then she reached with The Eyes, seeking Mojag and Gurice's thoughts.

Sure enough, they were in the market. Gurice was pretending to be an elderly woman shopping with Mojag, who guided her through the crowds with ease. He was zeroing in on one of Xerxes' people, hoping to get some answers from the soldier.

Shyla changed his mind by calling him to her.

Over here.

Back wall.

Be casual.

She repeated the call until a figure darted right by Rendor and tackled her. They tumbled to the ground.

"Mojag…can't…breathe."

"Sorry." He loosened his grip. "I knew you weren't dead."

"Are you going to explain why everyone believes you are?" Gurice asked. She stood next to Rendor.

"Yes, once we're someplace safe."

The siblings followed them back to the castle. Since the King wouldn't be going to his sleeping chambers for a while, they found a secluded spot in the unused section of the castle to fill Mojag and Gurice in on all the details.

"Wow," Gurice said. "You're lucky you're not dead for real."

Shyla agreed.

"Can we get them back?" Mojag asked, clearly worried about the Invisible Swords. He rubbed his shoulder where their symbol had been drawn.

"We're going to do everything we can to free them."

The "we" seemed to get through to him. Mojag straightened from where he'd slumped against the wall. "We are." The words sounded like a promise.

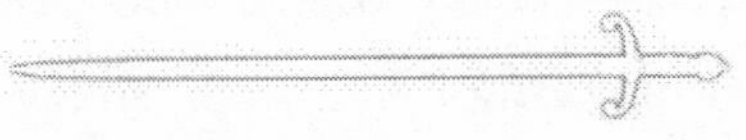

When they followed the King into his hidden sleeping chambers, Mojag gaped at the water. Then, when introduced to the King, he blurted, "But you're so young!"

The King laughed. "So are you. And you should know youth doesn't always mean a person is inexperienced or irresponsible or not intelligent. You're a perfect example. Because of you, the taxes are secure instead of in Xerxes' hands."

"Happy to help." Mojag beamed.

Gurice bowed to the King but seemed incapable of speaking. Shyla elbowed Rendor. She'd never seen her friend so flustered.

"I'm glad you're both here to help. More people to read through the old scrolls. Mojag, don't get too close to the pool or you'll—"

Mojag fell into the water with a splash. He thrashed,

panicking. The King gestured and the water parted so the boy could climb from the pool. By the time he reached them, he was dry.

"Thanks." He patted his clothing as if he couldn't believe they weren't sopping wet.

"You just couldn't resist, could you?" Gurice scolded.

"I've never seen that much water. Ever. I just had to touch it!"

"Until you learn to swim, don't go near there again or you might drown," the King said.

"Swim? Drown?"

"Shyla can explain it. I've work to do." He nodded to them and then went up the ramp. The water followed, blocking the passage.

Mojag walked over to the wall of water. He poked a finger into it and jumped back as if it would collapse and flood the room. "I wonder if I can move water, too." He rolled his shoulders as if loosening up.

"Before Mojag manages to drown us, what do you need us to do?" Gurice asked.

Shyla explained about the scrolls as she led them to the Room of Knowledge. After she opened the mural, she showed them the words they were seeking. They were no longer searching for information on the pendants but on the mural and its construction. Also for anything referring to where the sunfire and blackfire were found.

After twenty angles, Gurice groaned. "I hate to say this, but I think I'd prefer hauling buckets of sand. At least then I can see my progress as I clear a room. This…ugh."

Shyla pointed to a tall pile of scrolls in the corner. "That's our progress. Seventeen sun jumps' worth."

Gurice groaned again. She stretched her arms and then scratched idly at her shoulder, a gesture she and Mojag had been doing off and on since they reunited. Shyla was about to ask if the siblings had picked up sand fleas when Mojag hopped up and handed Shyla a scroll. "There's that funny word with that weird-looking K."

He referred to the ancient spelling of sunfire. Shyla scanned the document and sat up straighter. This might explain exactly how the sunfire worked.

"A good one?" Mojag asked.

"Yes."

"What does it say?"

"I need to translate it first."

Mojag sprawled on the rug. "Wake me when you do."

"Oh no, rat. You keep on working until Shyla says stop," Gurice ordered.

Shyla ignored them. The passage had her full attention. It reported about the original sunfire being much larger than the one in the pendant. It was found while digging the first underground city of Koraha. And when they cracked it open, they found a blackfire at its core. The blackfire had been surrounded by—

"Stop," Rendor said. "It's almost time for Najib's meeting."

It about killed her to put the scroll down, but she wouldn't risk the only advantage they had. Reluctantly, she left the room and settled in the hallway with Rendor, Gurice and Mojag.

When the sloshing sounds of the water echoed, Mojag leaned to get a peek around the corner. Gurice yanked him back with a scowl. He crossed his arms and pouted.

The King and Najib's voices soon reached them. Najib claimed he'd launched a full investigation of the stolen taxes.

"Commander Xerxes is back in Qulsary," Najib said. "He'd like an audience with you to discuss reforming the elite squads."

Shyla hoped the King would delay the meeting as long as possible.

"You know we don't have any coins to pay him or his soldiers," the King said.

"I made him aware of the situation and he offered to help us recover the taxes. He also mentioned he's been doing freelance work in other cities and that has kept his people employed. That must be what Shyla meant by 'taking over' the cities." Disgust dripped from Najib's voice.

"It can't hurt to talk to the man," the King said.

"That's what I thought. I'll schedule him for angle twenty."

No. Shyla exchanged worried glances with Rendor and the others. They weren't ready.

"I'd rather wait and meet with him in a few sun jumps, Najib," the King said.

"Why? The longer we wait, the smaller the chances of finding the stolen taxes."

Seven hells. Najib had him there.

"Yes, of course, you're right. I'm just tired."

"I understand, sire. Here, I brought your favorite blend of

tea."

They discussed other business, but Shyla no longer listened. The four of them would need to be in the King's office during that meeting. Perhaps all disguised as guards. Would Xerxes notice? They needed to devise a plan on how to stop Xerxes if he tried to kill the King.

Rendor squeezed her hand, pulling her from her panicked scheming. He pointed to his ear. She listened.

"...sorry, Najib." The King yawned. "I don't...know..." He slurred his next words.

"No need to apologize. Lie down, sire. I can see myself out."

Scorching sand rats. Had Najib just poisoned the King? Or drugged him so he wouldn't return the water to the upper chamber? That would allow anyone to just walk down and kill him!

They couldn't remain here while the King needed them. Coming to the same conclusion, they all stood. Rendor gestured for them to wait while he retrieved his weapons. She hoped Najib had already left. Mojag could fetch the King's physician.

The thud of heavy footsteps sounded and they all froze.

"What took you so long?" Najib demanded, still in the chamber.

"It takes time to sneak a large force into the castle," Xerxes said. "Is he dead?"

19

The situation had turned from critical to dire in a matter of heartbeats. Perhaps she hadn't just heard Xerxes' deep voice. Maybe it was someone else. But, by the pained and serious expressions on her companions' faces, she hadn't just had a bad dream.

"No, he's not dead," Najib said. "His magic would neutralize any poisons. And you've only a couple of angles before his magic burns through the drug and wakes him."

"Then stand aside," Xerxes said. A ring of steel sounded.

Whether they were ready for a confrontation with Xerxes or not, that was their signal. They burst from the hidden hallway and stormed into the King's main chamber. The King was sprawled on his sleeping cushion with Xerxes looming over him.

The commander spun and cursed. "You said they drowned," he snarled.

"They did," Najib insisted. "They triggered the booby trap. I—"

"Underestimated me," Shyla said. "Step away from the King, Xerxes."

"No."

Rendor threw his knife at the commander. Xerxes dodged with ease. He yanked his pendant out.

"Don't look at it," Shyla ordered, averting her gaze.

"Why not?" Mojag asked. "It's pretty."

No! Fear ringed her heart.

"Are you the boy who moved the dunes?" Xerxes asked.

"I am," Mojag said with pride.

"Come here, Dune Mover."

Gurice grabbed her brother's shoulders, holding him back. But Mojag knocked her hands off and dashed toward Xerxes.

"No!" Shyla shouted, grabbing for his arm.

But Mojag was fast. He darted around Rendor and was next to Xerxes in a heartbeat.

"If you value this young man's life, you'll put down your weapons," Xerxes said.

"Kill the King first and then we'll deal with them," Najib ordered. "Time's running out."

Xerxes turned, crouched next to the cushion, and drew his knife back. Before he could plunge it into the King's chest, Mojag tackled Xerxes, knocking the man into the pool.

Shyla froze a moment in surprise. Mojag had been strong enough to resist the sunfire's compulsion. Then Gurice rushed to Mojag, helping him up. Shyla kept an eye on Xerxes who, of course, knew how to swim. He reached the edge of the pool. Uh-oh. Rendor stalked toward Najib, who yanked out his pendant.

And there was surprise number two. A large sunfire, not a blackfire, shone from its center.

"That's close enough, Captain," Najib said.

Rendor froze, staring at the stone. Son of a sand demon. Najib was working *with* Xerxes, not *for*. No wonder he'd ordered Xerxes to kill the King.

"Now that I have your attention," Najib said, brandishing the pendant.

Shyla glanced at the siblings. Gurice and Mojag both stared at Najib. The sunfire was twice the size of Xerxes'. The big man climbed from the pool. Dripping wet, he glared a promise of pain at Mojag.

"Everyone *will* keep their distance from me and the commander," Najib ordered them with the magic of the sunfire. "Xerxes, finish the job."

Except Shyla felt no pressure to obey. Instead of keeping back, she dove for Xerxes. He spotted the motion and turned just in time to deflect her. She landed on the floor. Xerxes now loomed over her. She'd thought him massive before, but from this perspective he was a giant. With a blur of movement, he looped a blackfire pendant over her head and held the stone so it captured her gaze. It glinted with its iridescent shine but didn't tug her soul. Huh. Finally something going right for her.

Then Xerxes staggered to the side as Rendor shoved him away from Shyla.

"You all right?" Rendor asked.

"Yes."

Rendor pulled his sword.

Xerxes aimed the sunfire at him.

"Haven't you figured it out yet?" Rendor slid into a fighting stance. "That doesn't work on us anymore."

Shyla glanced at Najib. Mojag had pinned him against the wall. The tip of his knife rested on the advisor's neck.

Gurice gave her an I-don't-know shrug. "It's a beautiful stone, I couldn't resist staring at it. But it's not that engrossing. Mojag, were you pretending to obey Xerxes?"

"Of course. It's the only way I could get close to him."

Finally catching on, Xerxes dropped the pendant and drew his sword.

Rendor's grin widened. "This is going to be fun."

Xerxes lunged at Rendor, who sidestepped. "I've seen you fight, Captain. You're no match for me."

"Then it's a good thing I'm not alone." Rendor stabbed forward.

Gurice stood next to Shyla as they watched the fight. Shyla was always amazed over Rendor's speed. Xerxes used his strength to his advantage. Neither man wasted any more breath to goad each other. They were professionals, using quick, efficient, and brutal strikes aimed to disarm the other. No fancy moves and no wasted energy.

"Do you think Rendor will let us have a turn?" Gurice asked her.

"Not until he's ready to share."

Xerxes ducked under Rendor's feint and slammed him into the wall. Shyla cringed in sympathy.

Gurice smirked. "I think he'll be ready soon."

"Oh no, it'll be a while. Do you want to know why?"

"Don't keep me in suspense."

"Rendor's angry about being enslaved by Xerxes. He's going to beat that man bloody. And then it's my turn."

Sure enough, the cuts on Xerxes' arms, legs, and torso multiplied as his blood coated Rendor's sword. He shuffled in close and stabbed Xerxes in the shoulder of his sword arm. Xerxes' weapon clattered to the ground. But it didn't stop him from charging at Rendor. Xerxes ducked under Rendor's sword and rammed him into the wall.

"It's a good thing I'm not alone either," Xerxes said, then he yelled, "Vilma!"

Shyla turned toward the ramp, bracing for an attack. Now she understood the significance of Xerxes' comment about sneaking in a "large force."

Except a single set of boots came down, revealing Jaft. "Uh, yeah. About that…" Jaft scratched his shoulder. "Vilma and the others are otherwise engaged."

Xerxes growled a curse as Rendor took advantage of the commander's momentary lack of focus by punching him in the stomach.

Relieved but wary that Vilma's unit might show up soon, Shyla asked Jaft, "Engaged in what?"

"Engaged in contemplation over a lifetime of poor choices. Maybe some regret over joining forces with Xerxes. Most definitely fretting about their futures or lack of them."

Shyla stared at him. It seemed too good to be true. "You captured them? How?"

He beamed at her. "Once the compulsion disappeared and we could think again, the Swords decided to play along with the madman until the perfect opportunity arose." He gestured to them. "I'd say this was about as perfect as it gets. And…sorry, but I just need…" Jaft strode to her and hugged her tight. "I'm so very glad you're both alive. Burying you in the desert—"

"Sunbeam." Rendor's strained voice interrupted them. "Your turn." He blocked Xerxes' hammer fist with his forearm. Rendor had lost his sword. Covered with sweat and blood, he panted for breath.

Jaft released her and stepped back. Shyla gathered her magic and aimed it at the commander.

Freeze.

Xerxes froze. He struggled mightily, but Shyla wielded both the power of The Eyes and her magic. A double whammy.

"The sunfire no longer protects you from me," Shyla said. "Sit down, Beast."

He plopped onto the ground.

"Give me your pendant."

His muscles strained against the command, but he took it off and handed it to her.

"Thank you. Put your hands behind your head."

He laced his fingers together.

"Stay, Beast. Good boy." She patted his head. "What do you think is worse? Being well aware that you're being forced to comply, or having both your mind and body compliant? Becoming someone else with a new name and identity?"

Xerxes glared at her.

"Answer my question, Beast." She added more heat.

"This is worse," he ground out.

"Oh? I disagree, but…" She removed the blackfire from around her neck and donned the sunfire pendant. "It's your choice. Hands down. Head bowed."

Xerxes obeyed even though he tried to resist her commands. Guess she was angry, too.

"Wow, look at those muscles," Gurice said, fanning her face. "Too bad they're wasted on you."

When Shyla bent down to put the blackfire on Xerxes, he said, "Stop. Please."

"The please is nice, but it no longer matters what you want. It's what *I* want. Isn't that what you've been doing all along?"

No answer.

"As far as punishments go, that's a nice bit of revenge," the King said. "But I'd like a turn." He'd pushed into a sitting position on his cushion. His hand was rubbing his forehead as if it throbbed. His gaze moved to where Najib was still pressed against the wall. "After I deal with the traitor."

"That's fine," Shyla said, pocketing the blackfire pendant. "Beast isn't going anywhere." She patted his head again. "Do you want me to compel Najib to answer your questions?"

"No," Najib said, horrified. "I'll talk."

Mojag escorted Najib before the King and forced him to his knees. Najib glanced around, but he was outnumbered and no doubt the King would turn him into a raisin if he tried to escape.

"Why?" the King asked.

"You stole my power. I should have been king, not you. I'm

smarter."

"Not smart enough to remember that I didn't steal anything," the King snapped. "The Sun Goddess chose."

"It's not a choice. I've done my research. It's *always* the first person to make the oath who becomes King. You went first." It sounded like an accusation.

The King kneaded his temples. "Yes, I did, because you were scared about what was going to happen and I went first to show you it wouldn't be that bad." He balled his right hand into a fist.

By volunteering to go first, the King showed he had courage and empathy. It was a good way to pick a ruler. Shyla approved.

"How could you break your oath?" the King asked.

"I couldn't," Najib spat. "That's why I collaborated with the commander. He could do all the things I couldn't. Although my oath shouldn't have been binding—I took it when I was eight circuits old. I didn't know it would force me into a life of servitude."

The King's angry expression melted into sadness as his shoulders relaxed. "Servitude? I thought we were partners. Brothers. Best friends."

"You thought wrong."

"How did you hide your thoughts from me?" Shyla asked.

"They were buried deep. They had to be in order for me to do my job. Besides, I knew you wouldn't go that deep. You're not that ruthless."

"I am if I'm pushed." She glanced at Xerxes. His head was still bowed. Maybe she should make him grovel. "But I still would have picked up on the sunfire."

"That's why I didn't wear one until now."

"You plotted to kill me in order to get your magic back?" the King asked.

"Yes."

"What if it didn't work?"

"It will work."

"How do you know? Did you research it? Has it happened in the past?"

"It will work."

"In other words, you were willing to risk every single person's life in order to get what you wanted." The King sighed. "I've no choice. Due to the magnitude of your crime, you must be executed."

Najib hopped to his feet with a cry. He thrust the sunfire forward, capturing the King's attention. "Your immunity doesn't work on the sunfire. You *will drown* everyone here except me, you, and the commander."

The King's expression turned blank. He swept his arm out. A column of water arced from the pool. Shyla lunged toward Najib, reaching for the sunfire. The traitor stepped back and she missed. But then the King's sapphire necklace glowed with a blue fire. It hurt to look at it. Shyla averted her gaze as the entire chamber filled with the incandescent light.

"No!" Najib screamed as his sunfire dimmed and darkened, turning black.

The one on Shyla's pendant also turned opaque.

Najib charged the King, but the column of water swept Najib off his feet and carried him into the depths of the pool. When the advisor failed to surface, Shyla glanced at the King. The glow had faded and his hand was pressed to the necklace.

"I'm glad I listened to the old king. He told me to never take this off."

"Sapphire," Shyla said with a groan. "That's what the water in the mural is made of. It can counter the sunfire." All that research and the answer was right there in front of them this entire time.

"That's great for the King, but how did *we* counter it?" Gurice asked.

Good question. Shyla searched her memories. Why didn't the sunfire work this time? What changed?

"The King's oath," Rendor said. "We pledged ourselves to the King so the sunfire was no longer needed to ensure our loyalty."

"But we didn't take the pledge," Gurice said, gesturing to Mojag and Jaft.

True. Shyla asked Jaft when the compulsion disappeared.

"About seventeen sun jumps ago," he said. "It was quite the surprise. Suddenly it felt as if I'd been pushed down a long shaft. The landing hurt." He rubbed his shoulder. "And we almost revealed ourselves. That Vilma is beyond intense. But all the Swords managed to pull it together. We figured we had to wait for reinforcements or a signal or something. The six of us were outnumbered and living in the belly of the beast. One wrong move and we'd be enslaved again." He shuddered and wrapped his arms around his chest.

"It was around seventeen sun jumps ago when I felt like

someone punched me in the shoulder," Mojag said. "Hard. I fell off the wagon."

"Gurice?" Shyla asked.

"I don't remember when, but my shoulder suddenly felt bruised and tender." She pushed up her sleeve, revealing her upper left arm.

The Invisible Sword's symbol glowed on her skin. It was visible to only those who could wield magic.

"Hey, hers has changed!" Mojag yanked up his tunic. "Did mine?"

"Yes." Shyla explained the changes to those without magic, "It has another sword." Then she relayed what had happened when she and Rendor swore the King's oath, showing them the scar on her palm.

"Does that mean we're married, too?" Mojag scrunched up his nose as if disgusted by the idea.

"No," the King said, pointing. "Yours only has three swords, one for me, you, and the Invisible Swords."

Shyla thought it was interesting that the King could see the symbol but not too surprising since he wielded powerful magic.

"But I didn't swear—"

"We swore our loyalty to the Invisible Sword," Gurice said. "Shyla is our leader. Since she took the King's oath, it counted for all of us. Right?"

"It appears so," the King said. "Good thing too, as it protected you from being compelled by the sunfire."

"What if one of us wanted to…" Jaft cleared his throat. "Marry another Invisible Sword. Would we get another sword in our symbols?"

Shyla glanced at Rendor. Who did Jaft wish to marry? He shrugged.

"I don't know, but there's one way to find out." Shyla peered at Jaft. "Who's the lucky person?"

Jaft blushed and stammered, but just shook his head.

"This can all be sorted later," the King said. "What's happening in my castle? Do we need to help fight the intruders?"

Jaft straightened. "No, sire. Once we learned about Xerxes' plans to assassinate you, we recruited the monks that arrived with the decoy caravan and we enlisted Captain Kilab's help from Qulsary. Also, as our wielders helped the force sneak into the castle, we tipped off your loyal guards."

"How did you know which ones were loyal?" Mojag asked.

"They were all the ones Vilma was avoiding."

Considering the dangerous circumstances, Shyla's chest expanded with pride for her Invisible Swords. They'd accomplished so much on their own. She asked Jaft, "Where are the others?"

He waved a hand at the ramp. "Probably helping with the cleanup. Once we ambushed the…er…ambushers and I knew Vilma's squad had no chance of winning, I took off after Xerxes and Najib."

"Who could have killed me by then," the King muttered.

"Not a chance, sire." Jaft's tone was slightly insulted. "Rae, one of the Invisible Swords, spotted Mojag and Gurice at the market with Shyla and Rendor." Jaft tapped his hand on his chest. "Seeing them alive was a jolt of joy for all of us." He pulled in a deep breath. "Rae followed them to the castle. We assumed they were protecting you and we trusted the four of them to keep you safe. Also things moved quickly after that. Mojag's disappearance forced Xerxes to enact his plans right away. He needed those taxes and he figured he could force Mojag to give them to him."

Mojag huffed. "Not a chance."

"No? You wouldn't have handed them over even if he threatened to kill Gurice?"

"Not even." A stubborn determination stiffened his posture. "Shyla only."

Gurice grunted. "Love you, too, rat."

Shyla smiled. She'd been right to entrust the coins to Mojag.

"Will you deliver them to me?" the King asked Mojag. Amusement sparked in his gaze.

"No. Shyla only. She can decide what to do with them."

He laughed. "Now that's loyalty." Glancing around the room, his good mood faded when he studied Xerxes. "It appears the commander's loyalty was to Najib. I'm tempted to drown him, but I'll interrogate him first." He met Shyla's gaze. "Will you assist me?"

"I'd be happy to, sire."

While the King followed Jaft to check on his people, Shyla helped Rendor clean and bandage his wounds. Then they escorted Xerxes to the King's office. Actually, she ordered the commander to follow her and he obeyed. Fun.

Also fun was when the rest of the Invisible Swords caught up to them in the corridor. Shyla and Rendor were immediately surrounded by happy, smiling faces. Breathless explanations were exchanged. When the news of their union was revealed, Rae squealed and hugged Rendor while Vashi swept Shyla off her feet. Balin and Nard slapped Rendor on the back and congratulatory handshakes abounded. Shyla met Rendor's stunned gaze and gave him an I-told-you-they-are-your-family look.

He nodded in acknowledgment before telling Rae she had done a good job of following them. "I never spotted you."

She smirked. "I know."

After everyone settled down, the Invisible Swords went to sample the cook's famous gamelu sausages while Shyla and Rendor took Xerxes into the King's office.

"You have two choices," the King said to Xerxes after the traitor knelt in front of him. "We can compel you to answer my questions, or you can volunteer the information. Which will it be?"

"Does it matter?" Xerxes asked in a rough voice.

"Yes. If you cooperate, I might not drown you."

Xerxes glanced at Shyla.

"Your choice," she said. "Just remember, I'll know if you're lying."

The big man deflated. "Ask your questions."

With Shyla monitoring his emotions—a mix of anger, disbelief, and fear—Xerxes explained the plot to assassinate the

King. Najib had discovered information about the power of the original pendants in the King's Room of Knowledge. The old king had been fond of the curious boy and encouraged his studies. Seemed Najib was a talented researcher and his efforts often helped the old king while also helping himself.

Najib searched for sunfire and blackfire stones that had been stored as artifacts in the various monasteries. He collected them all. As the old king became increasingly erratic, Najib recruited Xerxes, who brought on Lonato—who was currently waiting at the Qulsary monastery for news of the assassination.

The three of them had the magical stones cut and made into pendants. The plan was to take over all the cities of Koraha and the monasteries, then assassinate the King. Najib wanted complete loyalty from all the people in Koraha before the assassination. Therefore no one would protest his ascension and he wouldn't have to worry about being killed in turn.

"Wait," Shyla said to Xerxes. "If you weren't going to become the next king, why did you say I could have been queen?"

"Najib wanted you as his queen. You're the second most powerful person in Koraha." He pointed to her hand. "You were supposed to swear that oath to him."

That seemed worse than being enslaved by the sunfire. She met Rendor's gaze. His fierce expression agreed that outcome would have been horrific. And by the way he fisted his hands, she'd bet he'd like to punch Xerxes just for uttering those words.

"What other schemes did Najib have once he became king?" the King asked.

"Najib planned to kill the new king-in-waiting so his magical protection would last longer." Disgust sharpened Xerxes' tone. "I refused to be a part of it, but he believed he'd find someone to carry out his orders."

Shyla hadn't thought her opinion of Najib could get any lower, yet it dropped. Killing an innocent child to extend your own life was the lowest of the low. Najib should have been staked in the sand and cooked. Drowning was too good for him.

"Why did you agree to help Najib? What were you promised?" the King asked Xerxes.

"The five circuits before the old king's illness worsened, his missions for his elite soldiers were demeaning and degrading—a complete waste of time and resources. I was ready to quit when Najib told me his plans. He promised our assignments would return to doing important work—helping people."

"And you didn't stop to consider that *I* might also do the same?"

"I did, but he also guaranteed consistency."

"Consistency?"

Xerxes sighed. "Yes, consistency. Currently, each city handles their problems in different ways. There's corruption and greed everywhere, and the training of the guards is inconsistent. With all the cities under our influence, we could finally get everything to the same level. Crime would be rare. Vagrants would be assimilated into the general population. No more bribing the high-ranked officials, or favoritism, or all those extra perks for the rich citizens. No more black market. No more bandits and pirates. People would know exactly what to expect if they broke a law. It would be the exact same punishment if they were in

Apanji or in Nintri." Xerxes gestured to Shyla. "It's considered murder to leave a sun-kissed baby out on the sand in Catronia, but in Zirdai, it's encouraged. That needs to stop!"

Surprised by Xerxes' genuine desire to change the world, Shyla's initial reaction was to agree with him. Their world had many problems. And she hated to admit she was impressed by Xerxes' passion, his desire to make Koraha a better place to live. Admirable, except his methods were unconscionable.

"We were all frustrated by the old king's lack of action. However, I'm planning on fixing many of those injustices," the King said.

"You can try, but you'll be dealing with all those Water Princes and Princesses that have been doing things their way for circuits. Dealing with corrupt Heliacal Priests and Priestesses. Dealing with guards who won't want to stop collecting the coins the black-market dealers give them to look the other way. Dealing with entitled rich people who refuse to help anyone but themselves. You can try all you want, but nothing is going to change." Xerxes sank back on his heels. His posture was one of a tired, defeated soldier. "Not unless you force that change. Najib's plans limited the amount of force needed. Limited bloodshed." He glanced at Shyla. "How many people died for Zirdai to be free of those two tyrants? Over two hundred?"

Two hundred and sixty-four. She'd never forget.

"Unfortunately, that was during the old king's reign. I'm not going to let something like that happen again," the King said.

"You can try. But without the sunfires, you'll fail. Nothing will change."

Xerxes had a bleak view, and while Shyla trusted many things would improve under the King's leadership, she knew some of those issues would remain.

Utopian societies were pure fiction.

"I'm more optimistic," the King said. "I agree that there will be failures, but there will also be successes. Free will can be unpredictable, but it's also more interesting. Not to mention morally correct." He stepped closer to Xerxes. "I'm curious. In your perfect world, what would you do to a traitor who tried to assassinate the king?"

Xerxes didn't hesitate. "Drown him. He can't be trusted and it'll make other potential assassins hesitate because they'll know the consequences of failure."

"I'll consider it." The King motioned to his guards. "Take him to the prison."

"I'd rather die," Xerxes said, hopping to his feet.

Freeze, Shyla commanded.

"Which is why being confined is a more fitting punishment." The King studied the big man. "For now. I can always flood your cell with water if you're too much trouble."

The guards surrounded Xerxes. They manacled his wrists behind his back but stepped back from him as if afraid he'd try to fight.

"Beast, obey the guards and cooperate with the jailors," she instructed, freeing him from her earlier command.

The four guards' postures relaxed slightly. They escorted Xerxes from the office. When they were gone, the King turned to Shyla. "Once he is secured in a cell, please release him from your control."

"He'll be a difficult prisoner to keep confined," Rendor said.

"I'm sure. Even though he deserves it, taking a person's will is still wrong."

"At least he had a taste of what he put others through," Shyla said. "I hope he remembers it."

"If he proves to be too difficult, perhaps you could remind him," the King said. "That is, if you were serious about wanting to stay? You were under a great deal of pressure at the time. I'd understand if you'd rather not."

She couldn't fault the King for questioning her. His best friend betrayed him, claiming his pledge was invalid because of how young he had been. "I'm afraid, sire, that you're stuck with us. All of us. The Invisible Sword is at your disposal."

The King sank into his cushion. "Thank the goddess. We have so much to do. We need to make traveling safe again and find homes for the people squatting in the shelters. But we also need to free those cities still under the sunfire's influence. And I have to introduce myself to the citizens of Koraha. And—"

"First we need to send a force to capture Lonato and destroy all the sunfire and blackfire pendants. Then Mojag needs to recover the taxes. After that we can plan from there," Shyla said.

"Oh, yes. Of course. I'm getting ahead of myself. See? You're already being a great advisor."

"Advisor?"

The King smiled at her. "You wield The Eyes, Shyla. It's meant to be. But if you'd rather another title…I can think of something." He glanced at Rendor. "Not queen, though." They shared a smile.

"But I'm the leader of the Invisible Sword."

"Why would that change? Can't you do both?"

"I might be needed elsewhere."

"Ah. Being my advisor doesn't mean you can't leave my side. I've just learned a very painful lesson not to be overly dependent on one person. I plan to have a few advisors. Well…I'll see who I can afford. Do you know anyone who is good with numbers? Najib could balance the budget in his sleep."

A huge weight lifted off her chest. "I'll ask around."

"Good." He suddenly snapped his fingers. "Commander! That's a perfect title for you."

She stared at him in shock. "I…" Shyla cleared her throat. "I think I like advisor better. I'm committed to the Invisible Sword."

"Exactly! And since you're also committed to me, it means the Invisible Sword is now my elite force. You are already their leader. And I'm assuming you'll want to expand the membership and train them. The monks can also do more than just collect information and you could oversee that as well. Don't worry, you can still give me advice."

"She's not worried about that," Rendor said. "She'll give advice whether you want it or not."

Shyla's glare said if he didn't keep quiet, she'd have more than advice to give him. Unperturbed, Rendor grinned.

Everything was happening rather fast. She drew in a breath. "I'll think about it." She also needed to talk to the rest of the Invisible Sword.

"Good. All right, Commander, I need—"

"I said I would *think* about it."

"Yes, yes. Think all you want. But I'm the King of Koraha so…" He shrugged. "One of the perks of my job."

She rubbed her face as all that weight settled back on her shoulders.

"It's a title, Shyla," the King said kindly. "I can call you the Grand Master of Sand or the Chief Magic Wielder or Prime Advisor. It doesn't matter; your job remains the same regardless. Using Commander just makes it easier for everyone else. They'll know right away who they are dealing with."

When he put it like that…it still seemed like a great deal of responsibility. However… Shyla met Rendor's gaze. He would be beside her along with the Invisible Swords, who proved to be quite capable of dealing with problems without her. The responsibility wasn't all on her, but on *them*.

"What did you need me to do?" she asked.

The King beamed at her. "Please assemble a strike force and take care of that infection called Lonato."

"Yes, sire." Shyla turned to Rendor. "Captain, any ideas of how we should proceed?"

He considered her question for a moment. "Lonato is expecting good news. Since he doesn't know Jaft and the others are free, we can pretend to be sent from Xerxes to get close to the monk."

"Sounds like a plan. Let's find the others. We'll leave for the monastery at angle zero."

With four magic wielders, Shyla, Rendor, and the rest of the Invisible Sword, it was rather easy to reach Lonato and his loyal monks. Once his sunfire was removed and exposed to the King's sapphires, the people the monk influenced were freed from his compulsion. This result gave her hope that the Water Princes and Princesses who had been enthralled by Xerxes were now also free. She and her Swords would still have to visit those cities and monasteries to ensure everyone had regained their free will.

After the attack, Mojag led her to the taxes hidden under the sand on the other side of the mountains. They filled the three wagons with the coins and ensured every single one was deposited into the King's vault. The steady *plink, plink, plink* was the sweetest sound. Then and only then did she and Rendor collapse onto the oversized cushion in the guest quarters.

Voices woke her…later. She was alone, but the fur was tucked tight around her. It took her a moment to realize there were a few people in the other room. And another to note that the King had someone deliver their belongings. Glad that they no longer had to hide in the King's chambers, Shyla stretched and thought about food.

"…don't want to go back to Zirdai!" Mojag's strident voice cut through her peaceful contemplation.

She peeled the fur back and headed to the common room. Mojag stood, looming over his sister, who sat cross-legged on a cushion. Her expression matched his—both stubborn. Rendor and the rest of the Invisible Swords watched the siblings with various degrees of amusement.

"Calm down, Mojag," Gurice said. "You'll wake Shyla."

"Too late," Shyla said from the doorway. "What's going on?"

"Just making plans to return home." Gurice shooed her brother back to his cushion.

Mojag plopped into it with a huff. "I'm not going."

"It's not your choice. We're the Invisible Sword and we belong in Zirdai." Gurice crossed her arms as if that settled the matter.

Shyla entered the room and joined them. "About that." She explained that they were now working for the King. "We're no longer going to just protect Zirdai but all the cities of Koraha. I'm moving our headquarters to Qulsary."

While Mojag cheered, Gurice gaped at Shyla. The others' expressions showed mixed emotions.

"But what about Jayden? And your parents?" Gurice asked her.

"And we did all that back-breaking work to make that old temple livable!" Jaft cried.

"I can visit my parents anytime. We're not stuck in Qulsary. In fact, we'll be traveling quite a bit." Something she was looking forward to. "I also plan to have…bases in each city so we can keep an eye on everyone. The monks are going to be more active in helping the citizens in each city. They'll be coordinating their efforts with ours so I want a couple of our people in the monasteries as well. Gurice, if you want, you can be in charge of the Zirdai force."

"And miss all the action? No thank you," Gurice said.

"I'd like that job," Jaft said. "I've family in Zirdai. And…" He glanced at Rae and her cheeks reddened. "I think we should have at least one magic wielder in each city."

Ah, so Rae was the lucky person who'd caught Jaft's heart. "That's a good idea. I'll send a message to Zirdai and bring the rest of the Swords to join us. We'll work out all the details then and find a new location for our headquarters."

"How are we going to pay for all this?" Vashi asked.

"Tamburah's treasure will cover all the initial expenses," Shyla said. "The King will eventually pay us a salary."

"Eventually?" Lamar asked.

"Xerxes and Najib stole two circuits' worth of taxes. The poor man has quite a bit of debt. We don't need to add to his problems."

"But he expects us to solve them," Balin said.

"No. We are helping the citizens of Koraha, making their lives better. That's what the Invisible Sword was created to do." She told them about how The Eyes were supposed to be woken by the King's advisor.

They discussed the various issues and complications that the move to Qulsary was bound to cause, but Shyla wasn't worried. They'd been through worse and they had each other.

When the impromptu meeting broke up, the others headed out in search of food.

Before Mojag left, Shyla called him back. Gurice waited for him in the doorway.

"Why don't you want to return to Zirdai?" Shyla asked. "I thought you and Jayden—"

"It's not him," Mojag said. "Even though it won't ever be the same with him, I'm not avoiding him. Well…not as much. No. There's just too many bad memories in Zirdai. Here, I'm freer. And it's a challenge! I can navigate Zirdai with my eyes closed. Boring." Then he grew even more animated. "I'd love to be able to navigate every city in Koraha with my eyes closed. That'd be a good thing to know for our new job, right?"

"Yes. It would be." She smiled at him. He'd come a long way from the vagrant boy who whined about life not being fair. "I'm glad you're excited about the changes."

"It's like you said, we're supposed to be doing this." He tapped his chest. "My heart agrees."

"My stomach agrees that we need to eat. Coming, rat?" Gurice asked.

"Your stomach has gotten us into more trouble than Shyla," Mojag grumbled, but he dashed after her.

"I think you were just insulted," Rendor said.

"I disagree. I've seen Gurice when she's hungry. It's not pretty."

He conceded the point then grew thoughtful. "Mojag will be the next commander."

"Mojag?"

"He has the passion and the power."

"Not the maturity."

"Oh, he has it when he needs it. He just ignores it the rest of the time."

"Why are you thinking about the next commander? Are you worried I'll—"

"No," he rushed to assure her. "I'm thinking about when you slow down. And maybe have other responsibilities."

"Other responsibilities?"

"The King did bless us with a dozen children. We're going to be busy." He swept her off her feet. "We should get started right away."

Desire swept through her just as fast. "I'm not agreeing to a dozen."

Rendor carried her toward their sleeping cushion. "Pity. Half a dozen?"

"No."

"Four?"

"Getting closer."

"Two?"

"Yes."

"All right, two dozen it is!"

"Rendor," she scolded, but he ignored her. "And no children until we get the Invisible Sword network set up and have fixed a number of problems. And I can still work when I have children. Mojag can have my job when I'm older. Much older."

"Yes, Commander," Rendor said, laying her down on the cushion.

She smirked. "I outrank you."

He laughed. "Sunbeam, you've outranked me from the moment I met you."

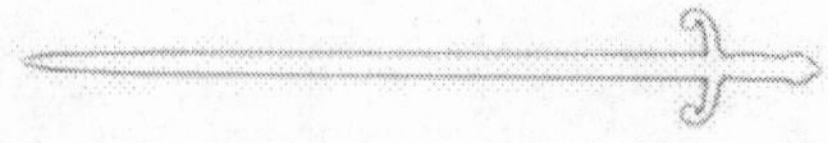

THANK YOU

Thank you for choosing *The King of Koraha*, the third book in my award-winning Archives of the Invisible Sword series. I hope you enjoyed this fantasy series set on the hot desert sands of Koraha. Please consider leaving an honest review of my books. They are super helpful along with spreading the word about me and my books. That's the best way you can help keep an author in business!

If you'd like to stay updated on my books and any news, please sign up for my free email newsletter here:

http://www.mariavsnyder.com/news.php

(go all the way down to the bottom of the page). I send my newsletter out to subscribers three to four times a year. It contains info about the books, my schedule and always something fun (like deleted scenes or a new short story or exclusive excerpts). No spam—ever!

You're also welcome to come join your fellow MVS fans on my Facebook reading group called Snyder's Soulfinders. Why Soulfinders? Because according to Plato, "Books give a soul to the universe, wings to the mind, flight to the imagination, and life to everything." The Soulfinders are all about books, especially mine, but also others as well! It's a great place to find fellow readers and make friends from all over the world. There are perks, too, like exclusive give aways, getting all the news first, and an insight into my writing process. Please answer at least 2 of the 3 questions as we don't want any trolls in our group, just Soulfinders. Here's a link:

https://www.facebook.com/groups/SnydersSoulfinders/

Please don't be a stranger, stop on by and say hello. You can find me on:

- Facebook: https://www.facebook.com/mvsfans
- Goodreads: https://www.goodreads.com/maria_v_snyder
- Instagram: https://www.instagram.com/mariavsnyderwrites/

ACKNOWLEDGMENTS

I've been doing fun puzzles instead of typing out my eternal gratitude to all the people who have aided me in making *The King of Koraha* the best book possible, and all those who supported me throughout the process of writing my twenty-first book. If you've been paying attention to my acknowledgments, you should find the clues to the Acknowledgment Crossword Puzzle on the next page!

I also wanted to express my appreciation for all the hardworking people at my publishing house in Sydney, Australia whose names I might not know, but who I know worked hard to turn my manuscript into this beautiful book. Also thanks to Wendy Bos, my Australian audiobook narrator, who did a fantastic job narrating my Archives of the Invisible Sword series.

And speaking of support, no acknowledgments would be complete without a shout-out of thanks to my parents (bonus points if you know their names), my sister, Karen, and her husband, Chris, and my close friends who keep me sane and don't whine too much when I'm too busy to hang out (you know who you are!).

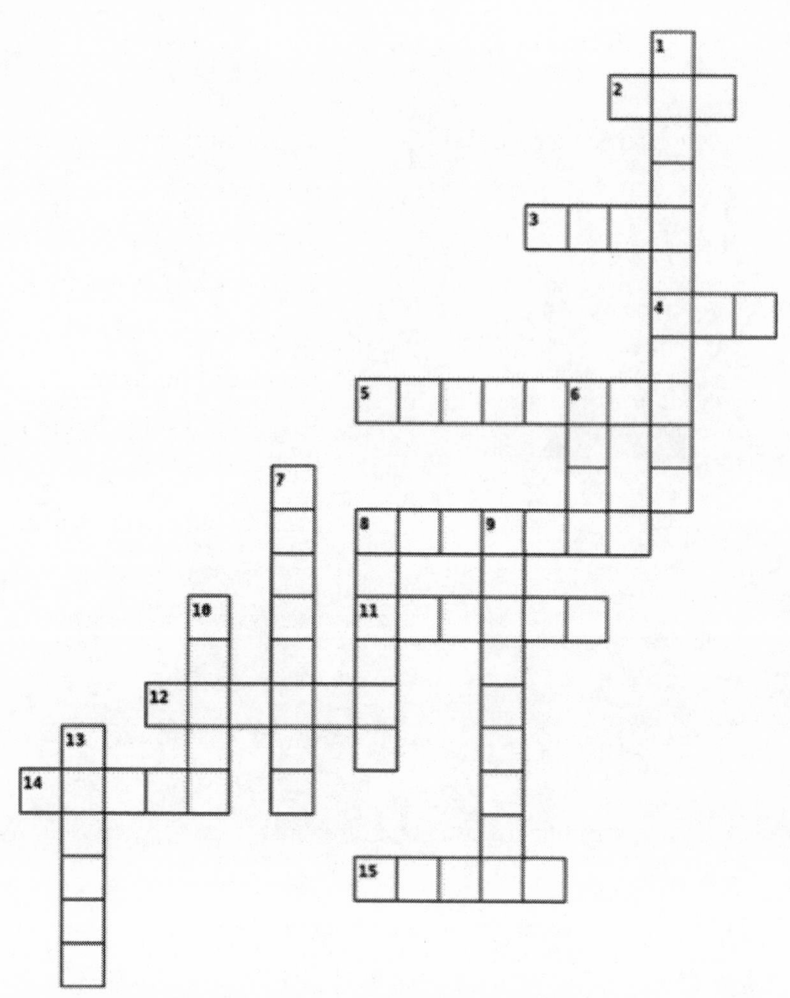

Across

2. My talented US cover artist
3. B&N manager who stocks all my books
4. My Chief Evil Minion
5. The owner of Cupboard Maker Books and friend
8. My publisher & my editorial dream team
11. The amazing Australian cover artist
12. The person who schedules my Australian events and promotes my books
14. The audiobook goddess who narrates my US books
15. My beautiful and intelligent daughter

Down

1. My loyal readers who bring me joy
6. My smart and snarky son
7. My virtual assistant
8. My supportive and wonderful husband
9. My publishing house in Australia
10. My big picture editor
13. My eagle-eyed proofreader who hunts for inconsistencies

ABOUT THE AUTHOR

When Maria V. Snyder was younger, she aspired to be a storm chaser in the American Midwest so she attended Pennsylvania State University and earned a Bachelor of Science degree in Meteorology. Much to her chagrin, forecasting the weather wasn't in her skill set so she spent a number of years as an environmental meteorologist, which is not exciting … at all. Bored at work and needing a creative outlet, she started writing fantasy and science fiction stories. Over twenty novels and numerous short stories later, Maria's learned a thing or three about writing. She's been on the *New York Times* bestseller list, won a dozen awards, and has earned her Masters of Arts degree in Writing from Seton Hill University, where she is now a faculty member.

Her favorite color is red. She loves dogs, but is allergic, instead she has a big black tom cat named … Kitty (apparently naming cats isn't in her skill set either). Maria also has a husband and two children who are an inspiration for her writing when they aren't being a distraction. Note that she mentions her cat before her family. When she's not writing she's either playing volleyball, traveling, or taking pictures. Being a writer, though, is a ton of fun. When else can you take fencing lessons, learn how to ride a horse, study martial arts, learn how to pick a lock, take glass blowing classes and attend Astronomy Camp and call it research? Maria will be the first one to tell you it's not working as a meteorologist. Readers are welcome to check out her website for book excerpts, free short stories, maps, blog, and her schedule at MariaVSnyder.com.